THIS ABOVE ALL

OTHER COVENANT BOOKS AND
AUDIOBOOKS BY DANA LeCHEMINANT

The Thief and the Noble

"A Twist of Christmas" in *The Holly and the Ivy*

CALLOWAY SERIES

What Dreams May Come

This above All

Never Doubt I Love (coming August 2025)

THIS ABOVE ALL

A Regency Romance

DANA LeCHEMINANT

Covenant Communications, Inc.

Cover image © Abigail Miles / Arcangel

Cover design copyright © 2024 by Covenant Communications, Inc.

Published by Covenant Communications, Inc.
American Fork, Utah

Library of Congress Cataloging-in-Publication Data

Name: Dana LeCheminant
Title: This above all / Dana LeCheminant
Description: American Fork, UT : Covenant Communications, Inc. [2024]
Identifiers: Library of Congress Control Number 2024933635 | ISBN 978-1-52442-535-7
LC record available at https://lccn.loc.gov/2024933635

Printed in the United States of America
First Printing: July 2024

30 29 28 27 26 25 24   10 9 8 7 6 5 4 3 2 1

To my parents

Thanks for proving that true and lasting love exists and for always letting me be my true self.

Chapter One

Staffordshire, England
October 1815

Nick Forester loved a good adventure as much as the next man, but despite Miss Barton's thrilled insistence that they were bound to be set upon by a highwayman, he hardly considered waiting on the edge of the road an adventure. Nearly an hour in and they still hadn't managed to get the coach unstuck from the mud.

He was tired, thirsty, and covered in mud, and the blasted woman had been talking almost nonstop since leaving London. It was enough to make him consider remaining a bachelor for the whole of his life. Surely not every woman in the world was like Miss Barton; otherwise, he would most certainly remain single for lack of a worthy partner. True, he had been searching for a wife for years, and the unending loneliness of being on his own wasn't something he wished on his worst enemy. But at least on his own he could hear himself think.

Unlike now.

"Can't you just picture him riding in from the woods there?" Miss Barton said, pointing with a flourish to a tiny copse of bare trees that hardly offered an ounce of shade, let alone enough cover for a bandit. The landscape was wide and open, fields stretching out for miles beneath gray and gloomy skies.

"Doubtful," Nick said. He stretched his legs out where he sat on a fallen log, hoping his curt response would end her fantasy.

She was not dissuaded from continuing. "On his black horse, of course."

"Of course," he grumbled.

"With his pistols blazing."

"I do not think you understand how pistols work, Miss Barton."

"Oh, hush." She giggled, batting her eyes at him. "Would you rescue me, Mr. Forester?"

Nick knew she was testing him, trying to see how far she could push the lines before he finally gave in to her temptations. He had considered it once, but this journey from London had been enough to prove how incompatible the two of them truly were. She was beautiful and moderately wealthy, with a good name and family behind her, but if he tried to picture the rest of his life with Catherine Barton at his side, the whole scenario made him shudder in horror and consider hopping onto a ship to the Americas. He could start a new life on a farm, and all his problems would be solved.

He grimaced. If he thought he was lonely now . . .

Gritting his teeth, he tried not to sound at all interested in Miss Barton as he said, "If the occasion called for rescue, I suppose I would."

"You are a gentleman through and through, I see! It is a wonder you haven't married long before now. Has no lady taken your fancy, sir?" She batted her eyelashes again, as if her simpering smile would be enough to induce him to propose right there on the spot.

Rather than giving in to her obvious wishes, Nick stood in order to put some distance between them.

He had done his best to ignore the other passengers of the coach, a Mr. and Mrs. Franks, who were neighbors of Miss Barton and acting as her escorts. They had been happy to accompany her for propriety's sake, as her parents were required to return to their home in Suffolk instead of traveling with her to her cousin's. But now the Frankses were both watching Nick with uncertainty as they huddled together for warmth inside the coach with Miss Barton's maid. The weather had taken a definite turn since they'd left London, the skies threatening more rain after a night of downpour, and Nick was rather convinced that the only reason Miss Barton was not shivering like the rest was because her fast tongue kept her warm.

Still, if the expressions of the Frankses were to be believed, both of them considered Nick's indifference to be quite appalling. He would need to do something with Miss Barton, whether to encourage her or tell her he was not interested and likely never would be. As if that might persuade her to stop her pursuit.

"Miss Barton," he said with a sigh.

"Oh look! I do believe our driver is returning!" Miss Barton waved to the approaching wagon, where the coach's driver sat among several large men from the town a few miles up the road.

"Thank the heavens," Nick muttered.

Mr. Franks had complained of a poor back, and Nick and the coachman alone had been unable to push the coach free after it had stuck itself deep in the mud. The driver had offered to walk to the town in search of help, leaving Nick with the incorrigible Miss Barton and a pair of scandalized onlookers. He should have gone with the coachman, but he had realized as much too late.

"Everybody out, please," the coachman said as he hopped down from the wagon, and he offered his hand for Mrs. Franks and Miss Barton's maid.

Within five minutes Nick and the four townsmen managed to free the coach and get it back onto solid ground, and everyone clambered back inside the coach in the hopes of finding some warmth from the chill autumn air.

Everyone except Nick. And, of course, Miss Barton.

"Oh, do help me, Mr. Forester," she said, gesturing to the minuscule amount of mud still underfoot. "I would hate to dirty my hem before we arrive at Harstone Court."

Why Lord Harstone had thought to invite Miss Barton for a visit, Nick would never know. Nor would he ever comprehend his own decision to accompany her to Staffordshire, where his old friend lived, rather than making the journey on his own. The thought of sharing the fare had been far too tempting, and he was too poor a rider to risk taking a horse on his own. But surely he had not been so blind as to think a journey of this sort would make him like Miss Barton more after her many attempts to convince him they would make a good match.

Nick cursed himself as he considered that thought. Of course he was blind. His entire future rested on securing himself a wife, and he rejected more and more prospects every week. His options were running thin, and Miss Barton was one of the few he hadn't yet rejected outright, despite having met her several years ago.

She knew this as well as he did, which explained her tenacity.

"Miss Barton," he said with a slight bow of his head, then offered his arm. When she didn't move beyond widening her grin, he gritted his teeth and reminded himself that she was as much a guest of Lord Harstone as he would be, and it would hardly do to make her an enemy before they even arrived at their destination. That would certainly make the next few weeks unbearable, far from what he hoped for.

This visit was supposed to give him some moments of peace, away from the pressures of London Society, where everyone knew he was on the hunt for a wife.

"If you'll allow me," he growled, then slid a hand behind Miss Barton's back. She responded in turn and wrapped both arms around his neck so he could lift and carry her to the waiting coach.

"Oh, you are too kind," she whispered in his ear, sending a shudder down his back that had nothing to do with the October chill.

Miss Barton was going to be the death of him, he was sure. As he settled into his seat next to her, he closed his eyes so he would not have to endure her sickeningly sweet smiles and batting eyelashes. He could survive a few days with her if it meant he could be away from the rest of London. Compared to some of the husband hunters who had attacked him over the last couple of Seasons, Miss Barton was as tame as a lamb.

The woman did not stop talking for the next two hours, however, and even Mrs. Franks was grimacing as if she thought walking would be an agreeable alternative to being trapped in the coach with Miss Barton. Somehow Mr. Franks had managed to fall asleep just like Miss Barton's maid, who must have grown accustomed to her lady's unstoppable tongue, and Nick envied the pair of them.

He would never sleep with Miss Barton prattling on like this.

"And do you remember at Lord and Lady Lucas's ball?" Miss Barton said, though the only reason Nick even comprehended her words was because she'd touched his arm and made him flinch.

"I do not believe I attended that one," he said. That was a lie. He had attended every event since returning to London in June. It was the only way he might find a suitable wife.

"Nonsense," Miss Barton replied.

Well, he had tried, but she was more intelligent than most of the *ton* and would not be so easily deceived. There was one point in her favor.

"You danced with Miss Newman twice that night."

And more observant as well, apparently.

If Mrs. Franks had fallen asleep like her husband had, Nick might have been a little harsher with Miss Barton, but their aging witness being very much awake meant he had to remain civil.

"Perhaps you are right, Miss Barton," he grumbled. "You seem to have a far better memory than I do."

Miss Newman had been quiet but charming, and Nick had looked at her more closely than he generally allowed himself. But, like so many others, she had fallen prey to the gossip that surrounded him and focused on the parts that were the most untrue. Namely, that he was wildly wealthy and influential. Two things he most certainly wasn't. Plus, she had somehow found out about the fortune he was set to inherit from an old friend of his father's. The unentailed lands had been promised to him years ago, as the man who owned them had no male relations to leave them to.

Nick clenched his jaw. Without that inheritance, he was lost. But without a wife, the inheritance would be lost. The whole thing was impossible.

"But surely you remember what happened with Sir Edgar," the incessant woman continued. "You know, when he challenged Mr. Platt to a duel?"

Under different circumstances, Nick might have kept his mouth shut and let her keep talking as she had been, but his patience had been pushed to the limit. Mrs. Franks or no, he could no longer sit and listen to the gossip of Town when he had been the subject of it himself for the last three years. Could people not concern themselves with their own business instead of bothering with his?

"Ah," he said, feigning thoughtfulness. "I do believe I know why I do not remember that evening. That was the night I challenged a man to a duel myself, and I was a bit too preoccupied with that to pay attention to anything else that happened that evening."

Miss Barton's eyes went wide. "You did not," she gasped.

"I most certainly did. You can ask Mr. Mansfield."

"I do not know Mr. Mansfield."

Nick forced himself not to smile and kept his expression grave. "Of course, even if you did, it would be difficult to ask him now, seeing as I shot him."

Mrs. Franks let out a gasp of her own, and Miss Barton pressed her fingers to her mouth.

Perhaps Nick had pushed this one a bit too far. He would need to backtrack before all of London believed him a murderer. They had believed much more sensational falsehoods about him, and it wouldn't surprise him to find the ladies only found him more intriguing than before. Everyone loved a dangerous rogue.

He had decided last summer that he needed to stop perpetuating all the lies that surrounded him, but that was turning out to be more difficult than he had imagined. Clearly his lying had become a habit, and he knew deep down that it would take more than his own power to clear the air of all the falsehoods that had followed him the last three years.

Now that he had committed to this duel nonsense, he supposed he might as well make the most of it.

"Oh, but rest assured," he said, "I did not kill him. My aim is not that true, no matter what people say. He simply had to return to his country estate for a time to, ah, recover."

"Were you hurt, Nicholas?" Miss Barton whispered and took hold of his arm.

Nick stared at her fingers, more concerned by the notion that she did not seem to care about the fictional Mr. Mansfield than the fact that she had just used his given name in public company. She had spoken his name once or twice before, but only when they were out of earshot of others, something Nick had done his best to avoid lately.

"I was unharmed," he said slowly. Would she still pursue him if she thought he *had* killed a man? Perhaps he would need to make such a claim if she did not give up her pursuit before long.

"Whyever would you challenge someone?" Mrs. Franks said suddenly, and then she winced when she realized she had not said that quietly.

Miss Barton quickly scooted back to a respectable distance as she released Nick's arm, which must have meant she had forgotten they were not alone. It was impressive, given the volume of Mr. Franks's snores.

Nick only just managed to hold back a wry smile. "Because he insulted my cravat," he said as seriously as he could.

Mrs. Franks's eyes widened behind her spectacles, and she drew a little nearer to her husband.

He knew he was being unfair, both to Mrs. Franks and Miss Barton, but he had endured three years of everyone assuming they knew all they needed to know about him. That had apparently pushed him to a breaking point. Why should they care that he hoped for a love match, not simply a marriage of convenience, when he was set to inherit the whole of Mr. Mackenzie's property despite not being his blood relative? Why should they care that he hated being the center of attention when a failed engagement had forced him onto Society's stage? He was not nobility, nor was he as wealthy as everyone seemed to think he was, but since then he had become one of the most talked-about men in England.

He had enjoyed the attention once, but he had recently come to realize that all he truly wanted was a comfortable life with a woman he loved and children to adore. He hardly needed people to believe him to be both a rogue and a hero, and at this point he couldn't predict which fantastic rumors a person might believe about him, which made it deucedly difficult to navigate Society. What good was notoriety when he spent every night alone in an empty apartment?

Though the coach had been quiet for some time, which was a welcome relief, Nick could feel Miss Barton's eyes on him. Mrs. Franks finally seemed to be succumbing to the same sleepiness as her husband and the maid, and that would leave Nick and Miss Barton practically alone.

"You grow more and more interesting by the day, Nicholas," she whispered.

Nick kept his eyes locked on the window and prayed they were almost to Tutbury. He wasn't sure how much longer he would last.

Chapter Two

Emma Mackenzie walked arm in arm with her cousin, Elias Drake, but she was considering leaving him behind and continuing through town on her own. As she often did, she had brought up the subject of being an independent woman, and today Elias was having none of it.

"You will speak this topic to death, Emma," he said with a groan. "You know why your grandfather cannot leave you Mackenzie Manor and its assets. Not on your own."

"Because I am a woman." Emma scoffed. "Aside from my sister, I am the only relative he has left, Elias. Even distantly. If not to me, where are his lands supposed to go?"

Elias paused to examine a hat in the window they passed, though he was far too sensible a man to purchase such a thing when he had a perfectly acceptable hat already atop his head. There was no one as practical as Elias. In all ways he was her opposite, and Emma figured it was the only reason they had managed to remain close throughout their lives. Otherwise, she might have gotten bored of him.

Shaking his head at the hat, Elias gave her a tug and moved on down the street. "I thought Mr. Mackenzie had already promised the estate to that Forester fellow."

Emma clenched her hands into fists at the mere mention of the man. "Oh yes, the *wonderful* Mr. Forester, Grandfather's favorite charity case." He was not even related to her grandfather—merely the son of Grandfather's close friend, and yet Grandfather had promised him everything beyond Emma's small allowance. Surely a woman inheriting an estate was preferable to giving the land to someone not even of Mackenzie blood.

She huffed. "As far as I know, Mr. Forester has been in Tutbury only once in his life, and I am just as capable as any man might be. Why should he have what I cannot?"

Elias chuckled. "Emma, you cannot change the world out of spite, though I know that won't stop you from trying."

"You can hardly blame me for complaining when my only solution is marriage."

"You could be a governess. Plenty of ladies of high birth have become so when necessity dictates they do."

She had considered the idea once, but her thoughts had been fruitless. "Grandfather has forbidden it, and I don't have the heart to disappoint him. He thinks taking up an occupation is beneath me. Yet another thing I cannot do because of what I was born to." Though, she knew she could hardly complain about being the daughter of a gentleman. She truly was fortunate, but was it so wrong to want more for herself?

Patting her arm, Elias seemed to think over his next words before he spoke them, something he had taken more of a habit to as they grew older. He had grown wise when talking of subjects that riled Emma. And there were many. "What is so terrible about marriage?" he asked finally.

Emma wrinkled her nose. "You think me foolish, don't you?"

"I am just trying to understand. Surely now that you are grown you are more inclined to it."

"Now that I am grown I realize it is simply another form of imprisonment."

They had reached the square in the center of Tutbury, and Elias pulled Emma to a stop so he could look her in the eyes. "You know," he said, "I am rather looking forward to marriage once I find myself a good wife."

Emma snorted a laugh and was glad to see Elias chance a smile. He was not the most expressive of people, so she loved when she could get him to give her an outward show of his happiness.

"It will be difficult for you to find a wife if you never venture outside your house, Elias Drake," she teased.

He was not injured in the slightest. "I am out of the house right now."

"With me. That hardly counts. But no matter your thoughts on marriage, you cannot dissuade mine."

"Marriage is *not* imprisonment, Emma."

"Did you know Mrs. Hudson has never made a single choice in her married life? From the moment she is woken in the morning to the instant she falls asleep, everything she does is dictated by Mr. Hudson."

Elias made a face of irritation and amusement, apparently caught off guard by Emma's example. "That isn't true, and you know it," he said before fixing his calm expression once more. "Mrs. Hudson spends her days how she likes and is usually out socializing."

"That does not mean she doesn't have to get permission to leave the house first. That much is true, at least."

"I will admit some men are stricter than others," he said with a sigh. "But it makes sense for a man to want to protect his wife, and to care for his lands and house. But every woman in your situation has a say in her household, so stop complaining about how women have nothing."

Taking his arm once more, Emma pulled him in the direction of the millinery. "Wealthy women don't need men in their lives," she argued. "So why should I marry?"

"Because you are not wealthy."

"Yet."

When they reached the shop, Elias pulled himself free and fixed Emma with a look of long-suffering yet withering patience. He spoke quietly, which Emma appreciated when he mentioned the one fact she hated most about her life. "You seem to have forgotten that your grandfather has told you that you must be married before he will turn the estate over to you. As far as I am aware, you are unwed and have firm plans to remain so."

Emma huffed again, folding her arms, but there was nothing she could say to argue his point.

"I am going to post my letter," he added more loudly, gesturing toward the post office. "Try not to make a nuisance of yourself while I'm gone."

"I am never a *nuisance*."

Emma gritted her teeth. It was not in his expression, but she could see the laughter in her cousin's eyes. The only reason she had been able to come to town at all was because he was with her; Grandfather did not trust her to be in the village on her own. He expected rakes and bandits around every corner, and Emma could do nothing to persuade him otherwise. He was a good man, but he couldn't seem to see how little she needed a man in her life.

She smacked Elias's arm when his lips twitched with a smile again. "You are asking for trouble, Elias Drake," she warned.

"You *are* trouble."

Waiting until he had disappeared inside the post office, Emma slipped inside the millinery and considered their conversation. Marriage was not all bad, if she was to believe the picture of happiness her elder sister painted with her husband, but Emma had seen far too many miserable unions to think she could be guaranteed happiness. At least with an estate to manage, she could live without being subject to a man's dictates.

Unfortunately for her, Grandfather had gotten it into his head that she required a husband to manage the estate for her.

She picked up a fetching bonnet lined with blue ribbons, though she hardly gave it much notice in her frustration.

If she could not convince Grandfather to leave her more than her little dowry and a barely livable yearly allowance, she would be forced into a marriage when he was no longer around to look after her. That fate could very well happen soon, given his old age. And the thought of being in an unwanted marriage made her stomach hurt. If she could marry for love, then all would be well, but that was asking a good deal.

Who would want her? She was no heiress, and she would not call herself a rare beauty. She liked to think she was more than passable, but her one Season in London had hardly given her hope for rich and handsome men flocking to her side like they did with the noble women of grace and poise; they all seemed to find her tenacity a fault. She had made plenty of friends but never had any prospects worth pursuing. Anyone who thought to court her had been far from the ideal she hoped for. Besides, she hated leaving Staffordshire when everyone she loved was here: her sister, her grandfather, her three adorable nieces.

Single men in Tutbury were few and far between, and it was not as if prospective husbands appeared out of thin air.

"That would look marvelous on you."

Emma jumped, spinning around to find an unfamiliar man leaning against the wall in the corner of the shop. He was mostly shadowed, though a beam of sunlight landed on his smile.

"I beg your pardon?" she asked.

His smile grew. "Forgive me. I hadn't intended to say anything. I'm hiding, you see. But the bonnet would match your eyes."

This was most peculiar, and Emma glanced around the shop, curious to know from whom he was hiding. She really shouldn't have been speaking to him, seeing as he was a stranger and she was on her own, but this was Tutbury. Nothing bad ever happened here. And aside from the shopkeeper, the building was empty.

Emma knew she should retreat and go find Elias, but her curiosity kept her in place. "You're hiding?" she asked, returning the bonnet to its stand. "From what, may I ask?"

He shifted his stance, folding his arms as he tucked one foot over the other as if he hadn't a care in the world. His well-tailored clothing spoke of wealth, and his demeanor spoke of pride, two things Emma didn't especially like. "From something truly frightening. You didn't like the bonnet? Is it because I said it would look well on you? Usually people believe whatever I say."

Scoffing, Emma inched a little closer to the man, hoping to see his face. He had the voice of someone both old and young, like he had seen more years than her but didn't necessarily show it in the way he spoke. "What reason would I have to believe you when you are a stranger to me? Good day, sir."

Just as she dipped into a curtsy, the bell above the door jingled, signaling a new arrival in the shop. Emma turned to see if it was someone she knew but had hardly had a chance to look before the man behind her cursed and ducked down behind a display of hats beside her.

"I beg of you, stay where you are," he hissed, looking up at her with wide blue eyes.

Now that she could see him better, she guessed he was several years her senior. He looked rather ridiculous, crouched down as he was, as he was nearly too tall to fit behind the display in the first place. The only reason he was hidden was because Emma stood there.

The two ladies who had stepped into the shop looked around, and Emma guessed they were likely looking for their gentleman companion. The finer of the women certainly dressed as well as the man, her dress made of bolder colors than Emma ever saw out here in the country. She rather looked like a peacock as she rose up on her toes to see across the shop.

Emma busied herself with the nearest hat, though she was sorely tempted to see what would happen if she gave up the man's hiding place. "I cannot see why you're so frightened of a couple of women," she muttered as quietly as she could. "Especially when one of them is a maid and the other looks like a fine woman indeed."

The man snorted. "Miss Barton is no mere woman."

"She looks innocent enough to me."

"You all do, but none of you are." He cringed. "I didn't mean that."

"Then, why did you say it?"

"Because I say a good deal of things I do not mean. Is she still searching for me?" He peeked around the edge of the display, though he would hardly be able to see the women from his low vantage point.

Emma glanced over. Lady Peacock—Miss Barton—was now admiring an overtrimmed bonnet while her maid looked ready to fall asleep on her feet. They must have been traveling through Tutbury on their way to somewhere else; people rarely came to the little town to visit.

"She seems to be enamored by a rather horrendous bonnet," Emma said with a shrug. She could only pretend to be interested in the hat display for so long before she was noticed, and Elias would return at any moment and likely judge her for speaking to the man. "I take it you are traveling with her?"

His eyebrows rose as he looked back at her. "Indeed."

"Then, won't you need to be discovered eventually? I doubt you would like to be left behind."

"At this point, that might be preferable." But he sighed and twisted his hat in his hands. "I suppose I am only delaying the inevitable, though I thank you for assisting me, even if my efforts were in vain. What name might I give my beautiful protector?"

Emma frowned. Speaking to him was one thing; introducing herself was another. "I hardly think that is appropriate, sir."

The grin that stretched across his mouth made him look far more handsome than he had a right to look. With the way his eyes crinkled at the corners, he seemed to be a man who smiled often. "And here I was hoping you would be different," he muttered before rising to his full height.

Lady Peacock noticed him immediately. "Nicholas!" she said before clapping a hand over her mouth and turning bright red. Apparently she hadn't meant to call him by his given name. "There you are."

Nicholas nodded toward Lady Peacock before giving Emma one last grin. "I commend your propriety," he told her as he set his hat atop his blond head, "but if I might offer a suggestion?"

Emma couldn't decide whether she should be offended or pleased by his continued attention. "Are you going to tell me to purchase the bonnet?" she guessed dryly.

He chuckled, looking at the item in question as he walked slowly backward in the direction of his companions. "While I stand by my assessment that you would look quite handsome in it, my suggestion is unrelated."

"What is it?"

He smirked. "If given the option, always be a nuisance."

Emma let out a little gasp. Did that mean he had heard her conversation with Elias outside? Before she could think up some clever response, Nicholas escorted the other ladies outside, leaving Emma on her own.

What a peculiar man! Emma hadn't been around anyone new in quite some time, especially anyone who clearly spent a good deal of time among the *haute ton*, but the gentleman had been entirely improper. He must have assumed she wouldn't be versed in Society's rules and decided he could do as he pleased.

At least she wouldn't have to see him again, as a man with so little regard for politeness could hardly bring anything good to Tutbury.

The door opened once more, bringing Elias into the shop. He must have seen something in her expression because he frowned slightly as he approached. "Did something happen?" he asked, looking around the shop as if he might find evidence of whatever he suspected. "Have you found what you were looking for?"

She could tell him about the strange man, but she chose to keep that moment to herself. Elias would only worry and tell her grandfather, and she would undoubtedly lose what little freedom she had. Grandfather would likely forbid her from coming into town at all.

"I was simply waiting for you," she said, looping her arm through his. "You are far better at colors than I am."

He lifted one eyebrow but said nothing about her deflection, instead pointing to the blue-trimmed bonnet Nicholas had commented on earlier.

Emma snickered. There she was, judging the man for acting outside of the rules while she went and thought of him by his Christian name. She neither had the right to know his name nor cared to remember it. "You like it?"

Elias shrugged. "I believe the color would suit you, though it is certainly overpriced."

Indeed it was, but that only made Emma more inclined to purchase it, even if it would forever make her think of the strange man. She received a generous allowance from her grandfather, but not enough to live off of, and purchasing a bonnet she didn't need was one of the few things she could do on her own.

"Yes, I believe you are right," she said, and then she picked up the bonnet and strode to the front to pay for it. As soon as she finished, she led Elias back onto the street and said, "I would like to visit my sister today."

Elias didn't respond, which meant he was more than happy to join her. Emma was glad her sister lived within walking distance, because who else could she tell about the mysterious stranger passing through? Tabitha's husband, Lord Harstone, neé Alvaro Rowland, might even know who he was, and Emma praised the fact that her sister had managed to marry a particularly friendly and social viscount. Though the gentleman named Nicholas was likely only passing through, if by chance he was visiting someone in the area, it would be far easier to avoid him if she knew his surname as well as his given. Alvaro would know it.

Emma had been only eleven when Tabitha married, but she remembered quite clearly the first time she'd met Alvaro Rowland. At the time, he had barely come over from Spain after the tragic deaths of his cousins and was still settling into his new role as heir to the Harstone Viscountcy near where the Mackenzies lived. He had gotten himself lost traveling to his country home from London. Tabitha and Emma had been out on a walk, and he'd stopped to ask them for directions.

Emma had liked his calm and friendly nature from the start, and Tabitha had been smitten from the first moment she'd laid eyes on him. Mr. Rowland had not once looked away from Tabitha during the whole of the conversation, and he had called on her that very evening.

Two months later they were married, and three years after that Alvaro had inherited his uncle's title and become Lord Harstone.

Ten years down the road of their relationship, they were still the most perfect couple Emma had ever seen. If she had to have a husband, how she longed for one who cared for his wife as much as Alvaro did!

Ideally, she wouldn't need to search the ends of the earth for a husband at all. She hardly needed one, and in her experience, men were far too often like the man in the shop; they felt themselves important and necessary to a woman's everyday decisions. Yes, perhaps Nicholas had been correct in saying the bonnet was a good choice for her, but that didn't mean he had the right to tell her so. And without even an introduction? Emma didn't always follow the rules of Society, but he seemed to push far beyond the boundaries she'd set for herself. That made him dangerous, so she would have to ensure she never saw him again.

"I feel as if you are scheming something," Elias muttered as they walked.

Emma grinned. "You always think I am scheming."

"You always are."

She wouldn't call this a scheme, but she was determined to learn more of the man if she could. Her gut was telling her she needed to be wary of his warm smile and bright eyes.

* * *

Just as Emma hoped, her sister, Tabitha, was in the nursery at Harstone Court with her three girls, each of them attending to their crafts. Lucy, the littlest at five, seemed to have run into a spot of trouble with her needle and thread.

"Here," Emma said, taking hold of the embroidery before the girl twisted the knot even tighter. "I've always had a hard time with thread."

"I did not expect you to visit today," Tabitha said without looking up.

Beside her, eight-year-old Sophia seemed to be matching her mother exactly, from the perfectly straight way she sat to the speed at which she stitched. Every so often, Sophia glanced over at her mother to make sure she was doing everything as she should.

Emma couldn't help but grin. Sophia would make a fine lady one day. "I visit nearly every day, Tabitha. Don't pretend to be surprised. Besides, I heard one of the servants say you had a guest arrive today, and I thought I could help with entertaining."

Tabitha gave her a grateful smile. "Grandfather is here as well. He came an hour ago in the carriage, so I am guessing you walked?"

"It is not so far."

"But that would mean you brought poor Elias with you."

"*Poor* Elias is happily sequestered in your library, as always," Emma said with a laugh. "Honestly, I think he enjoys coming here as much as I do simply because you have all the books he could possibly want to read."

"The two of you have that in common. And how was town on your way over?"

Emma fought against laughing as she remembered her encounter with Nicholas. Now that she was removed from the moment, it all felt rather ridiculous. "Town was . . . surprising," she said.

Tabitha finally looked up, her brow furrowing in interest and concern. "Surprising? Is that good or bad? What happened?"

Though Emma knew it would serve her better to speak the direct truth, she could hardly pass up a moment to embellish the story a bit, particularly with her three nieces peeking up from their cloths in interest. They adored their aunt's stories, and Emma liked nothing better than telling them.

"Well," she said dramatically, then laughed when Tabitha scoffed, knowing exactly what was coming. "There I was, walking down the street and considering what I might bring back for my three favorite little girls—"

"We're not little," Dora said and jutted out her chin. At six and a half, she liked to think she was older than she was.

Emma bit her lip before she laughed. "Of course not, my darling," she said. "I was trying to think of what gifts I might bring back for my three favorite nieces, when suddenly I was attacked!"

The girls jumped when Emma raised her voice for the last word.

"Attacked, were you?" Tabitha asked calmly. She kept her eyes on her sewing, but a smile played at her lips.

"Indeed," Emma replied. "It was as if he came out of nowhere, this beast, and he grabbed hold of me before I could run."

"That sounds truly frightening," Tabitha said in the same calm tone.

Dora was not so calm. "What did you do, Emma?" she whispered.

Even Sophia had paled a little as she waited for the story to continue.

"I did what I have been taught to do," Emma said. "I fought the creature off! Surely you girls have been trained in fisticuffs?"

Tabitha let out a sigh. "Oh, Emma, now they are going to want to learn."

Winking, Emma ignored the comment and continued. "I fought valiantly, as any lady should, and I had nearly freed myself when the witch appeared."

"Witch?" Lucy whispered. "What is a witch?"

"She is the cruelest of beings, full of dark magic and evil spells. No one who encounters her comes out the same, and as soon as I saw her, I realized the beast was not a beast at all, but a man who had been cursed! Cursed to roam the land as a beast until someone could save him."

Sophia scooted just a little closer to where Emma sat, her embroidery forgotten, and she spoke so quietly that Emma barely heard her. "Save him how?"

Emma grinned. "Why, with a kiss, of course!"

"Of course," Tabitha said under her breath.

"Did you kiss him?" Dora asked with wide eyes.

"I most certainly did not!" Emma replied and jutted out her chin in the most proper manner she could muster. "Beast or not, my kisses are far too valuable. I told him he would have to earn my kiss if he wanted it."

"That is a relief," Tabitha breathed. Surely she didn't think Emma would have kissed a man she'd met on the street.

The nursery doors suddenly burst open, and Alvaro jumped inside the nursery with a shout that made all three girls shriek and scatter before he rushed inside to catch them.

Emma had been startled as well, but Tabitha hardly reacted, despite the sheer noise level in the room. This sort of thing happened often.

As the girls ran away from their father, Tabitha reached for Emma's hand and pulled her onto the sofa next to her so she could be heard. "I take it you met a gentleman in town today," she said with a soft smile.

Emma nodded. "A most peculiar man."

"And handsome, if your blush is to be believed."

"So very handsome," she admitted, though she didn't want to. Nicholas could be as handsome as he'd like, but that didn't change his impropriety.

"What was this gentleman's name?"

That question was harder to answer; Emma could hardly tell her sister she knew only the man's Christian name. What would Tabitha think of her then?

Luckily, Lord Harstone had cornered one of his girls, which meant the shrieking stopped as the other two burst into laughter. He had caught Dora, and apparently that meant the game was over and it was time to return to normal.

"Papa," Dora asked, still shrinking away from his outstretched arms, "is it true that a kiss can turn a beast into a man?"

Emma snorted a laugh.

Not at all taken aback by the odd question, Alvaro grinned and pulled Dora up into his arms. "How else do you think your mama tamed me?" he said as he brought Dora back to the center of the room, where the others waited. "I would have remained a beast forever without her lips." He bent over and placed a kiss on Tabitha's smile as if to prove his point. "But I will hear of no kisses until you are grown, yes?"

"I don't want to kiss any beasts," Lucy said with a pout.

Sophia, on the other hand, seemed to consider the idea with interest, and Emma laughed again.

As if he couldn't help himself, Alvaro kissed his wife once more, much to the disgust of their children. Dora even squirmed away, trying to get out of his arms and away from the affection between her parents. Satisfied, he stood straight again and planted a kiss on Dora's cheek despite her protests.

"Ah, if I could but stay here with my girls all day," he said with a dramatic sigh. "But I have a guest to entertain, so I must steal your mama from you and leave you with Miss Howard."

The nursemaid in question seemed almost relieved to have something to do. She spent a good deal of time watching Lord and Lady Harstone raise their own children.

"Mi cielito," Alvaro said and took Tabitha by the hands to raise her to her feet. "You are needed in the guest wing. Miss Barton had some questions about her room."

Emma had been considering remaining with the girls, but her head snapped up at the name *Miss Barton*. That was the peacock she had seen in town, unless there was another Miss Barton traveling to the area. And if Miss Barton was at Harstone Court, what if that meant . . .

Would Emma again be seeing the improper Nicholas?

"Yes, of course," Tabitha said, then touched a soft kiss to the hair of each of her daughters. "You girls behave, and I will return to tuck you into bed."

"But I want to meet her," Sophia said with a frown. "You said I could meet Papa's cousin."

How Tabitha managed to withstand that trembling lip, Emma had no idea, and she waited for her sister to crack. Tabitha was made of stronger stuff than that, though, and she put on a smile before tucking her hand beneath Sophia's chin. "I will not go back on my promise," she told the girl. "You can meet her tomorrow when she is refreshed. We must give her a chance to settle in before we surprise her with how much you've grown."

Sophia nodded, though still disappointed, and returned to her sewing. She looked more and more a young lady instead of a little girl, and Emma wished they didn't have to grow up so fast.

Unless she found love and a husband who would not treat her as property—unlikely—Emma would have to be content to watch her nieces, rather than her own children, grow up. And that would have to be enough.

Chapter Three

Nick had been to Harstone Court once before, during the hunt years ago, and he had fallen in love with the countryside almost immediately. It looked just as he remembered, though perhaps a bit colder and browner, and he took to exploring the grounds as soon as he arrived, rather than going inside right away. It gave him a chance to truly take in the countryside and consider what his life would be like when he inherited Mr. Mackenzie's land.

Assuming he could keep up his end of the bargain.

There was something wild about this place, Nick thought as he crested a hill that overlooked the sprawling house. He could not see his future home from here, but he knew it was close and would have similar terrain. Not that he'd ever actually seen the estate up close, but this part of the country simply felt more real than London. It far surpassed the little home he had grown up in back in Derbyshire.

Nick breathed in the fresh air and let a smile play at his lips. Once he found himself a wife—one who wouldn't drive him mad—this could be home.

If he was lucky, he might even find himself a wife who already knew the area.

As it had for the last hour while he meandered, Nick's mind returned to the charming and beautiful woman he had met in Tutbury. She had surprised him, engaging him in conversation without first knowing who he was, and she had held her ground when he'd pushed the bounds of propriety. Not many young ladies did that, and she'd done so with a confident gentleness that had felt as contradictory as it was fascinating. That strength, combined with her beauty, had him enchanted.

He would have to ask Harstone if he knew her; his friend was a viscount and likely knew everyone in the surrounding area. Nobility had a habit of knowing more than they should, something that had always bothered Nick because they tended to use that power to their own advantage. Thankfully, Lord Alvaro Rowland, Viscount of Harstone, was nothing like that and had been a true friend to Nick since the day they'd met in London. Despite inheriting a prestigious title and an obscene amount of money, Harstone had never lost sight of his humbler beginnings. He and Lord Simon Calloway, a baron and Nick's only other close friend, were both of a good sort, their friendship something Nick had refused to lose over the years because it kept him from getting a big head.

It was one of the reasons Nick had been so eager to come to Harstone Court in the first place. If anyone could help him forget about the pomp and circumstance of London, Harstone could. The fact that Miss Barton had also been invited had nearly changed Nick's destination to Oxfordshire, but Calloway was too busy with his new wife to entertain a guest he, as of late, barely tolerated to begin with.

Why did Nick have only married friends? Were there no bachelors of thirty anymore? Surely the men in his extended social circle had enough sense to choose their partners wisely, take their time.

Nick sighed. Perhaps he was alone in wanting a perfect marriage and he would do better to lower his standards a bit so he was not the only lonely man in all of England.

"You may be that already," he told himself with a frown. It seemed everyone else of his acquaintance was either happily settled or cared little for the notion of finding a partner to keep through life.

As much as he wanted to admire the countryside for hours, the afternoon was quickly giving way to evening, and a chill had settled in the air. He would have to face Miss Barton again eventually, and he would prefer not to be frozen to the core when he did.

"Into battle, then," he muttered and pressed forward.

The butler opened the door just as Nick arrived and let him inside, and Nick offered up his hat and coat as he took in the expanse of his friend's house. It was just as grand as he remembered from six years earlier, though it had a different feel to it. Then Harstone had only just inherited, and the massive house had still felt like someone else's. It had had an air of majesty left behind by the previous Viscount Harstone, who had been as coldhearted as he was wealthy.

Now that the new Lord Harstone had lived in the house for more than half a decade, it felt more like a home and less like a castle dungeon. There was a warmth to the house that had nothing to do with the fire blazing in the parlor to Nick's right, and he smiled as he considered just how important a happy marriage was to a home. He liked knowing his theory was correct, even if it did complicate the matter of his inheritance.

"Forester!" Harstone's booming voice echoed in the entryway from the balcony above, making Nick grin even wider. For a man who had been entirely out of place when he first arrived in England, Harstone had never been one to play himself small. "I thought I would have to send out a search party, no?"

When Harstone reached the entryway, Nick clasped him in a tight embrace that was as much a testament to Harstone's cheerful disposition as it was to the closeness of their friendship. They didn't have the ability to see each other often, but Nick had considered Harstone one of his dearest friends from the beginning. Though they hadn't seen each other for several months, since the last time they were both in London during the Season, their relationship had not dimmed.

"You're looking well, *Lord* Harstone," Nick said when they broke apart. He emphasized the title, mostly because he knew his friend hated being esteemed above others when he had simply been born into it. Lord Calloway was the same way, and Nick—a mere mister—loved them for it. "I thought you'd look older."

Harstone glared at the unnecessary title, but a grin quickly replaced his displeasure as he examined Nick. "My girls keep me young. London does not do the same to you, I think."

"Tell me something I do not already know," he said with a sigh. Every day he seemed to have aged another year, and he certainly wasn't getting any younger. Before long his search would be entirely fruitless, and that prospect sounded grim indeed. He wanted a family. As big as he could get.

"Your Miss Barton was quite distraught when you disappeared upon arrival," Harstone replied. "My cousin was most worried for your fate."

Nick clenched his hands into fists and counted to five before he spoke, and even then he did so through gritted teeth. What might she have said when he was not there to temper her fantasies? "She is not mine, I assure you."

Harstone's eyes danced with laughter. "Have you told her that?"

"Many times." At least, he had given her no reason to think she had a chance of winning his affection. Perhaps he would finally have to be direct with the woman, but she was of a sweet enough disposition that he could imagine the hurt in her eyes when he told her they would never suit.

Wanting to avoid her tears hadn't done him any good at this point, however, so he would have to work up the courage, and soon.

"Mr. Mackenzie is here for dinner," Harstone said.

Nick straightened up. "Is he?" He had expected he would need to seek out the man who had been his patron since he was a boy, as he had important matters to discuss with the old man—the other reason he had come to Staffordshire—but if Mackenzie was here at Harstone Court, that would speed things up a bit. Nick had worried he would have to wait to have this conversation, one he was eager for.

If the man was so adamant about Nick finding himself a wife before inheriting, surely he could at least offer some assistance in procuring a good one. Nick's funds were dwindling, and he would not last through another Season's rent in Town without Mackenzie increasing his allowance. If he had to worry about only himself, that would be one thing, but his little allowance still had to pay the living expenses of his old housekeeper.

It wasn't Mrs. Murray's fault she was no longer needed when Nick's estate had fallen to ruin, and now she was too old to find a position elsewhere. She had no children to care for her and her husband was long gone, so Nick had stepped in. If only he could afford to do more.

"He is in the upstairs salon, if you care to see him after you change," Harstone said, referring to Mackenzie.

It was a not-so-subtle hint that Nick was an absolute mess after the incident with the carriage, but Nick knew he would only get more and more anxious if he didn't get right to it.

"Thank you," he told his friend and clapped a hand on his back. "It's good to see you, Harstone."

"And you."

Following Harstone's direction, Nick quickly made his way up to the salon, forming his arguments as he went. Mr. Mackenzie was a fair-minded old man, if a little odd, so Nick hoped he would at least listen. If all went well, the man would see reason and grant Nick his rightful fortune before he was reduced to begging. He needed to be firm. Confident. He needed to prove that he was worthy of inheriting Mr. Mackenzie's estate on his own. No other man had such ridiculous stipulations for receiving what was promised to him, and Nick clearly did not have the ability to follow through. If the past three years weren't enough time to prove that marriage simply wasn't an option, at least not in the near future, Nick wasn't certain the old man would ever believe him.

He was not opposed to begging, if it came to it, but he would rather keep his dignity intact if at all possible. There was enough talk about him in London as it was.

True, most of that was his own doing, but Nick could only control so many rumors. The fact that so many in the country knew how heartily he searched for a wife had always been a thorn in Nick's side, and no amount of storytelling could dissuade the Society tabbies from whispering about his future behind their fans as they threw their daughters in his direction.

If he had known how difficult his lies would make all of this, perhaps he wouldn't have hidden behind them for so long. Then again, creating a fake persona and life for himself had been the only thing he could think of in his desperation to protect the remainder of his broken heart after his engagement had fallen apart.

He found Mr. Mackenzie sitting in a well-stuffed chair by the fire, reading a letter, with his spectacles perched on the end of his nose. He looked up when Nick entered, and Nick felt a queasiness enter his stomach. He didn't know the old man well, despite being his heir, and Nick always found Mr. Mackenzie to be more than a little intimidating. The man's lands were prosperous and coveted, and his fortune was vast enough that it had sent swarms of ladies Nick's way when they'd learned he was to inherit the whole of it.

He still hadn't figured out how that information had gotten out in the first place.

Clearing his throat, Nick approached cautiously. "Good evening, sir."

Mr. Mackenzie scrutinized Nick, as if searching for something to criticize. He had never been a cruel man, but Nick had always felt lacking in his presence, though he wasn't sure why. Hadn't he given Mackenzie enough reason to be proud of him? Perhaps it was simply the mud that stained his clothes, and suddenly Nick wished he had followed Harstone's advice and changed before coming to the salon so he could be a little more presentable.

He shifted his weight between his feet, not sure how best to approach the subject. "Are you comfortable? Can I get you any—"

"Oh, stop pretending you care about my health, boy."

Nick drew back in surprise. "I care."

Mackenzie finally smiled, his eyes crinkling at the corners and making him look far more devious than any old man had a right to be. "The bare minimum, perhaps," he said. "But the sooner I die, the sooner you can contest my will and get your hands on my fortune."

Nick was about to say he had never planned on contesting the will, but his words stuck in his throat as his mind caught up to what the man had just said. Cocking his head to the side, he pondered that for a moment. "Why would I need to contest anything? I am to inherit, am I not?"

Mackenzie laughed, the sound deep in his chest, if a little rough. "That depends," he replied, which made Nick's blood run cold. What was that supposed to mean? "You do remember I have two granddaughters, don't you?"

Nick had to admit he had quite forgotten the second one. The elder had married Harstone and was now the viscountess, but the younger had never truly been anyone of consequence to Nick. As a woman, she would take only her dowry and a small yearly allowance when Mr. Mackenzie passed.

Or so Nick thought.

He sank into a chair, frowning as he processed this information. "You're telling me Miss Mackenzie is stealing my fortune?" he said warily. But that shouldn't be possible.

Mr. Mackenzie chuckled. "Technically, it is still my fortune, Forester. And no, she is not, no matter how determined she is to remain independent and care for the estate herself. You'll have your money if you keep your end of the bargain."

"So if I do not find myself a wife, you'll give everything to your granddaughter and leave me with nothing? I am already stretched thin as it is." He had been counting on this inheritance; he had gotten nothing from his own father, and Nick refused to imagine a future in which he was left entirely destitute.

True, if he had married before now, he would have no concerns, but that only complicated the matter.

"You could find an occupation," Mackenzie said.

"You owe me—"

"I owe you nothing, boy."

Nick flinched, surprised by the harsh tone of the old man's words. Mackenzie was right, though, and Nick had no reason to expect anything from him. If his own livelihood was the only one in jeopardy, he would be less reluctant to take up an occupation, but he had the security of Mrs. Murray to worry about. Where would she go without the quarterly funds he sent her?

Sighing deeply, Mr. Mackenzie pushed himself up to his feet and leaned heavily on his walking stick as he peered into Nick's eyes. He seemed to be searching for something, though Nick had no idea what that might be.

"I have known you since the day you were born, Nicholas Forester," Mackenzie said. "And I loved your father as if he were my own son. But if you are anything like your father, then I will see to it that you have someone with a good head on her shoulders who can keep you moving in the right direction when it comes to your finances. I will not have the Mackenzie fortune wasted on poor investments made on a whim."

Nick wanted to argue against such a blatant insult to his father, but the alarmingly small number that represented the worth of his assets was nothing less than full proof. Nick's father had been hasty when he came across an opportunity, and it had cost the Forester name everything. Without Mr. Mackenzie on his side, Nick possessed nothing but a profitless estate.

He thanked Providence that no one in London believed that part of his life, or he would have even more difficulty in securing a wife. He hated that his mistaken wealth proved both helpful and detrimental in his search. Without a fortune, no lady wanted him. Those who sought his fortune rarely cared about the man behind it.

How could he win?

"Sir." Nick let out his breath all at once as everything sank in, leaving him dizzy. He had been counting on this inheritance, and he had no plan beyond it. Even if he sold his land, losing his status as part of the landed gentry would far diminish any minuscule profits that may come from the sale. His father may have made a bad deal, but he'd been a gentleman through and through. Nick could only hope he could be the same and honor his name.

What would he do if he was cut off entirely? He stuffed his hands into his hair as anxiety sent his heart racing. What occupation could he possibly take up without besmirching the Forester name? There were only so many vocations that could be considered appropriate for a gentleman of his status, and among those only one or two Nick could actually do. None of his skills would give him what he needed.

He had gotten a good education at Cambridge alongside Calloway, but his studies had been general, and no education or intelligence could save his land at this point. Only money. The steward who had managed the lands until Nick came of age had told him there wasn't enough money to make repairs to the tenant cottages after several bouts of poor weather soon after his parents passed when he was twelve years old, and all his tenants had moved on over the years. With no income other than the small stipend Mr. Mackenzie had given him each year, Nick had had nothing to use to try to return the land to something profitable.

Had he told Mr. Mackenzie any of this? Of course not. He had felt guilty enough when he had to let all his staff go, especially Mrs. Murray. She had looked after him before he came of age, like a replacement mother after his had died. It was the very reason he paid for her living expenses, which hardly felt adequate to repay what she had done for him. This inheritance had felt precarious enough as it was, and he hadn't wanted the old man to think him incapable of managing the Mackenzie estate just because he hadn't had a chance to save his own.

It seemed pride would be his downfall.

"Why is it so hard for you to find yourself a woman to marry?" Mr. Mackenzie asked, still grinning with amusement as he returned to his seat. "From what I hear, there are women aplenty throwing themselves at you."

Slowly dropping his arms, Nick stared at Mackenzie and was horrified as he considered what gossip could have traveled this far north from London. Just how many people talked about the uncatchable Nicholas Forester? Perhaps Mackenzie had simply observed it all for himself when he was in London last summer. "Not every woman does a good wife make," Nick said warily. Surely the man understood that, at least.

As Mackenzie sipped tea from a cup that sat beside him, a chorus of childish shrieks filled the air above them. Nick looked up in alarm, but Mackenzie merely smiled. "My granddaughter certainly found herself a wonderful husband, did she not? Lord Harstone is a most doting father."

Harstone was the cause of all the screams of laughter? That didn't surprise Nick, and he found himself smiling despite the situation. "I have never known a man better than Alvaro Rowland," he said softly. Then he perked up. Mackenzie couldn't possibly fight this argument: "I only want what he has," he said. "A loving wife. A happy marriage. A good family. But I cannot have that if I am as poor as a church mouse."

Mackenzie made a face that was made up of both amusement and offense. "Who says money is the source of happiness?" he said, the words a bit rough. "You cannot possibly believe the only happy people in marriage are those with fortunes behind them. If anything, one might argue the opposite is true."

"Then, what of my parents?" Nick asked. His last argument had apparently failed after all, and now he was simply exhausted. He leaned his elbows on his knees as a headache built up behind his eyes. He had come into this room hoping to expedite his inheritance, and instead he had only succeeded in practically losing it. "Mother and Father were impossibly happy together, and they had a fortune to call their own." A fortune Nick would have had if Father hadn't been given poor advice and lost everything to that bad investment. That had begun a series of unfortunate events that had left Nick parentless and penniless.

Mackenzie huffed. "You cannot claim an exception as the rule, my boy. Your parents were lucky."

"And yet you will not allow me to find my own luck?"

"Do you think you could possibly be so lucky by the first of December?"

Nick's head snapped up. "Six weeks?" he gasped. "You're giving me only six weeks?" Surely he was not serious.

The old man chuckled again, unconcerned by the sheer panic in Nick's voice. "I have given you three years, Nicholas. A man of your quality should have found a wife long before now."

"But—"

"I told you this back in June, my boy. My decision has been made." Mackenzie spoke with finality, and he rose to his feet once more with some measure of difficulty. "The papers have already been drawn. If you have not made a respectable man of yourself and found a bride before December arrives, everything I possess will go to my younger granddaughter."

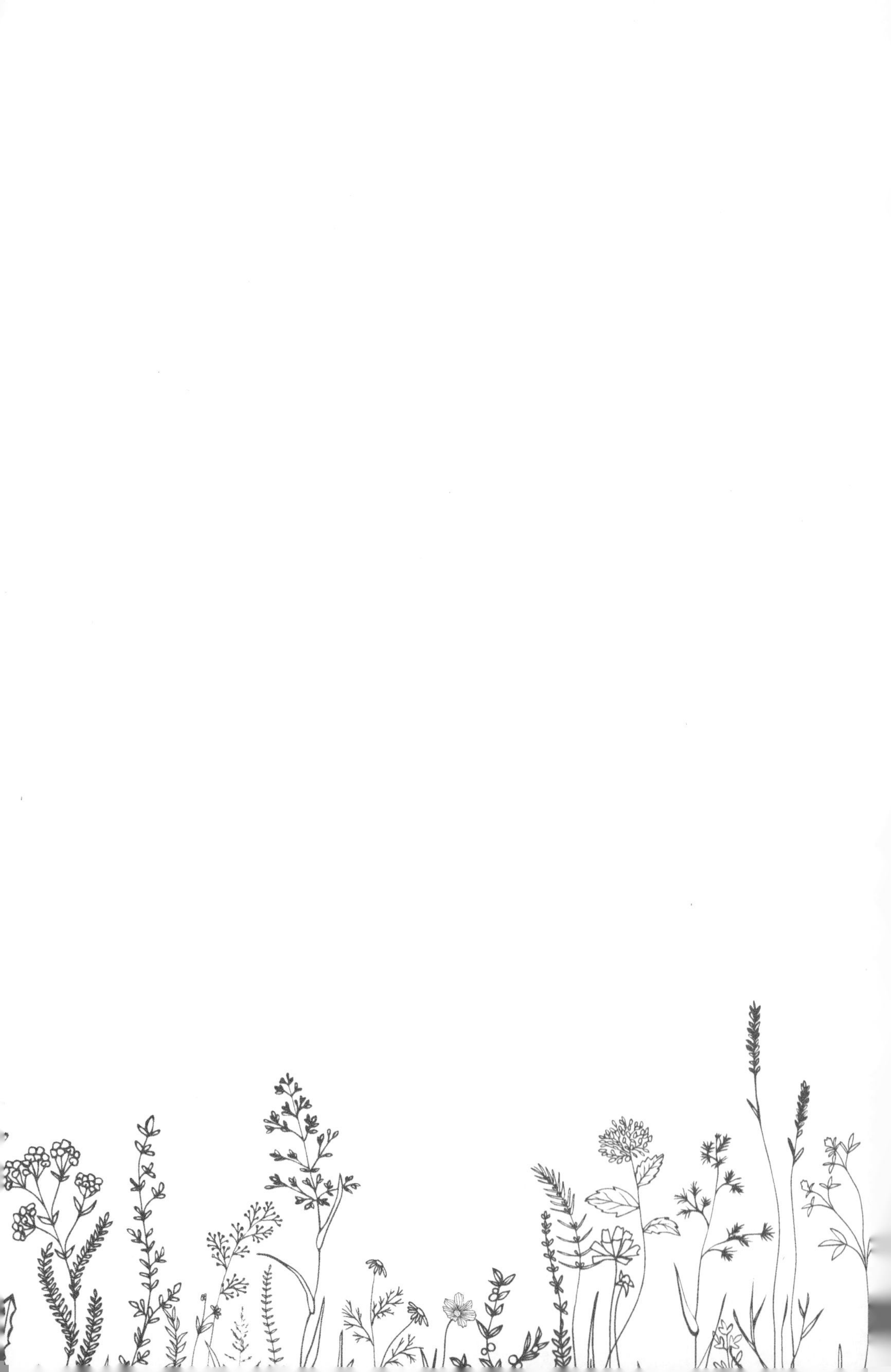

Chapter Four

Sure enough, the Miss Barton who'd spent ten minutes discussing curtains with Tabitha was the peacock from Tutbury. Emma had joined her sister in greeting the newly arrived guest, mainly because she hoped to catch a hint of whether Nicholas was also here without asking directly.

"All in all," Miss Barton was saying, "they simply will not do."

Emma glanced at the curtains in question and could not for the life of her figure out how they could possibly be unsuitable. Supposedly, Miss Barton required complete and total darkness when she slept, and nothing but the blackest of curtains could assist her with that.

If the blazing fire in the grate was to remain as it was during the night—the nights could get rather cold this time of year—Miss Barton would have to consider more than only the moon's light as she slept.

Tabitha, as always, was a most gracious host and offered to fetch the darkest curtains from one of the other rooms so Miss Barton could be as comfortable as possible.

Eventually, Miss Barton realized there was someone else in the room, and she scrutinized Emma for a moment before she said, "Did I see you in town earlier?"

"I believe so," Emma replied. "It seemed you had lost someone." She bit her lip to keep from laughing about the incident at the millinery; the memory of Nicholas hunched up behind the display made keeping her amusement to herself difficult.

Falling onto the chaise longue quite dramatically, Miss Barton sighed and looked for all the world as if nothing was going her way. Her tragic expression seemed to be saying, *First Nicholas and now curtains*. "Indeed," she said, her voice almost musical with dramatics. "That frustrating man has a habit of disappearing at the most inconvenient times. And now he has disappeared again. Who knows what may have happened to him!"

Emma couldn't help herself, and she spoke before she could hold her tongue back. "Perhaps something drove him away."

Miss Barton lifted her eyes and narrowed them, as if sensing a challenge in Emma's words. "He would never simply leave me on my own," she said slowly. "He is the best of men."

Coughing before she said something to the contrary, Emma nodded as if Miss Barton had said something quite profound. "I am sure he is," she lied. "Though, it is unfortunate for him to have disappeared like a, er, beast in the brush."

Tabitha coughed as well, which meant she had just discovered Miss Barton's role in Emma's earlier recounting of her trip to town. "Let me see about getting you some better curtains, Miss Barton," Tabitha said and tugged the bell pull.

As soon as a maid had been summoned and given instructions to replace Miss Barton's curtains, Emma took Tabitha by the arm and led her from the room before either of them cracked. When they had reached a respectable distance, she flashed her sister a knowing smile that made them both snort in laughter.

"She is rather eccentric, isn't she?" Tabitha said quietly.

"She reminds me of Mrs. Thatcher," Emma replied. "Do you remember how particular she was about her hems? Terrorized the dressmaker enough to make her leave town."

"Mrs. Clifford left because she got remarried," Tabitha said, shaking her head. "Sometimes, Emma, I wonder if you have begun to confuse fact with fiction."

Emma knew she had a habit of embellishing things, but the plain old truth was never very exciting. "Fiction is more fun," she argued.

"Which is why Miss Barton has become a witch in your eyes, is it? And who is this mysterious beast?"

Heat spotted Emma's cheeks, and she hoped Tabitha didn't notice. "I did not get his name."

"I see." Tabitha frowned, as if she knew something Emma didn't, and busied herself with brushing her skirts.

"Perhaps Alvaro knows who he is," Emma suggested, though she was tempted to ask whether her sister was keeping something from her.

"I will ask him if there is anyone new in town. Regardless, he may likely know the man. He has far too many friends."

"Your husband has far too much of a lot of things." Another round of squeals echoed through the corridors of the house. "Energy being one of them."

Sighing, Tabitha shook her head and held on a little tighter to Emma's arm. "If I did not love the man with all my soul," she muttered, "I would hate that about him. But I cannot begrudge my girls having a loving father when we were not so lucky."

A darkness settled around them, as it always did when one of them mentioned their late father. The man had never been cruel, but loving had not been one of his more dominant traits, despite his having been born of a man as kind as Grandfather. It was one of the reasons Emma was so reluctant to marry. Unless every potential suitor she came across could be as good a man as Alvaro Rowland, she feared she would never be content with any man.

Their mother had managed perfectly well on her own after her husband had left the three of them behind in pursuit of some wild dream to be a world traveler. His death abroad had not hurt any of them, outside of the required mourning period and its horridly plain dresses. If Emma had any say in the matter of her future, she would leave her care to no one but herself.

Just as they reached the entryway landing, one of the maids hurried up to the pair of them and curtsied. "Mr. Mackenzie would like to speak to you, miss," she told Emma. "He is in the library. And Cook was asking for you, my lady," she said to Tabitha.

Sharing one more smile with hidden laughter behind it, Emma and her sister parted ways, Tabitha to the kitchen and Emma to her grandfather.

Emma saw Elias first, tucked away in the corner behind a book, as he often was whenever he visited Harstone Court. Grandfather was in the chair next to him, and though they didn't seem to be in conversation, the two of them shared a look before Elias closed his book and rose.

"I need to ask Lord Harstone if he will let me borrow this," he said, though his voice wavered enough that Emma knew it was simply an excuse to get out of the room.

That was concerning.

Elias paused at the door, however, and glanced back to give Emma a brief smile. "I have been invited to stay for dinner," he said. "Think you can bear my company a little longer?"

Emma let out a sigh. "I am not going to grace that ridiculous question with an answer, Mr. Drake."

Smiling again, this time with a little more emotion to it, he bowed his head to Mr. Mackenzie and left the room, leaving Emma and her grandfather alone.

"Mr. Drake is a good man," Grandfather said.

Elias was the son of Mama's brother and therefore not related to Grandfather, but the two men had formed a bond after Papa left and Grandfather took over the care of his daughter and granddaughters. Grandfather treated Elias like the grandson he'd never had.

Nodding, Emma took up Elias's vacated seat near the fire, watching Grandfather's face to gain any sort of indication of what he might have summoned her for. It could not have been to talk about Elias.

"Are you well, Grandfather?" she asked quietly. If it were a trivial matter, he would not have sent Elias away, and he could have spoken to her about it when they returned home to Mackenzie Manor down the road.

Mr. Mackenzie huffed when Emma tucked her hands in her lap to stop herself from fidgeting. "Oh, stop looking so nervous, child." Setting aside the book he had been reading, Grandfather studied her with his rich brown eyes and took a slow, deliberate breath. Whatever he had to say, it seemed to carry some weight to it. "Well," he began and let out all the air in a sigh. "I'll just come right out and say it, as I would imagine you do not already know. Mr. Forester is in town."

Emma tensed. "Mr. Forester? He is in Tutbury?" That man had been nothing but a thorn in Emma's side since the day she was born, it felt like, as he was to inherit almost everything from Grandfather simply because he was a male. He wasn't even related to Grandfather, and yet he was the one who would take over the Mackenzie estate.

Surely even Elias would be a better option than someone unconnected to the family, but no.

Grandfather nodded gravely. "He is in Tutbury," he confirmed.

"But why?"

"Because he is a dear friend to your viscount brother-in-law."

Had Emma known that? Surely Alvaro or Tabitha would have mentioned something. "I suppose . . ." She forced herself to sound calm and unaffected, even though she would inevitably come face-to-face with the one person standing in the way of her independent future. "I suppose it will be nice to finally meet him," she said, feeling rather pathetic. The last thing she wanted was to meet her enemy. "Will he be in town for a while, then?"

"I believe so."

Emma rose, her mind spinning as she processed this unfortunate information. What if he was the man in the millinery? But no, surely this was all just a coincidence.

"Thank you for warning me," she said, curtsying before she took a step toward the door.

"That is not why I called you in here, Emma."

Emma immediately sank back into her chair.

At least Grandfather smiled, his eyes crinkling at the corners and leaving nothing but warmth and kindness in his face. "My dear, I know what you must think of me, leaving everything to him when you are my grandchild."

Emma didn't open her mouth for fear of insulting the man who had taken her in when her mother had died unexpectedly, when Emma was only ten.

"I do not often approve of Society's traditions being as set as they are, but . . ." He trailed off, his eyes distant. "In this case, I can only do so much if I want to secure your future happiness. You are a woman, and I have no near male relations. Naming Forester as my heir allows me peace of mind, knowing our family's lands will be well cared for without the risk of greed getting in the way. And without me, the young man has nothing. You, at least, have your dowry to help you find a worthy husband to care for you."

She had feared this part—dreaded it—and even though she had known it was coming, she had hoped she would at least get the chance to make her case. To gain something from the man who had himself declared her his most treasured companion. Clearly all her hoping had been in vain, and she fought the tears that filled her eyes. She would have to move to another plan, then, whether that involved finding herself a husband she could tolerate or seeking employment to pay her way through the rest of her little life. Her yearly allowance would only get her so far, and there was no telling what Forester might do when he inherited.

"Emma." Grandfather's tone had gotten stronger, and when she looked up at him, his eyes twinkled a bit. "I have no intention of sending you out onto the streets when I am gone. I have a plan, if you can but be patient."

"I do not understand," she admitted, her voice wavering.

"I have given Mr. Forester a task with a deadline. The stipulations of his inheritance are clear; if he cannot procure himself a wife by the first of December, he inherits nothing."

Emma brushed away a stray tear that had escaped to her cheek. "So . . ."

"So if Mr. Forester proves to be just as fickle as he has been these past three years, you have every chance of besting him in this game I have created. It is a fair enough opportunity for him to take what he thinks is his."

She hardly thought so, but she was not about to tell Grandfather that. A game indeed. Not fully understanding the rules, Emma wasn't certain how giving Mr. Forester a deadline was fair to either of them, and it simply meant delaying the inevitable. Emma would receive nothing, but she would spend the next month and a half wondering whether she might have a change of luck. Surely a man of any sense would snatch up the first beauty he came across in order to secure his fortune. The small matter of marriage was nothing compared to obtaining the Mackenzie estate.

Chuckling, Grandfather leaned forward and patted Emma's hand. "Do not look so morose, child. Anthony's son is of a predictable sort, and he is as much disturbed by my decision as you are—which means he fears he will be unable to make a lasting attachment in such a short space of time. He has had three years to find himself a suitable wife, and surely you have heard of his lack of success."

Even in Staffordshire Mr. Forester was often the subject of gossip. Just this year he had supposedly spurned three prominent ladies hoping to win his hand, and despite him being one of London's most eligible, he had hardly given anyone more attention than what was polite. Emma had, admittedly, taken a keen interest in the man's adventures simply because she wanted to know the sort of man who would receive everything she hoped for.

And his adventures were many, if all the stories were to be believed. Apparently the man spent most of his time saving babies and fighting battles, despite rarely leaving London. What utter rot!

She had always disliked him, thinking him the most odious man to walk the earth. What sort of man thought himself so above others as to perpetuate so many lies to make himself appear grander?

"You think he will not succeed?" she whispered, barely daring to hope.

Grandfather smiled and gave her hand a squeeze. "I think there is hope for you yet," he replied.

There was another matter that was bothering her, though she was afraid to ask in case it complicated things even more. Still, it would be best to go into the next several weeks knowing exactly what she was up against. "And am I under the same obligations as Mr. Forester?" she asked warily. "Will I need to find myself a husband before I can inherit?"

Grandfather pierced her with a look of long-suffering. "You have always known my stance on this, Emma. No matter how sensible you may be, the law gets muddy when it comes to a woman owning property. Especially at your young age, I fear anything I give you would be taken away from you otherwise."

She wouldn't lose anything. The lands were unentailed, which meant he could give them to whomever he pleased. Emma was nearly at the age of majority and knew enough to keep the lands well maintained and prosperous.

Whatever risk he thought he saw, it wasn't there. Unless . . . unless he had given Forester the deadline of her birthday for a reason. Surely he could have no fears once she was old enough to make her own decisions. Perhaps it was wishful thinking on Emma's part, but it was the best she had.

He sighed, reaching out to cup her cheek. "My wish is to see you find someone to love and cherish you as you deserve, my dear. Whether here in Tutbury or somewhere else, you are more than kind and beautiful enough to find yourself a good and happy life. Mr. Forester, on the other hand, needs all the help he can get in life."

What he needed was someone to prevent him from finding a wife so he could be forced into fixing his own problems. Emma would turn twenty-one at the start of December, which coincided with Mr. Forester's deadline. If he couldn't find himself a wife, surely Grandfather would leave it all to her, with or without a husband. Any other outcome would leave her hopeless and heartbroken.

Chapter Five

Thank goodness for the sheer size of Harstone's house. Nick had been pacing for nigh on an hour now, his thoughts whirring and his stomach twisting and his boots stomping through an empty wing of the house as he sorted through the revelation Mr. Mackenzie had sprung on him.

Less than two months?

Surely the old man could not mean that. What sort of man entered into an agreement in six weeks?

Nick growled to himself. *Everyone.* Everyone did that. Nick had known courtships to last only long enough for the banns to be read, and only because a special license was out of the question. He had known men to take one look at a lady and declare right then to be madly in love with her and in two months prove the sentiment true. Lord Calloway, a man who left his country home only when on business and was all things practical, had found himself a wife within a week. Nick had seen a man propose within twenty minutes of meeting a woman, for heaven's sake, so what the devil was wrong with *him*?

He had meant what he'd told Mr. Mackenzie, that he wanted to marry for love. How could he not, after seeing how happy his parents had been together? Even seeing Harstone and Calloway with their wives told Nick that anything less would only make him miserable, and that was hardly worth the small fortune he would gain from an unhappy marriage.

The small fortune that was the only thing keeping him from entering the poorhouse.

He kicked the nearest wall and immediately regretted it when his toes collided with the wood with a lot more force than he'd expected. Hopping on one foot in pain, he grumbled curses to himself and considered how much it would injure Harstone if he decided not to stay.

How could he? His blasted rival would be just down the road throughout his entire stay, silently tormenting him whether she knew the stipulations of

Mr. Mackenzie's will or not. Just her presence was enough to send Nick into a panic. If she had not existed, he would not be in this predicament. Why couldn't she have found herself a ridiculously wealthy viscount like her elder sister and saved Nick all this trouble?

He cursed again, far more loudly this time.

"Oh," a gentle voice said.

Nick froze, one leg still in the air. Who had just stumbled upon him and witnessed him in the worst possible state? Not only must he look ridiculous, but he had also been using ungentlemanly words just then. Dropping his foot, he took a deep breath and spun to face his captor.

He immediately smiled. "It's you!"

The woman from town narrowed her eyes, just as skeptical as she had been before. Now that she was no longer trapped beneath the shadows of a bonnet, Nick could see that her eyes were just as green as they were blue, and her honey-colored hair gave her a soft appearance that he rather liked. "Am I interrupting something?" she asked.

Goodness, she looked even more beautiful than she had in town, which left him tongue-tied. That was a foreign feeling, and he hated how quickly any sense of wit left him. He fought for something to say. *Anything.* "No, of course not. Merely a frustrating conversation with myself."

"I see." She turned to go back the way she had come.

"Wait!" Thankfully, she looked at him again, and Nick smiled. "You really won't tell me your name? You already know mine."

She scoffed. "Hardly."

"You're right. I abhor being called Nicholas. I would rather you call me Nick."

"I'm not going to call you anything. Not without a proper introduction." She raised an eyebrow, looking him over. "Perhaps not even then."

Despite the indirect insult, Nick laughed. "My, but you are stubborn, aren't you?"

Folding her arms, she seemed to fight a smile as she stood there. "What else would I be?"

"Without knowing who you are, I could hardly say," Nick replied. "But I did not say stubbornness was a bad trait."

Her pink lips twisted upward despite her attempts to keep her smile from appearing. Nick had a feeling he would treasure her smile. "Is that so? You think it admirable?"

"I suppose that depends on the circumstances."

"What about now?"

Nick chanced a step closer, pleased when she didn't flinch. He appreciated her ability to keep to her principles. Or perhaps he appreciated interacting with someone who didn't already know who he was. He couldn't remember the last time he had gone anywhere without admirers flocking to him. "Now," he said, taking another step, "I think your stubbornness should step aside long enough for me to learn your name so I might know what to call you when I tell you that you are utterly beautiful."

Her cheeks brightened with a handsome pink at the same time her smile broke free, and Nick had never seen a more enchanting smile. Whoever this woman was, she had captivated him.

"There you are!"

Nick jumped at the sound of a voice down the corridor and only realized how close he had gotten to the alluring woman when she slipped away to a respectable distance. Curse Miss Barton and her ability to drive him absolutely mad! He was usually more aware of his own actions.

"I was worried you had gotten yourself lost," Miss Barton said, completely ignoring their companion.

Nick gritted his teeth. "Me? Lost?" he said. "Certainly not. I simply saw a ghost down this corridor and thought to hunt it down and learn her history."

Miss Barton laughed, though it sounded more like the high-pitched twill of a chaffinch. "Do not tease me so, Nicholas," she said. "You know how interested I am in spirits. Was she a wayward soul?" Her eyes searched the empty corridor, as if she might catch a glimpse.

"Nothing of the sort," Nick replied. He only then realized her fingers had somehow wrapped around his arm, and he frowned down at his elbow. How had she managed to do that without him noticing? He must be losing his mind. "It was simply the ghost of a cow who must have wandered this land before the house was built."

"You know," Miss Nameless said. Her voice was so much smoother than Miss Barton's, and far more pleasing to the ear. Or perhaps it was simply a voice he had not heard far too much of today. "I have often seen that cow wandering around during my visits to Harstone." She barely concealed her grin, and Nick was once again fascinated by the woman. "It seems to be looking for something."

Miss Barton's mouth opened wide. "Looking for something?" she repeated in awe. "Whatever might a cow be wanting?"

"Perhaps her bell?" Miss Nameless suggested.

Nick had to bite his cheek before he laughed. "I don't believe I saw a bell around her neck," he agreed. "Perhaps we need to find her one so she can move on to what comes next."

"Where are we supposed to find a bell for a phantom cow?" Miss Barton said, and she seemed genuinely concerned.

Miss Nameless, on the other hand, bit her bottom lip and met Nick's gaze with her dazzling one. "I do not think we need an actual cow bell," she said with false solemnity. "I am certain simply the sound of one will do. One of us should attempt it before she wanders to another part of the house."

Oh, that wicked girl. Nick could no longer hide his grin, so he turned away before Miss Barton saw his expression. "I do believe she is nearly to the end of the corridor," he said with mock alarm. "I have never heard the sound of a cow bell, however, so I shan't attempt it."

"And I believe my name is being called downstairs," Miss Nameless replied. She threw one quick grin to Nick and hurried away, her skirts swishing behind her until she vanished around a corner.

Did the woman have any idea how enchanting she was? And how much hope her playful smile had given him in this moment of desperation? Such a lady, assuming she was unattached and even interested, could solve all his problems for him.

He needed to learn her name as soon as possible.

Just then, Miss Barton made the strangest sound Nick had ever heard, like a mix between a turkey's gobble and the sound one makes when hitting a bare toe against the corner of the bed in the middle of the night. He stared at her, bewildered, until he realized she was attempting the sound of a cow bell.

The attempt was absolutely horrendous.

"Miss Barton!" he said sharply, his voice cracking, and he coughed before he pulled his arm free and put a hand on her shoulder. "I do believe the ghost has moved to another part of the house." Perhaps he should have said she succeeded in sending the nonexistent cow to the beyond. Anything to stop her from making such an awful noise again. "I expect dinner will be served soon, so we should—"

"Oh dear," Miss Barton said with a sigh. "We shall have to try again tomorrow. Perhaps Miss Mackenzie will be able to assist then instead of being called away like she was now."

Nick froze, a sort of buzzing filling his ears. "What?"

"Miss Mackenzie," she repeated, furrowing her brow at him. "After all, it was her idea to make the sound of the bell, was it not? Perhaps she will have better luck."

Nick's mouth had gone dry, the buzzing now a roar. "Miss Mackenzie?" he said. Surely not.

Miss Barton laughed again and smiled at him as if he were a child. "My, you are entirely out of sorts today, Nicholas, and I have no idea why. Come. As you said, we should rejoin the others before we are missed. I am half-starved after traveling all day, aren't you?" Without a care in the world, she pulled him down the corridor toward the drawing room, and he stumbled blindly after her.

Mackenzie? How had he not recognized the one person in the county he was sworn to loathe? Well, of course he had not recognized her. With no other basis for comparison than her sister, who was clearly several years her senior, Miss Mackenzie could have been anyone.

A part of him knew this could turn out in his favor. Pursuing Miss Mackenzie would give them both what they wanted. Mr. Mackenzie had said something about her wishing to remain independent, but surely any woman of moderate intelligence would see this as an opportunity. And yet the thought didn't sit well in his stomach. He knew next to nothing about the woman, but he had a feeling her mind would not be easily changed. What if she didn't wish to share the land?

That would make them enemies. And Nick would a hundred times over rather be poor than trapped in a marriage with someone who would find him an inconvenience rather than a partner in life. That was the whole reason he hadn't already found a wife and secured his future, and he couldn't very well settle for less now. Even with his deadline.

Miss Barton had apparently already been introduced to the other dinner guests, as she took it upon herself to introduce Nick to each of them as they made their way around the crowded drawing room. The group was quite a bit larger than Nick had expected—though he should not have been surprised given the amiable nature of Lord Harstone—and yet it seemed no matter where he looked, there she was.

Miss Mackenzie.

He studied her carefully as she laughed with Harstone, as if she had not a care in the world. Why would she? She was only a few weeks away from being wealthier than most single women had the chance to be. Her brightness left a slightly bitter taste in his mouth, so much so that he could hardly focus on what Miss Barton was saying to the gentleman they had just fallen into conversation with.

Conversation being a loose term, of course, as Miss Barton was not one to let anyone get a word in with her fast-flying tongue.

Had Miss Mackenzie known who he was from the start? Perhaps that was why she had refused to give him her name. Nick had no doubt she was capable of acting, with the way she had dealt with the phantom-cow situation, but surely she could not have faked that smile of hers. It had lit up her eyes in the most genuine manner, just like it did now as she conversed with her brother-in-law.

Why had Harstone not warned him? But Nick knew the answer to that already. Harstone didn't know about the marriage stipulation or Mackenzie's ultimatum. No one knew.

The more Nick thought about it, the more he decided there was no possible way Miss Mackenzie knew who he was, the way she had smiled at him. Her wariness had been due to nothing but propriety. Dread weaved its way through his veins as he watched the woman laugh. This was not going to end well, even if he tried proposing marriage as a solution for them both. She didn't strike him as a woman to jump easily into a binding relationship any more than Nick was willing to risk a loveless marriage simply for the sake of money.

No amount of attraction could compensate for differing goals.

"Mr. Forester?" Miss Barton nudged his arm, giving him a pointed look.

Nick cleared his throat and turned to the man before them. "I am terribly sorry," he said, refusing to be embarrassed a third time. First in town, then in the passageway upstairs, but he would not be set down here in a crowd. If Nick was good at anything, it was charming strangers. "I had quite the long walk after I arrived today," he explained. "And then, what with the bandits and all, I—"

"Bandits?" Miss Barton cried.

The whole room went silent, and Nick realized his mistake. In a crowded ballroom at the height of the Season, the *ton* generally concerned themselves with their own business, all of them on the hunt, whether for a spouse or better connections. Here, at an intimate gathering, it was far more difficult to hide.

It was a good thing Nick had had plenty of practice hiding his true self; he never would have survived his years of wife-chasing without it.

"Did you say bandits?" Harstone said from the other side of the room.

Beside Harstone, Miss Mackenzie smiled and looked thoroughly amused by Nick's antics. It seemed his rival was indeed as ignorant of his identity as he had been of hers.

Clearing his throat again, Nick quickly sorted through the details of his story and got to it, all the while hating himself for falling into old habits yet again. "Truly," he said, "though they were new to the profession, from what I could tell. Didn't use a weapon or anything of the like."

"Bandits, here in Staffordshire?" someone whispered in alarm.

Nick would have to waylay that fear before he sent the whole room into a panic. "Not to worry, Mrs. Kirkham," he told the frightened woman. At least, he was pretty sure that was her name and hoped he hadn't heard Miss Barton wrong. "They were practically children. Hardly dangerous."

Miss Mackenzie had moved to her sister's side and was whispering something to her, her amused smile still intact.

A bad feeling churned in Nick's gut, and he could hardly focus. "After they tried to rob me—" he said, but his words faltered when Lady Harstone whispered something back to Miss Mackenzie.

Her smile dropped instantly, making way for an expression full of fury.

She knew. And that was not the look of someone who might be willing to compromise.

"After they tried to rob me," Nick said again, "I sat them down and showed them the error of their ways."

"Did you now?" a sharp voice said, and Nick winced. Miss Mackenzie was not going to mince words, it seemed. "I rather wonder at your ability to confront some young bandits when you are so frightened by smaller foes."

He met her gaze, which had turned so cold that he wondered how he had ever thought her charming. This was a woman who would not go down without a fight, nor be cowed by her opposition. This was a woman who seemed to be considering murder as an alternative to missing out on a livelihood she did not need.

Nick gulped and sent Harstone a silent plea for help.

The blessed man understood, announcing dinner was ready with a faltering smile and a look to his wife, as if hoping for reinforcements.

Miss Mackenzie's glare only turned harder as the other guests gathered to head into the dining room.

For the first time in his life, Nick considered feigning a headache and retreating.

Chapter Six

Just as Emma was walking into dinner after a quick but heated conversation with her sister, Nick stepped into her path. No, not *Nick*. Mr. Forester. The dreaded rival who threatened her every happiness. The *impostor*. The man whose presence Tabitha had kept a secret. Though her sister had apologized for not warning her, Emma had been quick to voice her displeasure at being left in the dark. Now she was trapped. As tempted as she was to ignore him and continue onward, her feet remained glued into place by the intense look he gave her.

"Miss Mackenzie," he greeted, bowing his head slightly.

She gritted her teeth. Niceties required that she reply, but she had no desire to be polite. "Forester," she said as sharply as she could. "At what point did you intend to tell me you were determined to steal everything from me?" She felt so foolish for writing his presence off as coincidence earlier. Of course he was Mr. Forester! At least her first impression of him had been correct, though he had nearly changed her mind with his playfulness in the corridor.

He let out a single, humorless laugh. "Right about when I discovered who *you* really were. You could have said." Folding his arms, he stood a little taller—wasn't he already tall enough?—and shook his head. "I suppose there isn't any point in me trying to convince you to—"

"You won't convince me of anything, Mr. Forester." Emma tried to match his height, though even she, who was taller than most women, barely reached his nose. She had to look upward to meet his gaze, which made her feel like he was looking down on her. Still, she would do her best to stand her ground. "I know what you will say."

"Is that so?"

"You think you and I should marry and allow us both to get what we want." The thought made her shudder.

Mr. Forester must have seen that shudder because he narrowed his eyes. "I was going to say nothing of the sort."

She exhaled through her nose. "Good. The Mackenzie lands are *my* home, and I have every intention of keeping them that way. Now, if you will kindly get out of my way, we are needed in the dining room."

He allowed her space to pass and followed her in, but to her frustration the only two place settings left were directly across from each other. It seemed she would have to continue interacting with him, though she would have to put a good deal of energy into keeping herself from childishly kicking him beneath the table.

He would probably take a silly kick as a sign that she was not a true opponent.

Well, Emma thought to herself, *he is most certainly wrong on that account.* She generally worked hard to ensure everyone was happy and included, but now her future was at stake. She couldn't be friendly with this man any more than she could see herself marrying the likes of him, with all his arrogance and exaggeration.

She had no idea how she would win, but Emma Mackenzie would not back down from this sudden call to arms. Not until she had her independence in hand. She only had to stave off his impending wedding—to whomever it might be—for six weeks, and then she would be free.

Easy.

Except Nick Forester was not a man to be trifled with, something she realized the instant he sent her a charming smile over the first course.

"Miss Mackenzie," he said with absolute ease and indifference, "Miss Barton here thinks you are the solution to our little problem in the east wing."

Emma gripped her napkin tight in her lap, twisting it so hard that she feared the servants would never get the wrinkles out. "Is that so?" She could see Elias watching her from the seat beside Miss Barton, and she knew he would ask her about the incident the first moment he could. She was riled up enough that he was likely quite worried about her.

"Miss Barton, were you not just saying Miss Mackenzie was the perfect candidate?" Mr. Forester said. He practically shouted it, as Miss Barton was clear on the other end of the table, and it pulled all attention their way. Did the man have no idea how dinner etiquette worked?

Miss Barton seemed thrilled to be addressed by the man and sent a ridiculous smile his way. "Indeed, Mr. Forester."

"What is wrong with the east wing?" Tabitha asked, and her concern came out clear in her thin voice.

Emma twisted her napkin even tighter, imagining it to be Mr. Forester's cravat around his neck. "Mr. Forester thought he saw a ghost," she said before either he or Miss Barton could turn it into anything more. What, had he roped that poor girl into his schemes as well?

Alvaro chuckled at the head of the table. "A ghost? You do not believe in ghosts, Forester."

"But of course he does," Miss Barton argued with wide eyes. "He swore he saw the spirit of a cow not an hour ago."

Mr. Forester's face turned pink, but it was not nearly enough for Emma to feel satisfied. This battle had only just begun. "He also said he was attacked by a couple of miniature bandits but managed to strike fear into their hearts," she said matter-of-factly.

Mr. Forester narrowed his eyes at her and seemed to be gathering his own arms to truly begin sparring. "Are you calling me a liar, Miss Mackenzie?"

"I am certainly not saying you've spoken any truth since you arrived. Bandits in Tutbury? Ghosts of cows? Preposterous."

"But you saw the cow as well, Miss Mackenzie," Miss Barton offered. "You said you've seen it many times."

Elias ducked his head to hide the smile playing at his mouth. Several others, Emma noticed, did the same.

Emma was tempted to throw her spoon at the insufferable Miss Barton and only refrained because Tabitha looked near to the breaking point. This was not how her sister had hoped their dinner party would go, and Emma was letting her own personal feelings get in the way of what was supposed to be an enjoyable evening. No part of this feud was Tabitha's fault, nor did it affect any of the other guests, who couldn't seem to decide whether they should laugh or choose sides.

It was time to take the battle to the background, away from anyone else. At least that way Emma would have a little more control and would not have to endure the ever-so-slight smile that curled Mr. Forester's lips. Apparently he seemed to think he had won this round.

Taking a deep breath, Emma turned to Alvaro and swiftly changed the subject, ignoring Miss Barton's comment entirely. "Do you think it will rain this week, Lord Harstone?"

Conversations immediately picked up again, and Emma breathed a sigh of relief as Tabitha smiled.

Without meaning to, Emma met Mr. Forester's gaze and scowled at him when she realized he was perfectly unaffected, despite the fact that some of the party now thought he believed in ghosts. She had to remember that the man had spent the last three years deep in the heart of social London and would not be overcome by one little oddity. From what she had heard, he had plenty others, and the man likely was used to being whispered about.

Emma, however, was not.

Mr. Forester lifted his wine glass in a toast, and though he spoke too softly to be heard, Emma could read his words well enough: "To the victor."

To the victor indeed. Nick Forester would rue the day he thought Emma would give up so easily.

* * *

After supper some of the guests moved to the parlor to play cards or engage in small conversations while some chose to return home before it got too late. People in Tutbury did not exactly conform to the fashionable traditions of remaining out until late in the night. Grandfather was snoozing in the corner, and Tabitha and Alvaro sat deep in discussion with their neighbors, Mr. and Mrs. Marshall. With Elias playing whist with Miss Barton, Miss West, and a man named Mr. Leeds, that left Emma and Mr. Forester, unless she wanted to speak to Miss West's mother. That would be a bad idea. Mrs. West continuously obsessed over the notion that she was suffering from some sort of ailment, which changed weekly. Emma had been caught in too many overly personal discussions over the years and now felt as if she knew as much of Mrs. West's body as the woman herself did.

Unwilling to interact with Mr. Forester unless it was necessary, and uninterested in talking to the supposed invalid Mrs. West, Emma settled into a chair in the corner and picked up the book sitting there—not with the intent to read it, as she had neither the patience nor the desire to read about flora and fauna, but in the hopes of appearing fully occupied until she could return home.

Mr. Forester ignored her attempts, settling himself next to her on the sofa. "I did not take you for a plant enthusiast, Miss Mackenzie."

Emma gripped the book so tightly that her thumb pulled at one of the pages, tearing it at the top. She winced. She refused to look at him, knowing his smirk would only make her angrier. "You know nothing about me, Mr. Forester."

"Pray, which flowering shrub is your favorite?"

"Was there something you wanted?"

He chuckled, the sound rumbling through his chest. Emma hadn't realized just how close he had sat until his jacket sleeve brushed her arm as he leaned nearer. "You know exactly what I want."

Though keeping her eyes on the book had become quite the feat with Mr. Forester so near, Emma managed it. "I also know you have plenty of time to get it. Pray, do you have plans in December?"

He stiffened, the first sign of weakness. "He told you?"

She couldn't resist looking at his expression, pleased to see the fear in his eyes. "My grandfather has my best interests at heart. Of course he told me." Even if his methods were a bit questionable.

The muscles in Forester's jaw strained as he examined her. "So it truly is to be a war?" he growled. "You should know I have no intention of standing down, Miss Mackenzie. I *will* be master of the Mackenzie lands." Gone was the lighthearted man Emma had seen in the corridor upstairs; a true beast sat in his place.

If the brute could convince a woman to take his hand, she would be a poor soul regardless of the fortune that would come with him.

Slamming her book shut, Emma turned to face the man. "Mr. Forester, need I remind you that you have no claim to those lands beyond my grandfather's charity?"

He winced at the word *charity*.

Emma pushed forward. "Are you so heartless as to leave me with nothing? Mr. Mackenzie's flesh and blood? Mackenzie Manor is my home. Without it, I have *nothing*."

"You have your dowry, don't you?" he snapped.

"My husband, should I ever find one worth consideration, will get my dowry."

His argument died on his tongue, which was a point in his favor. He had precious few of those. Clenching his jaw again, he turned his focus to the whist game on the other side of the room, where Miss Barton seemed to be trying to convince Elias to smile. "Miss Mackenzie," he said on a sigh. "I understand your situation. I really do. But I will not—cannot—step aside."

Emma hadn't expected anything otherwise. He could pretend to understand all he wanted, but as a man, he had freedom to take care of himself and do whatever caught his fancy. He would never know the struggle of being a woman subject to the whims of men.

"I do not think we need to continue discussing this topic," she said, no matter how much she wanted to shout at the awful man.

"We are in agreement."

"We most certainly are not. Otherwise, you would concede."

He groaned, rising to his feet and for once looking ruffled as he scrubbed a hand across his jaw. "Miss Mackenzie, please."

"I may not know your reasons for being so determined to take what is mine, Mr. Forester, but—"

"I thought we were no longer discussing the subject."

Her body tensing, Emma tried to ignore the way his eyes pierced hers with an intensity she'd never seen in anyone before. No matter how many lies surrounded him, there had to be some truth to the rumors about the man. From the little she knew about him, he was charming, friendly, and quick-thinking. He may not have saved lives every day like the rumors said, but perhaps he had become skilled at manipulating those around him to get what he wanted. The sharpness of his stare contained years of experience she would never have.

This battle would not be easily won.

She took a careful breath, wishing she had had some sort of military training. Alas, yet another reason women continued to be a step behind men.

"Mr. Forester," she began, "believe me when I say I will not easily give in."

"So you are saying I simply need to try harder. Noted."

"That isn't what I—"

He suddenly took hold of her hand, drawing a gasp out of her with his surprisingly gentle touch. He held it just long enough to plant a kiss against her knuckles, and then he returned her hand to her lap.

She hoped he didn't notice the tremble in her fingers.

"You have no idea what game you're playing," he murmured, speaking so softly that she leaned in. That intensity was still there, like a shadow had passed over his blue eyes. "You may think you're clever, Miss Mackenzie, but you are going to lose. A rose may have thorns, but they are never more than an inconvenience. Keep to looking beautiful; at least then you'll have done something worthwhile."

Though a flash of regret crossed the man's face, Emma refused to listen to any more of his nonsense. She leaped to her feet and hurried to Grandfather's side to gently shake him awake. "We should go home," she told him.

He grunted in response, but then his eyes landed on Mr. Forester, who still frowned as if Emma was being entirely unreasonable. "I see the two of you have spoken," Grandfather said with a chuckle.

"There is nothing humorous about this," she replied. "I wish you would have told me sooner that he would be here so I could have known to remain at home and avoid him." Although, now that she had met Mr. Forester, she had a better idea of what she was up against.

Surely no one would be daft enough to accept him when he was so unfeeling and selfish. He would be in Staffordshire for a few weeks at least, from what she gathered from Tabitha while the men had lingered over port, and all Emma had to do was provoke the man into showing his true colors every time he met a new lady. Not one of the women in Tutbury would be foolish enough to consider him if Emma had anything to say. What could he truly offer anyone? Charm? That would likely be his strongest asset, as he had plenty of it. His demonstration had given her that knowledge firsthand.

Mr. Forester had called her beautiful again, and she had felt his words to her core. She knew it was merely his most recent strike, but she still felt the whisper of his kiss on her fingers, as if his lips had left a searing brand behind.

She shuddered. No, no one would ever see anything admirable about the man, so no one would seek out his affection. No matter how charming he may be.

"Mr. Forester! You must come replace Mr. Drake."

No one except Miss Barton.

As she helped her grandfather to his feet, Emma watched carefully as Mr. Forester turned his attention to the young woman, hoping not to see any hint of attachment. He had literally run away from her that afternoon, but Miss Barton seemed of a persistent sort. She would likely be Emma's downfall if given the chance.

"What are you scheming now?" Elias asked her as he approached. "You know I don't like that look."

Emma waved him away. She would tell him about everything later, when Grandfather would not be able to overhear her plans. "Nothing at all. I simply wondered if you would be accompanying us home."

He frowned, as his family's home was just across the hedge from Mackenzie Manor. "You know I planned to."

"Wonderful."

"Good night, Grandfather," Tabitha said, kissing his cheek as they passed. "You'll come for tea tomorrow?"

Grandfather smiled as he accepted Elias's waiting arm. "Of course, dear. And thank you, Mr. Drake. You are too good to me."

Elias turned slightly red at the praise. "It is nothing, Mr. Mackenzie. I only wish to help where I can."

"We need to find you a spouse as well."

The heat in his face blossoming, Elias glanced back at the game of whist, as if wishing he had remained in the game rather than joined this conversation. "Eventually," he said, leaving it at that.

With Grandfather taken care of, Emma paused in the doorway and looked back at the card table as well. Three of the players were deep into the game, but one had his eyes locked on her.

It was a shame Mr. Forester was so handsome. His bright-blue eyes and striking jawline would only make it harder to keep him from finding a wife, and somewhere beneath his cold exterior was a wide smile that lit up his whole countenance. A smile like that, alongside his charm, could prove to be a valuable ally on his side of the war.

At the moment, he hardly wore an expression at all, and it brought a shiver to Emma's spine. She had a feeling she had only scratched the surface of this man, and she was afraid of what she might find if she dug deeper. And she would have to dig if she had any hope of securing her future.

Chapter Seven

Nicholas Forester was a cad. Though, perhaps he was doing himself a disservice by thinking so as he and Lord Harstone rode across a misty field. He had technically done nothing to Miss Mackenzie the night previous, and yet his chest ached with guilt. No, he had misstepped horribly. He had lost his temper in his frustration, something he never wanted to do, and he had fumbled through a pitiful attempt at softening the blow by telling her she was beautiful, though he knew that hardly made up for his cutting words.

Miss Mackenzie hadn't seemed to appreciate the compliment as he had hoped, though he didn't blame her.

Nick, fool that he was, couldn't help but admire the fact that she seemed to care little for vanity. He could hardly say she truly possessed an ounce of humility—he didn't know her well enough—and yet his measure of the woman continued to rise each time they went head-to-head in battle.

That attraction would do him little good when she was determined to take what small chance he had of making something of himself.

"This is the first time I have ever heard you so quiet, my friend," Harstone said as they crested a hill. To the east, the sun strained to break through the thin layer of clouds that threatened rain, leaving the air thick with moisture. "Has my cousin worn you down so thoroughly?"

Nick narrowed his eyes. "Miss Barton is the least of my problems, though she does have a knack for getting on one's nerves." The horse beneath him shifted nervously, clearly sensing his agitation. Nick had never been much of a horseman, or he might have given the beast its head and let it run to its heart's content. He certainly wished he could do the same.

As Harstone looked over the lands of his sprawling estate, he smiled with the ease of a man with a good life. "She cannot be that bad, no? I have known her for years and always enjoy her company."

Growling in his throat, Nick fought back an insult to the lady so as not to regret it later. He was dealing with enough of that emotion as it was. Besides, it wasn't Miss Barton's fault she had set her sights on a man so ill-equipped to choose a partner in life. She could have been the most perfect woman in all of England and Nick would likely have found a flaw in her. That seemed to be his pattern. "Yes, well, you, my friend, could enjoy the company of a halfwit and not notice the difference between him and the Prince Regent himself. You are uncommonly good."

"Calloway wrote to me." Harstone's smile hadn't dimmed. In fact, it seemed to have grown with each passing second.

Nick groaned. "And what did the good baron say? Did he tell you I've ruined all my chances of finding a wife and need to stop telling falsehoods if I ever hope to settle down?" Though he spoke with bitterness, Nick couldn't fault his friends for talking about him. Calloway was his oldest friend and had looked after him from the day they met at Eton. Nick had hardly done anything to deserve that friendship, but he treasured it, just as he did his friendship with Harstone. "Did he tell you he hardly recognizes me anymore?"

"He told me I should invest in silk," Harstone said with a chuckle. "But, since you brought up the subject, I hear Mr. Mackenzie has changed the rules."

Still tempted to ride off until he was miles away from his problems, Nick nudged his mount forward, all the while knowing Harstone would follow. "I suppose you all know my impending fate," he muttered. "Is nothing kept secret anymore?"

"This from the man who has his whole life on display? Emma told Tabitha, who naturally told me."

"Naturally," Nick grumbled, though he'd never had a confidante so natural in his life. Not even Calloway was privy to the inner workings of his soul, which left Nick to carry his own burdens without aid. No woman in England had been someone he could trust with his heart. Not since . . .

Clearing his throat, he pushed his horse a bit faster so conversation would be more difficult. Anything was better than dwelling on his failed engagement. "I suppose you will side with Miss Mackenzie on the matter," he grumbled.

"Why do you think that?"

The question caught him so off guard that Nick tugged on the reins, jerking the beast to a stop and nearly throwing himself straight over its head when it obediently complied. "What?"

A bit of mischief played in Harstone's eyes as he came up beside Nick far more gracefully. "You assume I support my wife's sister, yes? But I would sooner see her happily settled with a man worthy of her."

Nick scoffed. "The woman is twenty years old and refuses to go to London, and from what I hear from that bookworm cousin of hers, she is quite against the very idea of matrimony." Well, he had heard it this morning from Miss Barton, who'd heard it from Mr. Drake, which very well might have made the statement wholly untrue. Gossip hardly ever mirrored fact.

Chuckling, Harstone turned his mount to return back to the house. "Yes, Emma delights in independence. It is the reason she stays with her grandfather instead of with us."

"For which we are all grateful," Nick said under his breath. If he had been staying under the same roof as her, he might not have survived. Having Miss Mackenzie in the same town would be detrimental enough, particularly if her magnetism affected others the same way it had gotten to him before he'd learned her identity.

If the knot in his stomach was any indication, he would not likely find himself a bride in Tutbury. Was this entire visit going to be a waste of his limited time?

"But I believe she would accept a man's hand," Harstone continued, "if she found the right one."

"And then she wouldn't *need* my inheritance," Nick said, clenching his jaw as he followed his friend. As far as he was aware, she was under no marriage constraints like he was, but likely the only thing to convince her to surrender would be a better choice. Something more valuable than the Mackenzie lands.

Nick laughed bitterly. "It would take a fine man indeed to handle a wife such as that. All the money in the world wouldn't account for the bravery required to tie oneself to a woman like Miss Mackenzie." That wasn't necessarily true. He still found her terribly alluring, all things considered, but she hadn't even given him a chance to try to find a solution that would benefit them both. She had decided war was a better alternative to compromise, forcing him to fight fire with fire.

"You met her only yesterday, no?" Harstone seemed on the verge of laughing.

"Believe me, our small interaction was enough to tell me all I needed to know. I could spend the rest of my life never seeing her again and die happy." Also untrue, but Harstone didn't need to know that.

Beautiful though she was, Nick could hardly attach himself to someone who hated him.

"Pity. She will be joining us tonight at the Barlows'."

This time Nick's mount seemed to intentionally attempt to throw him, and he forced himself to relax. Not easily done when the prospect of another battle loomed before him. "Does she often invite herself to dinner parties?" he choked out.

The Barlow family had been more than happy to invite Nick to meet their two marriageable daughters, and he had been looking forward to a chance to meet the young ladies and, hopefully, get a good idea of his options here in Tutbury. But if Miss Mackenzie was to be in attendance, she would surely commandeer the evening and make herself an obstacle to his every step.

Throwing him a grin that contained far too much amusement for Nick's liking, Harstone shrugged a shoulder. "Tutbury is a small village, Forester, and Emma is well liked. You won't find a home unwilling to open their doors to her within twenty miles."

Oh, he didn't like the sound of that. "Surely not *everyone* enjoys her company."

Harstone had no response, and they rode the rest of the way back in silence.

That did not bode well.

* * *

The Misses Barlow were young and beautiful, both barely out in Society with only one Season behind them. The twins, blessedly, looked nothing alike, something Nick particularly appreciated when he learned their names did little to distinguish them. Miss Lily Barlow, elder by seven minutes, possessed a thin nose and close-set eyes, her features delicate and fair, while her sister, Millie, looked more robust, her hair of a chestnut shade and her round eyes dark. Both were immensely beautiful in their own ways and equally kind and gracious.

At least, Nick assumed as much. Dinner had been filled with stories from Miss Mackenzie—apparently a common occurrence—leaving him to sit and eat in silence because the ladies on either side of him had become too enthralled with the tales. Even now, in the drawing room, both girls had latched themselves to the insufferable woman and hung on her every word. Along with most of the room.

He had spoken at length to Mr. Barlow over port and found him to be a decent chap, but when he and the rest of the men in attendance had rejoined the ladies, their conversation hadn't continued to any topics beyond small-talk. With everyone else engaged in conversations or listening to Miss Mackenzie, Nick had migrated to a corner to rally his courage before he made any moves. It would likely be a losing battle, but surrender was not in his nature.

If those in attendance so enjoyed listening to Miss Mackenzie prattle on, surely he could command their attention for a moment or two. He had occupied entire ballrooms before; he could handle a country dinner party. He only needed to find his entrance.

"It was such a thrilling tale," Miss Mackenzie said, letting out a deep sigh as she smiled at her audience. "Who would have thought one could find such adventure on the sea? Almost makes me want to join the navy."

"I would never want to be a sailor," Miss Barton said, apparently quite scandalized as she sat with Miss West at the pianoforte. They had been looking through the music but had yet to play anything, too interested in what Miss Mackenzie was saying. "All that time at sea? I would be positively sick for the whole of it."

A few chuckles echoed around the room.

"You couldn't be in the navy even if you wanted to be," Mr. Oldman, a middle-aged bachelor neighbor, said with a scoff. "Can you imagine, a woman on a ship?"

"There are plenty of stories about lady pirates," Miss Mackenzie countered. "Some were quite fearsome."

"Legends," Mr. Oldman argued, but his disbelief caused the ladies in the room to scowl at him, which he realized quickly and shut his mouth tight.

Miss Mackenzie grinned, her eyes alight with amusement. "I think you will find women are just as capable as men in many instances, sir," she said lightly. "Perhaps more so. Why, I heard about a young woman who stole away on a ship just a few years ago and became first mate to the captain within months. She made herself a fortune shipping sugar from the Indies and retired here in England last year."

"Oh, you mean Miss Stanton?"

Heads swiveled to where Nick stood, and for the first time in his life he felt the weight of their gazes. He was always so comfortable with attention, so why did he have the sudden urge to pretend he hadn't said a word? He had made his entrance; now he had to justify his interruption. He clenched a fist behind his back, schooling his expression into nonchalance, despite the cool glare coming his way from Miss Mackenzie.

"You know this woman?" Miss Millie asked him, clearly in awe.

"I know her quite well," Nick replied with a wink, and his smile elicited a few giggles behind gloves. *Excellent.* "Though, I don't recall her ever setting foot on a ship. I do believe that was her brother, Lieutenant Stanton, was it not, Miss Mackenzie?”

Her face flushed a fetching shade of pink, making her look far more alive than the pale and delicate women around her. Ready to do battle.

“Miss Stanton does not have a brother, Mr. Forester,” she said calmly. “She merely posed as a man, which is why they let her on the ship in the first place. She *is* Lieutenant Stanton.”

“Oh, but I have met the lieutenant many times,” he argued, fighting a smile. For all he knew, this Stanton woman really did exist, but with the way Miss Mackenzie glowered at him, he had a feeling she was as adept at spinning tales as he was. “He and Miss Stanton are quite humorous together and have a habit of discussing his time at sea. She is quite proud of her brother and his accomplishments.”

Miss Mackenzie’s shoulders sank, but she showed no other signs of surrender. “No, you must be thinking of her cousin, the prominent actor, Mr. Stanton.”

The heads in the drawing room seemed as if watching battledore, their eyes bouncing back and forth between the two of them and waiting for one of them to miss the shuttlecock.

Nick’s smile only grew wider, though the game was far from finished. “I do believe your memory is failing you, Miss Mackenzie. I have been to the Stantons’ house on Wheeler Street many times and enjoyed countless meals and evenings with Lieutenant and Miss Stanton. She is a seamstress, is she not? And you must be thinking of Mr. *Scantion*, who was quite remarkable in his depiction of Hamlet last summer. You were there for that one, were you not? Oh, but I forget—you have not been to London since your unsuccessful Season several years ago. Perhaps you have mixed up your facts.”

Immediately upon those words leaving his mouth, Nick tensed. Nauseating guilt pulsed through him from such unkind words, and the tears that sprouted in Miss Mackenzie’s eyes only made things worse, though she still sat tall.

You’re a scoundrel, he told himself, clenching his jaw. Insulting a woman about circumstances beyond her control couldn’t possibly ingratiate him to the locals; it merely made him look an uncaring bounder. The silence in the room proved his fears, and he ducked his head, wishing he could turn back time to several days ago so he could do things all over.

Thank goodness for Miss Barton, who was likely feeling left out and jumped in with, “Oh, I adore Shakespeare! Mr. Forester, do you remember at Sir Henry’s party when Miss Grace completely butchered Sonnet 106?”

Nick cleared his throat, keeping his eyes away from Miss Mackenzie. "Indeed, though it can often be difficult to keep things straight when one has so many good acquaintances."

"Miss Barton!" Miss Mackenzie leaped to her feet. "I have seen you eyeing that pianoforte all evening, and I was hoping you would favor us with a song. With your permission of course, Mrs. Barlow."

"Yes, we must have music!" Mrs. Barlow said, clapping her hands.

Miss Barton practically glowed with pleasure as the others in the room expressed their desire for the same thing. She certainly seemed the sort to be glad of attention, and she shooed Miss West off the bench they had been sharing. "Mr. Forester," she said, looking over at him through her lashes, "would you be so kind as to turn the pages for me?"

"I believe Miss West was in the perfect position for that a moment ago," he replied coolly. He could hardly stomach her on a good day, and his uncharacteristic cruelty had drained him of any desire to be social. What was wrong with him for such unkind words to slip so easily from his tongue? "Besides, I am rubbish with music. I would turn the pages at all the wrong times."

"But you turned pages for Miss Hunt not two weeks ago," Miss Barton complained, and she completed her argument with a pout that made her look like a child, rather than a lady of accomplishment.

Would the woman never stop? "I assure you, Miss Barton," he said in a low voice, "I did nothing of the sort. Miss West, if you would oblige her."

"Allow me." To Nick's relief, Mr. Drake stepped up to the instrument, receiving a smile from Miss Barton before she began her piece.

Nick retreated back to his corner to wallow until the moment he could return to Harstone Court. He remained alone for less than thirty seconds before Lord Harstone approached, the man's smile intact but wary.

"Don't say it," Nick growled, refusing to make eye contact with his friend.

"I would like to remain in my wife's good graces," Harstone replied easily. "Therefore, I have come to censure you."

"I did not intend to—"

"To thoroughly insult my sister-in-law? You do not have to like her, Forester, but I cannot abide meanness."

Nick turned to him, raising an eyebrow. "Do you even know how to recognize meanness? I did not think it was in your repertoire."

Chuckling, Harstone shook his head. "I do not know why you think I am so perfect, my friend. But you have always been a good man. Why—"

"I become a beast around Miss Mackenzie," Nick said, sighing. "There is no explanation for it."

For some reason, that sparked amusement in Harstone's expression. "A beast, you say?" His eyes flicked to Miss Mackenzie for a moment. "I happen to know Emma rather likes beasts."

"So her tears were a positive reaction to my insult? That is a relief."

At least Miss Mackenzie seemed to have recovered. She was back to smiling as she spoke with the Misses Barlow, though still with that attractive color in her cheeks, and most of the room had turned their attention to the pianoforte, where Miss Barton had begun to sing as she played.

Sighing, Nick rubbed the tension out of his neck and shook his head. "Something tells me I am not going to find myself a wife here in Tutbury. If Miss Mackenzie is near, I fear I will forget myself and act a cad, so rest easy; I will not be around to cause your wife distress much longer."

"You know you are always welcome to stay," Harstone replied. The fact that he said nothing to the contrary about Nick's inability to find a wife seemed to seal Nick's fate.

As Lord Harstone returned to his wife's side—she sent Nick a powerful glare before smiling at her husband—Nick watched Miss Barton and considered the efficacy of walking home rather than enduring the evening's entertainment. He would undoubtedly be horrible company regardless of what transpired for the rest of the night, and he deserved the humiliation of walking through the rain.

Unfortunately, his thoughts circled too many times, and before he could make a decision, Miss Mackenzie was on her feet and approaching him with fire in her eyes.

Nick spoke before she could. "You need not censure me, Miss Mackenzie. I know what I have done."

"You made me look like a fool."

"Yes."

"Is that your plan? To make yourself so intolerable that the entire county turns against you? I hardly see the value in such action, though I will not speak against it when it can only serve to my benefit. No woman in her right mind would choose a man so unfeeling and cruel."

Gritting his teeth, Nick did his best to keep his voice even. "I hardly expect you to believe me, but I had no intention of hurting you. I crossed a line, and I apologize."

One delicate eyebrow lifted high, leaving her looking both surprised and amused. "You're right," she said shortly. "I do not believe you. But I accept your reluctant apology, if only because I know Alvaro likely required it of you to stay in his house."

"I will not be staying."

The other eyebrow joined the first. "Oh? I did not expect victory to come so easily."

Swallowing the urge to say something along the lines of allowing her to win out of pity, Nick shook his head. Counted to five. "Tutbury *will* be my home someday, Miss Mackenzie. I have not bowed out of this war, nor will I ever give up. But you have made it clear you have the advantage here, and I am not so foolish as to think I can overthrow your reign. I will return to London, where there are ladies aplenty not so easily taken in by little stories."

Stories that were clearly well told, though Nick refused to think he might be jealous of her talent for captivating her audience. Where he was an outright liar serving his own purposes, she was a storyteller determined to entertain.

He had been like her once, and he wondered if he ever would be again. He feared he had flown too close to the sun, like the fabled Icarus, and now his wax wings would melt and send him crashing to his doom.

Miss Mackenzie scoffed. "Ladies like Miss Barton? You forget, sir, I have seen your reaction to ladies of Town, and I hardly think I have anything to fear. You, on the other hand, have everything to fear if you think a man of your caliber could be desirable."

Nick couldn't stop the growl that rose in his throat. He was humble enough to admit his faults in what he'd said earlier, but he had no desire to roll over and submit. He let out a humorless laugh loud enough to draw attention their way, then spoke so quietly that only Miss Mackenzie would hear. "You forget, madam, that London *adores* me. I need only announce my presence, and the women come flocking. That inheritance will be mine. Good evening."

With a curt bow to the room in general, he slipped from the room and made his way out into the rain to begin the long trek back to Harstone. He may have won this battle, but he hardly felt victorious.

A beast indeed.

Chapter Eight

Emma should have been happy. It had taken only one dinner party to chase away the insufferable Mr. Forester, and yet the victory felt empty. Like it wasn't real. Shouldn't she have been pleased by the outcome? Her nemesis had taken the first coach out of Tutbury the morning after the dinner with the Barlows, running like the coward he clearly was, with his tail between his legs. And yet Emma had met the news when she arrived for tea with nothing but an ache in her midsection.

Perhaps her breakfast had not agreed with her.

"Oh, Miss Mackenzie, is this not the most dreadful of days?" Miss Barton flopped onto the settee beside Emma, who had been trying to read in the empty library with little success; her mind kept wandering to her battles, few though they had been. "I cannot bear it!"

If Miss Barton wished to pretend they were good friends instead of barely acquaintances, Emma would oblige. For now. "Whatever is the matter?" she asked, tucking a ribbon into the book to mark her place.

Miss Barton's blue eyes widened. "Mr. Forester's absence, of course! He only just arrived, and now he is gone. Forever!" She grabbed hold of Emma's hand and squeezed so hard that Emma winced.

Emma tried to school her features before her expression accidentally insulted the distraught woman. She had never been skilled at masking what she felt, but she hardly wished Alvaro's cousin added pain to this supposedly traumatic afternoon. "He has only gone to London," Emma said to reassure her. "And he is good friends with my brother-in-law and will likely—"

"You don't understand!" Miss Barton sank low into the settee with her legs stretched out, her dramatics growing worse by the minute. "It may not be the Season right now, but that does not mean there are not plenty of women in London. Half the *ton* is in love with him already, and I cannot return to Town until the spring. Who will keep them from turning his head?" Miss Barton rolled over and pressed her face into Emma's shoulder. "Mark my words, Miss Mackenzie. He will be engaged in less than a week."

"A week?" Emma croaked. The book slipped from her lap. Could that be true? Grandfather hadn't been all that convinced in Mr. Forester's ability to find a wife—she had assumed that was Forester's reason for coming to Tutbury—but from what Grandfather said, Forester hadn't seemed to believe in the deadline when he was in London before.

Surely he would not be so fastidious now that he knew he had only less than a month and a half to procure a wife.

Miss Barton, who had begun crying, nodded. "That is why this is the most dreadful day. I am in mourning for the future I might have had with the man I love with my whole soul."

If Miss Barton, dramatic as she was, could look past Forester's obvious flaws, other women would as well. And if they knew the fortune he was set to inherit—Emma's fortune—they would be all the more eager to catch his attention.

It was no wonder Emma's victory had tasted sour. It was not a victory at all!

"If you'll excuse me." Leaving Miss Barton on the settee, where she sobbed into the cushion, Emma hurried from the library in search of her sister.

A week? That was hardly enough time for Emma to make a plan, let alone execute anything, and that was assuming she even found a way to London. She hadn't been to Town since her one and only Season three and a half years ago, and the city had hardly made a good impression on her. After meeting some of the most dishonest, selfish, and cruel members of the upper crust, she had vowed to remain in the country among the humbler people of fewer means. At least in the country the good outnumbered the bad, which was not something she could say about London.

But the prospect of losing her independence, which she treasured above everything else, was reason enough to break that vow.

"Tabitha!" Emma found her sister in the nursery with the girls, the four of them enjoying tea together. "I must speak with you."

Raising her eyebrows, Tabitha glanced at the curious girls and then rose to her feet, gesturing for the nurse to take her place. Once they were out in the corridor, she gripped Emma's hand. "What has happened? You look as if you've seen a ghost, and I know you do not believe in those."

No thanks to Miss Barton and her loose tongue the other night. Emma swallowed, trying to calm herself. She needed to sound rational if she wanted to convince her sister of her makeshift plan. "I think we should go to London."

Tabitha's eyes went wide. "You want another Season?"

"Heavens no!" Emma managed a little laugh. "But perhaps a short stay before winter could be pleasant."

"You hate London."

"It's been years."

"Because you hate it." Tabitha pursed her lips, studying Emma, as if hoping to decipher the reason behind this surprise request. "London is such a distance," she said eventually. "Surely you can wait until—"

"This cannot wait. And you know I will not be able to convince Grandfather to go when he barely tolerates London in the first place."

"Yes, the two of you have that in common."

Emma could feel her panic rising, like a hot stew bubbling up inside her chest and threatening to spill over. But if she told her sister the real reason she wanted to go to London—to sabotage a man's every attempt at finding a wife—Tabitha would think her bound for Bedlam, no matter that she knew all about the will and Grandfather's stipulations.

A sane woman did not put so much effort into controlling a man's life.

Then again, most women were perfectly content to live their lives according to their fathers and husbands. Emma was not most women, and she refused to give up her dreams so easily. If she had a chance to save her future, she had to take it.

"Please," she said, squeezing Tabitha's hand. "When have I ever asked you for anything?"

Though Tabitha laughed, she seemed unable to come up with an answer to that question as her expression became more thoughtful. "Have you *ever* asked me for something?"

No. She hadn't. Because even though she was several years her sister's junior, Emma had always done everything herself. She asked for Elias's help only when she knew her cousin would benefit at the same time, and Grandfather more often than not asked for Emma's opinion or assistance than the other way around.

"This one thing," Emma said. "I know a stay in London is nothing small, but—"

"Honestly, Alvaro would likely jump for joy if I suggested it," Tabitha said with a sigh. "I think he gets lonely in the country, no matter how much he pretends otherwise. He loves spending time with the girls, but they cannot compare to the friends he has in Town. We have been in the country since July, which is longer than what he is used to."

Emma held back a grin. That hadn't been an agreement, but it was close.

Glancing around the empty corridor, Tabitha was quiet for a long few seconds before she said, "Perhaps we could find you a proper suitor at last, without so many unworthy prospects crowding the ballrooms, and you can finally settle down."

"Perhaps," Emma agreed, knowing she would be focused on anything but. She was convinced no man would fit the bill, as no man wished to have a wife who forged her own path. In her experience, men preferred simple women who did as they were told. If such a contrary man presented himself, she would consider him, but the chances of that were slim to none.

"I will speak to Alvaro," Tabitha said with a little shrug. She wasn't entirely fond of London either, Emma knew, though she had acclimated to the city after years of joining her husband while Parliament was in session. "Two weeks should be enough time to prepare for—"

"Two days," Emma practically shouted. "The sooner we can go, the better. Before winter sets in."

"Two days!"

Emma gripped both her hands. "Please."

Sighing again, Tabitha nodded. "Very well. If Alvaro agrees, we will leave as soon as we are able. But you know this will put Miss Barton out. She planned to stay with us for—"

"We could take her with us!" Biting her lip as she grimaced, Emma tried not to imagine being stuck in a coach with that woman for the entirety of the journey. It was no wonder Mr. Forester had hidden while he could. Miss Barton was perfectly sweet, but even a storyteller like Emma could only handle so much drama in one dose. "She was just telling me how much she wished to be in London. We can keep each other company as we go about Town."

Besides, if Miss Barton truly loved Mr. Forester as much as she professed, she would be crucial in keeping the man from ruining everything.

"You're going to London?" Elias appeared at the end of the corridor, his expression rather calm for someone who spoke with a good deal of alarm in his voice. "Why?"

Emma could see the wariness in his eyes, as if he knew exactly her reasons. He had been an unwitting accomplice in too many of her schemes and stories for him not to have at least some suspicion, and she had told him all about the inheritance yesterday.

"She still hasn't told me her reasons," Tabitha said with a shrug, making Emma cringe. "Though, I will be doing my best to find Emma a husband while we are there. It will do her good. Would you care to join us, Elias? We are, apparently, leaving as soon as the arrangements can be made, and I imagine we will return a few weeks before Christmastime."

"My estate needs my attention," Elias said, frowning a little. "And it seems unwise to leave your grandfather here on his own for so long. You will be taking Miss Barton with you?"

Emma chuckled at his concerned frown, perhaps a little too grateful that her cousin wouldn't be there to stop her from going to battle against Forester. "Yes, you will have your peace and quiet restored, Mr. Drake."

"That isn't . . ." He cleared his throat, shifting back into his usual expressionless self. "I suppose I will go find some books to hold me over until your library is available again. With your permission, Tabitha."

"Of course. Alvaro never reads them anyway, so you are welcome to anything that interests you."

"Miss Barton is in the library," Emma warned with a grin, and Elias returned a small smile before disappearing. Then she turned to Tabitha, taking her sister's hand. "I know I am acting strange, but I promise my reasons are good. Should I not be allowed to secure my future as much as anyone else?"

She hoped Tabitha would take that as an agreement to pursue a match while in Town, rather than inferring any sort of sabotage when it came to Nicholas Forester and the inheritance. Emma wasn't very comfortable with the idea of ruining the man's chances, but what choice did she have? He had had more than enough time to secure his place as heir, and now it was her turn.

It was time for her to take charge of her own life.

Chapter Nine

Perhaps it was merely the circumstances of the will addling his brain, but Nick was convinced London was far emptier than usual for this time of year. At the very least, Lord Gregory and his wife were not nearly as popular as they had been last year, with their musicale attendees being less of the nobility and more of the gentry, who apparently cared little to be on the land that had given them their status in the first place.

Although, as he surveyed the guests already congregated in Lord Gregory's music room, Nick supposed he would have to count himself among those whose land hardly appealed to them. He couldn't remember the last time he had spent more than a week at his estate.

He grunted at the edge of the room, reminding himself that his focus needed to be on the ladies in attendance tonight, not on the land he had neither the knowledge nor the funds to improve and make profitable again.

Upon entering the house, he had spotted a few young ladies he hadn't met yet. *Young* was a key word regarding their descriptions, however. They couldn't be older than seventeen or eighteen, and Nick, at thirty, was not comfortable with pursuing girls who had scarcely entered Society. Whoever his wife would be, she ought to be at least somewhat near his own age and would have to know how to weather the gossip storms of London that were never far behind him.

He had stalled long enough, and unless more guests were set to arrive fashionably late, Nick had seen his only options. Five miserable days in London had given him little hope for success, but he would hold his head high and face the crowd that had finally realized he was standing at their outskirts.

It was time to perform.

He had taken only one step toward Lord Gregory to garner an introduction to the ladies when a horrifyingly familiar voice cut through the chatter.

"Yes, Mr. Forester was quite convinced the ghost of a cow was wandering the corridors! Can you imagine such nonsense? A cow!"

As his blood turned cold, Nick mirrored several gazes turning to the far corner of the room. She couldn't be . . . But yes, Emma Mackenzie stood next to a small gathering of people, Mrs. Hatch, one of London's premier gossips, among them. And judging by the way Miss Mackenzie smirked at Nick, she knew very well that she had spoken just loudly enough to catch the attention of most in the room.

What on earth was that blasted woman doing in London?

"A . . . a cow?" Mrs. Hatch repeated, her eyes wide beneath the ridiculous feathered headdress she had donned for the evening. "How fascinating."

Miss Mackenzie smiled wide, and Nick tried to ignore how much he liked that dimpled smile. Her happiness could only mean misery for him. "I myself do not believe in spirits, but he was quite convinced it required his help."

Would he never live that down? It had been a ridiculous utterance to escape Miss Barton, something Miss Mackenzie knew well.

As eyes swiveled to him, Nick forced a smile. "If I recall, Miss Mackenzie, it was your idea to discover what the poor creature was lacking."

"Only to humor your concern," she shot back. "You seemed ever so upset. And after the bandit attack as well!"

"Ah yes, the village youths who thought to rob me."

"Thought to? They succeeded, did they not? You were so fearful when you arrived at the house, running from the depraved souls who frightened you into hiding when you arrived in Tutbury."

Nick choked when he realized she was speaking of Miss Barton, all too aware of the heads bouncing back and forth between the two of them. Miss Mackenzie had a knack for using the truth to her advantage, it seemed. Though it wasn't his usual tactic, he thought it might work to his benefit to do the same. "The bandits got to me *after* I had arrived at my destination, if you'll recall, Miss Mackenzie. I believe you are thinking of the lost child who waylaid me while I was in town. The poor thing hardly knew what to do with herself, all alone in the village like that."

Why was he engaging? Miss Mackenzie wasn't known in London, and she could say whatever she wanted; no one had any reason to believe her. He needed to stay focused and let her realize she was entirely out of her depth among the *ton*. These were not country folk who hung on her every word. They had spent the last three years listening to *him*.

He made it one more step toward Lord Gregory before Miss Mackenzie said, "It is a pity you were forced to leave Tutbury."

The murmurs of the other guests made him pause. Forced? Was she going to turn him into some sort of villain, chased back to London with torches and rifles like some unwanted beast?

"Yes," he said slowly, all too aware of the many eyes on him. "I would have liked to stay, but when I heard my good friend fell ill, of course I had to return to Town."

She pursed her lips as if deep in thought. "Do remind me. Which friend was that?"

He could give any name. Any name he wished, and she wouldn't have a clue. But the rest of the *ton* . . . The people in this cursed city liked to think they had the right to know everyone else's business, and Nick spent far too much time perusing the gossip columns and betting books to ensure he didn't lose track of where he stood. The last three years of his life had been lived for the consumption of others, and he needed to remember that.

Emma Mackenzie knew no one in London outside her family; the rest of those in the room knew *everyone*.

"Mr. Mansfield, of course," he said, not quite with the confidence he hoped for. Miss Mackenzie had gotten under his skin already.

"The man you dueled?"

Oh heavens, Miss Barton is here too.

Pasting on a smile to avoid looking utterly horrified, Nick found the woman just behind Miss Mackenzie, as if the two of them had become good friends over the course of the last few days. Heaven help him if that were true.

"You have a good memory, Miss Barton," he said, hoping she didn't remember the reason he had given her for the fictional duel. He seemed to recall something about a cravat, which was a ridiculous reason for dueling someone he had now claimed to be a dear friend. Had he always been this awful at coming up with new lies? Why had Society ever believed a word he said?

He cleared his throat, standing a little taller. "The friend I speak of is that Mr. Mansfield's brother. But it seems Lord Gregory and his wife are eager to begin the evening's entertainment, so I shan't bore you all with the details."

With one nod of his head, he had the crowd scrambling to take their seats. At least he could still direct a group, which would come in handy if Miss Mackenzie was to remain in Town for the rest of his timeline. Did that mean Lord Harstone had come as well? Who had escorted her this evening?

A hand planted on Nick's shoulder as if in answer. "This will be far more entertaining than the chaos of the Season, no?" Harstone murmured before stepping past him to take a seat with his wife.

It was only then that Nick realized he should have been selecting his own seat, preferably next to the newly out ladies. But each chair had been filled too quickly, leaving one seat for him—directly between Miss Mackenzie and Miss Barton.

Both seemed all too pleased by this arrangement, for vastly different reasons. Miss Barton would surely continue her attempts to gain his affection, and Miss Mackenzie . . . well, there was no telling what she might do. The woman was entirely too confident this evening, and it seemed she had already made some allies. Her intelligence and friendliness could easily spell his downfall, and as Nick lowered himself into his seat, he told himself to stay strong.

This battle had only just begun.

Chapter Ten

The instant the first musician began her piece on the pianoforte, Emma leaned close to Mr. Forester. "Surprised to see me?" she whispered.

He kept his eyes on the instrument ahead. "Hardly. You do not strike me as a woman to give up easily."

"I am not."

"I would call it an admirable quality if you were not such a thorn in my side." The words growled out of him, as if he were trying not to let them free. He certainly was a man who liked to be in control of a situation, and it seemed Emma had made that rather difficult for him.

She smirked when he clenched his jaw. "Thorns are merely inconveniences, sir," she said coolly. "I mean to be far more than that. I only need to keep you unmarried for a few weeks; beyond that, we never have to see each other again."

"I look forward to the day."

Emma sat straight, fighting against the smile that had been on her lips from the moment Forester realized she was there. He had been scanning the room with such an appraising eye, as if he knew nothing could hinder him in his search. Though she had planned to surprise him later in the evening, she couldn't help announcing herself and watching the fear enter his eyes.

It had been entirely coincidence that the Harstones received an invitation to tonight's musicale. They had only just arrived in London when Lord Gregory rode past the town house, and he'd stopped with excitement to greet Alvaro. Tabitha had not been exaggerating when she said her husband had many friends; though they had been in London for only a day and a half, they had already received an inordinate number of invitations to events.

Tabitha had agreed to most of them because she wanted Emma to meet as many eligible men as possible. Emma had agreed because she knew she needed to get to every event Mr. Forester might attend.

"Do you intend to follow me around Town all day, every day?" Forester murmured after the next performer began.

Emma scoffed. "That hardly seems necessary. I only need to enlighten these people and show them who you truly are."

"Enlighten? *These people?* Do you think yourself above them?"

Though Emma opened her mouth to disagree, the words caught on her tongue. She had arrived at Lord Gregory's door with little care who she met, as long as she could use them to tear down Forester's popularity. Did she think herself above them? Perhaps she did. Goodness, this war was getting to her already, and she needed to humble herself before things got out of hand. There was a difference between confidence and arrogance, and she had no desire to take the path toward the latter like Mr. Forester obviously had.

He smirked at her silence, looking far too handsome. The young ladies on the row in front of them kept looking back, not as discreetly as they likely thought. They had probably heard many rumors about the man, and his attractive features only made him more desirable. Emma had not been in London an hour before hearing Forester's name. Though that had only made her more determined to keep him off the Marriage Mart, it also meant she was in over her head.

London had been overwhelming when she'd *wanted* to be here three and a half years ago. It was even more stifling now, and the stakes were so much higher.

"You cannot pretend to know me, Mr. Forester," she said, keeping her gaze away from him.

"Of course I can," he replied, shifting closer so their shoulders brushed. "I can pretend anything I like. But I don't need to imagine who you are when you are so incapable of hiding anything."

The audience broke into applause, and Miss Barton turned to face them. "Was that not beautiful, Mr. Forester?"

"A breathtaking performance," he agreed, though he couldn't have paid attention enough to have heard any of it. Emma certainly hadn't.

Miss Barton, dramatic as she was, had already proven herself useful in this battle. She seemed to know everything about Forester and his habits, whether from her own observations or her use of servants' talk, and she was so determined to become his wife that she would likely do all the heavy lifting when it came to keeping Forester unwed.

He clearly could not stand Miss Barton—he had been shifting closer and closer to Emma's chair—and she was more tenacious than anyone Emma had ever known. Having her with them in London would be Forester's downfall.

"Miss Mackenzie, I would love to hear you play," Lady Gregory said.

Emma's head snapped up to meet the baroness's kind eyes. "Pardon?" Was it impolite to decline such a gracious invitation?

"Yes," Forester agreed loudly. "After all, no one has had the pleasure of hearing you perform, what with you being new in Town." He flashed her a brilliant smile that made his blue eyes glitter.

Curse her heart for deciding to beat the pattern of a racehorse's hooves. She had remained rather calm until that satisfied smile hit her square in the chest. Did he know she couldn't play anything? Or had he simply seen her fear? Regardless, Emma needed to say something if she wished to endear herself to the people of London.

And perhaps she could wipe that smug smile off the man's face while she was at it. "Unfortunately, I do not play an instrument," she said with what she hoped looked like a shy smile. "But I have heard so much of Mr. Forester's talent on the pianoforte that I will happily sing if he will accompany me."

The color drained from his face, his smile dropping as his eyes flicked to the crowd around him. Ha! The unflappable Nicholas Forester had no idea what he had gotten himself into when he'd decided to go up against Emma Mackenzie.

"Oh," he said, taking in the dozens of stares focused on him. "No, I don't think . . ." But he paused, his intelligent eyes taking in the eager expressions of the room. He seemed to realize how much the other attendees wanted to see a rumor come to truth, and if he wished to remain in their good graces, he would need to either admit the truth or somehow prove he had a skill he clearly did not possess.

"What do you say, old boy?" Lord Gregory said brightly. "Care to accompany the delightful Miss Mackenzie? I should like to hear her sing."

What if Forester found a way to convince someone else to play? Miss Barton, perhaps? Miss Barton had kept close to Emma since the moment Forester left Harstone Court, and now she and Emma were—according to her—the best of friends. She would probably jump at the opportunity to do more together if given the chance. And for all her desire to cut down Mr. Forester, Emma did *not* want to sing in front of a bunch of strangers.

She'd only meant to call his bluff, and now she feared she would be the one to lose.

Tugging at his cuffs, Forester suddenly relaxed, shifting from the stiff and uncomfortable man he had been a moment ago into a carefree dandy with an easy smile. "I suppose I could play a song or two, though I warn you I am out of practice," he said lightly. "You know how much I abhor being in the spotlight, but Miss Mackenzie has the voice of an angel. I would hate to disappoint you all."

Then he rose and offered his arm to Emma.

Oh goodness, she couldn't back down now. Declining would make Forester look far superior, and she needed all the sympathy she could get.

Taking the man's arm—and ignoring the strength she felt beneath her fingers—Emma plastered on a smile and let him lead her to the instrument.

He walked slowly, leaning his head close and whispering into her ear as they went. "It may come as a shock, but no one has ever mentioned me having musical talent, Miss Mackenzie. I cannot for the life of me understand why they believed you so easily."

"It seems the people of London will believe just about anything when it comes to you," she replied, hoping she didn't sound as breathless as she felt. "I look forward to seeing you fail, Mr. Forester."

As he took his seat at the pianoforte, Forester looked out over the crowd, clearly nervous. "Is there anything in particular you would like me to play?" he asked, loudly enough for the audience to hear.

If she chose a song for him, he could use the excuse that it was one he hadn't practiced. No, better to let him choose his own downfall. "Oh, I will sing anything you are inclined to play."

Forester picked up the stack of music that had been left on the stand, shuffling through them with his brow furrowed. He likely couldn't even read the music and was only delaying his humiliation. He paused on a piece that was particularly difficult to sing and held it out to show her. "Do you know this one?"

Emma held back a laugh. "If you can play it, I will sing it."

"This one it is," he replied and laid out the sheets, his eyebrows pulled down low as his fingers brushed the keys with unfamiliarity.

"You could admit defeat," Emma muttered, leaning in closer so as not to be overheard. "No need to cause yourself undue embarrassment."

Forester turned, hitting her with a smile so dashing that it knocked her back a step. "Where would be the fun in that?" Then he began to play, all hesitation and discomfort gone. His fingers flew over the keys with the ease of someone well practiced and genuinely skilled, leaving Emma stunned.

When he paused, she realized she should have begun singing. "Oh," she breathed, feeling the sting of her loss when a few people chuckled.

"Shall I start again?" Forester asked, laughter in his voice.

Emma straightened. She would not have this insufferable man take both her livelihood *and* her dignity. "Please."

Her first words came out stilted and strained, but as Forester continued to coax such beautiful sounds from the instrument, Emma found herself falling into the music. The song was one of her favorites, but she'd never heard it played the way he played it, with emotion guiding each note. The words came more easily to her as she sang along with such beautiful music, and her fear disappeared with each measure.

Everything disappeared. It was as if the room vanished as Emma inched closer to the instrument, like the music coming from it could fill her soul and help her find the contentment she desperately wanted in life. No more time spent trapped beneath expectations and traditions, no more men telling her how to live her life, no more fears that she would spend her future alone, with no one but servants for company.

When the song ended, Emma's voice trailing off with the last notes of the pianoforte, she felt her heart beat with something new. Something like hope for a future without worry.

Then she met Forester's gaze.

He stared at her, his chest rising and falling like he had forgotten to breathe throughout the song, and Emma could hardly understand his expression. There was something akin to anxiety in it, but also awe. Admiration?

The audience broke into applause, and Emma jumped, startled from his unwavering gaze. Based on how enraptured everyone seemed from their little performance, both of them had gained some attention tonight. Likely all of Town would be talking about them, which was good for Emma in her attempt to endear herself to as many as possible. But it also meant Forester had increased his value, and if the way the young women were eyeing the man was any indication, he would not be short of admirers after this.

And though Emma hated to admit it, tonight she had, for a moment, become one of them.

Chapter Eleven

It seemed Nick still had absolutely no self-control around Miss Mackenzie. At least he had not turned into a beast tonight, but he had shared the one thing he had vowed to keep to himself. No one was supposed to know he enjoyed playing the pianoforte, yet he had just performed in front of Mrs. Hatch, ensuring all of London would know about his talent by teatime tomorrow.

How did Miss Mackenzie get under his skin so easily? He could maintain his composure around anyone, Catherine Barton included, but put him in a room with Emma Mackenzie, and all his good breeding went out the window. Something about her ruffled him, kept him nervous, had him wanting to throw away all notions of the man everyone else knew and be something entirely different.

And yet she stood on the other side of the room, laughing and smiling as half the party fell in love with her. She didn't seem affected by him in the slightest.

The one person in the world who seemed to see the real man beneath all the pageantry, and she hated him.

"Do you not think so, Mr. Forester?"

Nick reluctantly dragged his attention back to the young women who had practically swarmed him as soon as the entertainment ended. He'd been correct about their ages, one seventeen and two eighteen years old, and yet all three seemed determined to snag the country's most eligible bachelor. Although, Nick hardly considered himself that anymore. He was too old, hardly flush in the pockets, despite everyone's belief, and not a soul in the world knew who he really was. Not even Harstone or Calloway, who were his closest friends.

Clearing his throat, he tried to think back to what their conversation had been about. Something about balls and gowns; he had been watching Miss

Mackenzie for longer than he should. "Most assuredly," he said, hoping his agreement was what they wished for.

The girls giggled, fanning themselves with practiced movements. "I thought so," one of them said. Miss Ashton. She seemed to be the leader of the trio, more precocious than the others. "I didn't think what they said about you could be true."

Oh goodness, he probably should have been paying attention. It was difficult enough to keep up with the rumors he'd started himself, let alone those started by others. "That depends on what they said."

Miss Mackenzie laughed again on the other side of the room, the sound as lovely as her singing voice. She hadn't been nervous enough before she started to indicate her being a terrible singer, but as soon as she'd opened her mouth, he was captivated. He had nearly stopped playing so he could simply listen to the way her voice floated through the notes. But that would have made her stop, and no one deserved to be deprived of a voice like hers.

He would have to devise a way to hear her sing again.

"We heard you are a scoundrel," Miss Ashton said with another giggle, followed by echoes from the other two girls. "Mother told me you break hearts wherever you go."

That shouldn't have made her more interested, but the way she batted her eyes at him had Nick wishing he could run away. "Perhaps that is true," he murmured, and he meant that. So many women had fancied themselves in love with him, and he had rejected them all.

"But surely you would not call me beautiful if you did not believe it."

Coughing, Nick fought for a response. Was that what he had agreed to? He hadn't paid enough attention to have formed an opinion on whether these women could be potential candidates, and he didn't want to lead any of them on without doing his due diligence. No heartbreaking allowed this time around. "Stating fact could be done by even the worst of men, Miss Ashton," he said, giving her a smirk that made her blush. *Too much.* He took a step back, hoping that counterbalanced his smile. "Are you all enjoying London thus far?"

"Oh yes!" Miss Ashton said, grabbing his arm.

Nick froze. Was she really going to be so bold in a roomful of people? He shifted, tucking both arms behind his back and taking another step away from the girl.

"I'll admit I do wish I had made my entrance during the Season," she continued, undeterred, "but I can easily say London is far more exciting than anything back home in Shropshire."

"I am sure you're right."

"Oh, Mr. Smith, you are too much!" Miss Mackenzie said across the room.

Nick turned without thinking, locking his eyes onto Miss Mackenzie as she laughed with Charles Smith. Somehow the crowd around her had doubled, essentially leaving Nick alone with the three ladies and their hovering chaperone, Mrs. Ashton. How did Miss Mackenzie do that? Usually it was Nick at the center of attention, even when he didn't want to be.

"Oh, do continue your story, Miss Mackenzie," Smith said. "My apologies for interrupting."

Ah, she was telling stories again? She did seem to be good at that, though he couldn't fathom what could be so amusing to keep even Smith's interest. The man was an utter bore and considered himself a cut above the rest, hardly deigning to notice anyone beyond his close circle of friends because he had a good deal of money to his name. But there he was, hanging on the woman's every word like a lovesick puppy. He looked as if he might propose on the spot.

Well, there's an idea . . .

"Do forgive me," Nick muttered and bowed, only realizing as he walked away that Miss Ashton had been in the middle of saying something. As a knot settled in his stomach—he had likely ruined his chances with any of the girls by being so incredibly rude—he skirted around the crowd and took his leave of Lord Gregory, who hardly gave him a passing glance and a nod. He, too, had been ensnared by the charm of Miss Mackenzie.

Nick slipped out into the corridor, trying to keep up with the plan that had sparked to life just now. While he waited for a footman to collect his things, he stood just outside the music room's open doors and studied the men surrounding Miss Mackenzie. She had them at her mercy, and he had a feeling she didn't even know it. She was too caught up in her storytelling to see Mr. Holden edge in closer with every breath or the glares Smith gave anyone who laughed loud enough to gain a smile from Miss Mackenzie.

There had to be a reason she hadn't gotten herself married yet, but who could turn down an offer from someone who would provide a lavish life? Smith earned three thousand a year from his shipping company. Holden owned acres upon acres of high-yielding farmlands. Any one of these men could give Miss Mackenzie so much more than what she would receive from her grandfather.

If Emma Mackenzie found herself a husband in possession of a considerable fortune, she would have no need of Nick's inheritance.

"You are either a fool or a genius," he muttered to himself, taking his hat from the footman and stuffing it onto his head. But while he worked on securing himself a lasting love with a woman he adored, he would find the same in a man for Miss Mackenzie. It would not be easy, what with her apparent aversion to the idea of marriage. At the very least, he would find her someone she could tolerate enough to accept. Choosing to put any of his limited energy and time into finding her a husband would mean gambling on her good nature—not a very sure footing for him, he knew, but should he succeed, she might just give him a chance to argue his case: if she didn't need the Mackenzie lands anymore, surely she would give them to him. He wouldn't have to rush to find himself a wife, and they both could get what they wanted.

As he stepped out into the cool evening air, Nick shook his head. "I fear you will end up the fool," he muttered to himself. With his luck, Miss Mackenzie would either reject any man who came near her or fall in love with a penniless man, leaving Nick with no chance at all. But what choice did he have? He had to try.

Chapter Twelve

"İf I never have to greet another stranger again, it will be too soon." Emma groaned, rubbing exhaustion from her eyes. It had been three days straight of introductions and small-talk, with no sign of letting up. "I thought visitors were supposed to stop by unannounced only during your at-home day."

Tabitha pursed her lips, fighting a smile as she leaned against her husband's arm. They made quite a pretty picture, sharing the sofa with their hands clasped together. "Alvaro has never followed the rules," she said with a yawn. Clearly, she was just as exhausted from hosting as Emma was. "For us, every day in London is an at-home day."

"Unless we are not actually at home," Alvaro threw in with a wink.

Emma couldn't help but smile. She was friendly, and she truly enjoyed interacting with people, but no one socialized like Alvaro Rowland. Everyone had come to welcome Lord Harstone back to London, and he had given each the same bright smile and warm greeting. He treated them all like old friends, no matter their status, and Emma wondered if he truly did consider them all friends.

"Well," she said, glancing toward the door as if someone might walk through it. At this point, anyone else would push her past her limit. "If it is agreeable to you, I think I will take a walk."

She wasn't as lucky as Miss Barton, who had received a letter an hour ago and excitedly disappeared to read it rather than remain to greet all the visitors.

Tabitha yawned again, dropping her head onto her husband's shoulder. "I think that is a lovely idea. Grayson?"

The butler stepped into the room. "Yes, my lady?"

"We are no longer at home. I think I would like to spend the rest of the afternoon with the girls."

"Yes, my lady." Grayson left with a small smile, clearly accustomed to the unorthodoxy that was Lord and Lady Harstone.

"You'll take your maid with you?" Tabitha asked Emma as she rose, Alvaro right behind her.

Emma fought back a laugh. She knew as well as anyone that wandering the city on her own was far from proper, though she was certain she could look after herself if she did so. "You think I would do something scandalous?"

Tabitha shook her head. "The only reason you brought Mr. Drake with you everywhere you went in Tutbury was because Grandfather required it, and I have a feeling you spent a good deal of time on your own regardless of his wishes."

"You could never prove it," Emma countered with a grin. "Do not fret, Tabitha. I'll bring Jenny with me. Although, finding myself alone with a gentleman could be a fantastic way to catch myself a husband."

"Unless that gentleman is a good-tempered duke with vast wealth, I do not recommend that course of action," Alvaro said with a chuckle. "And I guarantee there are none of those in London this time of year."

Emma grinned. "How unfortunate."

"We will find you someone worthy of you," Tabitha assured her, and then she and Alvaro slipped from the parlor.

"I doubt that," Emma muttered, rising to seek out her maid. "I doubt there is a man in existence who could tempt me into matrimony."

By the time Jenny helped her dress and they were on their way to Hyde Park, it was the peak of the fashionable hour. Though nothing compared to when Emma had been here during her Season three and a half years previous, a good number of people still walked about along the Serpentine, dodging horses and conveyances and forming little groups of acquaintances.

Emma paused at the park entrance, questioning her decision to come to this park at this time of day. "Perhaps we should walk elsewhere," she said, tugging lightly on the ties of her bonnet.

Jenny flinched as a gig passed close to them. She'd spent her whole life in the country and had likely never seen this many people at once. "Oh, but this is so exciting, miss," she said, her voice wobbling.

Emma laughed. "You do not have to pretend you are excited for my sake."

"I *am* excited! Maybe a bit nervous, but . . . if my mama could see where I am, she'd be right jealous."

"I'm more jealous of your mama." Emma pursed her lips, trying to decide whether a walk in the park was even worth it. No one here knew her except those who had come to Harstone House, as it had been several years since she was last in Town and she doubted she had made a lasting impression. But would that make her an object of interest or someone to be ignored? Social niceties would require an introduction if she wanted to speak to anyone, which would make it easier to blend in and walk in peace, but— "Oh drat."

Emma spun in a half circle, turning her back to the busy park, but she had a feeling she had not hidden her face quickly enough. No, she knew she hadn't, because Forester's smile had grown the moment they'd made eye contact. *Of course* he was out during the fashionable hour. *Of course* he would ruin her day with his nonstop falsehoods and insults. *Of course* he would look even more handsome out in the sunshine, his hair turning to the color of burnished gold.

"Ah, Miss Mackenzie, I thought that was you beneath that lovely blue bonnet. I was beginning to think you had gone back home."

Gritting her teeth, Emma counted to five before she turned and flashed a smile. Why had she chosen to wear the bonnet he had encouraged her to buy in Tutbury? "It has been a few days," she agreed.

Forester bowed far more deeply than necessary. "Too long."

"Not long enough," she growled back under her breath.

She hadn't been too overwhelmed with visitors to note the fact that she hadn't seen Mr. Forester since the musicale earlier in the week. It hadn't helped that every new acquaintance said something about the man. Emma had done her best to paint him in as poor a light as she could to dissuade ladies from considering him, but even when she spoke absolute lies, no one was surprised. It seemed Nick Forester had done and seen everything a man could possibly do, his own tall tales setting him up as a paragon among London Society.

It was as if he couldn't be touched.

Forcing herself to keep smiling, Emma glanced at the man she had only just noticed standing a pace behind Forester. "It seems you have neglected your friend," she said with a nod.

The gentleman turned a deep shade of red, his eyes fixed on the shiny points of his boots.

Laughter painted Forester's voice with amusement as he said, "Forgive me, Miss Mackenzie. I would like to introduce Sir Thomas Morland. Sir Thomas, Miss Emma Mackenzie, Lord Harstone's sister-in-law."

That perked the man right up, his head lifting as soon as Forester mentioned Alvaro. "Lady Harstone's sister, you say?"

Emma wanted so badly to laugh at the unhidden interest, but she held it back. She didn't want to be rude. Not toward anyone but Mr. Forester, anyway. He looked far too smug to be unaware of what influence her relations would have on any admirers she might come across. She would never hold their interest for long—at least, they would never hold *her* interest—but the Harstone name always drew them in.

And she couldn't fathom why Forester would encourage anyone to pursue her unless he had no idea that she was under the same marriage requirement that he was—a requirement Emma still hoped would disappear as soon as she came of age. She intended to keep Forester unaware of the stipulation, else he would likely take advantage of it just as she was doing with him.

"Yes, she is my sister," Emma said, dipping into a curtsy. "It is a pleasure to meet you, Sir Thomas." She didn't have Forester's innate talent for lying— she was genuinely amazed that anyone had believed her as she'd spun stories about him—but at least the gentleman didn't seem to notice her disinterest. "How are you acquainted with Mr. Forester?"

He blinked once. Twice. Three times, so evenly spaced out that it was as if he counted the seconds between each blink. "Oh, Forester and I are not—"

"We are new acquaintances," Forester cut in, clapping Sir Thomas on the back. "He heard about my expedition to India two summers ago and simply had to know more."

What a load of nonsense! "India?" she replied, faking curiosity. "Was that before or after your great-uncle shot you in the leg?"

His eyes—such a bright blue—practically sparkled as he gazed at her. "Someone has been talking about me behind my back," he accused, though it seemed to delight more than worry him. "You know it is unwise to listen to gossip, yes?"

"Shouldn't you be off finding yourself a wife?" Emma asked, eager to return to the town house and spend some time in the library. Even a room by herself was better than being around Nicholas Forester. "I do not think Sir Thomas can fill that role, nor would he want to were he a woman."

Sir Thomas spluttered, turning red again.

Forester laughed, shaking his head with a grin instead of looking like he felt the censure she had intended. "Oh, there are many ways to find oneself a partner," he said, turning his smile to Sir Thomas. "Sir Thomas was just telling me how much he desires to meet more eligible women, and I thought to teach him my ways."

Emma let out a single laugh. "I suggest looking elsewhere for assistance, Sir Thomas. Mr. Forester has been searching for a wife for years and has yet to be successful. I do not think that speaks much to his credit."

His eyes sparkling, Forester threw an arm around the obviously uncomfortable Sir Thomas, who stood as still as a statue. "Ah, but see, you cannot find anyone more qualified than me to tell you what *not* to look for in a wife! I have seen it all, my good man, so never fear. We'll find you someone in no time."

"Have you taken up matchmaking for others now that you have realized you are incapable of finding a match for yourself, Mr. Forester?" Emma asked, lifting an eyebrow. "How generous of you."

"Perhaps I have already found myself a wife."

Emma's heart stumbled in her chest, though surely she would have heard a rumor about that over the last few days. Nicholas Forester settling down would hardly go unnoticed. "But you haven't," she guessed, trying to sound confident rather than questioning.

Rather than responding, Forester tightened his hold on Sir Thomas as he said, "Sir Thomas only recently became a baronet," as if Emma had any desire to know more about the man who seemed content to be spoken over rather than hold his own in the conversation. He had spoken fewer than a dozen words thus far, despite being the subject of conversation. "His poor father succumbed to illness only last year," Forester continued. "One would hardly guess it, seeing how confidently the new Baronet Morland has managed the estate in his absence. I daresay no lands in Devon are finer."

"Dorset," Sir Thomas mumbled.

"Yes, that is what I said. Miss Mackenzie, I believe they may rival your grandfather's lands."

As Forester leaned in to whisper something to Sir Thomas, Emma clenched her hands into fists, recognizing the challenge for what it was. Or perhaps Mr. Forester simply wanted to remind her of the reason she had made a mad dash for London in the first place, and it was not to have a leisurely walk in solitude. No, she needed to stop letting this man control every situation and start doing more to undermine his attempts to steal what was hers.

"I am pleased to hear your lands are doing well, Sir Thomas," she said, then dipped into a curtsy. She had a plan to make. "If you will excuse me, I—"

"Will I see you at Almack's this week?" Sir Thomas said far more loudly than necessary. Several people looked their way in interest, causing heat to burn in Emma's cheeks.

Almack's? Even during her Season she hadn't set foot in the exclusive social club, never having garnered an invitation. She hadn't wanted one to begin with, so she had asked Alvaro not to secure her one. "Oh," she said, fumbling with her reticule. "I don't—"

"Of course she will be there!" Forester announced, clearly intending for as many people to hear as possible as his clear voice rang out over the park. "I guarantee Miss Mackenzie is sure to be at all the best events this autumn, as she is always eager to be the center of attention."

Oh, Emma wanted to slap the man! Perhaps at home, where she was comfortable with all the people, she enjoyed being a source of amusement. But this was London, where a single misstep could turn an idol into a pariah with one well-placed whisper. Forester likely knew this better than anyone, and he was showing his advantage. In Staffordshire Emma had had the upper hand, but now he had the high ground.

But if he thought one little challenge would be enough to send her running back home, he had seriously underestimated her drive to win.

"Yes," she said, putting on a smile that made Sir Thomas blush. "Barring any unfortunate incidents, I will be there. Good afternoon, gentlemen."

Just as she turned to leave, Forester did something wholly unexpected. He stepped to the side, looking beyond Emma and catching the attention of Jenny.

"Ensure your lady wears blue that evening," he said, and then his eyes traveled over Emma, from her head to her toes, before resting on her face. "While she looks marvelous in anything, blue is her best color. Good day to you, Miss Mackenzie." With a tip of his hat, he led Sir Thomas back the way they'd come.

And Emma stood there, confused by the heat that spotted her cheeks even after he was out of sight.

Chapter Thirteen

In all honesty, forcing Miss Mackenzie to attend Almack's would do nothing to benefit Nick, and he knew it. He would do better to ensure she never occupied the same space as him and therefore eliminate the possibility of her sabotaging his attempts at finding himself a wife. Deep down, he *knew* this. And yet that didn't stop him from climbing the steps to Harstone's lavish town house on Tuesday evening to see if Miss Mackenzie's brother-in-law had managed to secure her an invitation. It wasn't as if Nick had more social power than the *ton*'s most friendly viscount, so if Harstone had not obtained a voucher for the woman, there was going to be a rather disappointed Sir Thomas Morland at Almack's.

Nick chuckled as the Harstone butler opened the door for him, letting him into the entryway before directing him to the study. Sir Thomas wasn't a talkative man, by any means, but his interest in Miss Mackenzie had been written all over his face. And Miss Mackenzie couldn't have appeared more *un*interested if she had tried. Despite Nick's best attempts to push them together, he knew Sir Thomas was hardly the right sort of man to tempt her into matrimony.

That wouldn't stop him from trying. He had yet to figure out what sort of man *would* tempt her, and if nothing else, Sir Thomas would keep her occupied for the space of a dance and leave Nick free to find his own partner.

"Ah, Forester, I was not expecting you so late in the evening." Harstone bounded into the study, a man of endless energy. "I would have thought you would be deep in one of London's many social events. That is why we are all here, no?" He gestured for Nick to take a seat in one of the plush armchairs he kept in the comfortable room. "You, in particular, have always been at the heart of entertainment."

Nick forced a smile. Once upon a time, he had enjoyed being the center of attention, attending as many parties and balls as he could. Yes, to find a wife, but also because he had delighted in the company of friends new and old. But that had been before all the rumors and lies. Before Lady Lavinia had forced him to turn into something he wasn't when she made it clear their engagement had meant little to her.

Helping himself to a drink from Harstone's stock, Nick remained on his feet rather than sitting, feeling the need to be able to run from the conversation should it not go his way. "I may have overstepped the other day," he said and then swallowed a healthy portion of brandy to ease the sting of admitting his mistake.

Harstone's expression didn't change, still light and happy, as always. "Is that so? What have you done this time?"

"I convinced half of London that your sister-in-law would be at Almack's tomorrow."

"Only half?" Again, Harstone's smile remained intact, though that was hardly surprising. For being a man far from his home country, he had settled in to his new home with ease and never questioned his decision to remain. He could have easily accepted his title and returned to Spain, leaving a steward to look over his lands, but he had never given any indication of missing his Spanish countrymen. He was clearly content with his life in England, no matter how much it shifted and changed.

Nick had always admired his resilience.

"You seem able to convince London of a good many things," Harstone said with a chuckle. "What I do not understand is why you are telling me this. Do you want me to warn her of the expectation?"

Nick threw back another swallow of brandy before throwing himself into a chair beside his friend. "I want you to do whatever you can to ensure she is able to attend. I have injured her too many times to find any comfort in her being the subject of gossip should she not attend as I promised."

"How uncharacteristic of you."

That assessment stung more than it should, and Nick rubbed his chest as if he could rub the ache out of his heart. "I hope you think better of me than that," he muttered. He had already spent the summer withering under Lord Simon Calloway's censuring gaze, and he did not need the judgment from Harstone as well. He knew his lies were unbecoming, but there was only so much he could do to change his life now, much as he wanted to.

Steepling his fingertips together, Harstone seemed to study Nick for a long moment as the dying fire crackled in the hearth on the other side of the room. His energy had shifted, less buoyant and directed straight at Nick. "You are a good man, Nick Forester," he said after a long moment. Had it really taken so long to come to that conclusion? "But you do seem lost."

Nick let out the breath he had been holding. "'Lost,'" he repeated. As much as he agreed, he hated to admit such a thing. It would strip him of any sense of control over his life. "No one navigates London Society better than I do. Except perhaps you, who have the entire world at your fingertips because everyone desires your friendship."

Chuckling, Harstone shrugged and settled more comfortably in his chair. "There is nothing wrong with being friendly, and it is far better than manipulating my fellows."

Nick scowled. "I think I liked you better when you hardly spoke English."

"I can just as easily speak the truth in Spanish, my friend. And I have always spoken English."

"Yes, but your accent used to be stronger, so your words were above my level of intelligence."

"Why do you run from the truth, Nick?"

Groaning, Nick rose back to his feet and began a circuit around the room. His friends only ever called him by his preferred name when they were bothered by something, and those moments usually did not end in his favor. "I did not come to discuss my unfortunate life," he complained. "I came to ensure Miss Mackenzie would be able to attend Almack's."

"I procured her a voucher yesterday when she requested one."

"Oh." Nick paused his pacing. So he had come here for nothing? He should have known Harstone would have no issue obtaining a voucher for his sister-in-law—deep down, Nick *had* known. But he had come anyway, and his stomach churned as he considered the reason. It was far too late for a social call, even if Harstone had welcomed him without hesitation.

Apparently there were a lot of truths Nick was ignoring, and he didn't like the thought that even he was beginning to fixate on the lies. Had he really fallen so far?

Sighing deeply, he sank into his chair again and ran his hands through his hair. "You think I'm lost," he said again, letting those words sink in. "How long have you known me, Harstone?"

"Long enough that you used to call me Rowland."

Before Harstone had taken up his title as viscount. Before Calloway had become a baron to replace his late father. Before Nick's life had been altered so thoroughly by a decision made by a woman who likely hadn't given him a single thought in the three years since. Lavinia was happily married now to a man who *wasn't* Nick, so of course she wouldn't have thought about him over the years, though he'd certainly thought about her. Every rumor that circulated about him, whether he'd started it himself or not, was because of her.

"I've practically forgotten who I am," Nick muttered more to himself than to Harstone. "And I don't know how to get back to the man I was."

Was it even possible? After three years of perpetuating every rumor that surfaced and speaking more lies than truths, Nick wasn't convinced a normal life was even possible at this point. It was hardly any wonder he hadn't found himself a wife yet when he knew in his heart that any woman who caught his fancy would be caught in the same net of lies. No woman deserved that horrid life, and he couldn't fathom anyone choosing to face that battle with him.

Chuckling, Harstone rose and put his hand on Nick's shoulder. "You are an intelligent man. I am sure you will find a way back. Just remember that a journey is always better with a companion. It is late, and I should be returning to mine."

"Yes, of course." Nick followed him out into the corridor, already dreading returning to the silence of his rented room. He could probably find somewhere to go, some social gathering full of ladies to welcome him with open arms, but his heart wasn't in it. At least he could rest easy knowing Miss Mackenzie would not be ridiculed tomorrow.

But then again, Nick would be at Almack's as well to attempt to find her a different match, and the odds of him remaining civil with the headstrong woman were not in his favor. Not when that place held nothing but bitter memories. Perhaps, if he kept his focus on Miss Mackenzie and procured her a good number of suitors, he would not be forced to remember the day his life had fallen apart.

Chapter Fourteen

"But you have to come!"

As Tabitha wrapped her shawl more tightly around her shoulders, she poorly hid her frustration with a pained smile. "It is simply out of the question, Emma. If it were only me, I would endure the evening for your sake, but the girls are just as ill as I am. Worse. How could I leave them?" She gestured into the nursery, where the poor girls were curled up in their beds, all three of them miserable with coughs and fevers as their nursemaid attended to them.

Emma tucked her arms around herself as guilt ate at her stomach. "No, of course you cannot leave the house in your condition. You should be in bed just like the girls."

Shaking her head, Tabitha looked over her children with worry in her teary eyes. "I will never be easy when they are like this."

"The physician said they simply need rest." Emma knew that would not stop Tabitha from staying up all night to watch over her children, even though she shared the same illness. "That means you as well."

"Mi cielito, you should be in bed!" Alvaro, who had walked the physician to the door, hurried down the corridor and wrapped Tabitha up in his arms. For once, he wasn't smiling as he pressed a kiss to his wife's forehead. "You need to sleep. I will watch over the girls."

Though Emma always loved seeing how attentive Alvaro was as a father and husband—heaven knew her own father hadn't been—her heart sank. She had actually been looking forward to the evening at Almack's tonight, but then the girls had succumbed to their fevers this afternoon. She had held out hope that Alvaro would not fall prey to the same illness, but she had forgotten his devotion to his family.

Though she had no interest in Sir Thomas, Emma did feel some measure of pity for the disappointment he would feel when she did not arrive at the assembly for their dance. Plus, she wanted to prove Forester wrong about her. He had issued the challenge at the park, likely thinking she would fail to meet it, but she would keep her head high and show London that she belonged here as much as anyone.

If he wanted her at every social function, she would be at every social function, always right there to ensure no woman took him seriously.

"Emma, your hair is not ready!" Alvaro swept his eyes over her with moderate alarm. "Do you plan to arrive fashionably late? Miss Barton is waiting for you."

Emma frowned. "Late for what? Miss Barton and I cannot go to Almack's alone." Even if she wished they could. A man could attend without an escort, but a woman required supervision. It was as preposterous as it was insulting.

Though concern for his family still pulled at the corners of his mouth, Alvaro smiled. "But you will not be alone. Forester should be here any moment."

As she let out a laugh, Emma imagined what would happen were the two of them left alone for any length of time. They would cut each other to ribbons, and not just with their words. Every time she laid eyes on the man, she had the sudden urge to take up fencing.

"They cannot go with him on their own!" Tabitha said, speaking Emma's own silent argument.

"They will not be on their own," Alvaro replied with a scoff. "Mrs. Chatwell has agreed to accompany them."

"Mrs. Chatwell, our neighbor?" Tabitha asked. "She is ancient."

"And excited to get out of the house for a change."

"But—"

"Whether or not your ancient neighbor is to join us," Emma said, folding her arms, "it does not change the fact that I would rather prance around Hyde Park in nothing but my underthings than go anywhere with that horrid man."

Tabitha gasped. "Emma!"

And then the last voice Emma wanted to hear spoke just a few feet behind her. "That would be quite the spectacle, Miss Mackenzie."

Emma spun around to find Forester leaning one shoulder against the wall, a quizzing glass to his eye as he examined her with a smirk on his lips.

"Imagine the stories the *ton* would tell."

"Circulated by you, no doubt," Emma snapped, though her voice came out airy. She did not usually embarrass so easily, and she blamed the intent way Forester was looking at her. She knew she should not have spoken so brashly, but when it came to Mr. Forester, she could rarely hold her tongue.

"You wore the blue," he said with a broad smile that made him look far too handsome for his own good. "Your maid should be commended. Though, perhaps she could use some practice with hair."

"My concern for my nieces pulled me away before she could finish. Jenny is a *wonder* with hair."

"How are the girls?" Forester asked, genuine concern wrinkling his brow.

It was only then that Emma realized his examination had not once made her feel like he was imagining her statement about running around the park without proper clothing. She had encountered plenty of men whose hungry eyes left little to the imagination, but Forester had focused entirely on her gown. Conceited liar or not, he had never been a cad. Besides, Alvaro would never stand for a friend who treated women poorly.

Emma took her leave then, hurrying back to her chamber before she thought too hard about the genuinely worried look in his blue eyes when she'd mentioned the girls. It had been more attractive than the practiced smile he usually wore.

By far.

* * *

Though she hated to make Miss Barton wait longer than she already had, Emma told Jenny to take her time doing her hair. It would put out Mr. Forester as well as force him to remain with Miss Barton for company. Emma could only hope the young woman was still as in love with him as she'd been in Tutbury, as she would serve as an excellent deterrent to other women throughout the evening.

When she finally arrived downstairs to where her companions were waiting, she held back laughter at the sight of Mrs. Chatwell—as ancient as Tabitha had declared her—snoozing in a chair while Forester paced around the entryway with Miss Barton at his heels, jabbering away as she always did.

"And I couldn't wear the cream chiffon, of course," Miss Barton was saying.

If Emma had to guess, she was describing her entire wardrobe in detail, even though she had already done the same with Emma earlier in the day as she'd attempted to choose which dress to wear to Almack's.

"Of course not." Forester looked to be at his wit's end, his eyes shut tight as he circled the space. Just how long had he been pacing not to have to look where he was going?

Emma would have been content to watch the man's increasing frustration, but as the two of them turned to face the staircase, Miss Barton caught sight of Emma and let out a gasp loud enough to startle Mrs. Chatwell awake.

"Miss Mackenzie, you look a dream!"

Emma smiled, but the warmth from Miss Barton's praise fizzled when she locked eyes with Mr. Forester, who had pulled his eyebrows together as he looked at her. What fault did he find now?

"Is she not the most beautiful woman in London?" Miss Barton said with a doe-eyed smile. Oddly, she barely seemed to acknowledge Forester now that Emma had arrived, despite how intently she had pursued him back in Staffordshire. Had something changed?

Forester kept his gaze on Emma, as if searching for something. "I am not certain I could choose between the two of you," he said eventually, and then he offered his arm to Mrs. Chatwell. "But everyone knows Mrs. Chatwell will always hold the honor of most beautiful."

The old woman spluttered as she allowed Forester to help her to her feet. "Oh, well, I don't . . ."

"Shall we be off?" Forester said brightly, as if unaware of the way he had so easily charmed the gray-haired woman who had likely not been complimented so thoroughly in years.

Emma hated how much she appreciated his thoughtfulness. He had nothing to gain from charming a woman old enough to have grown grandchildren, and he had done so without hesitation, just as he had done when speaking to Jenny at the park despite her being of a far lower social standing. Jenny had mentioned her interaction with him more than once since, expressing her utter delight at someone like him speaking to a "nobody" like her.

Forester cleared his throat, glancing between Emma and Miss Barton. "You'll forgive me for not having a third arm," he said with a smile, "but I think it will be safer for me not to choose between the two of you and leave one without."

Emma hardly cared about having an arm to hold, but Miss Barton beamed as she latched on to Emma's arm. "You think of everything, Mr. Forester. As long as I get to dance with you tonight."

As he led the way outside to the waiting carriage, Forester dipped his head. "I would be delighted to stand up with you both. And Mrs. Chatwell, if she will let me."

Mrs. Chatwell swatted his arm but turned a healthy shade of red. "You tease, Mr. Forester."

"Yes, but only the beautiful."

Forester assisted all three women into the waiting coach, but he paused when it was his turn to climb inside, his eyes resting on the empty seat next to Emma. She would have preferred to be seated next to Mrs. Chatwell and left Miss Barton to talk the man's ear off, but the other ladies, apparently, had had other ideas and chosen to occupy the same bench.

"Just take your seat, Mr. Forester." Emma sighed, scooting as far to the other end of the bench as she could. Still, Mr. Forester was not a small man, and he filled the space quite thoroughly as he settled beside her. Despite him tucking his arms into his lap, his broad shoulders still pressed against hers. She had always paid more attention to the fine cut of his clothing than his build, but sitting next to him gave her a good idea of just how solid he was. One would never have guessed the man had as much strength as he had pride.

"Oh, are you as excited as I am, Miss Mackenzie?" Miss Barton said, bouncing in her seat and bouncing Mrs. Chatwell along with her. "I have never been to Almack's!"

As the young woman launched into a stream of exuberant proclamations and peered out the window at the passing streets, Emma tried to relax before she ended up sore from sitting so stiffly. Not especially easy to do when Forester leaned in closer, the clean smell of his soap filling her nose.

"Temporary truce?" he whispered.

Emma's eyes shot to him, even though Miss Barton was still talking. "For how long?"

He smirked. "How long do you think you can manage?"

"*My* fortitude has never been in question. I hardly expect you to hold your tongue long enough for us to arrive in peace."

"It is only a few blocks."

"Exactly."

Miss Barton chose that moment to turn away from the window and cease talking to herself. "Do you not think so, Mr. Forester?"

He didn't hesitate in the slightest, even though he couldn't possibly have been listening to what she'd been saying. "I rather disagree."

That seemed to catch Miss Barton off guard, bringing the coach into silence for the first time since they set off. "You disagree?" she repeated, her mouth hanging open slightly.

Now Emma badly wished she knew what Miss Barton had said. Whatever Forester's false opinion, it was apparently quite shocking. "Do tell us why you think so," Emma said, fighting a smile when his blank expression slipped into slight worry as he glanced between Emma and Miss Barton. "I am most fascinated by your opinion."

"Oh, leave the boy alone," Mrs. Chatwell said with a wave of her hand. "I too question the authority of Prinny now and then."

Emma pressed a hand to her mouth to hide her smile. Had Forester just managed to insult the Prince Regent somehow? She could hardly imagine how he would talk himself out of this one.

But Forester faltered for only a moment before his eyes lit up with amusement. "Why, Mrs. Chatwell, I never would have taken you for an anti-royalist."

The old woman harrumphed. "I take no issue with the monarchy, Mr. Forester. Merely with a man who has more hair than wit. I am too old to pretend otherwise."

Emma cleared her throat before a laugh escaped out of her, though she wished she hadn't made a sound when it pulled Forester's attention back to her as if to share in her amusement. Goodness, when he was holding back laughter as he was now, he looked like a man she could befriend.

"Oh, thank heavens we have arrived," Miss Barton breathed, apparently appalled by the disloyal sentiments of her companions. "And look at how many people are here!"

The coach came to a halt, and Forester pushed open the door before the footman could get to it, stretching his shoulders as soon as he was on the ground. He had evidently spent the ride trying to take up as little space as possible, just as Emma had. Once he had assisted Mrs. Chatwell and Miss Barton to the street filled with people on their way to the assembly, he held out his hand once more for Emma.

The look in his eyes made her pause. She had seen a good number of expressions on this man's face, but never a nervousness such as this.

"Well?" he said, stretching his gloved fingers closer.

Emma slipped her hand into his and allowed him to help her down. "If I did not know better," she muttered with a frown, "I would think you are anxious about the evening."

Someone called his name, and Forester flinched before nodding to the passing man. He hadn't yet released Emma's hand, even though she had a solid footing on the ground. "I do not get anxious, Miss Mackenzie."

"If I believed that, I would be even more of a fool than you."

He let out a sharp laugh before offering his arm; Miss Barton and Mrs. Chatwell had already started for the door. "Well, at least we made it through the drive. That must be a record for us."

Emma narrowed her eyes. "You did not answer my question, sir."

"You did not ask one."

"If Almack's makes you so nervous, why did you come?"

Forester's arm tightened under hers, but by then they had reached the entrance to the hall and joined their companions in greeting the patronesses. The noise of the assembly became deafening, reminding Emma of one of the many reasons she disliked London. She could hardly hear herself think, and there was no telling what might happen throughout the course of the evening.

Once inside, Forester directed their little party to a less occupied corner of the ballroom, assisting Mrs. Chatwell into a chair before looking around the room with wary eyes. For a man who always seemed to enjoy being at the center of attention, Emma couldn't understand why tonight he looked like he would rather hide.

"You didn't have to come tonight," she told him, hoping that would be enough to convince him to leave.

He chuckled. "I doubt your brother-in-law would have allowed you to come if I did not."

Emma huffed a frustrated sigh. "I didn't want to come."

"Neither did I."

"So why are we here?" Folding her arms, Emma scowled at the man until he met her eyes. "I know you told Sir Thomas to ask if I would be attending tonight. You are aware that I am trying to stop you from finding a wife, yes?"

"How could I forget?"

"Would it not have served your purpose better to *prevent* me from being here with you rather than guarantee my interference?"

Forester clenched his jaw but was saved from having to answer by a gentleman who approached Miss Barton and asked her to stand up with him in the next set. She gleefully accepted and took the man's arm with the look of someone who had just been told all her dreams would come true.

Emma wished she could live that way. To find joy in every moment and have so much hope for a happy future. But what did it mean that Miss Barton seemed to have given up on Forester? That was a valuable ally lost in her war.

"We are here," Forester said eventually, "so Miss Barton can finally dance with the man she has loved since childhood. He only just now came into his inheritance and can support a wife."

Emma's jaw dropped, and she watched Miss Barton and the man converse while they waited for the current set to end. But how had Forester known?

How could he have concocted such a plan to . . . She narrowed her eyes, turning to face Forester. "That was an utter lie."

He chuckled, a smile creeping up his face. "Of course it was. Do you really think anyone could spend a lifetime with Catherine Barton and still think of her fondly?"

"I happen to like Miss Barton."

"That is because you are not a single man of moderate means."

Emma couldn't stop her own smile from mirroring his. "No, I suppose she has no reason to try so hard with me. Though, I have no idea what she sees in you, Forester."

"Neither do I."

"Does she know that gentleman, at least?" Or did Miss Barton look at every eligible man with such interest?

Forester studied the pair. "They met last Season before she turned her sights so fully on me."

"Again, I have to wonder if she is of a sound mind. That gentleman looks far more agreeable than the likes of you."

Forester flashed a smile, though he didn't let it last long. "Ah, Miss Mackenzie. If only you could so skillfully cut down every man of London. Perhaps a humbler Society would be more bearable."

As heat crept into her face, Emma realized with some alarm that she was enjoying herself. Even conversing with Forester. After so many encounters that had left her frustrated, hurt, or angry, she wasn't sure what to make of this new civility. Civil for them, anyway.

"How do you propose I do such a thing?" she said, stumbling over her words a bit as she struggled to find her balance in this new situation. "In order to insult every man in England, I would have to speak to them all, and that is hardly possible when I am stuck talking to you." She took a deep breath when he didn't respond. "I suppose I should be embarrassed, as no one has asked me to dance," she said with a shrug. "But I am simply relieved that I have nothing to offer these men and therefore am not a target. I am not Miss Barton, who can draw a man in with a smile."

"You underestimate your appeal, Miss Mackenzie," Forester said without a hint of teasing. In fact, a scowl had taken over his expression as he looked out over the crush. "The only reason you have not been approached by every man here is because you are standing next to me."

What was she to make of that? First his compliment and then a seriousness she had yet to see from the man? She almost missed the insults; at least those she knew what to do with. Hoping to bring a sense of normalcy back to the evening, she spoke with measured sharpness in her words. "Are you truly that repulsive?"

The chuckle that rumbled out of him sent shivers through her. "As cutting as always, Miss Mackenzie. But, as always, you are also wrong. They fear me more than anything."

"And why is that?"

"Because, whether or not they all believe what they hear, no one has proven any of my claims to be false. And no one wishes to risk tarnishing their own reputation by compromising mine."

She couldn't determine whether he was proud of the fact or angry. His expression had shifted once again, this time into something much more difficult to read. "I find it hard to believe anyone could fall for your lies," she replied. "I don't believe a word I've heard about you."

Though a wry smile played at the corner of his mouth, he didn't look at her. "That is because you are more intelligent than most, Miss Mackenzie."

It was no wonder that the whole of England worshipped this man when he had such an ability to speak compliments in a way that made them impossible to disregard. Emma felt his praise from her head to her toes, even if she knew he likely didn't mean a word of it.

Still, she accepted the compliment and stood a little taller. "That is true."

Forester let out a laugh that sounded genuine enough for Emma to wonder if she had truly amused him. She shouldn't have cared, but she did. After feeling so out of place since arriving in London, she liked knowing she could make the country's most popular gentleman laugh. Perhaps she could navigate the rest of the *ton* with more ease than she'd feared if she worried less about being liked and more about being herself.

If she could gain some friends without losing herself in the process, perhaps she could find a solid enough footing to win this battle once and for all.

"You should be warned, Miss Mackenzie," Forester muttered, leaning ever so slightly closer. "While I have kept the men at bay with my presence, I have also piqued their interest by speaking to you for this long. In their eyes, if you have held my attention, it must mean there is more to you than beauty and an angelic voice."

Emma scoffed, though her face warmed at the praise. "I would hardly say there were enough in attendance at that musicale for any of these men to know—"

"Surely you cannot think all of London does not know of our performance together. If your goal was to avoid attention, you made a mistake in singing with me. Although, why else would you come to London if not to find yourself a husband? You need to secure your future, after all."

All good feelings vanished in a heartbeat, leaving Emma's hands cold with frustration. He had been charming her, lulling her into a false sense of security before striking. "Why would I need a husband when I will soon have the Mackenzie lands to care for?" she snapped back. "I believe there are a good number of ladies hoping to dance with you this evening, though heaven knows why. You should be on your way."

His smile didn't falter. "And I see Sir Thomas making his way over to claim his set. Good luck with the sharks, Miss Mackenzie. Should you need a reprieve, you know where to find me."

Did nothing affect the man? He wandered away, stopping to ask for a lady's hand as the current set finished. And Emma reluctantly turned to greet Sir Thomas, who looked just as dull as he had at the park.

Chapter Fifteen

How was a man supposed to focus on his dance partner when Miss Mackenzie was failing miserably at looking interested in hers? Poor Sir Thomas had never stood a chance with such a lively woman when the most exciting part of his life was choosing which knot to tie in his cravat. Miss Mackenzie needed someone interesting. Amusing. Someone who wouldn't bat an eye at doing something out of the ordinary.

Speaking of ordinary . . . Nick flashed a fake smile at Miss Giles as the dance brought them together, trying to remember why he hadn't interacted with her much since meeting her at the end of spring. She was quite pretty, if young, and she came from a good family. Her father owned a good deal of land in Shropshire or Cheshire or . . . wherever. It didn't much matter.

The lady's face burst into a deep crimson hue the next time he smiled at her, and he pursed his lips. Perhaps that was why he hadn't considered her; she was far too easily overcome. Did no women of London possess some backbone? Or were they all taken in by a smile or the prospect of a fortune?

"This dance is quite invigorating," Nick said when the steps brought them together again.

Miss Giles squeaked. "In-indeed."

He barely resisted the urge to groan. Just as he'd thought. The musicians had chosen to play so slowly that they were hardly dancing at all. Her agreement with his nonsense meant Miss Giles was more inclined to appeal to his vanity than to speak her mind.

"London has been unseasonably warm of late, don't you think?" he asked next, even though it had rained most of the last three days as autumn inched closer to winter.

Miss Giles glanced over the crowd, as if searching for assistance. "I suppose," she said, this time with some hesitation.

Would she agree to everything he said, no matter how ludicrous?

When next they came together, standing still for a longer moment, Nick forced his expression into something serious. "I was thinking of taking up embroidery but have no idea where to begin," he said. "Perhaps I might call on you, and you can teach me."

The poor girl turned so red that he worried she would swoon, as she completely lost focus on the dance and stared at him, open-mouthed. "Em-embroidery, sir?"

"Yes. You ladies make it seem so amusing that I've wanted to try for years. But I can't very well march into White's and ask one of my fellows for assistance, now, can I?"

As the dancers moved around them, Nick refused to move until she responded, which didn't seem likely to happen anytime soon. She probably thought him completely mad, but that was hardly any different from the way Miss Mackenzie treated him. The difference was Miss Mackenzie's utter disregard for his feelings. If he had said such a preposterous thing to her, she would have laughed in his face and said something to the effect of it being no wonder he hadn't found himself a wife yet when he was too busy painting himself a fool.

Nick smiled to himself at the thought, tempted to convince Miss Giles to spread the word that Nicholas Forester wished to take up a lady's pastime. It would reach Miss Mackenzie eventually and fuel their banter. At least with her, he had a worthy opponent. No one else had the spirit to match. Knowing Miss Mackenzie was not after his fortune through marriage had given him a chance to act like himself for the first time in years.

Miss Giles looked on the verge of tears as they stood there, clearly hating the attention being pulled their way the longer they remained motionless. "I suppose I could show you some things," she whispered.

Nick bowed his head and then took her hand to pull her back into the dance. "Perhaps I should not learn after all," he said with a dramatic sigh. "I would hardly wish to become better accomplished than you and have you regret teaching me."

The instant the set finished, he returned Miss Giles to her parents, apologized for his poor dancing skills, and then slipped into a relatively empty corner of the hall to take a moment to look out over the room. While Miss Barton had already found herself another partner, Miss Mackenzie was back with Mrs. Chatwell, apparently unaware of the half a dozen men eyeing her with interest. Nick knew each of them well enough to know none of them would appeal to Miss Mackenzie. Three of them thought far too highly of themselves, and the other three would run with their tails between their legs the moment she spoke to them.

Another gentleman caught Nick's eye, and though Mr. Parker had seemed not to notice Miss Mackenzie—hard to when he was too short to see over the heads of the crowd—he was at least amusing enough to hold a decent conversation. He would certainly be a better choice than Sir Thomas.

"Parker!" Nick held a hand out to the man as he passed.

Parker flinched as if startled by someone noticing him, but he quickly settled into a smile when he saw Nick. "Ah, Forester, I didn't see you there. It's awfully crowded tonight, isn't it?"

Nick laughed. "Isn't it always? I didn't know you were a patron of Almack's."

Parker shuddered. "I'm not, usually. I always feel as if Almack's is where the most odious of Society make themselves the loudest. But desperate times, eh?"

"Still searching for a wife?"

"Aren't we all?"

Nick couldn't have planned this better if he'd tried. While a good number of men were on the hunt, Parker seemed more eager than most. He would probably work a little harder to secure a partner, and it would assuredly take an effort to convince Miss Mackenzie to take someone's hand. Maybe Parker would be up to the task. He had always been tenacious in school, making up for his lack of stature with confidence and exuberance.

Putting his arm around Parker's shoulders, Nick steered him toward Miss Mackenzie, who thankfully hadn't been asked to dance yet. "I wonder," he said, "if you've met Harstone's lovely sister-in-law yet."

"I have not had the pleasure, no, though I hear she made quite a stir the other night."

Nick would need to look into what people were saying about her, in case anything turned negative. He needed her to be the most desirable woman in London if he was to marry her off in time to save his fortune.

"Ah," Nick said, "luckily for you, I am sure she would be delighted to give you a preview of what transpired last week if you ask. If nothing else, I am certain she would grace you with a dance. Miss Mackenzie!"

She startled, turning to him with a lovely pink rising in her cheeks, as if she hadn't expected anyone to speak to her. Then her countenance darkened when she realized who had spoken. "Mr. Forester," she ground out. "Not dancing this set?"

Nick grinned. "How could I enjoy a dance when I know you are on your own? May I present my friend, Mr. John Parker? Parker, this is Miss Emma Mackenzie."

Miss Mackenzie took a moment to examine Parker as she dipped into a curtsy. "Mr. Parker," she said slowly. "You have my condolences."

Parker took a step back. "Pardon?"

"For your misfortune."

Nick frowned, glancing between the two of them. Did she know something he didn't?

"What misfortune might that be?" Parker asked, standing a little taller. Unfortunately, he still stood below Miss Mackenzie, who was admittedly rather tall.

Miss Mackenzie nodded her head toward Nick, a fire sparking to life in her eyes. "Anyone who is forced to be Mr. Forester's friend has my pity."

Parker barked out a laugh, a smile breaking out on his face. "Yes, well, I suppose it must fall to someone. Are you engaged for this set, Miss Mackenzie?"

"Not yet."

"It would be my honor to stand up with you. What I lack in height I make up for in stories of Nick Forester's younger days."

"How could I refuse?" Miss Mackenzie took Parker's hand and sent a smirk toward Nick that made him laugh.

Perhaps finding Miss Mackenzie a husband would be easier than he'd hoped. "Try not to destroy what little esteem she holds for me, Parker," he said as the pair made their way to the dance floor.

Parker chuckled. "I make no promises."

As the music started up, Nick watched Parker quickly and easily bring a smile to Miss Mackenzie's lips with only a few words, undoubtedly sharing some unfortunate tale or other from when they were at Eton together. Miss Mackenzie laughed a moment later, and Nick shifted his feet as an unsettled feeling worked its way into his gut. What if they got along *too* well? Parker was a sympathetic fellow and not especially wealthy. If she told him of her predicament, he would likely conspire with her to keep Nick from inheriting. Not many would willingly say no to a small fortune to go along with a pretty wife.

"Don't forget the real goal," he muttered to himself. "You need a wife as much as she needs a husband."

"What are you mumbling over there?"

Nick turned to flash a smile at Mrs. Chatwell, who squinted at him from her chair. "Merely working up the courage to ask you to dance, Mrs. Chatwell."

She tapped her cane on the floor. "That tongue of yours will get you into trouble, young man." Still, she smiled at his jest. "I wonder why you did not ask Miss Mackenzie instead of handing her off to that small fellow."

Nick nearly laughed, though he refrained from letting his true feelings show so easily. It would take a miracle for the two of them to make it through an entire set in one piece. "Because she is too far above me."

Harrumphing, Mrs. Chatwell watched the dancers before turning her wrinkled gaze back to him. "The way you two go on, one would think you were made for each other. Miss Mackenzie certainly admires you."

He choked. "Excuse me? Are we talking about the same Miss Mackenzie? She despises me."

Her laugh lines deepened, though she had turned her attention back to the dance, as if she hadn't just said the most preposterous statement. "There is a fine line between love and loathing, Mr. Forester, and the pair of you have clearly begun to test the strength of it, seeing how close you can get before the line snaps."

As his eyes itched to find Miss Mackenzie in the crush, Nick forced his attention to remain fixed on the mad woman who was most assuredly losing her senses in her old age. "I believe the heat of the room is getting to you."

"I do find myself rather thirsty."

"Allow me to fetch you some lemonade." Nick hurried off before she could speak any other nonsense, but he couldn't shake her words. "Admires me?" he muttered to himself, shaking his head as he shuffled through the crowd. It was too loud for him to think straight, and the words slipped out of him against his will. He wasn't even sure where he was going, but it felt like something was chasing him. He pushed a little faster, as if he could run from Mrs. Chatwell's opinions. "Miss Mackenzie wouldn't hesitate to pull the trigger if I put a pistol in her hand and stood in front of it."

He slipped into a crowded room, wishing it were easier to find a moment to himself in this blasted place.

He was being unfair to Miss Mackenzie. She was not a cruel person, and nothing she had done was any worse than what he had done in turn. He even admired her strength where so many ladies of the *ton* would completely lose their personalities in an effort to be what men wanted them to be.

Tugging at his cravat, Nick took a deep breath and forced himself to relax. He could feel a good many eyes on him, and it would hardly be to his advantage to have so many see him so ruffled. His tug turned into adjusting the knot, and then he shifted into fixing his cuffs and brushing nonexistent lint from his sleeve.

"Having a good time, Forester?" a man asked.

Nick finally looked up as he said, "Always a bit of a struggle when ladies fight over me for a dance." But then he froze.

He had accidentally entered the card room, the one room in this cursed place he had vowed never to set foot in again.

The man who had spoken—Lord Blake—chuckled as he played a card. "Always the charmer, I see. Care to join in on the next game? Harrow here is quite cleaned out, and I'm eager to place another wager. Miss Lennox and I have been deucedly lucky tonight."

The woman across from him giggled behind her hand, nothing but flirtation in her eyes. An all too familiar sight.

As bile rose in his throat, Nick clenched his hands behind his back and forced a smile. "I'm afraid I've already promised the next set. I only came in here to hide from the ladies I had to disappoint."

"A pity," Blake said, though he hardly seemed to care as he smirked at Miss Lennox. "I would have liked to see how deep those pockets of yours go. One hears so many rumors."

Nick needed to leave. He could hardly twist any comments in his favor right now, with his head spinning, but his feet were planted in place. Blake sat at the same table Nick had played at three years ago. He could see the scene so clearly in his mind, with Lady Lavinia in the chair on the left and Lord Hayworth beside her. Nick had been so blissfully happy, thinking Lavinia would be his wife within the month, that he had ignored the way she'd laughed every time Hayworth spoke. He hadn't given any thought to the way she'd touched Hayworth's arm every few moments.

It was only later, when he'd found them entwined in an alley outside that he had realized his naivety.

"Everything all right, Forester?" Blake's words seemed to echo in his ears.

Nick dipped his head and stumbled from the room, only taking a full breath when he reached the outer doors and stepped into the blissfully cool air outside.

Chapter Sixteen

The instant Miss Barton dipped in a farewell curtsy to her current dance partner, Emma took her by the hand and dragged her from the ballroom before anyone else could request their hands for the next set.

"Oh," Miss Barton said, her eyes behind her, "I was hoping to—"

"Surely you could use a rest." In reality it was Emma who needed a respite, and she couldn't wander the assembly on her own, as much as she wanted to. Mrs. Chatwell was half asleep in her chair, so Miss Barton would have to do. "Just one set, and then we can return."

Thankfully, Miss Barton seemed to understand her need to take a breath; she allowed Emma to direct her to a sitting room full of ladies, who must have had a similar idea. The men of London were certainly eager tonight, and Emma hadn't had a moment to herself since Forester had thrust Mr. Parker at her. She had been as frustrated by that pairing as the last, though no one would ever be as tedious as Sir Thomas.

Mr. Parker had been amusing at first, but all of his geniality had been surface-level. Emma had done her best to find some depth of character, but the man seemed entirely too quick to laugh at misfortune and poke fun at things out of people's control. Emma dearly loved to laugh, but she hardly thought a young woman's measurements were something to ridicule.

Each dance partner after that had made Emma's frustrations with London grow, reminding her why she hadn't bothered to come back for another Season after her first. If she was ever to find a husband, she would not meet him here. At least, not now. There were good men among the *ton*—there had to be—but they likely avoided associating with those who were vain and unkind. They were probably all in their country homes waiting for the Season.

"Have you not been having the most wonderful night?" Miss Barton asked as they settled on the only empty sofa in the room.

Conversations buzzed around them, ladies whispering behind their gloves and giggling about who knew what.

Emma wished she could pull off her slippers and rub her sore feet. She had no true desire to impress any of these women, but neither did she wish for them to turn their gossip onto her. The best part of living in the country was having the chance to be herself, with no fear of judgment, and she already found herself questioning the value in remaining in the city. She had hardly done any good to deviate Forester's warpath for a wife anyway.

"You must have had better partners than I," Emma breathed, forcing herself to sit up straight even though she was tempted to slump down in her seat. "I found myself surrounded by fools and fops."

Miss Barton giggled. "Oh, Miss Mackenzie, surely they were not all bad! I saw you dancing with Mr. Parker. He's an amusing fellow."

Emma suppressed a laugh. "I hardly think so. He is more insulting than entertaining."

"Well, not everyone is perfect."

"Have you found anyone of interest?" Emma asked instead of addressing that worrisome thought. Just how low were Miss Barton's standards? The woman was in love with Forester, of all people, and if she thought Parker a suitable alternative, she would likely end up settling for less than she deserved. She needed someone calm and quiet, with the patience of a saint.

Letting out a dramatic sigh, Miss Barton let her eyes trail around the room as she spoke. "Oh, there are so many interesting gentlemen in London this year. More than I expected! I only wish Mr. Forester would ask me to dance. He is a *divine* dancer."

Several ladies suddenly burst into giggles, though they quickly pretended they weren't eavesdropping.

Emma clenched her jaw. Another reason to despise London: no one kept to their own business. "Perhaps Mr. Forester is only shy about his feelings for you," she said, though she immediately felt guilty for that. Forester certainly wasn't shy, and Miss Barton was hardly on his list of interests. Besides, Emma still wondered if perhaps Miss Barton had given up her pursuit of the man.

She was about to ask when two women turned in their seats to face Emma and her companion.

"Nick Forester is hardly shy," one of them said with a sneer. "If he hasn't asked you to dance, it means he hasn't given you a thought."

Miss Barton's face fell. "Oh, but he and I are good—"

"I've hardly seen him tonight," the other lady said, scrunching up her face in false worry. "Do you think he might be ill? He is usually at the height of attention."

"Perhaps he stole away with some fortunate girl," the first young lady replied.

"Oh, to be so lucky! I tried once to get caught with him and force his hand, but he is far too intelligent. Did you hear he was assisting Bow Street all summer, solving cases with the Runners?"

"Oh, he would look so good in red! But I thought he was in India all summer."

"No, that was last year."

"Of course! I do hope I can ask him about his travels one day. I would so love to hear all about Germany in the autumn."

"Was that where he won that horse race?"

Emma groaned as a headache formed behind her eyes, only realizing that she hadn't kept the sound to herself as much as she'd hoped. More than the two women turned their attention to her, leaving her feeling exposed as she fought to find an explanation for her irritation.

Might as well use the attention to try to get it into their heads that the Forester they thought they knew was a lying scoundrel. He had admitted that himself the first time she'd met him, when he'd told her that he said many things he didn't mean, and he had been proving that to be true ever since.

"Have you no pride?" she said, doing her best to ensure her expression was soft and warm instead of completely judgmental. As much as she wanted to ruin Nick's chances, she also wanted to help these women set a better standard for themselves. They deserved better. "Do you truly believe one man could accomplish so many ridiculous feats?"

A lady in the corner of the room scoffed. "What do you know of the man, Miss . . . ?"

Emma sat up as straight as she could. "Miss Emma Mackenzie."

A gasp blew through the room like a breeze.

"Mackenzie?" someone said as if in awe. "Are you the one who sang with Mr. Forester last week?"

Apparently, Forester had been correct when he'd said all of London knew about that little performance, and Emma resisted the urge to run from the room. She couldn't read everyone's expressions well enough to know whether they appreciated her performance or were utterly jealous of her being the only person in all of London to have sung with the man. Would these ladies be out for her head to rid themselves of competition? If only they knew how completely unsuited she and Forester were.

"Yes," she said after a long while, choosing honesty over following in Forester's shady footsteps. "Yes, that was me."

"So you are well acquainted with him? No one knew he could play the pianoforte."

Emma glanced at Miss Barton, who watched her with wide eyes. "Well, Miss Barton knows him better than I do, but I suppose—"

The whole room burst into excited squeals and moans of protestation, leaving Emma feeling uncertain of her own standing among these women. But as soon as she opened her mouth, all of them went silent, her audience captive.

This moment felt familiar yet foreign at the same time. These ladies weren't waiting for an entertaining story but for gossip, and Emma did not especially like being in this position.

"I know Mr. Forester well enough to know you shouldn't be so interested," she said carefully. "Why are you all so easily fooled by a man who hasn't an ounce of sincerity in him?"

Dozens of eyes blinked at her.

Wincing, Emma got to her feet because she did not want to deal with the inevitable battle that would come as soon as these women realized she was attacking their favorite gentleman. "I would imagine the reason you're in here instead of out there pursuing him is because he has already rejected you. Am I wrong?"

None of them said a word. Even Miss Barton was speechless.

Emma set her shoulders and headed for the door, pausing only to look back and say one final thing. "I do not know any of you, but I know you're better than stooping to gossip surrounding a man as worthless as he is superficial. If you have any self-respect, your attention is better directed toward someone who will adore you from the first moment he meets you rather than use you for his sport. Good evening."

With an abrupt curtsy, she hastened from the room even though Miss Barton still sat on the sofa. Hopefully the young woman would follow or at the least find herself a companion to walk back to the dance hall with, but Emma would be more than glad to find Forester and send him to collect Miss Barton so they could return home and end the evening early. She had most assuredly spoken too harshly just now, and she walked at such a speed that she hoped she could outrun the guilt that would be right behind her.

She had just about reached the ballroom when she collided with another person. A rather unladylike curse slipped from her tongue as she struggled to remain on her feet, but thankfully the person grabbed hold of her arms to steady her. She got halfway through a hasty apology when the other person spoke.

"Where did you learn a word like that?"

Head snapping up, Emma tried to remind herself that she hated this man, even if Forester's little smirk made him look far too handsome for his own good. Her churning stomach seemed to think otherwise, however, telling her that her words spoken in frustration were wildly untrue. Forester was a lot of things, but he wasn't worthless *or* superficial.

"Would you release me, sir?" she snapped.

Forester held his hands up, laughter in his eyes. "I believe you're the one who should be releasing me," he said with a dip of his chin.

Oh goodness, he was right. Emma had grabbed hold of the fabric of his jacket, though she had no idea how she'd grasped it at all when his arms barely fit within the sleeves. "Whatever do you do with your time, Mr. Forester?" she asked as she slowly stretched her fingers out, testing the reality of his muscle. Surely he could not be this strong as a man of leisure.

Chuckling, Forester took a step back to remove himself from her touch. "Because you do not play, you would not know the effort required to learn the pianoforte."

Though she had no idea why he wouldn't brag about the real reason he had built himself up so strong, Emma could feel her blush rising. Had she really just stroked the man's arms? She had, and if the rest of him matched his shoulders, she could well understand why their collision had been so painful.

"What is the real reason you are so strong?" she asked, surprised and confused as to why she so badly wanted to know the truth. Usually she didn't bother to separate fact from fiction because she hardly cared about the man behind the rumors.

His smile shifted, softening from a smirk into something more genuine. "Perhaps, if you dance with me, I will tell you."

When he held out his hand, Emma stared at it like it might cause her pain if she touched it. He wanted to dance with *her?* when he could have his pick of any lady in the building? It would serve neither of them to stand up together, and yet she found herself reaching out to take his hand.

But then her eyes caught on Mrs. Chatwell, fast asleep in her chair, and Emma shook away the strange spell that had fallen over her with that smile of his. "We should probably get her home," she said, choosing not to dwell on the disappointment that washed over her.

Even more so, she refused to acknowledge that Forester's expression seemed to match her own.

Chapter Seventeen

"What a fine day for a drive!" Miss Fairfax's eyes were bright, her cheeks pink in the brisk breeze, and she was everything sweet and delightful. Of everyone Nick had danced with last night, she was one of the few he hadn't already rejected, and he'd had good reasons for not considering any of the others in the past; from what he'd observed last night, those reasons still held up.

If he were being honest with himself, he wasn't sure he could still trust his own opinions of people. He had once had a good deal of friends, and he couldn't expect everyone in London to be awful. Perhaps he had raised his standards so high that they could never be met and he was only fooling himself into thinking he was any better than the rest of them.

He wasn't better. He *knew* he wasn't.

He had hardly slept last night, and as he navigated Lord Calloway's horses into crowded Hyde Park, he was regretting more and more his decision to ask Miss Fairfax to accompany him today when he was clearly struggling to maintain the status quo. At least Calloways' horses were well trained, as were his servants, who hadn't batted an eye when Nick had arrived at the baron's unoccupied town house and asked to borrow the curricle.

It was a good thing he had endeared himself to the London Calloway staff years ago, before he'd gotten himself into his ridiculous mess of lies. And perhaps equally fortunate that Calloway was too busy with his new wife to make the effort to come into Town unless he had to. With no animals or vehicles of his own, Nick was going to take advantage of the man's absence.

"Oh look, there is Mr. and Mrs. Allen!" Miss Fairfax pointed to a couple who were feeding ducks at the edge of the Serpentine. "Did you know they had to move into a smaller residence this year because their finances couldn't support where they were living before?"

Nick gripped the reins a little tighter. Hopefully this was only one observation and not an indication of Miss Fairfax's general nature. "Is that so?" he growled out. "Losing one of his ships must have taken its toll."

Thankfully, Miss Fairfax blushed with embarrassment, as if she hadn't realized until now that there may have been a reason for someone's finances taking a turn for the worse. "Oh, how sad!" she said softly. It was only a moment before she perked up again, pointing toward a young woman who walked with an aging chaperone. "Did you know Miss Gardner has a dowry of more than six thousand pounds?"

Nick didn't bother to respond to that comment. He had a feeling Miss Fairfax would continue on well enough without him.

"Oh, do you see the Duke of Tipton walking with his brothers? I heard he and Lord Alexander had a row in the middle of Vauxhall last week. No one knows what about, but I'm surprised to see Lord Alexander acting so genially toward his brother. He was rather upset with him last—"

"Miss Fairfax." Nick pulled the horses to a halt despite being in the middle of the pathway. He was already short-tempered as it was, and he needed to tell the girl to hold her tongue before he became any more irritable. Shifting where he sat to better face her, he took a slow breath before saying anything. This was not the time to get frustrated, as much as he wished to. He knew better than anyone how harmful gossip could be, but Miss Fairfax apparently did not. "I appreciate your knowledge of the *ton*, but perhaps spreading rumors is not the best use of your time."

Her eyes went wide. "But they are not rumors; they are truths. And surely you of all people would appreciate—"

"Have you ever actually met the Duke of Tipton or his brothers?"

That got her to close her mouth for a moment, her expression shifting into confusion. "Met a duke? No, of course not."

"And did you know anything of Mr. Allen's ship before I said something?"

"No." She had turned rather pink, likely realizing her folly in speaking of things she knew nothing about.

Maybe someday London Society would finally realize that spreading gossip did nothing to benefit anyone, but Nick wouldn't hold his breath. He had been the subject of that gossip for three years now, with no signs of that changing.

True, he had spread plenty of lies, but they had only ever been about himself. Never about other people.

Nick took another deep breath and ignored the glare he received from a man who had to direct his gig around them. "Miss Fairfax, nothing good comes of speaking about people so negatively. What should it matter that Miss Gardner has a large sum to her name when that has nothing to do with you? You should worry about your own qualities and hope no one is talking poorly of *you*."

Oh goodness, was she crying now? Miss Fairfax did her best to keep her composure, but tears were most certainly sprouting in her eyes as she focused her attention directly ahead of them instead of looking at him. Perhaps he had been too harsh, young as she was, but she would have to learn at some point, wouldn't she?

No, he had most certainly been too harsh, and he mentally kicked himself for letting his tongue fly free. The girl didn't deserve his frustrations simply because she had been raised in an uncaring Society. "Miss Fairfax, forgive me. I shouldn't have said . . ."

Sniffling, she blinked a few times before her eyes caught on something ahead. "Oh look, there is my friend Miss Sophie. Do you mind if we . . . ?"

Recognizing her need for something familiar and comfortable, Nick shook his head. "Of course we can say hello. Allow me." He hopped from the curricle and then assisted Miss Fairfax to the ground, cursing the way she pulled her hand free as soon as she was steady. He had no desire to make a match with the young woman, but neither had he intended to hurt her.

It seemed Miss Mackenzie had not been the cause of him becoming a beast after all; he was boorish all on his own.

Miss Sophie arrived only a moment later, and though Nick hadn't met her, she looked at him with a knowing glint in her eyes before greeting Miss Fairfax. The question was *what* did she know? "Miss Fairfax, so lovely to see you!"

The two women embraced, and then Miss Fairfax turned to Nick. "Sophie, this is—"

"Yes, I know who you are," Miss Sophie said, her gaze turning colder the longer she looked at Nick.

Well, that was certainly an unfamiliar reaction from anyone aside from Miss Mackenzie, and Nick found he didn't like it one bit. Despite the utterly improper greeting Miss Sophie had given him, he decided to hold his tongue and let her think whatever she wanted about him. Everyone else seemed to, but at least everyone else liked him.

"Might I speak to you privately for a moment?" Miss Sophie asked Miss Fairfax, and the two ladies scurried several feet away toward the lake, leaving Nick with the horses.

Normally, if he was left standing on his own, women took advantage of the opportunity and approached him in the hopes of befriending him or subtly convincing him to court them. Sometimes not so subtly. But as he stood in the sunshine, brushing his hand along the neck of the nearest horse, Nick watched several people pass without even sparing him a glance. Those who *did* look at him turned immediately to their companions and started whispering. Some people even glared at him, like Miss Sophie had.

"What new rumor has spread about me?" he wondered out loud.

The horse snorted in response, as if laughing at him.

"You're quite right," he agreed. "Surely there have been many, not just one." He would have to figure out what people were saying about him and ensure he twisted it to his favor, but no one was coming close enough for him to overhear any of the conversations happening around him. Perhaps Miss Sophie was relaying the information to her friend and Miss Fairfax in turn would tell him what she had heard. She seemed all too eager to spread whatever she knew about those around her. Once he knew the scope of the rumors, he would figure out a way to squash them. At what point would people start to question the validity of everything they heard?

Nick prayed that day came quickly.

As he waited for the ladies' conversation to cease dragging on, Nick continued to rub the horse's neck, marveling at the beauty of the animal. Lord Simon Calloway was as rich in money as he was in goodness, and yet he had never flaunted his wealth. *Probably* because *of his goodness*, Nick thought with a chuckle. The man was wholeheartedly kind and honest, and though he likely didn't know how often Nick stopped by his town house, his charity had clearly extended to his servants as well. Otherwise, they wouldn't have let him take the horses in the first place, as Nick had never met more loyal staff than Calloway's.

"Think he would let me take you home?" Nick asked the horse, chuckling to himself at the thought. What home? He could barely afford his rented room here in London, and his estate back in Derbyshire was quite literally falling apart. He hadn't set foot in that house in over a year, and the land was likely overgrown and overrun. Perhaps some brave soul had thought to take up residence and claim it for his own, but Nick doubted it.

The house had been in shambles even before his father had lost what money he had, and Nick had never been able to scrape together the funds to make any repairs *and* pay for Mrs. Murray's living, even with Mr. Mackenzie giving him a small yearly allowance to sustain him as a favor to Nick's late father.

Sighing, Nick leaned against the horse and tried not to dwell on how tired he was of relying on other people. Calloway had helped him through school; Mackenzie had helped him in the years since; Harstone was helping him now. What little coin he had was all he'd been able to stomach to take when Harstone had offered it to him upon his arrival in London.

Harstone knew well enough how much Nick had been relying on spending the autumn at the country manor rather than paying for a room in Town, and he had first offered to let Nick stay in his town house when he arrived in London.

But that would have required being in the same place as Miss Mackenzie, and Nick knew too well the danger in that.

"Though, she was almost pleasant last night," he told the horse, as if they were having a true conversation. "One almost has to wonder what manner of conversations we would have if we didn't have this inheritance between us."

Emma Mackenzie would certainly be far kinder to her fellows than Miss Fairfax, who was at last returning to the curricle with Miss Sophie on her arm.

"My apologies, Mr. Forester," she said, her voice thin. "I must return home as soon as possible."

It wasn't as if he was enjoying their drive together, but Nick couldn't help but wonder what had transpired between the two ladies to make her so skittish. "Is something the matter?"

"Hmm? Oh no, nothing at all. That is to say . . ." She shook her head. "I want to go home."

Well, he could hardly ignore the fear and worry in her eyes, even if she didn't wish to give him a real reason for cutting their outing short. "Yes, of course," he said, climbing into the curricle and then holding out his hand to pull her up beside him.

She seemed to take his hand with great reluctance, and her eyes fixated on Miss Sophie until he had flicked the reins and directed the horses forward. Then she sat stiffly, her hands twisting her reticule in her lap and her eyes downcast.

Nick waited as long as his limited patience allowed before he asked, "Miss Fairfax, is something—"

"Did you really captain a ship in the navy?" The question came out of her so quickly that it was as if she hadn't been able to hold it in any longer.

Nick had a feeling this conversation was not going to be in his favor. "Is that what they say about me?" he asked; perhaps being aloof would save him from the truth coming to light.

Miss Fairfax huffed. "You cannot be older than thirty, I should think. And the battle of Trafalgar was in 1805."

Nick's stomach clenched. "I believe it was, yes."

She narrowed her eyes, finally looking at him, even though he kept most of his focus on the busy street ahead. She did not live far, but her house was not nearly close enough. "So you would have me believe you captained a vessel at twenty years old?"

So much for wanting someone to question all the rumors. With the way she was looking at him, like he was the scum of the earth, Nick's guilt made him squirm and wish she weren't sitting in the curricle so he could drive away and hide. He urged the horses faster, taking the corner perhaps a little too quickly for the two-wheeled conveyance to travel safely. It teetered a bit, but he managed to keep it upright.

"Miss Fairfax—"

"What else has been a lie, Mr. Forester? Is anything about you genuine?"

For what felt like the first time in his life, he didn't have a response. What could he say? If he was truly trying to change his ways and begin living a more honest life, he couldn't very well argue against her sudden change in opinion. His lack of response seemed to be answer enough for Miss Fairfax, apparently, and she folded her arms, sitting so stiffly that he felt himself cowering beneath her anger.

It had to have been Miss Sophie who changed her mind, but why? Why was all of London suddenly looking at him like he had betrayed them?

"Good day to you, Mr. Forester." Miss Fairfax didn't even wait for him to help her down to the street when they reached her house. She hopped down on her own, slipping through the front door without a backward glance.

Swearing under his breath, Nick gripped the reins tighter and told himself that everything would turn out as it should. He could hardly lose his entire reputation in the course of one afternoon, and he would make it through this. Whatever *this* was.

Chapter Eighteen

THERE WAS NOTHING QUITE SO fulfilling as spending an afternoon with Tabitha's children, who had bounced back from their illness with remarkable resilience. The girls didn't care about fortunes or marriage or which man would bring the most notoriety to a match. They treated each other with fairness, most of the time, and were quick to praise and show their love and appreciation. Playing with dolls with her nieces had filled Emma's capacity to still see good in the world, and that was the only reason she had agreed to attend a dinner party with her sister and Alvaro.

That hadn't stopped her from trying to remain at home, however.

"Oh, but Lady Wilmore is a dear friend of mine. I am certain you will have a far better time than you're expecting." Tabitha had been making arguments for the last twenty minutes, unwilling to yield.

Emma scoffed as she held up another gown for Tabitha to judge. "I have yet to enjoy any social function in London thus far. What makes you think this will be any different?"

"Because you have only been to more public gatherings, and this will be a much quieter affair." Tabitha held the dress up against her body, studying herself in the mirror. "And Lady Wilmore has the best taste. No, I think the blue one will do for tonight."

Her lady's maid immediately began assisting her into the chosen gown with a satisfied smile.

Emma knew she likely wouldn't win this argument, so she should probably go call Jenny to help her dress, but that felt too much like admitting defeat. Besides, she had planned to wear a blue dress again, and now she would have to choose something different so she and Tabitha did not look too alike.

Then again, what did it matter what she wore? She hadn't even liked any of her blue dresses until . . .

Until Nick Forester told her it was her color.

Cheeks pinking, Emma cleared her throat and tried one more fruitless argument. "Surely you and Alvaro want more time to recover instead of escorting Miss Barton and—"

"Miss Barton has decided to remain at home this evening. It seems she has fallen behind on some correspondence."

Even if it made her seem juvenile, Emma still whined a bit as she said, "Why is Miss Barton allowed to remain at home while I am forced to go out?"

Tabitha laughed. "When did you become such a homebody? You hardly ever stay home when we're in Tutbury. Grandfather likely forgets you live with him because you are never there."

"You exaggerate."

"You are an overwhelmingly social person, Emma. Is something wrong? Why wouldn't you want to go out and meet more people?"

Sighing, Emma tried to find an explanation that would make sense. She could hardly tell her sister the real reason she didn't want to attend this dinner. Namely, because Nick Forester would be there. She hadn't seen him since Almack's the night before, but he hadn't been far from her thoughts.

He had acted so differently from the hateful man he had been from the first moment she'd discovered who he was. There had been something genuine about him, in the way he'd laughed at her jests and called her intelligent. Though Emma was certain he did not mean most of what he said on a day-to-day basis, she had felt he'd meant every word when he'd complimented her.

"Emma?"

"I feel so inferior here in London," Emma said with a wince. Was admitting that truly better than interacting with Mr. Forester again?

Settling in a chair, Tabitha fixed her gaze on Emma while her maid set to work on her hair. "Why would you feel inferior? You have as much reason to be here as anyone, and you are always so happy with friends. Surely it will not take you long to make new ones."

Emma sighed. She had already amassed a good number of admirers since her arrival, though she hadn't allowed herself to become attached to anyone. Whether because she would soon return to Staffordshire or because she feared being known, she wasn't certain. Perhaps it was both. "I suppose. But I think I've grown too comfortable with the familiar. I already know everyone in Tutbury, and they already know I am . . . odd."

"Who says you are odd?"

"I think my lack of husband speaks for itself." Emma picked at a string in her skirt, refusing to meet her sister's gaze. "I don't need a husband to be happy, and I know this. Mother did perfectly well on her own."

Tabitha spoke softly. "But?"

As she looked up, Emma braced herself for the chance, however small, that her sister would ridicule her for what she was about to say. "But if I am going to subject myself to marriage and give up the independence I hold so dear, I want it to be for the deepest of loves. How could I ask for anything less when you and Alvaro show me day after day that such a thing can exist? In any case, it isn't as if men are lining up to court the woman who speaks her mind freely and aspires to manage her own land."

"You don't know that."

Emma shot her a sharp look. "How many men do you see pursuing me, Tab?"

"Isn't this why we came to London? So you might find yourself a match? You cannot do that by hiding yourself away and cowering."

Emma sat up straight, feeling that judgment in her core. "I am not cowering."

"You have yet to show me otherwise. Why are you so certain there are no men in London who would not find your strong mind to be an asset rather than a mark against you?"

"If such a man existed, I would have found him three years ago, when I was actually trying to find a partner."

"And you are not trying now?"

Oh, Emma hadn't intended to admit that part. She already felt guilty enough about convincing Tabitha and her family to come to London, but she would rather be honest than continue to lie. "Not especially."

"Then, what are we doing here, Emma?" Tabitha asked, her eyebrows pulling low as she gazed at Emma through the mirror.

Could she really admit to the real reason she had come? It would make her sound like an awful person, but it would be accurate. Clasping her hands in front of her, Emma tried to look as repentant as she felt. "Because I worried Mr. Forester would find a wife if I didn't intervene."

Tabitha shared a look with her maid, who dipped into a curtsy and slipped out of the room. Apparently, this conversation had just turned serious enough to require privacy. "What on earth does Mr. Forester's life have to do with yours?"

"You know about Grandfather's inher—"

"And you thought sabotaging the man's chances would benefit yours?" Tabitha turned to face her, using the stern expression that always worked on the girls. Emma wasn't often on the receiving end of her sister's censure, and suddenly she could feel the ten-year difference between the two of them. "Just what sort of man do you think Grandfather is? Do you think he would leave you destitute simply because he wishes to assist a man of unfortunate circumstances?"

Emma tried not to wither where she sat. "There is a difference between having a generous dowry and having independence, and Grandfather refuses to give me independence without a husband. And yet a dowry does me no good without being wed, and even then it hardly does anything for me." She huffed a sigh as her frustration with it all grew. No matter which way she turned, marriage was her only option unless she convinced her grandfather to reconsider as soon as she came of age. "Besides, what right does Nicholas Forester have to lands that have been in our family for over a century? And all because his father and our grandfather were friends years ago! Why should he get something he hasn't earned and will never love as much as I do? The man is entirely incapable of being serious, and unless he stops telling lies to benefit his image and starts taking responsibility for his own life, he will be nothing but a handsome face with land as barren as his soul. I refuse to allow some poor, innocent woman to fall for his many charms only to be a means to an end."

To Emma's surprise, Tabitha nearly smiled as she sat there, as if she had come to understand something she hadn't known before. "Why are you so certain Mr. Forester will destroy Mackenzie Manor? Alvaro told me they spent a good deal out of doors when we were in Staffordshire, and Mr. Forester seemed a different man after exploring Grandfather's lands."

Emma folded her arms. "That means nothing. Mr. Forester has already made his own estate unlivable, and he will likely—"

"Mr. Forester's father made an unfortunate decision that drained the estate of all its finances, leaving Mr. Forester with nothing. His parents died when he was only a boy, and it is a miracle he has made it this far on his own."

Was that true? As that information hit Emma straight in the chest, she tried not to dwell on the feeling of pity that filled her gut. She hardly wanted to feel anything toward Mr. Forester aside from hatred, but she couldn't ignore the fact that she had been wrong. She had been so certain his circumstances were his own doing, that his frivolous nature had led him to squandering what he had.

Feeling small, Emma ducked her head. "I didn't know that."

A hand pressed against her shoulder just before Tabitha sat beside her. "I know Mr. Forester has a . . . large personality."

Emma laughed. "That is a generous way to put it."

"But Alvaro considers him one of his closest friends. With how many friends my husband possesses, that is not insignificant."

The more Emma thought about it, the more unfair she could admit she had been when it came to Mr. Forester. If she took away the inheritance and their feud, she realized she knew very little about the man. Partly because he was surrounded by so many rumors, but mostly because she hadn't yet bothered to learn where the truth lay. The one time they had been civil—standing at the edge of the Almack's ballroom—she had reluctantly enjoyed his company.

Could there really be something worth knowing about the man? It changed nothing about their circumstances, but perhaps she should spend less time trying to tear him down and more time considering her real reasons for avoiding attachment. What if there really was someone out there who would value her independent nature rather than abhor it? She had been so convinced that such a man couldn't exist that she hadn't given anyone a chance.

"Well?" Tabitha said, grasping her hand and giving it a squeeze. "Will you be joining us tonight?"

Wincing, Emma considered the alternative. Remaining on her own here at the house, with nothing and no one to keep her company except a woman who apparently had a good deal of letters to write and a history of being verbose? That sounded absolutely dreadful. And facing Mr. Forester after this little revelation from Tabitha seemed far less daunting than it had before. Perhaps they could continue their truce. Maybe even be friends. If she lost this war, she wanted to be able to return to visit the lands she loved so well, and she would need Mr. Forester's good favor to do that.

As she hurried to her room and called Jenny to help her dress, Emma couldn't help but smile at the thought of saying something tonight that would bring that handsome smile to Mr. Forester's mouth, like she had at Almack's.

"That," she told her reflection, "is going to become dangerous if you are not careful."

Chapter Nineteen

THE MOMENT EMMA STEPPED INTO Lady Wilmore's drawing room behind Tabitha and Alvaro, three different ladies greeted her with enthusiasm, as if they were long-lost friends. One of them Emma hadn't even met yet, and she struggled to keep up with their different conversations, barely managing to get a word in. Before she could try to gain some sense of control, she was introduced to several men, who each expressed an interest in getting to know her better after hearing so much about her.

Heard about her when? How? She had no idea, and she hadn't a clue what was happening. This attention was far worse than anything she'd gotten at Almack's the other night. Something had changed.

It was nearly half an hour before Emma's eyes flitted to the corner of the room, where she found Mr. Forester sitting on his own and looking especially gloomy. Had he been there the entire time? Usually he was at the center of everything, commanding attention, and seeing him with his gaze locked on the floor knocked Emma off-balance.

She had seen him angry and frustrated, but she had never seen him look this dejected. The sympathetic ache from earlier returned to her heart as she watched him, and she lasted only a minute or two before his frown pulled her in his direction, though she had no idea what to say to the man. It would probably be best to stay within their usual back-and-forth banter.

"Not flirting with all of London tonight, Mr. Forester?" she said as she neared.

His eyes snapped up at the same time his body went tense, like he hadn't expected anyone to notice him in his corner. "Miss Mackenzie," he said with a sharp nod. There was no trace of his smile, and Emma realized she had never seen him like this when in company. Even during their verbal battles, there had always been a part of him playing the role of carefree dandy. That mask was entirely absent tonight.

As much as Emma appreciated honesty, she wasn't certain she liked this cold and broken version of Nick Forester.

"What has you so out of sorts?" she asked, keeping her voice soft. She glanced behind her, confused by the sheer number of people watching their exchange with little attempts at subtlety. Was this conversation truly so riveting? Emma felt like laughing at the absurdity.

Mr. Forester, on the other hand, refused to make eye contact with anyone, even as he searched the crowd, flinching every few seconds, as if he could hear everyone's thoughts through the low buzz of whispered conversation.

"Some unwelcome news," he muttered, clenching his hands at his sides. "Nothing to concern yourself over."

But Emma *was* concerned. Anything that could dim the man's endless cheerfulness had to be bigger than a minor disappointment, and with how close Mr. Forester supposedly was to Alvaro and his family, she had to wonder if this so-called unwelcome news affected him solely or if she needed to worry.

"Mr. Forester, what—"

"I am in no mood to engage in battle tonight, Miss Mackenzie," Mr. Forester growled, turning his gaze back to her. "Don't you have some stories to tell? Gentlemen to enchant? Anything that would take you away from this corner so I may endure their judgment in silence?"

Stunned by the pain in his words, Emma looked behind her once again, heat spotting her cheeks as she realized the other guests were watching her as much as they watched Mr. Forester. Whispering about *her*. "Whatever rumor has you so on edge, Mr. Forester," she said, "I should think you, of all people, would know better than to listen to all the lies thrown about Society."

Something shifted in his demeanor, like he had been moldable clay a moment ago but had just come out of the fire, hard as a rock. "Lies," he repeated hoarsely.

Emma scoffed. "Surely you don't think anyone actually believes all those rumors. I certainly do not, and you can hardly expect—"

He was on his feet in a flash, towering over her with the fire in his eyes now. "What have you done?" he hissed.

She might have taken a step back if the intensity in those blue eyes of his hadn't rooted her to the spot. At least her tongue still worked, even if her feet did not. "Excuse me?"

"My reputation was perfectly intact until you came here on your little crusade to ruin me. What. Did. You. Do?"

"Your *reputation* was built on the gullibility of simple minds. Anything could have toppled it, so I do not know why you are so convinced I had anything to do with whatever this is." Emma waved her arm toward him, certain he had lost his mind—until she recalled what she had said to the women at Almack's last night. She glanced behind her once more. The whispers stopped immediately. "I did Society a favor," she said to defend herself, though she wasn't very confident. Not when Nick looked weary to the bone, like he'd lost everything overnight. "Now no one has any reason to believe the utter rot that is Nicholas Forester's sham of a life." Could one irritated comment really be enough to tear his standing to rubble?

He seemed to think so, if the way he glared at her was any indication.

"If you were honest for once in your life," she continued, "you might have found someone to love you years ago, but you are nothing but smoke, Mr. Forester. Insubstantial and insignificant. It is no wonder you have been left entirely alone in your life."

As soon as those words left her mouth, she regretted them. Why did he bring out the worst in her? Though Mr. Forester hardly reacted, his eyes turned deep and dark as he stared at her, and she felt as if she could see through them into his soul. What she found was nothing but pain. Pain and hopelessness.

And she had been the cause of it.

"I . . . I'm sorry," she whispered, shaking her head. She felt ill, knowing those cutting words were not ones she could take back. "I didn't mean—"

Someone cleared their throat, and Emma turned just as the butler announced that dinner was ready. As grateful as she was for the reprieve from this disastrous conversation, she only felt worse when she turned back to better apologize to Mr. Forester and found his corner of the room empty, a door to her left falling shut.

Chapter Twenty

"ALL THINGS CONSIDERED, IT COULD be worse." Nick kept telling himself that as he sat holed up in Lord Calloway's study, nursing a glass of brandy as if it could solve his problems. Unfortunately, his optimism went only as far as his voice could carry it, and there was no one else around to keep it from falling flat on the ground.

After that disaster of a dinner party tonight—not that Nick had stayed long enough to enjoy the meal—he had locked himself up here in Calloway's town house to wait out the social storm. He could hardly imagine what people were saying about him now that Miss Mackenzie had thoroughly insulted him. Hiding would do nothing to help his situation, but he had come to the conclusion that he was tired of pretending he had any control over what people thought of him.

He never had.

For the last three years, he had been deluding himself into thinking all the lies he'd spread were enough to cover up the truth, but now he knew better. Miss Mackenzie had proven there were people in the world intelligent enough to see through the scheme and find the real man behind the mask—the coward who was so afraid of losing what little he had that he had put it all at risk.

It seemed all of London had finally wised up.

"Nick Forester, you've got a long way to climb," he told himself, wincing as the strained sound of his voice filled the silent room.

He had tried filling the evening's silence by playing the pianoforte in the music room, but his fingers kept fumbling across the notes as he struggled to find a song that fit his mood. Everything had been too bright and cheery, and the instrument itself had reminded him of the way Miss Mackenzie had sung with him the week before. Blast it all, she had tainted one of the few things he could call his own, and Nick cursed the empty house around him.

It was too quiet with Calloway out in the country, and it wasn't as if the servants would sit and have a conversation with him. Miss Mackenzie had spoken truth when she'd said he was utterly alone.

A week ago he had been able to call upon any number of friends and acquaintances and take advantage of their hospitality. It was the only reason his funds had lasted as long as they had. But thanks to whatever Miss Mackenzie had said about him and how many people were now questioning everything about him, Nick feared putting his old relationships to the test. How many people would turn up their noses at the sight of him? He hadn't yet hit the bottom, as far as he was aware, but one misstep would send him crashing to the ground.

Unless he gave in and found himself an occupation that would leave his future children—assuming he ever got that far—with little opportunity, the inheritance from Mr. Mackenzie was all he had left. Taking the path of a laborer would affect Mrs. Murray as well, and though she constantly told him he did not need to pay her housekeeping wages now that she lived on her own in a little cottage, he still felt responsible for her well-being.

"Don't make me do this, Emma," he said before draining his glass. As frustrating as she had been since their meeting in Tutbury, the woman didn't deserve to be thrust into this unnecessary battle. If she would stop fighting and accept that she was already better off than him, Nick would be able to stop thinking of her as the enemy.

Truth be told, he'd hardly stopped thinking about her at all. It was as if Mrs. Chatwell's words about Miss Mackenzie being made for him had gotten stuck in his head, and when he'd seen her at the Lord Wilmore's tonight, smiling and laughing with the people who no longer saw Nick as one of the greatest men in London, something had shifted inside him, leaving him feeling unsteady. Even after all she had done to cut him down, she had somehow lodged herself in his mind as someone to admire.

No one had ever challenged him the way she did. She was clever and fearless, and she knew exactly what she wanted. It didn't matter what anyone thought of her; she went forth boldly in a way Nick envied.

He hoped the world didn't change her the way it had changed him.

Gripping his glass, Nick glowered at the row of ledgers that lined Calloway's bookshelves as if they had insulted him. He couldn't even properly hate the woman for ruining everything! Yes, he had hoped to begin dismantling the lies that surrounded him, but Miss Mackenzie had instead pulled the rug out from under him at the edge of a cliff, and she had no right to wonder why he'd ended up battered and bruised. And yet she had still looked at him with remorse when she'd apologized for an insult that had been entirely accurate. The regret in her eyes made her an infuriatingly good person, and he could hardly blame her for saying what she had when he had pushed her to it.

And now, though he hadn't been brave enough to venture elsewhere after leaving Wilmore's before dinner had even started, Nick knew all of London was questioning everything about him even more than they had that morning. The problem was they would be questioning the truth as well as the lies, and that left Nick with nothing to stand on. No way to get back on his feet and keep fighting.

Lud, he was tired. If anyone could fix such a mess of a life, he could, but at this point he wasn't sure he even wanted to. Maybe it would be better to start over, move to America, work long enough to buy himself a farm and pretend that that was the life he had always wanted. Perhaps Mrs. Murray would come with him, as he would not be able to look after her if she remained behind. His guilt over having to dismiss her in the first place would not be smothered easily. Not after she had cared for him before he'd come of age.

Unless he found himself an especially wealthy woman with a heart of gold, Nick was out of options.

He sighed. What was the point of trying to beat Miss Mackenzie at her grandfather's twisted game when there likely weren't any women left, of any status, who would even consider Nick's suit if he kept trying? He had already lost.

Lifting his empty glass into the air, Nick toasted Miss Mackenzie and then gathered up his discarded jacket and cravat. He needed to stop wallowing, go to bed, and get some sleep. Maybe in the morning he would be more inclined to make an actual plan for his future, one that didn't require him to abandon Mrs. Murray or give up his last connections to his family. Leaving England would mean leaving behind his parents' graves, and their names carved in stone were all he had left of them.

Calloway's London butler, Hastings, greeted him in the entryway with a nod of his head. "On your way, sir?"

Nick squinted at him. Calloway's servants were entirely professional, but Hastings always seemed to have a certain look about him whenever Nick showed up unannounced. It wasn't annoyance, but neither was it pleasure. Somewhere in between.

"Did Calloway ever tell you about the day he and I met?" Nick asked as he struggled into his jacket.

The butler cleared his throat. "Shall I call for the carriage, sir?"

Nick sighed, though a smile found its way to his mouth. "You truly are good at your job, man. I shall enlighten you. We were at school, and a fellow student challenged me to a race across the lake. We built boats and set off across the water. My boat capsized in the middle, however, and I refused to abandon my boat. A good captain should go down with his ship, so they say."

Hastings seemed to be fighting a smile, though he stood silent.

Nick narrowed his eyes, though he'd made it only halfway into his jacket. This conversation seemed more fun than making the cold trek back to his rented room, especially after how much brandy he'd consumed. "Calloway decided I should not die a noble death and jumped in to save me, though he hadn't yet learned to swim and nearly drowned before I pulled him to safety."

Clearing his throat again, Hastings reached out and helped Nick push his arm into his other sleeve. He adjusted the jacket, straightening the collar with little change in his expression. "Lord Calloway has been swimming since he was in leading strings. And I believe they were paper boats you launched across the pond. Sir."

Nick grinned. "So he did tell you! Did he also tell you that I am the one who cannot swim and that I was reaching across the water to save my boat when I fell in?"

The butler smiled, ducking his head. "He might have mentioned it."

Nick wasn't sure why that conversation made him feel better, but it did. Maybe it was admitting the exaggeration of the truth, but he felt lighter. More like himself again. Or, at least, the way he had been before Lady Lavinia had pushed him to weave his twisted web of lies. He liked to think he had been a man of honor once, though he wasn't certain he could claim that now.

"You're a good man, Hastings," he said, clapping the man on the shoulder. "Don't tell Calloway how much I drank."

Just as he took one wavering step toward the door—lud, he'd drunk more than he thought—the butler cleared his throat. "Lord Calloway insists that a room be made up for you all year round, should you have need of it. And I do not doubt Cook would appreciate making supper for more than the staff, seeing as Lord Calloway is spending more time at the Park now that he is married. Sir."

Tears pricked at Nick's eyes as his throat went tight, though he wasn't about to let a butler see him get emotional. Nick had always considered Calloway one of his dearest friends, but he had also always been too proud to admit he could barely care for himself, let alone anyone else. Calloway had more than enough money to bestow a little charity, and Nick could humble himself now that he didn't have a load of nonsense to hold up.

Perhaps, if he reminded himself of the man Calloway and Harstone had befriended—the one who was not too proud to accept help—he could get back to the good man he had once been. It wouldn't help him win any ladies' hands before December, but maybe he could still have a chance at happiness eventually.

"You know, perhaps it would be wise for me to spend the night," he said, feigning thoughtfulness. "I am a bit foxed, after all."

"Wouldn't want something to happen to you on the journey home," Hastings agreed with a small smile. "And should you choose to stay longer than tonight, sir, you need only say so."

As he sank heavily into a plush bed a few minutes later, Nick couldn't stop his mind from drifting back to Miss Mackenzie yet again. Though he had little chance of finding himself a wife in the next month, perhaps he could still succeed in finding Miss Mackenzie a husband so she might take pity on him and surrender. It was his last hope, and yet he fell asleep with his stomach twisting in discomfort. The idea of Miss Mackenzie falling for someone was the last thing he wanted.

Chapter Twenty-One

Apparently, most young ladies of London Society were perfectly content to sit in utter boredom. Or perhaps Emma was the one at fault, seeing as the other ladies who embroidered around her were having a grand time, giggling and grinning as they discussed who knew what while they sewed. Emma hadn't remembered spending an afternoon stuck inside quite like this during her Season, and she would much rather have spent the day in the library, pretending she hadn't gotten herself tangled in the middle of a gossip chain. She could understand why the other ladies enjoyed the activity, but embroidering had never been one of her talents.

This wasn't helping her feelings of inferiority among the women of London. They were all so prepared to take on households when they married, and Emma knew more about rotating crops than changing linens. For the first time, she felt as if she couldn't be her true self, and she hated it.

But Miss Barton had begged her to join her, and Emma hadn't been able to say no when the young woman had pouted and somehow managed to will tears into existence.

"Aren't you so glad you came?" Miss Barton asked quietly, grasping her hand as they sat side by side. "I haven't done anything like this before!"

"I am glad I could be your companion for the day," Emma replied, which was true. She would have preferred spending the day with Miss Barton away from the eyes of strangers, but that was out of her control. After Miss Barton had missed last night's dinner party, she had been desperate to get out and meet more people.

Miss Andrews, who had invited the pair, smiled at them from the sofa across from theirs. Though the small gathering of ladies had been embroidering for nearly twenty minutes now, this was the first attention anyone had given Emma since their arrival, which was a new sensation. "I am so glad you could come, Miss Mackenzie," Miss Andrews said, and her words immediately pulled everyone's attention away from their sewing, as if everyone had been waiting for this moment. "I have been wanting to speak with you for a long time."

Heat spotted in Emma's cheeks, but she was glad for the excuse to set her pitiful embroidery in her lap rather than continue. "I was not aware I was so interesting," she said with some hesitation. After how quickly the people seemed to have turned on Mr. Forester, she had chosen to be more cautious when in company. "Here I was thinking I was simply a country girl of little importance."

The room bubbled with giggles.

"Nonsense!" Miss Andrews said. Her smile seemed far too wide to be believable, but Emma didn't sense any malice in it. "You've made quite the stir since your arrival. This is your first time in London, is it not?"

How would they take to the news of her failed Season? Emma considered lying and agreeing with the woman, but her gut twisted at the thought. She had no desire to become as unsteady as Mr. Forester. "No," she said, sitting a little taller. "I had a Season a few years ago, but I decided I preferred life in the country to being here in Town."

Miss Andrews's delicate blonde eyebrows rose in surprise. "What brings you into the city, then?"

"What brings any of us?" Emma asked in reply.

That sent the dozen or so ladies in the room into even stronger fits of giggles, many of them turning to their friends and whispering behind their hands.

Miss Andrews translated: "There aren't as many options of the male sex this time of year, but there are still some admirable choices. Enough to keep us entertained, anyway. Have any caught your eye yet?"

Emma was tempted to see how they would react if she told them she had no intention of marrying anyone, but she wasn't quite brave enough for that one. She was lucky her direct insult to Mr. Forester last night hadn't turned her into an outcast alongside him, and she hardly wished to put herself in danger. The only way she would be able to keep herself in a good position to inherit was to appease the *ton* to ensure she remained in higher standing than Mr. Forester.

At this point, that was easily done. All throughout dinner last night, Emma had been catching snippets of conversations, most of them involving Mr. Forester in some way. It seemed her frustrated remark at Almack's had impacted Society far more than she could have expected, and no one seemed to know what to think about the man of lies anymore.

"Oh," Emma said, realizing everyone was still waiting for her response. "No, I haven't found myself interested in anyone in particular."

Why did that feel like a lie?

Face growing warm again, Emma ducked her head and pretended to fix a stitch.

"Not even Sir Thomas?" Miss Andrews sounded skeptical. "You danced with him the other night, did you not? Haven't you heard what he's rumored to be worth?"

Emma held back a scoff. "I suppose that is a fine recommendation," she admitted. "But—"

"If she's after wealth," another lady said sharply, "she could do better than Sir Thomas." Scooting forward on her seat, she practically bounced with excitement as she asked Emma, "Have you met the Duke of Tipton yet?"

"A duke?" Emma spluttered. "I hardly—"

"His Grace's brothers are far more handsome," someone else threw in. "Lord Charles may not be a duke, but—"

"If you're going for the duke's brothers, it's Lord Alexander you want. Not the youngest."

"But Lord Alexander is so quiet! Except, I suppose he wasn't the other day, when he and His Grace—"

"Oh, you weren't even there, Sophie. You have no idea what you're talking about."

Emma was going to get dizzy from looking from one person to the next as several women broke into an unintelligible argument, as if the personal affairs of a duke and his brothers were any of their business. And Mr. Forester enjoyed this life? He had been at the center of this for years, not just physically but as a topic of discussion. Perhaps that was why he was so jaded; Society had given him little reason to be otherwise.

"Oh dear," Miss Barton whispered, apparently realizing, like Emma had, that this argument was not likely to die down anytime soon. It seemed the eligible bachelors of London were more interesting than Emma's lack of a marriage prospect. "Suppose they would notice if we snuck out?"

Emma grinned to match Miss Barton's mischievous smile, and then she turned her attention to the clock on the mantel. "Oh, would you look at the time!" she said, loud enough for only those nearest her to hear. "My sister will be wondering where we are, Miss Barton."

"Yes, I hadn't realized it was so, er, late."

Biting back laughter, Emma left her abysmal sewing project on the sofa and stood with Miss Barton in tow. "We are so grateful you invited us, Miss

Andrews"—Miss Andrews was too busy telling someone about why Sir Thomas was better than either of the duke's brothers to notice—"but unfortunately we are late to meet Lady Harstone. You understand, don't you?"

They had nearly made it to the door when a pretty young woman with red hair hopped up and grabbed Emma's arm.

"Forgive me," she said, ducking into a quick curtsy. "I don't believe we've met. I'm Harriet Fairfax. I've heard a lot about you over the last few days, Miss Mackenzie."

Frowning, Emma checked to see if Miss Barton knew the woman—Miss Barton's smile seemed to indicate that she did—and then she said, "Is that so? I haven't paid much attention to what people are saying these days." That was a lie. She'd been paying *too much* attention, which was why she'd hoped to remain at home today.

Miss Fairfax pinked as she glanced behind her to make sure no one else had decided to join in their quiet conversation. "I also noticed you have spent a good deal of time with Nicholas Forester. It's all anyone has been talking about lately, and I wondered if you might provide some clarity."

Emma didn't like where this was going, but she had already been plenty rude to Miss Andrews in the way they'd snuck to the door. Perhaps she should be gracious in this instance. "Clarity in what way?"

"From what I've gathered, you are the one who opened our eyes to Mr. Forester's, ah, less-than-honest ways."

Emma had hoped everyone had forgotten her involvement, even if that wouldn't have lessened her guilt for what she had done. It would probably be a good idea to know what she was up against, however. Mr. Forester had been beloved by so many for so long that the chances were high she had created some enemies for herself by saying what she had. And perhaps she could find a way to fix things. Not enough for him to find a wife, but . . .

Goodness, this whole sabotage business was not for the faint of heart. Already she was beginning to wish things were different, though she had no idea how both she and Forester could win.

Dropping her voice even lower, Emma tried not to sound too accusatory. "All I said was we would be better off questioning some of the things people say about him. I never said—"

"Ah, I see!" Miss Fairfax's eyes brightened. "I thought perhaps you were hoping to manipulate the rest of us so you could have him for yourself."

Emma barely held back her laughter. "I have never wanted Mr. Forester, I assure you. And it would take nothing short of a miracle for me to change my poor opinion of the man."

"I thought you liked him," Miss Barton said, her voice thin. Small.

Emma realized her mistake when she saw the hurt in Miss Barton's eyes. She had encouraged the young woman to continue to pursue Mr. Forester back in Tutbury, and now it seemed as if Emma did not think her worth anyone better. Taking Miss Barton's hand, Emma forced a smile. "My opinion of Nick Forester has more to do with me than with him. He and I would never suit, but that does not mean he isn't perfect for someone else." She just hoped that that someone else did not make herself known before the month's end.

"We should go," Miss Barton said, still downcast and muted. "We are late, after all."

Silently cursing herself for hurting the poor woman, Emma nodded once to Miss Fairfax and turned to leave.

"It's probably for the better if you have no interest," Miss Fairfax said with a haughty sigh. "The more I think about it, the more I realize the man is an utter scoundrel for pretending to be something he isn't. I hope he crawls into whatever hole he came from and never returns. And I know the rest of London likely agrees with me. It was only a matter of time before we all discovered his lies, and I am glad he has been cut down and forced to quit his life here."

Emma's heart stumbled in her chest. "What? What do you mean quit?"

Miss Fairfax's eyes turned cold, as if that question had marked Emma as an accomplice to Mr. Forester's scheme. "I mean he has been forced to give up his rooms at Albany, and I would imagine he will be going back to his hovel in the country. Good day to you, Miss Mackenzie. Consider yourself lucky for not falling under his spell like the rest of us."

Thank goodness for Miss Barton, who led them out into the chill air without a word. The brisk breeze helped Emma focus her thoughts as she tried to understand what Miss Fairfax could have meant, but she still felt slightly dizzy from this revelation.

"Poor Mr. Forester," Miss Barton said as they began walking back to Harstone House. "I can't imagine how he must be feeling right now with so many awful rumors flying about."

Emma nearly groaned. "I am sure he is perfectly well. His whole life has been nothing but rumors, so he is accustomed to—"

"To being liked," Miss Barton interrupted. "I'll admit he has a habit of playing into the gossip, but he has been treated unjustly for something beyond his control. It isn't as if he could have stopped everyone from talking nonsense about him, so it only makes sense for him to have played into it and made the most of things."

Stopping dead in the middle of the pathway, Emma stared at Miss Barton as if seeing her for the first time. "You sound as if you've never believed all the rumors about him."

Miss Barton giggled. "Of course not! I am clever enough to know he never could have bred a champion racehorse or spent a year with the natives in the West Indies. And he never claimed to do any of the things people say he's done. Not genuinely. It's easy to spot his jesting when you know what to look for, but it's far more fun to play along than to call him a liar. Besides, I think it's easier for him to pretend he isn't hurting after everything that happened."

Emma hadn't known any of that, and she had gravely underestimated Miss Barton. And apparently Mr. Forester as well. "What do you mean?" she asked, allowing Miss Barton to guide her forward again. "After *what* happened?"

Miss Barton pursed her lips, keeping her gaze ahead. "You don't know?"

"Know what?"

"It was all anyone could talk about three years ago."

"That must have been after I returned to Staffordshire. What happened?"

But Miss Barton shook her head, smiling a little as they walked. "No, if you are ignorant, so much the better. Nicholas should have some allies in his life if he is going to weather this storm. If he wishes to tell you, that is his prerogative. I would rather not make his life harder than it already is."

Emma never would have expected such compassion from Miss Barton, and she found herself feeling more guilty than ever for what she had said about Mr. Forester at Almack's. Though she still didn't understand how she could have had such power over the whole of Society, she knew she had inflicted some real wounds.

Had she completely misunderstood her adversary?

"You really admire him, don't you?" she asked quietly.

Miss Barton nodded, brushing tears from her eyes. "I don't think he remembers, but we met several years ago, before . . . well, he was a different man then. Lighter. He used to use his charm to benefit those around him, and he brought so much joy into the world before he was forced to hide behind all the lies. The only time I have seen him act the way he used to has been . . ." She glanced at Emma. "Well, when he's been around you. I have resigned myself to knowing I am not destined to be anything but his friend, as much as I love the man he used to be. I only wish him well. It will take a special woman to bring back his light, and I hope she finds him soon." Another glance. "Whoever she is."

And Emma, as hard as she tried, couldn't help but wonder what else she had been wrong about when it came to Nicholas Forester.

Chapter Twenty-Two

"This was a terrible idea, miss."

Emma glanced at Jenny, who wasn't usually this outspoken when it came to things she didn't like. Though quick to agree with Emma, the maid generally kept her negative opinions to herself, especially when it came to Emma and her unusual notions of a woman's place.

Emma had to agree with Jenny this time.

Though it wasn't yet so late that the streets were empty, it had gotten dark. And it was certainly too late in the evening for Emma to be venturing out on her own, even with Jenny beside her. If Tabitha ever found out what she was doing . . .

"I need to apologize to him," Emma said, clasping her hands in front of her, as if that might make her look less terrified to anyone who passed. Truthfully, the longer she stood outside the building, the more suspicious she would look, and this wasn't such a poor part of Town that she had no chance of being recognized. Mr. Forester lived here, after all, so it had to be at least somewhat respectable.

Yet he was the reason Emma hadn't been brave enough to go inside and find his apartment. Mr. Forester, who had looked at her like she was the source of all his pain. Mr. Forester, who hadn't done anything worth Emma's complete ruination of his reputation. Mr. Forester, who did not, as Miss Fairfax had believed, rent a room at Albany. Emma had, thankfully, had the foresight to casually ask Alvaro where Mr. Forester lodged before setting out this evening. But now that she was here, looking up at the ill-maintained building with its cracking plaster, Emma was beginning to see the folly in her plan.

Yes, she wanted to apologize to the man. But she probably should have waited until the next time she saw him instead of sneaking out under the cover of darkness, and with only a maid to accompany her, no less. But after her afternoon with the young ladies of Society, Emma had been overcome with guilt, and she wouldn't have slept a minute tonight if she hadn't at least tried to make things right with the man. No inheritance was worth condemning a man to being an outcast when he already had so little.

Jenny cleared her throat, fidgeting as she glanced around them. "Should we go inside, miss?"

Emma sighed. "Yes. We came all this way, and I can swallow my pride for an evening." She didn't particularly like the way Jenny hid a smile as they stepped up to the dilapidated building.

As soon as they reached the door, however, Emma halted and stared at the wood. She had been so focused on getting herself here that she hadn't considered what she would actually say when she arrived. "I'm sorry" didn't seem to be enough for how thoroughly she had torn him down, and that was assuming he even listened to her. At this point, she would be lucky to receive a few seconds of his attention, and that would hardly be enough.

How did one tell a man she had been completely wrong about him but couldn't give him what he hoped for, no matter how much she wanted to? That inheritance was the only thing she had.

"I've made a mistake," she whispered, taking a step back from the door.

Jenny didn't hesitate with her response. "I will find us a carriage to return us to Harstone House."

As the maid hurried back to the busier street around the corner, Emma took her time in following, her mind stuck on the fact that she was always going to be an enemy to Nicholas Forester, no matter what she did. One of them would always be the winner, and her heart ached with the idea that her happiness would result in his misery and the other way around. What sort of cruel trick had Grandfather played by choosing one of them over the other?

"What have we here?"

Emma jumped, startled by a gruff voice in the growing darkness. It took her only a moment to know the man who approached her just outside the building would not be friendly. Why had she dawdled instead of keeping to Jenny's side? It wasn't as if the maid would be any sort of defense against a man twice her size, but there was strength in numbers.

Emma forced a brief smile. "Excuse me, sir." She attempted to step around him, but he blocked her path, forcing her back against the wall. "My companion is wait—"

"That little slip of a thing?" The man reeked of poor hygiene, his eyes dark pits against sallow skin, and Emma could hardly breathe. "We don't see many chits like you around these parts." His fingers bunched the fabric of her skirt as his eyes took her in from her feet to her neck. "All proper like. This dress would fetch a pretty price, wouldn' it?"

Heart pounding, Emma fought to get enough breath to scream, but then his hand slid up to her throat, cold fingers tucking around her jaw.

"Whoever you're comin' to see, I reckon he won't mind waitin' while I have a taste."

Before Emma could react, his mouth was on hers, tasting foul. She finally snapped out of her fear, shoving his chest and kicking and squirming, doing everything she could to get away from him. He was stronger, though, her protests pulling a growl of anger out of him, and he shoved her into the wall. Crying out with pain, Emma fought more frantically. She would *not* go down without a fight.

"Emma!"

Suddenly the man was ripped away from her, tugging her forward because one hand still gripped her dress, and she stumbled right as her rescuer threw a punch into the man's jaw. His grip loosened, but Emma still lost her balance and crashed to the ground in a heap.

That same voice shouted her name again, though her heart beat too furiously for her to place where she knew it from. Not until a gentle hand took her arm and helped her up to her feet.

"Are you hurt?" he asked frantically, his large hands wrapping around hers.

Emma lifted her eyes to meet his gaze. "Mr. Forester? No, I'm . . ." She struggled to take a deep breath. "Perfectly well."

He clearly didn't believe that, his eyebrows pulling low as he looked down at their clasped hands. "You're shaking."

Indeed she was. How else would he expect to find her when she had just been attacked by a true beast? "You saved me," she whispered, even her voice trembling. "I came to . . ." Why had she come? She couldn't think with Mr. Forester's eyes examining her with so much concern.

The man on the ground groaned, not yet unconscious, and Mr. Forester swore when he looked at him. "We need to get you away from here," he muttered, wrapping an arm around her waist without releasing one of her hands. "We can't let anyone see you in this state."

"What?" Only when they started walking did Emma realize her dress had been torn in her attacker's grip, several inches of her skirt pulled away from the bodice.

"You shouldn't be seen with me like this," she mumbled back, feeling rather numb all of a sudden as she realized what might have transpired if Mr.

Forester hadn't come to her rescue. And to think she had come here to try to make things better for him. "You are under enough scrutiny as it is, and—"

"I hardly think anything could make my situation worse than it already is, Emma. You saw to that. Is that your maid?"

She breathed a sigh of relief when she saw a hackney coach waiting ahead, a worried Jenny beside it. "Yes. Nick, I didn't mean to—"

"Get inside," he nearly commanded, and she found herself listening to him without question, climbing inside the coach with weak legs. She likely wouldn't have managed it without his hand wrapped around hers, and even when she sat, she still gripped his fingers like she might fall apart without the contact.

Had he really rescued her? After everything?

"You hate me," she whispered, staring at him as he stood outside the carriage.

He helped Jenny climb inside despite awkwardly standing in the doorway with his hand trapped, and then he sent a smile to Emma that didn't help her racing heart. She didn't deserve that smile.

"Now, Miss Mackenzie, you mustn't believe everything you hear. There's a good deal of untruth out there."

With that, he pried his hand free and told the driver to take her to Harstone, shutting the door and throwing Emma into darkness. Only when she was safely in her bedchamber and in her nightgown did she realize she'd never even thanked him for saving her from something truly terrible.

Some apology that had been.

Chapter Twenty-Three

It was far too early to be making a visit to Harstone House, and yet Nick hurried up the steps, desperate to know how Emma fared after last night's near disaster. As Harstone's butler placed Nick in the parlor and left him alone with his thoughts, he couldn't stop imagining the moment he had turned a corner and seen a woman fighting to be free of her captor. The sight had been horrific enough as Nick had rushed forward to assist, but then he'd recognized Emma.

He shuddered. He had only gone to retrieve his few belongings to set up permanently in Calloway's place, and if he had arrived even ten minutes later . . . Surely someone else would have come to Emma's aid, but that wasn't a risk he would have liked to take.

At what point had he started calling her Emma in his head? It must have been last night, though whether it was before he'd held her trembling hands or after, he wasn't sure. She'd been terrified, and rightly so, and Nick couldn't help but feel responsible for that. She'd been in that situation because she was trying to find him, after all.

"You don't know that," he growled.

But why else would she have been on Hatton Street? At that building? None of the other tenants were in the upper ten thousand (one of the reasons Nick had been living there), and Emma Mackenzie was not one to wander about a poorer part of Town for no reason.

"Could she really have been there to see me?"

"Talking to yourself, Forester?" Harstone chuckled as he entered the parlor, a daughter in either arm. "Have you run out of friends to bore with your endless chatter?"

"Papa, that wasn't a nice thing to say," the older girl censured.

"You are quite right, Dora," Nick agreed, scowling at his friend. But Harstone was in good spirits, which had to mean Emma was safe and sound.

He could breathe again. "The most agreeable man in London has turned to insults? I am thoroughly entertaining, and you know it."

Harstone laughed. "That is not what I have been hearing the last few days." He settled himself on the sofa, his girls tucking in next to him.

Nick tried to ignore the ache of jealousy in his chest at the happy sight, but he did a rather poor job of it. Securing Mackenzie's estate was not the only reason he so badly wanted to find himself a wife. The longer he searched for someone he could truly love, the less he believed such a person existed, and his chances of building a happy family like Harstone had were dwindling. Especially now that no one was willing to give him a chance anymore.

Emma had seen to that.

"I didn't take you for one to listen to gossip," Nick grumbled.

"I do not. But I cannot go anywhere in London without hearing your name. What happened?"

Nick almost wondered if Harstone had brought his girls to keep the conversation civil, and he appreciated the forced softening to his frustration. It wasn't Emma's fault. Mostly. "Your sister-in-law is particularly skilled at getting what she wants."

"That is a Mackenzie trait," Harstone replied with a grin. "The women, especially. Always a joy when I am surrounded by so many of them; the house is positively full of women at the moment."

"Speaking of women, how is Miss Barton?" Nick only mentioned her because he worried she would suddenly appear and make it more difficult for him to ascertain Emma's state of being. He had been enjoying his time away from Miss Barton since coming to London, but the woman was too persistent to leave him be for long. Or perhaps even she had turned away from him.

Harstone frowned. "She has fallen ill, unfortunately."

"Oh." Nick did feel some measure of pity, but he couldn't deny he was relieved. He hadn't the energy to direct her attention elsewhere again, especially when *his* attention seemed locked on the other young lady in the house.

"Papa." The younger girl, Lucy, tugged at her father's sleeve and then whispered something to him when he leaned down.

Harstone's expression softened as he looked down at her. "This is my friend, Mr. Forester. You met him last month."

"She's too little to remember," Dora said with confidence. "But I remember, Papa!" She turned slightly pink when she met Nick's gaze, and then she buried her face in Harstone's shoulder.

The littler one slid from the sofa and approached Nick's chair with wide brown eyes. She looked the most like her father, her brown curls bouncing around her head. "I'm Lucy," she said, dipping in a wobbly curtsy. "Please to meet you, Mista Fohstah."

Oh, she was adorable. Standing, Nick gave her a very proper bow and then crouched down to be closer to her level. He was still too tall, so he sat on the floor. "The pleasure is all mine. You know, I have a dear friend named Lucy."

Her eyes brightened. "Another Lucy?"

"She married my friend Lord Calloway."

"Did she kiss him so he wasn't a beast anymore?" Dora asked from the sofa, her eyes as big as saucers.

Nick had no idea how to respond to that question, and Harstone was too busy holding back laughter to be of any help. Nick could make a guess, however. "Of course. Everyone knows the only way to tame a man is to kiss him. But only if you know you are the right one to break his curse."

Dora still watched him with utter seriousness. "How do you know if you're right?"

He could remember how it felt to love Lavinia, even if the scars he bore went deep. He put his hand over his heart. "You know you're the right one when you feel as if you can't keep your heart in your chest when you're around them."

As if it agreed with him, his heart beat more strongly in reply before returning to its feeble attempts at keeping him going. He had felt that way once before; maybe he could feel so again.

"I should return you girls to the nursery before your mother thinks you have been snatched by fairies," Harstone said, scooping up the girls despite their protests.

"Will you come visit us, Mr. Forester?" Dora asked from the doorway. "You can tell us stories of beasts and witches like Emma does."

Realizing Harstone had paused so he could respond, Nick pasted on a smile. "I would love to," he said, though he had a feeling Emma would never let him anywhere near her nieces. It would likely turn into a battle of whose stories were best, and Nick had already disrupted Emma's life enough and would gladly stay out of her way once he had what he needed. If he could have the Mackenzie lands—and with them an actual chance to raise his own family—she could have her own family to herself.

Harstone returned only a few minutes later, and Nick hadn't yet moved from the floor. He'd gotten lost in thought, his eyes fixed on the rug, and he barely noticed the door opening.

"Oh." That wasn't Harstone's voice.

Nick's head snapped up, his heart picking up speed at the sight of Emma standing in the doorway. "Em—Miss Mackenzie!" He scrambled to his feet and brushed nonexistent dust from the seat of his breeches. "What happened to Harstone?"

She cocked her head to the side as she stepped into the room, seeming to study him as if she hadn't seen him in a good deal of time. "He wanted to read a book with the girls. He said I had a visitor, though he can't have meant you."

"Hardly," he agreed.

Silence hung between them for a moment before Emma said, "Why are you—"

"I wanted to see how you fared." Nick winced at his interruption, but at least it wasn't a lie. "You never said . . . Did he hurt you?" But he didn't need her to answer that question when he could see the bruises along her jaw beneath the powder she had used to try to cover them. Unconsciously, his fingers rose as if to touch the marred skin, but he held himself back. "He *did*. Emma."

She ducked her chin, tears spouting in her eyes. "He would have done far worse if you hadn't . . . Thank you, Mr. Forester."

He felt the formality like a slap to the cheek and took a step back. What was he doing? They were hardly friends, and she wouldn't want him calling her by her Christian name any more than he wanted her questioning his lies.

His heart thumped again, making him wonder if he was simply ill, like Miss Barton.

Meeting his gaze once more, Emma seemed to take a steeling breath before she said, "I went to your apartment to apologize, Mr. Forester. I never meant to ruin your life."

For some reason, that made him smile. And that smile brought a blush to the woman's cheeks. That couldn't be right. Was she also unwell? Feeling overheated? She couldn't possibly be blushing because he *smiled* at her. Still, he rather enjoyed seeing the warmth of her skin, and he spoke to keep himself from touching her cheeks to ascertain whether they were as warm as they looked.

"If we're being honest," he said, loving the little laugh that came out of her from that line, "I ruined my own life three years ago. Anyone could have made it crumble, so you shouldn't take too much credit."

That got her attention. "What happened three years ago?"

Since he had absolutely no desire to tell her about his failed engagement to Lady Lavinia, he kept talking as if she hadn't asked the question. "In truth,

I never thought my lies would last as long as they did, and I must confess to some measure of . . . relief."

She gasped. "Truly?"

"Some," he repeated with a wry smile. "I am rather put out with you regardless. Finding myself a wife who could stand the exaggerated version of me was difficult enough, and now I must rely on my own merits."

She rewarded him for that bit of cleverness with a smile that lasted only long enough for him to question why he considered her smile a reward. Her expression shifted, her eyebrows pulling low, and it was easy to guess where her mind had gone.

Sighing, Nick lowered himself slowly back into the armchair. It would be better to be up front about everything rather than cloak it all in lies and jests. "Miss Mackenzie, as much as I wish I could, I cannot concede in this war of ours."

She didn't look at him as she settled onto the sofa. "I know," she murmured. "But neither can I."

He had expected that, but Nick still wondered why she didn't try to find herself a wealthy husband. She had built up enough of a following here in London—she would have had to in order to convince all of Society to turn against him—that she could have her choice of gentleman. Perhaps not the dull Sir Thomas or the arrogant Mr. Parker, but there had to be *someone*. She couldn't possibly wish to be alone all her life.

He wasn't sure anyone could want that.

Regardless, she would continue to be his enemy unless he did something to change that. "I know neither of us can afford to lose," he said carefully, "but I wonder if we might be able to come to agree to some rules of engagement."

That didn't quite bring a smile out of her, but at least she looked up at him again, her eyes sparkling. "Terms of battle?"

"If we can agree to avoid sabotage, whichever of us wins will have done so with honor." And perhaps his conscience would no longer be burdened with guilt over the way he had been treating her. His father had raised him to be a better man than he had been the last few years, but he had forgotten how to be anything but what Society had made him.

"I am not certain how I can play this game of ours without sabotage," Emma admitted, though she seemed intrigued. "My entire goal was to keep any women from finding you desirable."

He grimaced. "Oh, I am well aware. Charlotte Denham nearly burst into tears at the mere sight of me last week."

Emma bit her lip, and Nick couldn't look away. She looked rather beautiful, sitting there in her excitement, something his heart seemed to agree on as it thumped a little more enthusiastically. "I may have told her you were seriously ill and not likely to last the fortnight," she said.

He choked out a laugh. "And she believed you?"

"I am quite persuasive. Though, in honesty, I did not particularly enjoy spreading a lie like that."

"It stings less the more you do it." That was a lie unto itself.

"Even so." Emma let her smile loose as she watched him. "I suppose there isn't much left for me to do against you at this point. You seem to have woven your web poorly enough to leave you with nothing to stand on."

He knew that far too well, but he still found himself smiling. He couldn't remember the last time someone had been brave enough to put him down so thoroughly. Emma deserved a round of applause for holding her own against him. "It's a miracle your grandfather has even given me a chance."

She sobered at that, clasping her hands in her lap. "How are we to proceed? Am I to sit idly by and hope you make a fool of yourself whenever in a lady's presence?"

"That is more likely than you seem to think. But no."

"You expect me to return home?" She frowned. "That is surrender, Mr. Forester."

He could hardly imagine a woman with so much grit tucking tail and running away. She was far stronger than that. "I expect you'll be plenty busy with your many suitors to worry about my side of the battle, but if you insist on an offensive strategy, you may do your own matchmaking."

"My own . . ." She jumped to her feet, her mouth hanging open. "You've been persuading men to court me!" It was not a question.

Nick laughed at how utterly offended she seemed. "I honestly thought you would realize long before now. It was only two men, mind you, but there are more where they came from."

"You think a proposal will be enough to persuade me to give up my claim." Again, not a question, though she didn't seem angry. She almost seemed on the verge of laughing, that sparkle in her eyes again. "You are far too confident, Mr. Forester, if you think there is a man in this world who could subdue my independent nature. I have as much desire to marry as you have to speak the truth."

"I have a chance at succeeding, then." It was true, then. She did not wish to marry, though he couldn't fathom why. Any man would be lucky to call himself hers.

Standing tall, her chin high, Emma looked down at him with determination. "Very well. I shall prove to you that no man will ever tempt me, and you will be so inundated with women hoping to be yours that by the time you've met them all, your deadline will have come and gone."

As if she could find any women left he hadn't already rejected. Still, he quite liked the idea of this challenge, far more than tearing her down and hoping it helped his own standing. "And if I somehow manage to find someone I can stomach to be around for longer than half an evening," he said, "I will give you whatever it takes for you to live out your independent life."

Her shoulders dropped. "What?"

As he stood to match her, he did his best to ensure his expression was as serious as he felt. "I do not wish for you to be destitute, Miss Mackenzie. I long for a wife and enough money to build a life and a family, and the Mackenzie lands have enough for us both to get what we want. I could find you a cottage somewhere in the neighborhood, where you can tell stories to your neighbors to your heart's content."

She had gone silent, as if she couldn't believe he would ever give her a shilling. It wasn't the same as giving her the home she so clearly loved, but he hoped it might be a compromise.

"My grandfather already gives me an allowance," she said eventually, with a good deal of hesitation in her voice. "I do not merely wish to live out my days with nothing to keep me occupied."

That didn't surprise him in the least. "A small farm, then?" He held out his hand, too afraid to watch her expression as she considered his offer. What if she said no? What if she continued cutting him down to nothing until she claimed that inheritance and left him on the streets? From the very start, he had hoped she would show him kindness if he secured her a future, and he prayed he wasn't wrong about her.

With a smile that left him breathless, she pressed her palm against his, her skin warm and soft, and he found himself unwilling to let go. That likely meant something, but he wasn't brave enough to wonder what that something was.

Chapter Twenty-Four

Emma was nervous, and she didn't like it one bit. It was just a ball, and a private one at that. Tabitha and Alvaro were both with her—Miss Barton was still feeling poorly—and Tabitha had assured her that the host and hostess were good and kind people. Emma supposed she was nervous because she had yet to hear whether anyone had seen her last night outside of Nick's rented room, and she had no idea what gossip she might be walking into.

Her nerves had absolutely nothing to do with Nick himself.

Nick. She had been thinking of him by his preferred name again ever since his thumb had brushed across hers when she shook his hand, as if that brief touch had suddenly made them become dear friends. He had touched her far more when he'd rescued her, wrapping his arm around her and holding both her hands, but she hadn't felt anything then.

Then again, her fear from the attack had left her numb, hardly the circumstances to notice the way heat had spread through her hand upon contact with Nick's fingers the following day.

As their carriage rolled across the streets of London, Emma clasped her hands in her lap and told herself she was being ridiculous. She had barely become friends with the man, if even that, and it would hardly do to entertain thoughts of his smile.

She groaned when his smile popped into her mind like it had been doing since he'd left Harstone House that morning. He had no right being that handsome when their friendship was so precarious. Emma would have to take careful steps when sending women his way to avoid injuring any of the ladies who became part of her scheme and prevent them from falling for his charms. Even with all the gossip surrounding him, his merits were not as limited as he seemed to think.

Perhaps she needed a different strategy, one that did not involve others.

When the carriage slowed to a stop, Emma was more than ready to climb out and stretch her restless legs, but neither Tabitha nor Alvaro moved. They seemed to be waiting for something.

"Just waiting for Mr. Forester," Tabitha said, as if sensing her confusion.

Emma glanced out the window. This was not the Hatton Street apartments. Instead they had halted outside a stately town house that clearly belonged to someone quite wealthy. For a moment, she thought she may have been mistaken when she showed up to the other place last night, but then she remembered it was her brother-in-law who had told her where Nick lived. Whose house was this?

Before she could ask, Nick stepped through the front door, laughing at something—and looking far more attractive than Emma wished—before he turned back to the door. A butler appeared, fixing Nick's cravat and handing him a hat as he said something with a smile. Laughing again, Nick clapped a hand on the butler's shoulder and then made his way down the walkway to the waiting carriage.

"Harstone. Lady Harstone. Miss Mackenzie." As he settled beside Emma, filling the small space with his broad shoulders, Emma couldn't help but remember the last time they had been in such close quarters. They had still been enemies then, though that had been their first truce. Now they had agreed to be entirely civil with one another. At least, Emma had decided upon that. If she wished to avoid adding to her guilt, she couldn't keep treating the man as an adversary.

Especially when he'd promised her an independent life regardless of the outcome of their battle.

"You are looking rather lovely this evening," Nick murmured, leaning close to her as the carriage began moving again.

Goodness, why did that make her blush? She would hear the same thing from every one of her dance partners tonight, assuming she still had some admirers, and she doubted any of them would affect her.

"You are in a good mood," she whispered back. Why she didn't want her sister and brother-in-law to be privy to their conversation, she did not know.

"I believe I have thought of the perfect man to be your husband."

Her stomach twisted itself into a knot at the thought. "I beg your pardon? *That* is the reason you are grinning like a fool?"

His eyebrows rose high. "Like a fool, you say?"

No, that wasn't really accurate, but it had been several days since she had seen him this relaxed and happy, if she had *ever* seen him quite like this.

Either their truce had taken a weight off his shoulders, or the collapse of his reign of lies had actually been good for him. This seemed more like the man Miss Barton claimed him to have been.

"Whose house was that?" Emma asked instead of trying to find any clarification on the man's mood. "Is it yours?"

He barked a laugh, finally sitting up straight again. "You think I would fight so hard against you if I owned a house like that?"

"I suppose not."

"It belongs to Lord Calloway."

"It's about time you used it," Alvaro said with a chuckle, telling them that their conversation had not been as private as Emma had believed. "The number of times he has complained to me about your stubbornness and pride would astound you."

Nick scoffed. "Calloway never complains about anything. He suffers in silence."

"Yes, which should tell you just how frustrated he has been with you." Then Alvaro muttered something to Tabitha in Spanish, and she pressed a hand to her lips to stifle a giggle.

Nick leaned close to Emma again, filling her nose with his clean scent. "Please tell me you've been around him long enough to know what he just said about me."

Snickering, Emma shook her head. "I am afraid my genius does not extend to Spanish, though that hasn't stopped me from trying. I am convinced they have purposefully prevented me from learning."

"Of course we have," Tabitha said as she brushed her fingers through her husband's hair, adjusting the dark waves. "It was the only way to stop you from eavesdropping when you were little." She muttered something in Spanish that prompted Alvaro to press a kiss to her temple, his eyes bright with happiness.

"I think now is a good time to throw myself from the carriage," Nick said, reaching for the door.

Laughing, Emma grabbed his hand. "I find it sweet that they still have affection for one another after all these years."

"All these years?" Alvaro said in mock offense. "I am hardly older than Forester."

Nick groaned in protest. "Five years is more than *hardly*."

Emma hadn't fully known Nick's age, and he was older than she'd expected. At five years younger than Alvaro, that put him at thirty, more than nine years her senior. Not that it mattered, as they were certainly never going to be a match . . . Still, she was surprised he had gone this long without finding himself a wife.

For the first time, she wondered if he had actually been *trying*. Or had whatever happened three years ago hurt him enough that now he saw only the flaws of a match rather than the potential?

"I am going to be sick," Nick grumbled, but he was smiling at the couple in front of him.

A romantic with little hope for his own chance at romance? Oh, but Nick Forester was quite the mystery Emma suddenly wanted to solve.

It was only when the carriage came to a stop outside the brightly lit mansion that hosted the evening's ball that she realized she hadn't released Nick's hand. And neither had he pulled away.

Chapter Twenty-Five

If Nick had known the *ton* would completely ignore him, perhaps he wouldn't have come tonight. He suspected the invitation had come to him only out of politeness anyway, which was more than he deserved. After all the lies he had told, he didn't blame anyone for looking down on him, but still. Did they have to spend so much energy glaring at him from across the ballroom?

He'd sequestered himself in an unoccupied corner almost immediately upon arrival, knowing it would save everyone the trouble of finding a proper way to tell him they had no interest in keeping his acquaintance.

Unfortunately, his solitude lasted only ten minutes or so before a group of young ladies approached him with the appearance of a pack of wild dogs hunting their next meal. He recognized most of them, and considering he had rejected at least half of them for one reason or another, he could only assume they were here to ridicule him.

Miss Andrews stood at their head and was the first to address him. "Mr. Forester, I am surprised to see you out among Society." She dipped into a curtsy that would have been too small to notice if Nick hadn't been watching her so closely.

"Miss Andrews, it is always a pleasure." Did that count as a lie if he was trying to be courteous? He greeted each of the other ladies as well and then bowed low. "Are you ladies enjoying your eve—"

"Is it true you have never left England?"

Nick held back a sigh. So it was to be more of this? "Yes, that is true."

Miss Andrews scoffed. "Therefore, you did *not* spend a summer in India with tigers and elephants?"

"No, that was Mr. Bonden."

"I thought as—" She cocked her head. "What?"

Nick nodded toward the man in question, who was deep in discussion with a few of his friends. "Mr. Bonden was in India for most of last year and returned only a few months ago."

The ladies began whispering amongst each other, as if they weren't sure they could believe him. Luckily, nothing he had just said had been a lie, and Bonden was far more adventurous than Nick had ever been. If these women were so interested in sights beyond England, they would do better with focusing on him.

"And what of the rumor that you once saved a child from being trampled by a horse?" Miss Tremblay asked from the back of the group.

Nick searched his memories for the source of that one. He was quite certain he had started it himself. But he had heard of someone else doing something similar just last month, though it had been a novice stablehand in danger rather than a child. The situation was similar enough, as well as the man's name. Nick wouldn't need influence or admiration to make himself believable, and he smiled. "I think you have confused me with James *Foster*."

Miss Tremblay's eyes lit up, along with the color in her cheeks. "That was Mr. Foster?"

The entire group of ladies shifted from whispering to giggling, several of them looking around the room as if in search of Foster. He wasn't high enough socially to be at a gathering such as this, but it seemed the women of London were fond of the man regardless.

"Do you expect us to believe you after all of your lies?" Miss Andrews asked with another scoff. She, it seemed, wasn't as easily taken in as her fellows.

Nick smirked. "No, I do not. But that hasn't stopped Miss Evans from asking Mr. Bonden herself, has it?" He nodded toward Miss Evans and the woman who had been beside her until a moment ago; both were obviously flirting with a clearly bewildered but excited Bonden. "Have you any other rumors you're interested in, Miss Andrews? I can point you in the right direction, assuming they aren't all complete nonsense. One can never be too careful when it comes to gossip."

Though the other ladies seemed eager to carry on with their lives—and perhaps start questioning everything they heard, even beyond Nick and his web of lies—Miss Andrews almost looked ready to challenge Nick on his offer. Unbeknownst to her, he had spent so long at the heart of Society and diving deep into the gossip columns and betting books that he would likely have a man in mind for anything she threw at him.

She must have sensed his confidence, however, because she dipped into an actual curtsy and herded the rest of the women away—to the relief of all the lingering men who had been hoping for a chance to ask them to dance. Each lady was picked off quickly, ensuring none of them could come back to question Nick more until the set was over.

Finally, he was able to observe the ballroom once more, and he found Emma in a crowd, charming a handful of admirers, as always. As far as he knew, no one seemed to have discovered her misadventure the night before, which left him breathing easier. That was one rumor he wouldn't be able to turn on someone else. He had done his best to keep her shielded last night to protect her identity, but it was impossible to know who might have been lurking in the darkness.

But she was safe. And, from what he could tell, she shone just as brightly as she had the moment she set foot in London.

As if she could feel his eyes on her, Emma looked over and met Nick's gaze. Though surrounded by people—the men likely wishing to court her and the women hoping to befriend her—she kept doing that. Watching him. Making him squirm. He was already having a devil of a time ignoring how much he had liked holding her hand on the drive over, and he didn't need to start convincing himself she thought of him as often as he was starting to think of her. No good would come of that, and yet—

"Blast," he muttered when he realized she was walking his way with a young woman in tow. He was in no state to be polite after using up all of his limited civility on Miss Andrews, but Emma had found one of the few women Nick had yet to meet, and Emma seemed to know it.

Lady Georgina was beautiful, but she had never shown an interest in Nick, so he had never bothered to gain an introduction. It seemed that was about to change.

"Miss Mackenzie," he said when the ladies arrived on his side of the ballroom. His voice cracked, and he cleared his throat.

Emma fought her smile as she dipped into a curtsy to match his bow. "Mr. Forester. I was speaking with the delightful Lady Georgina here when I realized she had yet to meet you. Imagine that."

"Imagine," he croaked back. "My lady, it is a pleasure."

Lady Georgina eyed him with wary interest. "Mr. Forester. I have heard so much about you."

"I told her she mustn't believe everything she hears," Emma said, her smile growing.

Nick held back a groan. He'd thought Emma's plan was to *avoid* sabotage, not cement her condemning words further. "Is that so?"

"Is it true you are quite proficient on the pianoforte?" Lady Georgina asked with the same hesitation. "Miss Mackenzie said you have quite the talent."

Nick took a step back in surprise, glancing at Emma. She had called attention to one of the truths? "Yes," he admitted. "My mother was very fond of music, and playing connects me to her."

He didn't miss the way Emma's mouth parted, as if she hadn't expected him to reveal something so personal. In truth, he was just as surprised as she seemed to be, but he kept his focus on Lady Georgina. He could examine his newfound ease in being open later tonight, when he wasn't in conversation.

Lady Georgina softened considerably with his answer, her smile small but warm. "How lovely," she said, inching closer. "I feel the same way. When I was a girl, my grandmother played the most beautiful songs on the harp. I haven't half her talent, rest her soul, but I feel as if she is listening every time I play."

"Would you care to dance, my lady?" Nick asked before his cowardice took control. The lady seemed to have formed at least a slight interest with their shared love of music, and he would need to take advantage of it.

Lady Georgina agreed, and Nick could hardly believe it as he led her onto the floor. Why would Emma bring him someone genuinely sweet and kind? Perhaps there was more to the woman than he had thus seen, but this was hardly inundating him with impossible matches. And he hadn't even thought to search for Mr. Wells and make an introduction to Emma in kind. Wells wasn't good enough for her anyway.

Besides, Nick had been hoping to dance with her himself.

"Are you well, sir?" Lady Georgina asked before the music began.

Nick nodded, but his attention was on Emma again. She seemed in a daze, not really looking at him, but there was no trace of a smile on her lips. As if she hadn't intended for the two of them to make a connection. Or perhaps she had, but she didn't like it. What was her game?

The orchestra began the first notes of a reel, and Nick forced his attention back to his partner. This could be his first chance in days to take a step in the right direction. Metaphorically, of course, seeing as he was failing to step in the right direction of the dance. Cursing his inability to pay attention, he shook his head and pasted on a smile, as if that would help him focus on the task at hand.

But halfway through the set, his eyes caught on Emma again, only she was no longer alone. She had been joined by none other than the Duke of Tipton, and Nick nearly tripped over his own feet. Why would the duke take an interest in her? And why was she smiling at him like that? His Grace had a reputation as gossiped about as Nick's, but for far worse reasons. Everyone knew Tipton had no qualms about pursuing women he had no intention of truly courting. He wooed them with false promises and had his way with them, leaving them heartbroken and worse. Too many ladies had been caught in his snares, but no one was brave enough to challenge a duke to a duel to defend them.

Surely Emma could see through his charming exterior. His Grace made her attacker last night look harmless, and Nick couldn't throw a punch this time to save her if he—

The dance pulled his attention away, though he did his best to keep an eye on Emma. Where was Harstone? Did he not realize his sister-in-law was speaking with the worst of men? Cursing the length of the song—the orchestra seemed to be playing at a glacial pace again—Nick debated leaving the dance early. Doing so would insult Lady Georgina most thoroughly, but perhaps she would forgive him.

He groaned. If he thought it was going to be difficult to find a wife before, a cut direct like that would only make it worse. Could he live with himself if something happened to Emma while he was busy caring about himself? But if he abandoned Lady Georgina, she would be completely humiliated. What if he ruined all *her* chances?

He spent so long agonizing over what he should do that the dance ended before he had made a decision, which suited him very well. Though perhaps a little too hasty in taking Lady Georgina's arm while she still clapped for the orchestra, he pulled her across the floor as quickly as he could without drawing attention their way. He found her parents easily enough, thanked the lady for the dance, mumbled something about calling on her for a walk through the park, and then took his leave. After colliding with a couple of men who shouted at him, Nick finally arrived at the place where Emma had been standing.

She wasn't there. Neither was the duke.

Heart pounding, he stood on his toes and sought out Harstone. "Blast." She wasn't with her family either. Had Tipton taken her somewhere? They weren't on the dance floor, which meant they had either gone into the corridor beyond the ballroom or out onto the terrace. He couldn't search the whole house, and though a little voice in the back of his head told him he should alert Harstone to the potential danger, his feet pulled him to the terrace.

As he stumbled through the open door, he thought his heart might beat right out of his chest until he caught sight of Emma leaning on the balcony that overlooked the gardens.

Alone.

"Oh, thank the heavens," he breathed, suddenly dizzy.

She turned with wide eyes and stared at him as he tried to catch his breath. "Mr. Forester? What . . . ?"

"What are you doing out here?"

She frowned, her eyes bouncing to the doorway behind him. "I might ask you the same thing."

Hurrying to her side, he searched her person for any reason to think he might be too late for a rescue. She seemed completely unharmed, but he wouldn't put it past her to hide any distress. "I saw you speaking with the duke, and then you were gone, and I thought—"

"You thought I was foolish enough to fall for his charms? How little you know me."

Now that he could breathe again, Nick leaned against the railing and managed a small smile. He had clearly overreacted, though his heart had yet to be informed. It still thundered in his chest like a racehorse. "No, I do not suppose I know you very well. It makes it inordinately difficult to find you a husband."

"I thought you said you had the perfect man in mind."

That brought a smile out of him. "I lied." He had needed a reason to be smiling so much that had nothing to do with how lovely she looked when he'd climbed into Harstone's carriage.

Emma scoffed. "Of course you did."

"As for not knowing you, it stands to reason that I should remedy the fact, do you not agree?"

"You wish to know me?" Why did that surprise her so much?

Though he was tempted to tell her it was because he badly wanted to be her friend, he kept to a reason she was less likely to question. "If I am to share half my inheritance, I should know who I am supporting."

"You mean half *my* inheritance."

She was unlike any woman he had ever known, stubborn and hardheaded, and Nick couldn't keep himself from grinning. He hadn't seen the evening going this way at all, mostly because he had planned never to mention the inheritance to her again. It would have been easier to pretend there was nothing preventing them from being more than recent acquaintances. "You intend to share as well?"

She seemed to think on that, tapping her chin as she studied him. "I suppose I should. It is only fair, after what you offered. But I will not give up the house. I will give you the money required to repair your estate."

"You know of my estate?"

She laughed, and Nick was reminded of how much he liked the sound. *Too much.* "I should think you would know by now that nothing about your life is a secret," she said. "I can work out the true aspects of all the rumors well enough, as I do not imagine you would willingly spread lies about your estate being unlivable."

Nick ducked his head, trying to keep his grin from widening. "Society tends to focus on the fantastic falsehoods rather than the mundane truths. It is a pity that no longer holds true, as no one will want to marry a penniless liar with a home in disrepair."

"I suppose that is a fair assessment."

They were both quiet for a long while. Though Nick usually hated silence, he found this one quite comfortable. He had nothing to prove to Emma, just as she had no reason to impress him. It meant they could simply exist in the same space, which felt rather peaceful.

So, naturally, he broke the silence with an unprompted question. "Why do you not wish to marry?"

That inquiry certainly caught her off guard, her eyes going wide and her cheeks flushing with color. She seemed just as surprised as Nick when she replied, "Because I have no desire to become a man's property. The moment I marry is the moment everything I own, everything I *am*, belongs to him."

He knew instinctively that she was speaking the truth, but he also sensed there was a good deal more to her reasoning than that. Too afraid to push, he pretended to accept her answer as the only one and presented his argument. "Surely there are men out there who will view that only as a technicality. I have always thought a marriage should be equal."

"You are a rarity, Mr. Forester."

"But your brother-in-law is the same. And my friend Calloway. There must be more."

She sighed. "Perhaps. But find me a man who not only tolerates my wit but also appreciates it, and I shall truly be impressed. No man enjoys sparring unless it involves a sword."

"I fence." Nick cleared his throat, feeling awkward because he had been about to admit that sparring with her was one of his new favorite pastimes. "You asked at Almack's why I am so strong. I fence. It is the only way I know to work out my frustrations without turning to pugilism, which I abhor."

She seemed to eye him with appreciation, though whether it was for his strength or his desire to avoid hand-to-hand combat, he wasn't sure.

He also wasn't sure why he was still thinking about how much he liked talking to her.

"You seemed eager to use your fist last night," she said, frowning.

"I had a good reason."

Emma seemed just as confused as he was, and that couldn't be a good sign. It was as if she was trying to see past his exterior and get into whatever lay inside, which made him feel very much like a fish about to be gutted.

"What are you looking for?" he asked, unable to help himself.

She cocked her head to the side. "I am not fully certain. I have heard so many different things about you since the day I first heard your name, and those who call you a friend seem to know a different man than I do."

What was he to say to that? "Is that a good thing or bad?"

"I suppose it depends on which man is the real one. My brother-in-law speaks so highly of you, and Miss Barton is convinced you are a good man. I can only assume your friend Lord Calloway is as fond of you as Alvaro is. Even my sister speaks to your credit. And yet . . ."

Nick fully understood her confusion. Not only had he behaved so abominably when they'd first met, but he had also not been himself for years. "And yet I have given you no reason to think well of me," he finished for her, dropping his gaze, as if that could hide him from her scrutiny. She had always been too intelligent to believe the mask he wore, but that didn't mean the man beneath was much better. "I admit I have forgotten the man I used to be," he said, the soft words tasting bitter. "Nor can I say with certainty that I used to be a good man in the first place. I like to think I was. But I am trying to be better, and perhaps someday you will find something good in me."

When he finally looked up, he found Emma still studying him, but her expression had softened. She likely still despised him, but perhaps the degree had lessened. He wasn't certain what to do with that.

He tucked his hands behind his back, pretending to admire the gardens despite being able to see only a small portion of them in the light shining from the house. He needed to bring things back to the way they usually were before he started getting dangerous ideas about Emma Mackenzie. *Too late for that.* "Speaking of good men, what else would you require in a husband were you to accept one?"

Emma took so long to respond that he looked at her again and found her fighting her smile. He wished she wouldn't hold back. She had such a beautiful smile. "Well, he must be tall."

"Tall?"

"Indeed."

"That is your only requirement?"

"Certainly not, but I cannot give away all my secrets tonight, now, can I?" She finally let out her smile, hitting Nick with its full, dimpled force, then made her way back into the ballroom.

Nick stared at the place she had disappeared from view, and he couldn't help but think about how *he* was tall. And he looked forward to their sparring more than he should. And there was a slight chance he was in grave danger of falling for Emma Mackenzie.

Which was a problem, because she was always going to see him as nothing but an obstacle in her quest for independence.

Chapter Twenty-Six

Once Miss Barton had recovered from her illness, Alvaro suggested they all go out to the pleasure gardens at Vauxhall. He said it was because the weather would be turning soon, but Emma suspected he had ulterior motives when he couldn't stop chuckling to himself. Though generally a jovial man, this was different. When he made the suggestion after reading a letter that had come in at breakfast, Tabitha shot him a look of surprise but quickly agreed when he pierced her with a stare.

There was most assuredly more to his plans than a simple excursion.

"I hardly care about the reason," Miss Barton said when Emma told her about her suspicions. She sat in front of a mirror, directing her maid as to how to do her hair for the excursion. "I am still angry that I missed my chance to meet a duke! If only I could be so well liked as you, Miss Mackenzie. Perhaps you will draw him back in at Vauxhall and I can be introduced!"

Even if the Duke of Tipton were there, Emma hardly wished to introduce him to sweet Miss Barton. The moment Emma had met the man—without a formal introduction, no less—she had seen his charm as nothing more than a mask to hide the scoundrel underneath. His Grace made Nick look like a saint by comparison.

"Have you truly given up on Mr. Forester, then?" Emma asked, brushing nonexistent dust from her skirt.

Miss Barton glanced at her in the mirror, her eyes narrowed. "I gave up on him as anything more than a friend just after coming to London. Why?"

Emma didn't exactly have an answer, not knowing where the question had come from, but she tried. "You were so enamored of him in Tutbury, and you spoke so highly of him the other day."

Miss Barton's lips pulled into a smile that made Emma nervous. "I will always admire the man, but my affection has, er, shifted." As her eyes darted to her jewelry box, Emma sat up a little straighter.

"Shifted where?"

Though Miss Barton laughed, the sound was shrill. Nervous. "Oh, nowhere in particular. It isn't as if a letter is the same as courting someone."

"A letter? Miss Barton, a courtship is exactly what a letter would mean. Are you writing to someone?"

"Come. We are going to be late!" Miss Barton leaped up and grabbed Emma's hand, pulling her to the door. "And it is probably time we stop being so formal around each other. You should call me Catherine."

Emma's thoughts were still stuck on the fact that Miss Barton—Catherine— was apparently harboring a secret love for someone at a distance. When had that happened? And how had she managed it? Surely Alvaro would have been concerned to learn his cousin was exchanging letters with a man when they were not engaged, which meant he likely didn't know. But all correspondence should have gone through him, unless Catherine had bribed one of the servants.

Catherine must have sensed Emma's wild thoughts because she moaned and pulled her into the empty music room. "I know," she whispered, wringing her hands. "I shouldn't have even entertained the idea, but we left for London so suddenly. And I thought, since he is your relation, there wouldn't be any harm in—"

"Elias?" Emma choked out his name in complete bewilderment. "You're writing to my cousin?"

Shushing her, Catherine watched the door for a moment, as if to make sure they were still alone. "I am as shocked as you are, Emma."

"I highly doubt that."

"You won't tell anyone, will you?"

Catherine looked so terrified that Emma knew she would never be able to share this secret. At least she knew Elias would never do anything to compromise the woman, though she would be giving her cousin a stern talking-to when she saw him next. It wasn't the strangest pairing she had ever seen, but it was high on the list.

Sighing, Emma squeezed Catherine's hand. "Your secret is safe. But I need you to be careful. I wouldn't want to see you forced into something you're not ready for. Either of you."

Catherine rewarded her concern with an embrace that knocked the wind out of her. "Thank you! And you're right. I will tell him in my next letter that we cannot sneak around any longer. If he wishes to court me, he must do it in the open." Then she tucked her arm through Emma's and led the way to the entrance hall to meet the others.

Catherine was still glued to Emma's side when they ran into Nick at Vauxhall, something that seemed to cause him a good deal of alarm, his eyes momentarily going wide. By the time he greeted Alvaro and Tabitha, however, he had managed to control his expression, smiling instead of looking ready to run.

"Ladies," he said, giving them a bow.

Emma did her best to curtsy with her arm locked with Catherine's, though she wasn't sure she managed it. "Mr. Forester."

"Quite a coincidence meeting you here," Alvaro said loudly.

Tabitha smacked his arm.

Ah, so he had wanted to come to Vauxhall to meet up with Nick. It made sense, though Emma wasn't sure why it had turned into an entire family excursion. Just as she didn't understand why Alvaro had told her she had a visitor the other day when Nick had been completely surprised to see her. She was beginning to suspect her brother-in-law thought he saw something that wasn't there and was playing his hand at being the worst matchmaker in the world.

"Who is your friend?" Catherine asked Nick.

Emma hadn't even noticed the man behind Nick, which was a bit ridiculous, considering that he stood several inches above Nick, who was by no means small. She must have been distracted by the look on Nick's face when they'd first arrived.

Stepping aside to allow his companion some space, Nick said, "This is Mr. George Seymour. I bumped into him earlier today and thought he might be interested in meeting you." His eyes landed on Emma before he added, "Both of you ladies."

"I am not sure why," Mr. Seymour muttered as he bowed.

Emma pursed her lips, unsure whether she should be scowling or laughing. If Nick truly wanted to get her married off and out of his way, he was going to have to try a lot harder than this. It was a miracle he still didn't know about Grandfather's marriage requirement for her, though she suspected he would still try to convince her to concede should she, by some miracle, find a match and earn the inheritance. Assuming she found a man with his own income, Nick would argue it was only fair that he have a living as well.

At this point, Emma was almost considering concession anyway, which didn't keep her stomach from tying itself into knots as she looked at the way Nick's eyes danced. If the likes of Nick Forester could find her someone worth marrying, he would deserve that inheritance and more.

"Yes, I suppose neither is a diamond of the first water," Nick said, giving Emma an examining look.

She might have felt offense, like Catherine clearly did as she wilted, but there was nothing serious in the man's expression. Choosing to say nothing, Emma was curious to hear Mr. Seymour's response.

He took his time, looking over both young women. Then he straightened, his chin in the air. "You're quite wrong about that, Forester. Both ladies are of the highest beauty."

Nick seemed on the verge of laughter, and Emma was quite certain she had figured out Mr. Seymour's character. She wanted to test her theory. "Mr. Seymour, it is lovely to meet you. And on such a pleasant evening."

He sniffed. "Actually, I find it rather muggy tonight."

"At least the gardens are beautiful this time of year," she said.

"If you appreciate dead foliage, then yes, but I am more interested in the spring and summer months."

"We were just walking the gardens," Emma said. "Are you fond of walking, like I am?"

"Not especially."

"A pity. I have rather been enjoying myself." Extricating herself from Catherine's hold, Emma slid her arm through Nick's before he could make any kind of protest. "Care to join me, Mr. Forester?"

He still held back laughter, enough amusement in his eyes to render him more handsome than usual. "I would like nothing better. Seymour, I know you do not enjoy walking, but Miss Barton—"

"I will gladly escort her."

Tugging Nick forward until they were a comfortable distance from the others, Emma burst into laughter, pleased when Nick joined in with her. And then she smacked his arm. "You are horrible!"

He held up his free hand, putting on an expression of innocence so far from believable that it made her laugh again. "I don't see what the problem is, Emma. Mr. Seymour is a man with his own opinions, which I know you value dearly, and he is tall. As far as I am aware, he is exactly what you—"

"You know very well that I require more than that to even think of considering a man. You are only making me less inclined to marry!"

Nick glanced behind them, likely to ensure they hadn't walked so far as to be out of sight. "I suppose you are right, but considering you refused to tell me more, I've had to come to my own conclusions. I happened upon Seymour this afternoon and couldn't help myself. He is a rather disagreeable fellow, but—"

"You are insufferable, Mr. Forester."

"And you deserve to be doted upon, I know."

Emma paused, thrown by that comment. But Nick seemed perfectly serious, like he meant every word. "Thank you," she said after a long while.

His arm tightened around hers ever so slightly, though he didn't seem to be aware he had done it. "I will find you a husband and convince you that you are wrong about marriage, Emma."

How long had he been using her Christian name? She hadn't noticed until now, which should have alarmed her. But her name on Nick's tongue felt familiar. She could almost picture a future with someone speaking her name with so much love and affection, something she'd never truly dared hope for. Nick seemed to think it was not only possible but likely.

Emma cleared her throat, trying to stay focused on the conversation instead of imagining a life in which she had someone who loved her. "Even if Mr. Seymour was only for your own amusement, you clearly have no idea what sort of man I—"

"Clever, kind, intelligent, slow to anger, honest. Am I close?"

Emma gaped at him, as she had not told him any of that. She hadn't even formed a list for herself, though she would appreciate all the things he listed. "Well, yes," she admitted. "Though, I do not believe such a man exists."

Nick grinned, making her heart pick up speed. He had always been handsome, but ever since she'd ruined his reputation, he had looked different. More open, less pretentious. There was something else in his expression as well, something almost mournful beneath the happiness. "I am certain he exists, Emma. Somewhere out there is a man who would give everything he possessed to make you happy. Excuse me."

The rest of the group reached them just then, and he gave her a bow before wandering off, leaving her completely befuddled.

"Odd fellow," Mr. Seymour said, clear judgment in his eyes as he watched Nick go.

Emma couldn't have disagreed more. A mystery, yes, but Nick Forester was anything but odd. In fact, she found him the most interesting man she had ever known, and she was desperate to know more.

Chapter Twenty-Seven

WHEN TABITHA TOLD EMMA THAT Alvaro was hosting a few political associates and their families for dinner, Emma's first inclination was to request a tray in her room and avoid interacting with people who would surely have heard all about her ruination of Nick's name. But then Tabitha mentioned Nick would be in attendance, and Emma suddenly found herself wanting nothing more than to attend.

According to her sister, each of the three men who were coming had a daughter of eligible age, and Emma knew she would need to keep them away from Nick.

At least, that was what she told herself, though she had small suspicions that her reasoning went beyond keeping him from her inheritance.

When the guests began arriving, however, Emma found herself wishing she hadn't changed her mind. With no sign of Nick, even when most of the guests had been shown into the drawing room to await the announcement of dinner, Emma was surrounded by the ladies in question, all of them apparently desperate to know her better.

"Is this your first time in Town, Miss Mackenzie?" Miss Weston asked, though she seemed more fixated on the house than on the conversation. Her eyes traveled the room as she spoke. "I haven't seen you here before."

Emma resisted the urge to sigh. "No, I had a Season a few years back, but my Grandfather doesn't especially enjoy London."

"You can't have had much opportunity, living in the country at your age," Lady Louise said with a haughty sniff. "My father almost never leaves London, so I am always at the center of Society."

"And yet you still haven't found yourself a husband," Miss Albury muttered under her breath, but not so quietly that the others didn't hear her.

Lady Louise glared at her. "You're one to talk, Miss Albury. This will be your third Season, will it not?"

Holding back a groan, Emma searched the room for anyone else she might talk to. She knew there were kind and sweet women in London, but somehow she always found herself surrounded by the ones who cared only for themselves. Where were the ladies like Catherine, who currently sat with Miss Albury's younger sister and seemed to be having a perfectly lovely conversation? Miss Weston seemed kind enough, but the other two . . .

"What do you think, Miss Mackenzie?"

Emma's head snapped back to Lady Louise. "I'm terribly sorry; I missed what you said." In fact, she hadn't been trying to listen.

Lady Louise scoffed, as if she hadn't expected more from a simple country miss. "I said it is no surprise that Mr. Forester has yet to make an appearance, after everything. The man must have finally realized he has no place in polite Society and will be ignoring invitations from here on out."

Emma frowned. "Perhaps he is merely running late."

"Mr. Forester is *always* fashionably late," Miss Weston added helpfully. She had perked up at the change in topic, and Emma had a feeling she would need to keep Miss Weston and Nick far apart from each other. "I do hope he makes an appearance. I haven't seen him since last Season."

"You mean when he rejected you?" Miss Albury said with a sneer. "One has to wonder if all these rejections of his aren't as truthful as we once believed. I'd wager any woman of value took his measure and realized he was made of nothing but false promises. Surely *they* rejected *him*."

"Did you hear he is neck deep in debt?" Lady Louise replied eagerly. "I heard he owes thousands of pounds and that is why he pays no heed to"— she threw a sharp look to Miss Weston—"*humbler* women."

"*I* heard he is completely mad and believes all the nonsense people say about him, as does anyone who calls themselves his friend." Miss Albury's cold gaze shot to Emma for half a second. "Anyone would be a fool to associate with such a man."

Lady Louise started to respond. "I heard—"

"Mr. Forester is set to inherit one of the most profitable estates in Staffordshire," Emma said, unable to listen to any more of their ridiculous gossip. Though the ladies stared at her, their expressions doubtful and wary, she continued forward. "From my grandfather. I'm assuming none of you have taken the time to have a conversation with him, or you would know he is one of the most intelligent men in London. Yes, there are a good number of things people have said about him that aren't true, but I know for a fact there is a good deal of truth as well."

Lady Louise raised an eyebrow. "Such as?"

Oh goodness, why did Emma's mind suddenly draw a blank? She had worked so hard to ignore all the rumors she'd heard that now she couldn't recall any of them. She would simply have to speak of what she knew for herself.

"He rarely speaks unkindly of anyone, and he is one of my brother-in-law's closest friends because of his good heart. He cares not one whit where a person comes from as long as they act with honor and kindness, and I daresay there are few men who rival him in cleverness."

"I am pleased to learn you think so highly of me, Miss Mackenzie."

Emma nearly jumped out of her skin at Nick's voice close behind her. She spun around so quickly that she lost her balance, but he steadied her, his hand lingering on her waist for a long few seconds before he took a step back.

"Mr. Forester," she breathed, confused that she could still feel his hand on her side even though he'd distanced himself from her.

"My apologies for arriving so late," he said with a small smile. It wasn't the bright and broad smile she especially liked, but this one pierced her just as deeply. As ridiculous as it sounded, she almost thought this warm smile was meant especially for her, because it shifted as soon as he turned his attention to the three ladies behind her, growing harder. "I had to do a bit of rescuing on my way here."

Miss Albury scoffed. "Oh, Mr. Forester, we will hardly believe that nons—"

"Who needed rescuing?" Emma asked, wincing a little when Miss Albury glared at her for interrupting. It was worth it when Nick smiled at her again.

His eyes danced as he said, "My new acquaintance, Mr. Humphrey." He gestured to a man who was in conversation with Tabitha but looked over when he heard his name. "The poor man is new to Town and was planning on scrounging up some food in Seven Dials, of all places."

Emma had heard of the slum but had no idea whether Nick's shudder was exaggerated or appropriate to the situation. She didn't especially want to venture to the neighborhood to find out; she had had enough of wandering places she didn't belong.

Mr. Humphrey bowed to Tabitha, then approached with an easy smile. "I will forever be grateful for the rescue," he said, clapping Nick on the shoulder. "My cook is a day behind me, and I didn't have the foresight to pack something for the road."

"American?" Miss Weston guessed from his accent, her eyebrows high. "What brings you all the way to England?"

"Business," he replied. "And I'm lucky I came across Forester here, or I might have been lost on the streets all night."

"How good of you, Mr. Forester," Emma said, her cheeks heating because the expression on Nick's face had her transfixed.

Nick leaned in closer, as if his response needn't be heard by the others. "Anyone would have done the same. Although, I rather enjoy rescuing poor souls who find themselves where they shouldn't." Then, louder, he said, "It is your dear sister who should be thanked, as I surprised her with our uninvited guest, and she welcomed him in without question."

"Any friend of yours is always welcome," Tabitha replied, though she blushed from the praise.

Emma's heart warmed, seeing her sister so happy, and she tried to silently tell Nick how much she appreciated his thoughtfulness. Whether he understood her expression, she wasn't sure, but she couldn't look away from his gaze.

Humphrey cleared his throat.

Blinking, Nick snapped to attention and tucked his arms behind his back. "Introductions," he said, as if he needed the reminder. "Humphrey, this is Lady Louise Hartwright, Miss Anne Weston, and . . ." He paused, cocking his head to one side as he studied Miss Albury and her permanently disgusted expression. "You'll forgive me, but I've forgotten."

Miss Albury turned pink, and her haughtiness finally slipped.

"Oh yes, Miss Mary Albury. I do beg your pardon for my momentary lapse, Miss Albury. Sometimes one forgets things when surrounded by so many *dear friends*." Nick didn't look repentant in the slightest, and his words seemed to be a warning. One Miss Albury must have understood because she dipped her head once.

"And this beauty?" Mr. Humphrey said, his eyes on Emma.

She didn't know what to do with that, feeling rather awkward as the seconds ticked on with Nick saying nothing. He simply watched her as intently as Mr. Humphrey did.

When she was sure she couldn't stand any more scrutiny, Nick finally spoke. "This is my darling friend, Emma Mackenzie, Lady Harstone's sister." He said it with such warmth and affection that Emma felt as if she caught on fire.

Though she sank into a curtsy, she kept her eyes on the floor. Nick considered her a friend? She didn't understand why she liked that idea so much, but she did. A week ago she had thought she hated the man, but now that he had been laid bare, she kept discovering more things to like about him. But what did he mean when he looked at her so intently? Oh goodness, and he had called her *darling*. She almost hadn't realized in her confusion over the idea of a friendship, but the word seemed to fix itself on repeat in her mind. *Darling. Darling. Darling.*

What did it say about her that she rather liked that he had attached that word to their friendship?

"Ah," Mr. Humphrey said, pulling her attention back up. "I heard a good deal about you on our way here, Miss Mackenzie."

Her face had most certainly gone bright red as she looked up again. Nick had spoken of her? "Good things, I hope."

"Well, Forester seems prone to exaggerate, I'll admit, but he didn't exaggerate your beauty. Perhaps there was truth to the rest."

"I am not certain I would trust his opinion so readily, sir."

"Indeed not. I intend to form my own opinions this evening, if you will give me the pleasure. Might I accompany you into dinner, if that is not breaking some rule of formality?"

She should have been flattered and enjoyed his compliments, but Emma stood there feeling uncomfortable with so many eyes on her. Mr. Humphrey was undoubtedly handsome, and thus far she had seen no reason to dislike him, but her thoughts about Nick were swirling around in her head, too jumbled to make sense of them.

Darling friend.

"Yes," she whispered after much too long. "Yes, I would like that. Mr. Forester, might I speak to you for a moment?"

As the other ladies jumped into conversation with Mr. Humphrey, Emma took hold of Nick's arm and dragged him several feet away to the sound of his chuckles.

He spoke before she could. "You cannot possibly already have objections to Mr.—"

"Why did you pretend to forget Miss Albury's name?"

Nick's eyebrows rose, as if he hadn't expected that topic of conversation. "Miss Albury?"

"You embarrassed her. But why? I never took you for a cruel man, Mr. Forester." Especially after she had praised his kindness so highly.

Clenching his jaw, he thought over her question. All traces of his smile had gone, though he didn't look angry. Simply thoughtful. "I have listened to far too many of her judgments to like the way she was looking at you," he said slowly, as if making sure he said the right thing. "Her tongue is as sharp as her finances are dismal, and I wanted to remind her of the value of kindness when she has little else to recommend herself. She can say what she wants behind her own walls, but I wouldn't have been able to bear her speaking ill of you, Emma."

Oh. Emma didn't know what she'd expected, but it wasn't that. "Th-thank you," she said, only now realizing her hand was still on his arm, because Nick had put his fingers over hers. "I would not have expected that from you."

"Because I am a beast?"

Emma's eyes went wide. Either he had heard of her story of the day they'd met, or he had guessed correctly what she thought of him. *Used to* think of him. "A beast?" she asked, slightly breathless.

He grinned wide. "Yes, it does seem a bit fantastical, but one of your nieces said something to that effect, and I thought it sounded appropriate. I have been a beast to you, and others, and I am trying to make amends where I can."

"That is very good of you."

"I thought so." He laughed when Emma swatted his arm. "You can't expect me to change my ways overnight, can you?"

Emma shook her head, her smile feeling permanently fixed in place. "Yes, I suppose that is asking far too much. It's a miracle I could think you might change at all."

"I wholeheartedly agree. I've been a beast for most of my life, and I haven't been lucky enough to find someone to break my curse before now."

Oh goodness, Emma hadn't expected him to say something like that. Even if he had no idea what she had said about kisses breaking curses, *she* couldn't help but think about the idea of kissing someone like Nick Forester. Would he be the sort to take his time, keeping his kisses slow and gentle, or would he take charge and dive in without hesitation? Excepting her horrid encounter with the man outside Nick's apartment, which she had done her best not to think about since for fear of falling into a panic, Emma had never kissed a man, and she hardly considered that a kiss in the first place. But she had seen how unafraid Alvaro was of showing his affection for Tabitha. Would Nick be the same way? He was so confident in everything else, and . . .

And he had called her his *darling* friend.

She had probably turned bright red again, and she could tell the moment Nick noticed the heat rising in her cheeks. His expression shifted from laughter to something more serious. Almost like interest.

He squeezed her hand, leaning in closer. "Are you well, Emma?"

She could hardly say. "I . . . Yes, I—"

"Trying to steal my dinner partner, Forester?" Mr. Humphrey laughed at his own joke as he held his arm out to Emma and broke her gaze, her heart racing with no explanation for it. Mr. Humphrey must have startled her with his sudden arrival, though she wasn't certain he had.

Nick hardly reacted to the interruption, but his smile grew, as if he knew the cause of Emma's sudden nervousness. "She is all yours, Humphrey, though I suggest watching your step. She may be beautiful, but her strength is in her mind."

"I shall do my best to keep up."

As Emma switched from Nick's arm to Mr. Humphrey's, she tried to shake away the fog that had settled over her. She had never struggled to converse with people; then again, she had never had anyone look at her the way Nick did. She had never had anyone give her such meaningful compliments. She had never . . .

She had never known anyone like Nick Forester. What was happening to her? She'd never imagined kissing someone, let alone a man she hadn't been able to stand a week ago.

Though her conversation with Mr. Humphrey throughout dinner was interesting enough, Emma couldn't help but glance at Nick every few minutes. He sat far enough away that she couldn't hear what he and Miss Weston discussed, but he seemed to be enjoying himself. So did Miss Weston.

Emma didn't like that.

Thankfully, the distance from Nick helped her relax and act more like herself than the confused and flustered woman she had been in the drawing room. Though she couldn't fathom why he would have made her act so strangely, she was glad to know his effects were only temporary. It made it possible for her to think clearly while speaking with Mr. Humphrey, which helped her come to the conclusion that she and Mr. Humphrey would not suit.

That conclusion had come rather quickly, after the man had waxed long on the uselessness of books and stories, claiming facts and physical labor were far more important than "silly fantasies," as he'd put it.

Nick must have heard that declaration as well, because he met Emma's eyes and winced.

By the time the ladies left the men to their port, Emma was glad to get away, finding herself a seat away from the other ladies, who inexplicably returned to their conversation about Nick and his many failings.

"You don't seem yourself tonight, Emma."

Emma looked up as Tabitha joined her, putting on a smile even though she knew her sister would see right through it. "I suppose I am not," she agreed. "I think I am simply tired from all the excitement since our arrival. We have yet to have a quiet day."

Pursing her lips, Tabitha studied her in the same way she studied the girls when one of them was keeping a secret. Though she'd married only a year after Mama had died and Emma had gone to live with Grandfather, that hadn't stopped her from mothering Emma just as much as their actual mother had done. She always knew when something was bothering Emma.

"I am not so certain it is London that has you out of sorts," Tabitha said finally.

Emma frowned. "What else would it be?"

"I think you're starting to wonder if you're wrong about your choice to stay away from love."

"I haven't chosen—"

"You can pretend all you want," Tabitha said, taking hold of Emma's hand. "I did the same thing before I met Alvaro. I believed I would grow up on my own and help you find the kind of happiness Mama didn't have. I would have been perfectly content to live out my days alone as long as you were happy."

Emma hadn't known that about her sister, and she furrowed her brow, trying to imagine it. Tabitha had been married for almost a decade, and she'd become a mother eight years ago when she had Sophia. Emma couldn't imagine her being alone.

"What changed?" she asked, even if she was uncertain about where this conversation might take her.

Tabitha's smile faded a bit as she said, "I realized that not every man is like Father."

Emma winced. "What does Father have to do with any of this?"

Though she fought to keep her expression light, Tabitha's eyes were sad as she squeezed Emma's hand. "I know you didn't know him well, but there were a few years when he was a good father. Before he got it into his head to see the world and find his fame and fortune, I believe he was content with the little life he had given us.

"I was around seven when he left the first time. I remember Mama crying most of the night, and I didn't understand why for a long time. Not until he had been gone for several weeks." Tabitha took a deep breath. "She loved him so much. Their marriage was arranged, but I am certain she loved him from the beginning. And when he left, I think he took a part of her heart with him."

Emma hadn't heard any of this. Mama had never said much about her husband, and Emma had learned not to ask. But she wanted to ask now. "When did he come back?"

"About nine months before you were born." Tabitha shook her head. "He stayed for only a few weeks before he was gone again, and then we didn't see him again until you were three or four." Brushing a tear that slipped onto her cheek, she tried to smile but did a poor job of it. "I think every time he returned, Mama was still hopeful he would stay, until . . ."

"Until he died," Emma finished. She'd been only eight when they'd received the news that he had been lost at sea, but she remembered so vividly that her mother was never the same after that, like her light had been snuffed out. "Perhaps you're right. Perhaps I am trying to protect myself from heartbreak. Mama was perfectly able to care for us on her own, and she could have been saved the ache of being left behind if she hadn't—"

"If she hadn't married Father and fallen in love, she never would have had us." Tabitha wrapped her arm around Emma's shoulders. "I don't think she ever regretted falling in love. And I *know* she wouldn't want you to be alone all your life simply because you are scared of what love might bring you. Just because she experienced heartbreak doesn't mean everyone does. I couldn't dream of a life without Alvaro now that I know what it is to have him."

"Yes, well, you were lucky and found a perfect man," Emma grumbled, rubbing her chest below her collarbone. It felt so tight, like she couldn't fully breathe. "Your love story is a dream."

Chuckling, Tabitha shook her head. "You think there aren't days when I want to wring that man's neck? Or moments when I wish he would leave me in silence so I can hear myself think? No love story is perfect, Emma, and we've had our share of bumpy roads. But that is what makes the journey exciting." She squeezed Emma's shoulders and then stood, crossing the room to join the wives of Alvaro's colleagues.

Emma sat there on her own even though the men began filing into the room. She hardly wanted to have any conversations right now, overwhelmed as she was, but she knew she couldn't leave Nick alone with the young ladies for too long. She doubted he would be interested in any of them, but in case Miss Weston was more interesting than she seemed, Emma intended to take up as much of Nick's time as she possibly could.

He couldn't fall in love with anyone if he was too busy talking to her.

"Miss Mackenzie, I was hoping to find you on your own."

Emma barely held back a groan as Mr. Humphrey took a seat beside her. She had barely spoken to him during the last half of dinner, focusing more on her pudding, but apparently her disinterest had not been enough of a deterrent. "Mr. Humphrey," she said, searching for an excuse to go speak to anyone but him.

He gave her a lopsided smile and seemed to waver a bit in his seat. "You truly are the most beautiful woman here," he said, his words slurring. How much had he had to drink?

"Thank you, Mr. Humphrey. If you will ex—"

"Did you know I have quite a fortune to my name? Far more than any of these English. Have you ever been to America?"

Emma bit her lip. "No, sir, I have not. I am quite fond of my English countryside."

"That is because you haven't seen Virginia. You will love it."

"Excuse me?"

"Forester said you are in need of a husband."

"Did he now?"

"He said you need someone who can *handle* you."

Scoffing, Emma rose to her feet, but Mr. Humphrey simply followed. "Sir," Emma said, "I need to speak to—"

He slipped around her, cutting off her path toward Catherine and Tabitha. A flash of memory from the other night sent her heart racing, though she hoped Humphrey would not be foolish enough to touch her. "I can offer you a blessed life, Miss Mackenzie."

"This is highly inappropriate, Mr. Humphrey."

"I have more land than you could dream of." Though Emma had been trying to keep her voice down, Humphrey spoke at full volume. "All the money you could hope for."

"I have no intention of settling down, sir. Now, please, kindly step aside so I may—"

"We could be on a ship tomorrow if you—"

"I think that's enough, Humphrey," Nick said, appearing at Emma's side with a cold glare in his eyes. He spoke quietly enough not to draw attention to their corner of the room, but there was no mistaking the warning in his voice. "I believe the lady has given you her opinion. Miss Mackenzie, I have come to remind you that you owe me a rematch on our game of chess."

Emma nodded, even if she had no idea what he was talking about. "Yes, of course, Mr. Forester. I know how wounded you were by your loss."

Nick let out a laugh, poorly disguised as a cough. "Exactly. You'd caught me on a bad day, and I need to restore my dignity. Humphrey." He nodded his head once and then offered his arm to Emma, leading her away without waiting for Mr. Humphrey to respond.

Emma let out her breath as soon as Nick helped her into a chair at the chess table. "Thank you," she whispered. "I didn't want to cause a scene and ruin the night for Tabitha and Alvaro."

Chuckling, Nick settled into his own chair and began setting out the pieces. It seemed he intended for this game to be real rather than merely an excuse. "I think Harstone could use a good scandal in his life," he said lightly. "The man is painfully perfect."

"It's a wonder the two of you became friends, being so different."

Despite the implied insult, Nick's grin grew as he looked up and met Emma's eyes. His blue eyes were so bright tonight, reflecting the candlelight of the room and giving him a mischievous look. He gestured for Emma to make her first move, and then he said, "I owe the friendship entirely to Lord Calloway."

As Emma moved a pawn forward, she was surprised by the honest answer. "Truly?"

Nick nodded, shifting his own pawn. "Calloway knows a bit of Spanish from his many business dealings on the Continent. He and I have been friends since we were boys, and he was one of the first people to accept Harstone into British Society. Harstone was probably glad to find someone who came close to matching his talent with languages, even though Calloway's Spanish is, so I hear, questionable." He laughed, his eyes slightly distant, as if remembering those days.

Emma couldn't help but grin along with him as she moved her next piece. They each made their moves quickly, which promised an interesting game. "I was so young when I met him that I remember thinking Alvaro was speaking nonsense when he first came to Tutbury. Tabitha thought his accent the most perfect thing in the world, and then she became obsessed with learning Spanish to match him."

"Your sister is far more intelligent than me," Nick said with a chuckle. "Harstone has always found it rather amusing to converse with Calloway in Spanish as often as possible because my language skills are dismal. I still can't understand any of it, no matter how hard I've tried."

Emma took his bishop, shaking her head. "You already know I am as help-less as you. I think he has lost much of his accent so I could better understand him when I was a child."

"He knew he would have to win you over as well because he was unfailingly in love with your sister the moment he met her." Nick said it with a groan, but his smile belied his pretended irritation. He captured Emma's rook with his knight, apparently unaware of the danger he had put himself in with that move. "I might have thought your brother-in-law mad if he wasn't the happiest man I know."

"It does seem incredible for someone to know so quickly that a match would be a good one," Emma agreed, quickly taking the knight with her own. "I don't believe I could be confident in my knowledge of a person without knowing him for a good while."

With a glance at Humphrey, who was glaring in their direction, Nick chuckled. "You mean you weren't considering the generous suit being offered to you tonight?"

Emma adopted her own glare, hoping Nick felt the brunt of it. "I have you to blame for that ridiculous man, Nick Forester."

He raised his hands in surrender. "I honestly didn't intend for him to be anything but a last-minute dinner guest."

"He said you told him I needed a husband. That I needed to be *handled*."

Groaning, he shook his head. "That is *not* what I said. I said there are few men worthy of a woman like you, and no man of sense would think he could ever control you. I said it would take a strong man indeed to handle your tenacity and independence." He frowned, as if reviewing his own words to ensure he hadn't said anything insulting. It was such a change from the quick-to-insult man she'd known before that Emma could only stare at him. "We men are fragile creatures," he continued, "and there are few of us who would be willing to admit they may not be the most intelligent person in a room."

She cocked her head to one side, trying to understand why he seemed so different. It was more than what he was saying; it was *how* he was saying it. There was no trace of the dishonesty that had followed him around before. "*You* would admit such a thing?"

"In a heartbeat. I know very well you likely do as much for the Mackenzie estate as your grandfather does, if not more."

Shocked, Emma stared at his expression, as if she might find some sign of him secretly laughing at her. But she found only sincerity. "How do you know that?" she asked. Her grandfather didn't even know how much she interacted with their tenants and worked with them to ensure their land was profitable.

Nick grinned. "I would never go to battle against someone without knowing them. And I know there is nothing you cannot do if you put your mind to it. You would never be foolish enough to take over from your grandfather without knowing what you are doing. That, my friend, puts you a cut above me, as I never had the opportunity to learn from my father. He was gone before he could teach me."

"My father abandoned my mother." Emma's eyes went wide. She hadn't intended for that to be her response, and yet it had slipped off her tongue so easily. It was as if Nick's praise had made her feel safe, and she was apparently still reeling from her conversation with Tabitha. "Forgive me. I didn't intend to say . . ."

Frowning, Nick seemed to be waiting for her to expound. "What?"

Did she really want to tell him such a horrible thing? Doing so would mean she trusted him to keep it to himself rather than use it to injure her as she had injured him. She ducked her head, taking a deep breath. "He made her believe that he loved her, but then he left and came back only when he wanted . . . I barely knew him. I watched my mother live each day with an aching heart until she was no longer strong enough to bear it. She died from a broken heart, Nick, and I never want . . ." She clasped her hands together, gazing at her fingers. "That is why I am so determined to take care of myself. Why I am afraid of marriage. My mother was an incredible woman, and she raised us on her own. She was so brave. I pretend I want to do what she did, and I know I would be strong enough to live my life without a partner. You apparently believe that as well. But . . . I don't want to be alone. That sounds miserable." She blinked away tears, praying she wouldn't lose her composure. "Yet I am terrified that if I let myself imagine having someone to share it all with me, I will end up just like her. Abandoned. Heartbroken. Lost."

Nick moved slowly, his eyes watching her so intently as he reached over and gently brushed her tears from her cheeks with his thumb. It was as if he was waiting for any sign that she might not want his touch, when in truth she craved more of it. "I do not think there is a man on this earth who could leave you behind, my dear Emma. Believe me."

She did believe him—she believed that *he* believed it, though her heart didn't beat strongly enough for her to agree. Unless she came across some miracle and found someone she trusted without question, she would have to remain on her own. That inheritance was her last chance.

But her only chance would leave Nick without one of his own.

She grimaced, wishing she had a different option. She looked down at the chess board, realizing their skills had been matched so perfectly that they were left in a stalemate, only their kings left in a game that could never be won. *How fitting.*

"I should go see if Tabitha needs any assistance with the rest of the evening," she said softly, rising to her feet.

Nick mirrored her, looking as if he wanted nothing more than to keep her there as he reached out. He didn't touch her, though, his hand lingering just beyond her arm. "Emma, I am sorry about your father. I hope you know that not every man is like him."

"Thank you for your rescue from Mr. Humphrey."

"I have the perfect man for you." Nick spoke so quickly that his words were barely intelligible.

Emma blinked. "What?" After all of that, he still wanted to throw men at her? "Nick, I don't want—"

"No more games." He pursed his lips, which didn't exactly give Emma much confidence in what he was saying. Still, his expression carried something she had never seen before, and he spoke with conviction, like nothing had ever been surer. "This one could really be the one. I know you're scared, and you have every right to be. But do you trust me?"

She shouldn't. She had only just come to consider the man a friend, and there was always the chance that he was trying to trick her to get the inheritance for himself. But she trusted him more than she had ever trusted anyone. "Yes," she said, feeling that word resonate throughout her body.

Nick's shoulders dropped in relief. "Thank you. And I promise you, Emma, this will be my last effort. If you do not believe with your whole heart that this man could make you happy, I will surrender. And if that ends up being the case, I only ask for your help in restoring my lands, though I hope we will not need to resort to those drastic measures. I have a good feeling about this match."

Too curious not to ask, Emma cocked her head. "Who is he?"

But Nick smiled that private smile from before and shook his head. "In time, dear Emma. Go see to your sister. I will convince Humphrey that it is in his best interest to make his way home for the night." He gave her one last smile, and then he was gone, crossing the room with determination.

And Emma slowly made her way over to her sister, her cheeks warm and her heart pounding because he had called her *dear Emma.* She rather liked that.

Chapter Twenty-Eight

"Are we playing billiards, or are you going to spend the evening staring at the wall?"

Nick blinked, tearing his eyes from the wallpaper that had, apparently, been so riveting. Just how long had he been staring? If Harstone's grin was any indication, it had most assuredly been longer than Nick would have liked. "Forgive me," he said, picking up his cue and moving to the table. "You are ahead, yes?"

Just as Nick leaned down to line up his shot, Harstone picked up the cue ball. "We can talk, if you would rather do that. I have too many points for you to try to win, regardless."

Nick groaned, pinching the bridge of his nose. "I am quite out of sorts this morning and terrible company. The only reason I came was because Calloway's butler was tired of me moping around."

Harstone chuckled. "I know. You told me when you arrived."

"Did I?" Nick dropped into a chair and sighed. "I have a lot on my mind, I suppose."

Making a sound of understanding, Harstone settled into the chair beside him. "You have less than a month before you forfeit Mackenzie's offer."

Nick glared as his stomach twisted itself into a knot. "I hadn't been thinking of *that* until just now," he growled. Mackenzie hadn't given him much time to begin with, but it certainly felt as if the last two and a half weeks had passed far too quickly. "I think at this point I might as well surrender now and save myself the stress."

Harstone said nothing, though his expression said plenty. He seemed to be waiting for Nick to read the judging look in his eyes and understand what he was trying to say.

Under normal circumstances, perhaps Nick could have gleaned his meaning, but he didn't have the patience for it today. "What?" he grumbled.

Shrugging, Harstone settled back in his chair, as if preparing for this conversation to be lengthy. "Perhaps I am wrong, my friend, but you seem to have already surrendered, no? You haven't been wife hunting since I arrived in London."

"I have!" But Nick cringed as soon as he said it. Even when he had been trying to connect with ladies, he hadn't tried very hard. "Or perhaps I—"

"What are you looking for, Forester?"

Nick grunted. "A wife. You know that."

"What *precisely* are you looking for? Even now, with your reputation in tatters"—Nick shot him another glare—"you could walk out onto the street and ask any woman to marry you. She would likely say yes. So I ask again. What are *you* looking for?"

Nick massaged his palm with his thumb, as if his only tension was in his hands rather than his entire body, and considered the question. He already knew the answer, but he could tell Harstone was trying to help him. What if he had been looking for the wrong thing? "I want to find love," he said eventually. "I always thought I would recognize it when I came across it, but now I fear I was entirely wrong. What if I found it already and had no idea?"

Harstone chuckled. "Love is not something you find in an instant, my friend."

"*You* did."

"I found *attraction*. But we *built* love. Together. Tabitha and I made something beautiful. You cannot *find* love, my friend, no matter how much you hope it will run into you on the street."

Harstone was wrong. Nick *knew* he was wrong because his heart swelled as he thought about the day he'd run into Emma on the street. Well, inside a milliner's shop. He had felt it then, and he felt it now. If anyone could be the woman he'd been trying to find, she could.

He had somehow fallen madly in love with her, and that scared him more than anything. What if he failed her? He would never willingly leave her like her father had, but what if he turned out to be too much like his own father and ruined everything with a bad investment? His father had meant well, trying to pull the estate from barely breaking even to profitable enough to provide his family with a more comfortable life, but his investment had turned out to be a misstep that had cost them everything. From when his parents became ill and passed away to now, Nick had been paying for that mistake.

Would his own children be the ones paying for his mistakes? He had made so many, and at this point he wasn't sure if even the Mackenzie fortune would thrive under his name or if it would fall as easily as his reputation had. Emma had been right when she'd said he was nothing but insubstantial smoke. His words were all he had, and they had done him no good.

"What if I'm not enough for her?" he croaked, looking up at his friend through the tears that built up in his eyes. He had never been this vulnerable in front of Harstone before, and yet he hardly cared how the escaping emotion made him look.

Harstone didn't ask for clarification; he clearly knew who Nick was talking about as he gave Nick a gentle smile. "What if you are exactly what she needs?"

"She's never going to trust me. After everything I . . ." Nick shook his head. He was fortunate she had agreed to allow him one more chance to procure a husband for her, but he couldn't expect her trust to go beyond that after all the lies he had told. He had been desperate for that last chance, but how was he supposed to convince her that *he* was the man who would treat her as he should? She hated him. Or, at the very most, she tolerated him.

Nick ran his hands through his hair, his frustration growing because he had yet to think of a good way to convince Emma to give *him* a chance. She was completely unraveling him! A week ago he wouldn't have touched his hair in order to remain flawless, but he had no reasons to be presentable anymore. Particularly because Emma was out calling with her sister and Miss Barton. He hardly had any reason to impress Harstone, so what did it matter if he made a mess of his hair?

"Emma deserves more than a ruffled-up, once-idolized man of thirty with no fortune who will likely never set foot in London after all this is over," he muttered. He doubted he could get that inheritance before his time ran out anyway. "Even if by some miracle I were to find another woman who makes me feel the way Emma does, I'll probably still give it all to Emma anyway." She would do far more with the Mackenzie lands than he ever could.

He looked at Harstone, who sat with an elbow resting on the arm of his chair and his fingertips pressed to his temple.

"Why aren't you saying anything?" Nick asked.

"You seem to be saying it all to yourself," Harstone replied with a smirk. "Don't let me get in your way."

Nick growled low in his throat. "You always seem to be full of advice when I do not want it, yet here you sit in silence when I need you most. You call yourself my friend?"

"I get the feeling you wouldn't want to hear what I have to say," Harstone replied lightly. "Therefore, I should keep it to myself, no?"

When Nick first met Alvaro Rowland, before he became Lord Harstone, the man never would have teased anyone like this. He had always been lighthearted, but he'd never been anything but completely kind. It seemed his time on English soil had tainted that kindness.

"You are acting too much like me," Nick grumbled. "I don't like it. Where is Calloway when I need him? He would agree with me."

"Calloway is enjoying married life with his darling Lucy, exactly where he should be. And you, my friend, are wasting your time here with me when I know you only came to see Emma." He tapped the side of his head with his finger as he seemed to study Nick. "I don't suppose you would be open to the idea of telling her how you feel?"

"And have her laugh in my face?" Nick shuddered. "I fear this situation requires more delicacy than directness."

Harstone nodded, his serious expression a bit too pronounced to be real. "Not a strength you possess."

"Thank you for your confidence in me. It is greatly appreciated."

That got Harstone to laugh and settle even more comfortably into his chair, stretching his legs out. "Do you want advice or no?"

"I'm considering how best to answer that question."

"You have never been in love." He held up a hand before Nick could protest. "I know how you felt about Lady Lavinia. You were as besotted as Calloway or I are with our wives. But you are not the same man you were then."

Though he knew Harstone was right, Nick still frowned. His friends hardly ever mentioned Lavinia, even though he knew they'd thought him a cad when he'd broken off the engagement. Nick had never told them the reason for it. "I wish I could go back," he admitted quietly. "To the time when I met her. I wish I could have asked some other woman to dance and spared myself all this trouble."

Harstone gave him a sad smile. "If you ever wish to talk about what happened . . ."

But Nick ducked his head. It had been three years since she'd broken his heart, and he wasn't sure he would ever be ready to face what had happened.

Harstone reached over and put his hand on his shoulder. "As I was saying, this is all new for you. You may pretend to keep your feelings to yourself, but Emma is no fool. She will see right through you and discover the truth soon enough. Wouldn't you rather she hear it from you than force her to read it in your eyes?"

Yes, but that wasn't the point. Whether he told her outright or she worked it out on her own, it wouldn't change the outcome. "I have nothing to give her, save what belongs to her anyway," Nick said weakly. "She has every reason to think being independent will serve her better than trusting someone else to hold all the power. And she has no reason to think my feelings might be genuine instead of a falsehood created to win Mackenzie's game. That hardly gives me confidence in a conclusion that works in my favor."

"Then, what are you going to do?"

If only he had an answer to that question. "For now," he said, pushing himself up to his feet, "I am going to go walk and clear my head. I should not have come here, when seeing her will only confuse me more. Good day to you, Harstone. Your advice is appreciated, if not heeded."

"Forester."

Nick paused at the door, glancing back.

"She will never be able to decide whether you are right for her if she does not know who you are. Who you really are."

As right as Harstone was, that was more terrifying than anything. Nick hadn't been vulnerable like that since Lavinia, and that had led to this whole mess. With his insides twisting into knots, he hurried from the room before his friend could speak any more harrowing truths.

He made it halfway to the front door when he nearly ran straight into Emma herself in the corridor. She must have only just returned, still wearing her cloak but holding her gloves in her hand. A rosy hue colored her cheeks and nose, rendering Nick slack-jawed.

"You are stunning," he breathed without even a word of greeting. A curl had fallen onto her cheek, and he barely resisted pushing it back. Apparently he had turned into a lovesick fool overnight.

She flushed an even deeper crimson, her greenish-blue eyes sparkling. "Ah, if it isn't the man who has terrible taste in friends and far too many compliments on the tip of his tongue. It seems you are always at the ready to assist the unfortunate players in your terrible game of matchmaking."

He smiled for the first time all morning, feeling it crack through the gloom that had been settling over him. "I mean every bit of praise I have ever said about you. And, if it makes a difference, I would not call any of those men my friends. Except perhaps Parker, though he can sometimes be a bit uncouth. As for Humphrey, he had better be wary if ever we cross paths again."

Emma ducked her head, though he wished she wouldn't hide those dazzling eyes of hers. They looked more green than blue today, matching the emerald color of her cloak. "I wish I had been able to rescue myself last night, but I am in your debt for recognizing my need for assistance."

"I am beginning to think you enjoy getting yourself into scrapes."

"I think the more likely explanation is you are rather fond of rescuing me and therefore create the situations."

He laughed. "I do enjoy being the daring hero, but I promise you I take no pride in being the cause of so much discomfort. I do not think I have ever met anyone quite as prone to needing assistance as you, my dear Emma. You may have the skills to look after yourself, but you're bound to send me to an early grave with worry anyway." And he would gladly live a shortened life if it meant he got to spend it with her. "You are too appealing for your own good. I am starting to wonder if I need to educate you in fisticuffs for the future."

She blushed pink. "That does sound amusing, I'll admit."

The corridor settled into a comfortable silence as they smiled at each other, and Nick felt a twinge of hope. She wouldn't smile at him so warmly if she felt entirely indifferent to him, would she? And she made no moves to excuse herself.

"Well," she said after a moment, "have you found my husband? You did seem rather confident you could find a man worth my notice."

He was nowhere near worth her notice, but he would still try to gain it. It was rather unfortunate he had no idea how to do that. "You think I would accept failure? It is as if you do not know me at all, Miss Mackenzie."

She pondered that, giving him a peculiar look as she studied him. "I do not think I do know you, Mr. Forester."

But would she want to learn of him? Harstone was right; she could never love Nick if she felt she didn't know him. He would have to give her reasons to want to know more. If he could stomach being his true self again, would she like what she saw? "That is true," he admitted. "If you did, you would know I much prefer being called Nick." Then he held his breath. He had been calling her Emma for some time now without ever getting her permission.

But she smiled, her fingers playing with the end of her scarf. "Actually, I did know that. It was one of the first things I knew about you, if you'll recall."

"You also knew me to be a coward."

"Or truly intelligent. Miss Barton is a pleasant enough soul, but she is better in small doses."

"And when she has someone else to show her interest."

Emma laughed.

This was good. They were joking together. Reminiscing about their first meeting, when there hadn't been any animosity between them yet. And she still had yet to give any indication that she wished to go up to her room and leave him here on his own. *This is good.*

Hopefully things would *stay* good. Now that he had realized how he felt, it was as if Nick was falling down a steep slope with no chance of slowing. All he could hope for was a soft landing at the bottom.

"Where is Miss Barton, anyway?" he asked. "No longer permanently attached to you, is she?"

Laughter still danced in Emma's eyes, though something else played there as well. Some kind of mischief. "She had an important letter to write when we returned and didn't wish to waste any time."

Emma seemed to hold back growing amusement, and Nick knew there was more to this explanation than a simple letter. "I haven't known Miss Barton to be much of a writer," he said, stepping closer.

Emma pursed her lips. "I believe this is a new pastime."

"Do you know who is lucky enough to be on the receiving end of such devotion?"

Emma shook her head. "We shan't talk of this, Nick. I promised Catherine."

While that was admirable, there could be only one reason a young lady wouldn't want anyone to know to whom she was writing. Nick may not have felt any affection for the woman, but he hardly wished Miss Barton harm. "Emma, if Miss Barton is corresponding with a man, she has put herself in danger of scandal."

Emma leaped forward and pressed her cool hand against his mouth, her other hand holding tight to his arm as well as her gloves. While her sudden bare-fingered touch had turned him completely mute, her eyes kept him captivated; they burned with passion. He couldn't have moved even if he wanted to, and he certainly didn't wish anything of the sort.

"I know," she whispered. "I've told Catherine the same thing. But she is writing to my cousin, and she promised she would tell him that they will only be able to interact in person from here on out. He will agree; I know he will. And she isn't as naive as you seem to think."

Nick reluctantly pulled his head back to free his mouth. "I never said she was naive. But writing to a man she hardly knows? I'll admit he is well-suited to her, but she is foolish to risk so much for a fleeting interest."

Emma shrugged. "Who are you to say she isn't in love with him?"

"She thought she was in love with *me* for years. Clearly she doesn't know a thing about love."

"And you do?" The hand that had covered his mouth now rested on his shoulder, something Emma didn't seem to realize as she stared up at Nick. Why else would she remain this close? "Tell me that you, a man who has spent years chasing a fantasy, know how it feels to love, and I will accept your expertise on the matter."

Now was his moment. He could tell her he knew exactly what love felt like because his heart seemed to be trying to beat out of his chest at the feel of her hands pressed against him. At the intent way she watched him. He ached to bend down and touch his lips to hers in a kiss. She was the only woman in the world who had ever met him step for step, and he couldn't let that go.

Nick swallowed, knowing his next move could ruin everything or make him the happiest man alive. Emma wasn't breaking her gaze, and she seemed to be waiting. For what, he didn't know. All he did know was that he had to tread carefully, or he was going to lose everything. He didn't have the time to keep playing a game, and now the stakes were so much higher than before. A week ago the only thing he stood to lose was a fortune.

Now he was in grave danger of losing his heart.

Three and a half weeks. He had three and a half weeks to convince her he wanted her love and not her money. Once his deadline arrived, he had little hope that he would be able to make her believe he wasn't merely after the inheritance that he had lost the moment he'd fallen in love with Emma Mackenzie.

Chapter Twenty-Nine

EMMA COULDN'T BREATHE. SHE HAD never been this close to Nick, and he had never been this quiet, and she had never been so completely overcome with conflicting emotions that she wanted to laugh and scream at the same time.

Nick was just standing there, his warm hand on her waist and his eyes digging right into hers like he was looking for a place to land if he jumped. What if he kissed her? She fought the urge to let her eyes drop to his mouth in curiosity, just to imagine what his lips might feel like against hers. Did she want him to kiss her?

Yes.

No.

Maybe?

Maybe she did want that. But the moment her eyes finally slipped to his lips, the spell broke. Nick hissed in a breath and took a step back, his hand dropping at the same time Emma's fell from his shoulder. *Oh.* He hadn't wanted to kiss her after all. Was Emma supposed to feel disappointed? She did, just a little. Perhaps more than she ought. This was Nick, after all, the man who had been trying to find her a husband since the day she'd set foot in London. Just last night he had begged her to give him one last chance to procure a candidate she might consider.

Thoughts of kissing him would have to stop before she got herself into a trouble he couldn't rescue her from.

"Would you care to take a walk with me, Emma?"

She blinked, surprised by the eagerness in his voice. "A walk? Now?"

His tempting lips twisted into a crooked smile. "I thought, since you're already dressed for the weather, now is as good a time as any. What do you say?"

"Yes." She sounded as eager as he did, and that brought a wave of heat into her face. Who needed a cloak when Nick Forester was around? Nobody.

She thought even her hands might end up warm next to him, and her hands were always cold. "Yes, I would like that very much." But she still needed to be careful before she got any ridiculous ideas, so she added, "I should fetch my maid and have her accompany us."

"I was going to suggest the same thing," he replied. "I'll meet you back here?"

Footsteps cut off Emma's response, and she jumped backward, even though there had been plenty of space between her and Nick already. Still, she didn't want anyone getting the wrong idea, especially when she realized it was Alvaro approaching them.

"Oh! Alvaro!" Emma winced at her own volume, forcing herself to speak in normal tones before her brother-in-law started jumping to conclusions. "I am going to be out walking with Mr. Forester, should anyone need me."

Alvaro raised an eyebrow, glancing between the two of them. "Is that so? Much to talk about?"

For some reason, that brought out a glare from Nick, one that Emma wished to temper as best as she could. She far preferred when he smiled. "We simply want to take advantage of the weather before it gets too cold for walking," she said, doing her best to sound nonchalant. She wasn't sure she managed it, because Alvaro seemed to be holding back laughter.

"You'll bring Jenny with you?" he asked.

Emma was glad she had thought of that on her own. At least she hadn't gone completely daft. "Of course. I was just about to send someone to fetch her."

"Perhaps Miss Barton would like to join you as well."

No, in fact, she would not. And Emma didn't want anything to interrupt this rare chance to converse with Nick without anything getting in the way. But how could she tell Alvaro that she was confident Catherine would rather stay behind without mentioning the reason?

"Miss Barton said something about writing to Mrs. Franks in Staffordshire," Nick said lightly. "Isn't that right, Miss Mackenzie?"

Emma met his smile with one of her own. "Yes, yes, she did. I would imagine she'll need you to frank it for her when she is finished, Alvaro."

"Of course," Alvaro replied. "I have a letter to send to Staffordshire myself."

"Who would have thought Miss Barton would have such affection for someone in Tutbury, of all places?" Nick said. He looked so mischievous that Emma wanted to smack him for nearly making her laugh. Thank goodness he seemed to have relaxed about Catherine's correspondence with Elias.

But, just in case he still worried, she figured she could add to the argument a bit. "Letters are such a good way to learn to know someone better, don't you think, Mr. Forester?"

His grin shifted, somehow growing both softer and brighter at the same time. She never would have guessed a man could have so many different smiles. "Indeed, Miss Mackenzie."

"Forester has always been fond of letter-writing," Alvaro threw in, reminding Emma that he was there. She had nearly forgotten in the last ten seconds, as she was so focused on Nick.

Emma's eyes widened. "You have?" She never would have guessed that a man so inclined to use his tongue would enjoy any other ways of communicating.

But Nick pursed his lips and ducked his head, as if embarrassed to have been exposed. "Yes," he admitted quietly. "After my parents died, my only companionship came from my school friends. During the summer holidays, I spent most of my time writing to Calloway to stave off the loneliness, and I never grew out of the habit. My old housekeeper and your unfortunate brother-in-law have been prey to my pen many times as well."

Alvaro reached out, clapping a hand on Nick's shoulder. "You know I am always glad to receive your letters, Forester. As is Calloway. They help us know you are well and happy."

Nick chuckled. "With my luck so far, you may never be rid of me long enough to receive another. I will be bouncing back and forth between your estates like an unwelcome purse-pinched brother."

Alvaro merely smiled. "I am content with that outcome as well. I consider you a brother already, and you will always have a room at your disposal. Now, I will go find Jenny for you so you can take your walk."

Emma watched him go, though she would rather watch Nick. When Alvaro had called him a brother, Nick's expression had filled with deep emotion that she was sure he didn't want anyone to see, so she kept her gaze away to give him some privacy.

"Your sister married an impossibly good man," Nick said in a hushed tone.

"How old were you when you lost your parents?" Emma grimaced as soon as the question left her tongue, and she peeked over at him to see how angry he might be.

He didn't look angry at all. Simply sad. "I was twelve."

"So young!"

He nodded. "They were my world, and watching them succumb to their illness felt like watching everything I knew crumble around me. I'm not sure I have ever felt whole since."

"Is that why you write to your housekeeper?"

"Yes. She cared for me until I came of age, and now I care for her. She is too old to work, so I do what I can to ensure she has what she needs."

Emma's heart ached for him. He had been on his own for so long, and suddenly she felt as if every one of his smiles was a miracle unto itself. How could she have misjudged him so thoroughly? Wrapping her hand around his wrist, she fought to find some sort of comfort she could offer. "*You* are an impossibly good man, Nick Forester," she whispered.

For several seconds, Nick's eyes remained fixed on her fingers. When he looked up to meet her gaze, there was something so vulnerable about his expression, like he was choosing to lay down every facade he had used to protect himself over the years and show her his barest self.

"Emma," he breathed.

"I am ready, miss!" Jenny's voice echoed down the corridor.

Before Emma could pull away, Nick put his hand over hers and held her in place, though his expression became guarded again. As Jenny approached, he shifted Emma's hold so her arm looped through his, and then he gave her a smirk.

"You do know we are going to cause quite a stir, walking together," he said as he led the way outside, Jenny a few paces behind them. "The *ton* is convinced we are enemies after you so thoroughly cut me down."

Emma winced. "Have I apologized for that yet?"

"You have."

But not enough. "Nick, I—"

He clicked his tongue, pulling her closer against him as they walked. Emma didn't mind, as his body protected her from the day's chill. And perhaps she enjoyed being this close to him. "None of that. I told you there was some good to come out of my fall from the sky, and I meant it."

She wanted to believe him, but that didn't lessen the guilt she still felt. From the moment she'd destroyed his reputation, he had been nothing but kind to her, and she wasn't sure she could say the same of herself. The longer they went on, the more she wondered if she was on the wrong side of this battle.

Unsure what she could say, she remained quiet until they reached Hyde Park. She hadn't been here since the day she was forced into going to Almack's, and everything looked different. Or perhaps it simply *felt* different. "The last time we were here together, you thrust Sir Thomas at me," she said.

Nick laughed. "The poor man never stood a chance. I don't think I've met anyone near as dull, but I wish him all the best."

As her eyes locked on a couple walking up ahead, Emma joined in his laughter and nodded toward them. "You may not have to wish for long."

Squinting, Nick stared at the pair as if he couldn't believe his eyes. "Is that Sir Thomas with Miss Weston?"

"She seems to be having a marvelous time." Emma couldn't decide whether the young woman was truly enjoying the conversation or was simply interested in Sir Thomas's apparent fortune, but both individuals looked rather happy. "I suppose there is someone out there for everyone."

"I'll believe that when I experience it myself," Nick replied. Something about his tone had Emma wondering if he really meant what he said, but he continued speaking before she could find a way to ask. "Do you see that lady up ahead? With the mauve dress?"

"Miss Lancaster?" Emma had met her only once and knew very little about her.

Nick nodded, a thoughtful look on his face. "I considered courting her until I realized she had a deep affinity for animals, and I cannot abide dogs. They make me sneeze."

Emma wasn't entirely sure why he would tell her that, but she enjoyed learning more about him. "Is it true you have considered nearly every woman in London?"

"Oh, don't say it like that," he groaned, though he didn't seem too put out. "You make it sound as if I've broken more hearts than I can count."

"Haven't you? Before I came along, it seemed any eligible lady would have gladly become your wife, yet none of them did."

"And then there was you. Emma Mackenzie, the only woman immune to my charms."

Snickering, Emma shook her head. Despite her first impression, she had, in fact, been somewhat taken in by his smile and wit when they'd met again in the corridor of Harstone Court. Had the inheritance never existed, she likely would have fallen for him weeks ago.

"Now you just sound boastful," she said, knocking her shoulder into his. "But I must know—what was your reason for turning down Miss Thurley?" She nodded toward the woman in question, who walked with her mother up ahead.

Nick crinkled his nose. "She was too happy."

"Too *happy?*"

"Yes, too happy. She sees the good in everything and everyone. I never would have been able to sulk if I married her, and I am quite fond of sulking."

Oddly, Emma could imagine him sitting in front of a fireplace, grumbling away after a long day of being cheerful and carefree. It was the same reason she enjoyed reading a book at the end of the day or telling an adventurous story to the girls. A way to express her frustrations without letting them build up inside her.

Eager to learn more, she pointed to the next couple ahead of them. "What of Lady Huntingdon? Did you pursue her before she married?"

Nick choked on his laughter, which drew the attention of *Lord* Huntingdon. He gave Nick a proper scowl before directing his much more pleasant wife to give Nick and Emma a wide berth as they passed. Emma had never met the earl, but she'd had a conversation or two with Lady Huntingdon back during her Season, when the woman was still Lady Marian and they were both newly out.

"I'd thank you not to put me on the Elusive Earl's list of enemies," Nick said with mock fear. "That man has never liked me." He glanced behind them, then genuinely winced when he realized Lord Huntingdon had done the same.

Emma met Lady Huntingdon's gaze, and the pair of them burst into laughter before directing their companions to keep walking rather than glare at each other. "I take it you did *not* take an interest in her."

"I might have hoped to dance with her once," Nick admitted warily, "but I could see as well as anyone that Huntingdon had already laid his claim. The man may be a mystery in everything else he does, but not when it comes to how he feels about his wife."

Emma had to wonder whether Nick would be the same way if he ever married. Would he scowl at anyone who came close to his wife? Or would he watch her dance with others with awe, as if he couldn't believe he was the one lucky enough to keep her when the dance was over?

Shaking away an image of being returned to Nick's side for the rest of her life, Emma forced her attention on the couple approaching them now. "And what of her?"

Nick stopped dead, his face going slack. He seemed to search the park for a way to escape, but the couple were too close, and the woman had noticed him, her eyes going wide. "Lord Hayworth," Nick said when the couple arrived. His voice came out strangled and smaller than Emma had ever heard it. "My lady. Congratulations on the birth of your son last month."

Lord Hayworth gave a reluctant bow, his jaw tight.

Lady Hayworth smiled, though nothing about her expression seemed happy. "Thank you, Mr. Forester. You are looking . . . well."

Emma gave his arm a squeeze, unsure what to do. He was clearly uncomfortable, standing stiff and tense beside her.

He gave her half a glance but nothing more. "May I introduce Miss Emma Mackenzie? Miss Mackenzie, Lord and Lady Hayworth."

"*Miss* Mackenzie." Lady Hayworth barely sank into a curtsy, her gaze sharp before turning back to Nick. "So the rumors are true? You are still searching for a wife."

Nick winced but said nothing.

"That must be quite the strain on your finances, not earning that precious inheritance of yours."

Whoever this woman was, Emma did not like her one bit. She seemed to willfully ignore every bit of politeness required in a conversation, as if she thought herself so far above Nick and his circumstances. Lord Hayworth—he now seemed fascinated by a duck in the Serpentine and ignored the conversation entirely—may have been a nobleman, but Emma had yet to see anything noble about his wife.

"It is only a matter of time," Emma said, drawing closer to Nick and putting on her sweetest smile. "I should count myself lucky that Mr. Forester hasn't settled before now, or I might not have had the chance to come to know the incredible man that he is. I have never met his equal."

She could feel Nick staring at her, but she couldn't seem to stop talking.

"Besides," she continued, "I believe you were misinformed, Lady Hayworth. Mr. Forester is far from purse-pinched. How could he be, living in Mayfair? In fact, he has been the talk of London since I arrived, and I am still bewildered that he chose to take me out today when he could have had his choice of lady. It is a pity you are already married, or I am sure he would happily consider you. You must be of the highest of the Quality to be his friend."

Lady Hayworth gaped at her as if she never would have thought someone would talk to her so boldly, and Emma felt rather proud of herself, until Nick leaned in close and muttered, "We should be going, my dear. His Grace is expecting us."

Though she shivered from his breath on her neck, she played along, sensing his wish to end this conversation. "Oh yes, I would hate to keep the duke waiting again. Do excuse us, Lady Hayworth. It was a pleasure to have met you after hearing so much about you from Mr. Forester. Perhaps you and I could get to know one another better, seeing as you are such a close acquaintance of his. I was thinking of hosting tea with Lady Harstone and Lady Huntingdon this week. Oh! But you would fit right in, being Lady Hayworth. All the Ladies H. in one place."

Nick tugged on her arm, nearly pulling her off her feet as she fumbled through a farewell, and he didn't slow his pace until they were well out of earshot of the lord and lady. "You, my darling, are completely mad." He said that with a wide grin, as if he couldn't believe his good fortune in having a ridiculous friend like Emma.

"I didn't like the way she spoke to you," Emma explained. "You seemed in need of your own rescue this time."

Nick glanced behind them, where Jenny dutifully followed, and met the maid's eye. "What did you think? Was I lucky to have made it out of there alive?"

Emma smacked his arm when Jenny turned bright red. "You don't have to answer that, Jenny," she said.

"Unless you wish to praise your lady," Nick added with a wink.

To Emma's surprise, Jenny cleared her throat and mumbled, "Miss Emma was right to stand up for you, sir."

"Ha! You *were* in need of rescue." Emma grinned, feeling a bit like laughing even though she had made a fool of herself with Lady Hayworth. But what did it matter? She hardly cared about the opinion of a woman she would likely never see again. Beyond Emma's family, the only person whose opinion mattered to her was Nick.

That idea was rather frightening, and she wasn't brave enough to consider just how deep that sentiment lay. And yet, as they continued their walk, Emma couldn't help but wonder what it would be like to be more than just a tentative friend to Nick. What if they were more than friends entirely?

Chapter Thirty

"Tell me more about this suitor you have in mind for me." They had been walking in companionable silence for several minutes when Emma blurted that out, when she couldn't hold it in anymore. Since their encounter with Lady Hayworth, she hadn't been able to stop thinking about what it might be like to truly be promised to Nick, and she needed something to distract herself. "What makes you so certain he and I would suit?"

Though he stared at her in surprise for a few seconds, he nodded once and then swallowed. "He understands your need for independence and would never make decisions for you."

"That I cannot believe. No man in his right mind would yield to his wife like that."

"I would. I've been beholden to other people for most of my life, and I know exactly how that feels. I wouldn't wish that on anyone."

Her heart blossomed at that, though she wished it wouldn't. Even though she knew he would never accept her, not after everything she had done to him, he was proving that such a man could exist. If Nick possessed all the qualities she would want in a husband, someone else could as well. Perhaps things were not as hopeless as they appeared and both of them could get the life they wanted in the end.

But first, she needed to know more. "Does this man enjoy reading?"

Nick thought about that. "I suppose, though he finds oral storytelling far more fascinating. There is something to be said for the magic of a performance, wouldn't you say?"

"And what of dancing?"

"Tolerates it. But he prefers conversation."

"His favorite food?"

That got a glorious laugh out of him. "You expect me to know every detail about this man? You must think I never leave his side."

"Well, that is certainly untrue, or he would be here right now. When am I going to meet this apparent embodiment of perfection?"

Emma wasn't sure if she imagined it or not, but Nick seemed to blush, his ears turning pink as he kept his eyes on the path ahead. "When he is ready, Emma. He has some things to work out first."

What was that supposed to mean? "How mysterious. But he knows of me?"

"He has never been more interested in a person than he is in you."

Though a part of her wondered if this man truly existed, Emma couldn't help but hope he wasn't merely a creation of Nick's imagination. After her conversation with Tabitha last night, she wanted to try to overcome her aversion to love and give herself a chance to find the kind of happiness Nick had been hunting for for years. If he believed so strongly in love, surely she could do the same.

"What will you do if this doesn't work?" she asked quietly, holding tighter to his arm, as if that might stave off her nerves. "If I can't fall in love with the man, and you don't find a woman to marry, what will you do? You've been searching for so long." And why did she get the feeling that Lady Hayworth was the reason for Nick's perpetual bachelorhood? It was as if with one disgusted sneer from her, he'd lost all sense of confidence.

When he gave no sign of answering her question, she was tempted to ask another. "Nick . . ."

He let out a deep sigh. "You want to ask about Lady Hayworth," he guessed. "I knew you wouldn't be able to last long."

"You don't have to tell me about her."

"Yes, I do."

Emma had been hoping he would say that. "Who is she?"

Clenching his jaw, Nick didn't respond until they had walked several paces. "She was to be my wife," he said, ducking his head when Emma gasped. "Three years ago. Lady Lavinia, as she was then, and I were engaged to be married. I loved her, or so I thought, and I considered myself to be the most fortunate man in the world when she consented to our marriage. Lavinia was every woman's idol, and I was the envy of every bachelor in London."

Emma could feel the growing tension in his arm, but she had to know more. "What happened?"

Nick scrubbed his jaw. "We attended Almack's together not long before the banns were to be read, and I found her outside with her now-husband. It was clear she had not been brought there by force."

"Oh, Nick."

He shook his head, coming to a pause and waiting until he was sure no one was around to hear him. "I broke off the engagement, hoping it would be a quiet affair with little fanfare. Hurt though I was, I had no desire to drag her through the mud. But this is London." He glared at the crowded park around them, as if all its visitors might feel the same pain Emma did as she listened to him. She wanted to hold him, comfort him, but she couldn't do that here.

"Society cannot keep to their own business," Nick growled, "even if their lives depend on it. All anyone could talk about was how I'd coldly abandoned my betrothed, leaving her to ruin without provocation. And I refused to let them speak of things they should not."

Emma's eyes went wide. "The rumors," she guessed.

Nick nodded. "I started spreading lies far more interesting than my failed engagement, not knowing how quickly they would take root. It didn't take long for me to realize how easily I could hide behind the untruths, and I started lying to myself as well, telling myself that I far more enjoyed playing Society's games than being the man I truly am."

"And then I came and exposed you all over again." Oh, she was a horrible person. If she had known . . . if she had known from the beginning, would she have done anything differently? Or would she still have told herself that Nick deserved everything that had happened to him? She likely would have believed the rumors instead of believing the man himself, and that made her feel awful.

He took her hands, bringing them up to his lips and offering a gentle smile that made her heart melt. "You freed me, dear Emma. You have no idea what that means to me."

A shiver ran through her that had nothing to do with the chill of the day. This could not be the look of an indifferent man, so why was he trying so hard to find her someone else? Why couldn't he just offer up himself? She supposed there was always the chance that he was trying to trick her somehow, to make her fall for him so he could take the inheritance that way. But Emma didn't want to believe that. She wanted to believe Nick was as good a man as he had shown her he was the last few days.

"We should get you home, miss," Jenny said, reluctance wobbling in her voice. Or perhaps that was because she was shivering as she stood there. Her hopeful smile as she looked at the pair of them seemed to indicate that she wanted this match as much as Emma was starting to want it.

Chuckling to himself, Nick tucked Emma's arm through his again. "Yes, I wouldn't want either of you to freeze out here. Besides, we have a duke to visit."

Emma grimaced. "Please tell me that was only a means to end the conversation."

"You don't wish to meet a duke?"

"I've already met one. I was unimpressed."

Laughing, he pulled her closer against his side as he guided her back home, and she was grateful for the extra warmth. A brisk wind had picked up, leaving her shivering as well. "You are the strangest woman I have ever met."

"I choose to take that as a compliment."

"You should. Your unwillingness to be like the rest of the painted peacocks is rather refreshing."

"Do you really think so?"

"I would never lie to you, Emma."

She actually believed him, which should have surprised her. But it didn't. For all his lies over the last few weeks, he had spoken nothing but truth when it came to the important things. Now that she was beginning to know him, she understood what Catherine had meant when she'd said it was easy to tell when he was being genuine.

"And what of my future husband?" Emma asked, testing him. "Would he agree with you?"

Nick paused, as if he really had to think about that question. "That I cannot say. But you are clever enough to recognize when a man doesn't deserve you. I have no doubts that whether you choose to accept the man I have in mind for you, you will never allow yourself to be diminished."

As her heart warmed the rest of her, Emma badly hoped her suspicions were correct and this mysterious man wasn't real. She hoped Nick could love her the way she was more and more certain she was beginning to love him.

When they reached Harstone House, Nick pressed a kiss to her hand at the door, lingering there until Emma felt as if she might burst. And then she watched him go, wishing she never had to say goodbye to Nick Forester.

Chapter Thirty-One

When a man received a summons from Mr. Mackenzie, he answered it. Though Nick had no idea why Emma's grandfather had suddenly decided to come to London so close to winter, he knew better than to ignore the request to meet with him. Not that Nick had any intention of ignoring it in the first place; any excuse to see Emma was one he would gladly take.

He hadn't wanted to leave her yesterday. After their walk, his heart was telling him she felt at least a portion of the affection he felt for her, and that had given him hope that all was not lost. Just a little more time, and he would hopefully be able to show her that he would give her everything she wanted if it meant he could have her love.

By the time he reached Harstone House, he was practically brimming with anxious energy. The butler directed him right to the library, and every step he took felt heavier than the last, until he finally arrived at the fire-warmed library and sank into a chair without any decorum. After a fitful night of dreaming about Emma, he was too tired to pretend he had any desire for pleasantries.

"You summoned me?"

Mackenzie chuckled, his hands on the top of his cane as he studied Nick from his own armchair. "I see you're still without a wife, Nicholas."

"Not for lack of trying," Nick grumbled. "It has not even been three weeks since we last spoke."

"And yet you have only three weeks remaining."

"At this point, I almost need a special license to be married by your deadline." But that didn't matter, because Nick knew Emma would never trust him enough in such a short amount of time. That notion had pervaded his thoughts all night. "I need more time."

Mackenzie studied him, his eyes sharp. He had always been a perceptive man, but Nick had always hidden as much as he could from him. He hated relying so heavily on someone who owed him nothing, and yet Mackenzie had always insisted on providing him funds and the promise of an inheritance. "Do you know why I put you in my will, Nicholas?"

Nick clenched his jaw. "Because you loved my father." He had heard the reason many times.

"My son, Matthew, was always headstrong and reckless," Mackenzie said, and Nick sat up straighter.

He had *not* heard this part, and he was eager to learn more about Emma's father. What sort of man could abandon his wife and children?

"I tried to teach him to be a good man," Mackenzie continued, "but there was always something wild about him. It was a part of him that he didn't want to let go, no matter how many people told him he should. One summer, he brought home a schoolfellow who couldn't have been more different from him. Anthony Forester had a good head on his shoulders and, more importantly, a good soul."

Nick swallowed the emotion that always crept up when he thought about his parents. He had marveled at the fact that he had been able to tell Emma about them yesterday with little issue, but he could barely hold back his misery today.

Mackenzie kept talking, either oblivious to Nick's tears or unconcerned by them. "Anthony didn't have a good father, something I learned fairly quickly, and he begged me to teach him how to run an estate. He spent hours every day at my side, while Matthew ran about the county, wasting time and playing with girls' hearts. Anthony came to Tutbury every holiday after that, always eager to learn more and become a better man.

"The day he met your mother was the day I knew without a doubt that he had become an admirable man. He wanted to give her the world; I'd never seen such love before. It was as if she had brought light into his life where there had been none before. I had never seen two people more compatible than those two, like they had been created to be two halves of a whole. And then they were blessed with a child, and Anthony begged me to look after his son should anything happen to him. I, of course, agreed without hesitation. He wanted for his child the same happiness that he had found, just as I did."

Nick didn't know what to say. He didn't know if he *could* say it even if he knew. His parents had told him their love story so many times, but a part of him had always wondered how much of the magic was real. Knowing that someone else had seen their love just as strongly somehow made it more tangible, and he swallowed the emotion that sat thick in his throat. That was all he wanted. A love so strong that it couldn't be denied.

"I need more time," he choked again.

"You have had more than eno—"

"I'm in love with Emma." As soon as those words flew from his mouth, he flinched, sinking deeper into his chair. Mackenzie watched him without speaking a word, his expression unreadable, and Nick could hardly stand the silence. "I am *desperately* in love with her," he continued. "I don't know how it happened, or when, but my heart is irrevocably lost to that blasted headstrong woman, and I *need more time.*"

Pursing his lips, Mackenzie seemed to study Nick for nearly a full minute, as if searching his face to see if he was speaking the truth. "She didn't mention a word about you last night when I arrived."

Nick's heart fell, though he tried not to read too much into Emma's silence. What reason would she have to talk about him? "I haven't told her how I feel."

"Why not?"

"Because . . ." How could he explain? "Because I treated her terribly when we met. This inheritance made us enemies, and we fought bitterly until I realized . . ."

"You're in love with her," Mackenzie finished calmly.

"Yes. And I have little hope that she feels the same, but I am trying. I need more time."

"You've said." He waved to a footman who stood by the door, catching his attention. "Some tea, I think. And call for Miss Mackenzie."

Nick shot up to his feet. "What? Why?" The footman was already gone, but Nick was not opposed to chasing him down and giving him different orders.

"Because you look like you could use some tea," Mackenzie replied. *"Sir."*

"Will you sit, boy? I am not going to confess your feelings for you."

That didn't make Nick feel any better, and the only reason he returned to his chair was because he felt as if his legs might give out beneath him. "You expect *me* to tell her how I feel? Here, with no preamble?"

The old man looked far too amused for the situation. At least Nick could assume he approved of the match, but that hardly made the circumstance any less mortifying. "I expect you to take control of your life, Nicholas. You have been living in fear for too long. Ah, Emma, you look lovely this morning."

Nick leaped to his feet again as Emma stepped into the library far too soon. His tongue felt like lead in his mouth, his knees wobbling, and a part of him was tempted to flee before he did as Mackenzie intended and confessed everything. The only reason he remained was because he couldn't stand the thought of leaving her now that he'd seen her. She truly was lovely, standing there in a pale-blue morning dress that brought out the pink in her cheeks and made her eyes look like the stormy ocean.

Blue had always been her color.

"You called for me, Grandfather?"

"Have a seat, Emma."

As she settled herself on the sofa between their chairs, Emma met Nick's gaze and seemed to be asking him a question to which he didn't have the answer. Mackenzie was up to something, but unless he found some way to force Nick to admit his feelings, Emma would remain in the dark for now.

"Is everything well, Grandfather?" Emma asked, her words timid. "You didn't say last night why you came to London."

"I have been hearing some concerning reports," Mackenzie said.

She glanced at Nick again, but now he *really* didn't know what was happening. "About what?"

"About the two of you."

Swallowing, Nick clenched his hands in his lap. Had their battle been spreading across the country? Or was this something else? Mackenzie hadn't seemed surprised about Nick's admission of love. Did he already know? But how? Nick had only just realized it himself.

"What sort of reports?" Emma asked, her voice thin.

Mackenzie harrumphed. "It seems neither of you have been trying very hard to find yourselves spouses, which leaves me in a difficult position. Your deadline is fast approaching, and yet I have nowhere to leave my assets."

Nick met Emma's gaze, frowning when she turned pink. She was under the same marriage constraints as he was! Why, then, had she been fighting so hard to remain single if that would leave her unable to inherit? He could only assume her reasoning was the same as his: a marriage without love would cost more than what the Mackenzie estate was worth.

"Grandfather," Emma said weakly. "I am nearly twenty-one. I thought perhaps I wouldn't have to—"

"You have known the terms of my will from the start," Mackenzie said sharply. "If you do not procure yourself a partner, I cannot in good conscience leave everything to you without fearing it will be taken from you."

As tears filled Emma's eyes, Nick barely restrained himself from slipping over to the sofa and pulling her into his arms. She must have been so certain that Mackenzie would change the rules as soon as she came of age, but the old man was clearly too stubborn to see that his granddaughter didn't need anyone by her side to thrive. He understood, in part, Mackenzie's fears—the law was not always kind to women—but what good did it do to set a deadline neither of them could meet? Yes, Nick knew next to nothing about running an estate, so having someone by his side to talk things through made sense. Nick had seen how much confidence and fresh perspective Calloway's wife gave him. But Emma? She could probably run that estate with her eyes closed.

Blast it all, why had it taken him this long to see how perfect she was for him? If only he had swallowed his pride and tried to court her instead of going to battle.

Emma didn't seem to breathe as she stared at her grandfather, as if everything inside her had fallen apart and left her empty. "You're giving me less than a month to find a husband I do not despise," she whispered. "A month for a man to claim everything that is mine, or I get nothing."

"Correct."

Did the man not see the reason for Emma's tears? The very light had gone out of her. It was as if Mackenzie had lost his mind, and Nick wanted to shout at him. Curse him. Throw a fist into his old and wrinkled face because this was going to help *nothing*. Was this his way of forcing Nick into revealing everything? Emma wouldn't consider his declaration a relief but a slap in the face. She would think he meant to marry her only to take everything for himself, because he had hardly given her many reasons to trust him.

"Do not be so dramatic, child," Mackenzie said as he struggled to his feet. "I will oversee the marriage settlement myself and ensure you are well taken care of."

"Assuming I have a groom," Emma mumbled, and then she turned her teary gaze to Nick, all of her desperation shining in her eyes.

He knew what she was asking. She was asking if this mysterious suitor he had invented was still an option. And, coward that he was, he nodded.

"You should rest, sir," Nick said through clenched teeth, helping Mackenzie to the door. "You clearly have some big decisions ahead of you, and we wouldn't want you to overexert yourself."

The old man paused just beyond the doorway, still as calm as ever. "I know my granddaughter," he said, his voice a soft rumble. "And I know what Matthew's actions did to her. Her mother raised her well, but Emma has always been afraid to make attachments."

"I know this already," Nick growled.

"What you do not know is how perfectly suited the two of you have always been. The older she got, the more I came to realize that you and Emma would make a good match. Far more than that Lady Lavinia would have."

Nick frowned as he processed that thought. "You thought we should be together?"

"Why do you think I enlisted Lord Harstone to ensure you spent as much time with Emma as possible? Why do you think he invited you to stay with him in Staffordshire in the first place?"

"You enlisted . . ." Nick shook his head, feeling off-balance. "But why did you never say?"

"Because you were both too stubborn to accept the truth if I had come right out and told you. You had to come to that conclusion yourselves."

"I suppose you are right." Nick groaned, glancing back at Emma. She sat stiff-backed and shaking, not yet letting her tears fall, though she seemed on the edge of breaking. "This is precisely why I asked for more time."

"But *I* do not have time." Mackenzie sighed, leaning heavily on his cane. "I am old, Nicholas, and I am tired. I can feel my end coming, and I wish to see my girl happy and cared for while I still can. I wish to see you *both* happy and cared for. Please."

Nick clenched his hands at his sides, but he could hardly argue against something like that. "You haven't told her you're dying," he said, not needing confirmation. "Losing you will break her."

Mackenzie's eyes were sad as he peered back into the room, like he was getting his fill. "I need to know she will have someone to hold her together when I am gone. Marriage will ensure she doesn't lose what I have given her."

Nick considered his words carefully. "You are leaving it all to her regardless," he guessed. That filled him with some measure of relief.

But Mackenzie shook his head. "No."

"Why not?"

"Because I fear it would all be taken from her, just as I have told her many times. Everything will go to Lord Harstone, who I am certain will give her full autonomy of the place."

That was almost as good as leaving it to her directly. "Why wouldn't you tell her as much?"

"Because my granddaughter is more stubborn than you are, something I never thought I would say. I couldn't bear the thought of her being alone the rest of her life, and I fear the only way to get her to see reason and find a partner is to force her hand. Otherwise, she will see no need and never allow herself to be cared for as she deserves." The old man smiled a little, though it was colored with sadness. "I need her to be happy, Nicholas, and I know you can make her happy. You already have."

"I'm not so certain of that," Nick muttered. "I've done everything wrong."

"The granddaughter who greeted me last night was so much brighter—stronger—than the woman who left Staffordshire a fortnight ago." Putting on a smile, Mackenzie patted Nick's shoulder. "She may not realize it yet, but she is mad about you, my boy. She only needs a little push."

"I hope you're right," Nick muttered. "I am not sure she will ever trust me."

Mackenzie sighed, patting Nick's arm. "You do not give yourself enough credit. With the way you've commanded the attention of England for the past three years, I am certain you will think of something. You have so much of your father in you, my boy. In the best way. Let Emma see that side of you, and you will have nothing to fear."

Nick swallowed. "Thank you," he said, knowing those words hardly encompassed everything he owed to the man. "For Emma's sake, I hope you are wrong about the time you have left."

"As do I," Mackenzie agreed, and then he shuffled off.

Someone would be arriving with tea shortly, but for the time being, Nick and Emma could be alone. He would have to use that to his advantage. When he stepped back into the library, Emma looked up at him. One tear slipped down her cheek, and that was enough to propel him forward and scoop her into his arms in an embrace.

She melted into him as she broke into sobs, pressing her face into his cravat. Closing his eyes, he sat beside her and held her tight. He wanted to tell her everything—how he felt about her, her grandfather's fading energy, Harstone's part in the inheritance—but he could see why he couldn't. She was still so afraid of being left behind, and she needed someone she could trust with her whole heart to never leave her.

She barely knew Nick, and he needed to change that. As quickly as he could. How had Shakespeare put it? *To thine own self be true.* Nick hoped the Bard knew what he was talking about.

"How could he do this to me?" Emma moaned into his shoulder, trembling in his arms. "What reason could he have to ruin my chances without considering my happiness?"

"They're not entirely ruined," Nick murmured. Though he hated the reason behind his current situation, he couldn't help but cherish the way he was able to hold her, like he was the only thing keeping her in one piece. If only he could hold her like this always.

Her future was secure no matter what happened, but Emma would never be content if her brother-in-law owned what she so desperately wanted. What if she started to resent Harstone? What if she felt so betrayed by her family that she left them behind? She would be more alone than ever, and that would break her heart into pieces.

Nick feared she would give up on love entirely if he didn't convince her to take him before the deadline arrived.

"Who could possibly want to marry me in such a short space of time, Nick?" Emma whispered into his shoulder. "You heard Grandfather. *Married.* Not engaged. Unless I somehow procure a special license or run away to Gretna Green, that gives me less than a week to convince someone to propose. You've won. Exactly as he wanted you to."

Clenching his jaw, Nick silently prayed that he could do right by this woman. She had already dismissed him as an option on the first day they met, and he knew she would have to choose him. He only prayed that he could show her enough of his heart for her to see the man he hoped he could be. The man who would love her for all that she was. He had to prove to her that he would never be like her father.

He took a slow breath, holding it in his lungs as he tried to be brave. "I haven't won just yet." When she tensed in his arms, he wondered what that meant. "You forget that no woman has agreed to marry me. Besides, you still haven't met your mystery suitor."

Forcing a breath, Emma sat back and shook her head. "Surely you, of all people, should understand that if I am going to subject myself to a union such as marriage, I require love. I will not give myself to a man with anything less."

He did understand, and if she could only believe him if he told her how he felt about her . . . if he could only find the courage to offer up his heart right now despite the risk of it being broken . . . "All is not lost. I cannot bring him to you yet, but he can write to you."

She scoffed. "Write to me? And if anyone should discover us? I will *not* be the subject of scandal."

Nick couldn't help but smile a little. "Oh, it is not so bad," he said, taking hold of one of her hands. "I rather enjoyed my first year of scandal."

Thankfully, she laughed a little through her tears. "You are unique among men, Nick Forester."

"I should hope so. And this man I have for you is just as singular. Trust me when I say he knows my opinion of you and could easily fall in love with you if given the chance. Do you?"

She sniffled. "Do I what?"

"Trust me?" Though he had already asked that question the other night, he needed to know if this would even work. He had plenty of practice in writing his thoughts to those he cared about, but never had he been unsure if the recipient shared his regard. Calloway and Harstone were stuck with him, and Mrs. Murray thought of him like a son. But Emma? He lifted her hand to his lips before pressing a kiss to her forehead because he wanted more. Emma could be his undoing. "I promise you will get your happy ending, my darling. Without scandal. Do you believe me?"

As she gripped his hand between both of hers, she seemed to be searching his face for something. She must not have found it, because she wilted. "Do I have any other choice?"

That question put a crack in the hope that surrounded his heart. But no matter. He still had a few days to show her who he really was. He barely had half a plan, but it would have to be enough for him to prove his love and earn hers in return.

"Do not lose hope yet, dear Emma. I will take my leave of you and return with a secret letter."

He paused in the doorway and looked back, meeting Emma's gaze. She looked at him as if he were all she had left, and it gave him courage. Maybe they both could win after all.

Chapter Thirty-Two

EMMA STARED AT THE LETTER on her vanity like it might fall apart if she touched it. Nick had brought it last night when he'd joined the family for dinner, slipping it to her in secret and reminding her that she couldn't allow anyone to see it. Particularly because she had never met the man who wrote it, she was putting herself in far more danger than Catherine had in writing to Elias, which was bad enough.

Her cousin had come to London with Grandfather, and in the brief moments they had had a chance to talk, he had made it quite clear that he intended to court Miss Barton under the watchful gaze of Alvaro as her temporary protector. He told Emma that he had already written to Mr. Barton to express his intentions, and he and Catherine had hardly left each other's sides since his arrival.

Emma hadn't even noticed them connecting in Tutbury; she had been so completely focused on Nick and their feud.

She was still focused on Nick, but her heart felt torn in two now that she had tangible evidence of the mysterious suitor. This letter was everything she could have wanted and more, and yet a part of her wished he hadn't written so eloquently.

A part of her wished *Nick* had written it.

If she was being honest with herself, she hadn't fully discounted the idea that Nick himself *was* the mysterious suitor. Though she didn't know why he would play such a game, it wouldn't surprise her to learn that he was the man behind such beautiful words. Alvaro had said Nick was fond of writing letters, but what would Nick's motive be in concocting such a scheme?

She picked up the letter, reading again the lines that had her so torn.

To the lovely and illustrious Emma,

May I call you Emma? I know this situation is hardly conventional, and should this letter fall into the wrong hands, it could lead to your downfall, so using your name is dangerous. That is a lot of trust to put into someone, and I am honored that you would trust me without knowing my name. But to call you anything other than what you are feels as if I am trying to change something about you, which is far from my intention.

As I understand it, you are in need of a husband in order to receive an inheritance. Rest assured, no matter the outcome, I will be discrete and tell no one of your circumstances. Ladies already have little enough freedom, and I have no desire to make things worse for you. As it so happens, I am in need of a wife, though I have nothing to add to your impending fortune. In the spirit of honesty, I have little to my name beyond what I carry in my mind and my heart. I would be relying entirely on your good fortune should we make a match of things. I am not opposed to laboring for my bread, though I admit I have not always been so humble, and you would be required to teach me how to care for an estate, as I have little knowledge of such things. From my understanding, you are more than capable, so I have no fear in that regard. I only wish you to know the full scope of what you would be getting into.

I suppose you would like to know more about me. I can say but little about myself, as there is little to say to begin with, but I was raised by wonderful parents who taught me to value love and partnership above all else in a marriage. I have only ever wanted the same for myself. A husband and wife should be equal, even if most of the world may not agree. I have seen enough happy marriages to know such a life is possible, and therefore I refuse to settle for anything less. Of course, no marriage can be perfect, but from what little I know about you, I fully believe we could come close. Forgive me for such a presumption, but I've been told you are rather pressed for time. You may not agree that we are complements after you meet me, but I am choosing an optimistic approach. If you allow me the honor of assisting you in your future endeavors, I will do everything in my power to see that you have the life you have always dreamed of, however that may look.

To aid in your decision, as I am unable to do more than write to you at present, I offer a list of things I do not especially enjoy: cold weather, too much talking when one is reading, dogs, men who treat women as possessions, boiled turnips, and spending too much time on my own. In contrast, here are a few things I adore: the sun on my face, enjoying a riveting book (or several), cats, women with strong minds, roasted goose, and laughing with a good friend.

As I do not wish to overwhelm you, I will end my list here, though I feel as if I could write to you all the thoughts of my heart and never wonder if they would remain safe with you. Nothing about this situation is ideal, but I promise, Emma, that you and I could make something great if you find it in your heart to accept a man you will, I pray, come to love in time.

For now, know that I have heard enough about you around London to know you are wonderfully friendly and kind, and your spark for life may turn out to be one of my favorite things about you, although, I am sure there are so many qualities to love that I will forever be changing my mind. Ah, there I go, being presumptuous again. Do not pay my eagerness any mind, as this decision is entirely up to you.

I pray with all my heart that I receive an answer from you, dear Emma. Until then, I am yours.

Affectionately,
A man foolish enough to hope

Emma sighed. If this man, who hadn't given his name, was in London, why could they not meet? She would like to put a face to the ideals, if nothing else. At the moment, she was imagining him with Nick's face, and she would be quite disappointed if he didn't turn out to be half as handsome.

She couldn't imagine why Nick would go to all this trouble instead of being forthright when she all but asked him if he could settle for someone like her, which was the reason she was so torn about this whole thing. He had been searching for someone for so long; he must not have seen Emma as an option, or he would have presented his hand as a solution to both of their problems after their conversation with Grandfather. So perhaps he *wasn't* the letter writer.

Oh, but this whole thing was going to drive her mad!

Her finger stroked the edge of the letter, and she knew she needed to respond. There was little time to waste; she wanted to ensure this man, whoever he might be, knew all the particulars of her circumstances before they made any decisions. Namely, how little time she truly had. But what could she say that wouldn't make her sound desperate? She *was* desperate, so perhaps she simply needed to be honest.

By the time she finished her letter—it was far longer than she had intended—she was practically starving, and she barely gave Jenny enough time to put her hair into a quick chignon after she dressed before she scurried down to the breakfast room with the letter tucked into her sleeve. With no address, she wasn't sure how to get it to the man, but she would find a way.

The way presented itself when she reached the breakfast room and found Nick alone, filling a plate with food from the sideboard.

"You're here!" Emma said.

He turned, flashing his brilliant smile. "I have been eating too much of Calloway's food and thought I might spread the—"

Emma rushed over to him, nearly knocking the plate out of his hand as she shoved her letter at him.

Laughing, he held it against his chest like it was precious cargo. "I take it you enjoyed his correspondence?'

"You knew I would."

"I hoped. There's a difference. What did he say?"

She had already shown too much eagerness as it was, so Emma lifted her chin. "Nothing that concerns you."

"And here I was thinking we were friends."

"We *are* friends." Even if Emma wished they were more. Oh goodness, *did* she wish that? She did, and that frightened her as much as it thrilled her. For all their bickering when they met, they really were quite suited to each other.

Placing his food on the table, Nick fingered the letter for a moment with curiosity clear in his eyes.

"Don't you dare think about reading it, Nicholas Forester."

He laughed. "But you gave it to me. And it has no name."

"He didn't give me a name."

"No?" His eyes danced. "That is interesting."

Emma watched him for any sign that he might be the man behind the mystery, like she suspected, but he was too difficult to read this morning.

Nick was his own sort of mystery, and she would be disappointed not to unravel it as well as figure out who seemed so perfect on the page.

"Perhaps you could tell me his name," she said as casually as she could manage. Then she could ask Alvaro about him.

But Nick shook his head as he tucked the letter into his jacket. He was far too amused by this situation, given the circumstances of it all. "Where would be the fun in that, dear Emma? If he has chosen not to tell you his name, he must have a reason. I will take credit for pushing the two of you together, but I will go no further than acting as delivery boy to keep your secret."

This was so confusing! Emma sank into a chair, too caught up in her swirling thoughts to remember that she was hungry. If Nick *wasn't* the mysterious suitor, she would have to wrap her head around the idea of agreeing to marry a stranger without meeting him first. The banns would have to be read for the first time on Sunday to keep a wedding within Grandfather's time line, and that left only three days including today to form an attachment.

If Nick *was* the man who had written the letter, Emma had a lot of conflicting feelings. As much as she hated to think it, there was still the chance it would end up being a manipulation. A way for him to guarantee he could get what he wanted. He could also have genuine affection for her, and that thought filled her with warmth. Two days ago, before their walk, she had been sure he was about to kiss her before he'd stepped away.

Regardless of who had written the letter, Emma knew in her heart that Nick felt some affection for her. She simply wasn't sure how much. Curious, she decided to press for more information.

"Shall I fill a plate for you?" Nick asked, noticing she hadn't done so for herself before she sat.

Emma smiled at him, watching for any sign of a reaction. He seemed more concerned for her well-being than affected by her smile, but that was no matter. "Yes, thank you. I am afraid this whole thing has left me out of sorts."

"I can't imagine how you must be feeling."

She thought carefully about what to say next. "I tried to convince my grandfather to give us more time, but he would have none of it."

That made him pause, a spoon of jam halfway between the bowl and her plate. He seemed to be staring at nothing, his eyes slightly glazed over. "'Us'?"

Emma bit her lips to keep from grinning, though she could do nothing about the warmth that entered her cheeks. "Though, you seem to have given up on wife hunting of late."

The spell breaking, Nick cleared his throat and then set her plate in front of her. "On the contrary," he said, though his words came out sounding hesitant.

Still, Emma didn't like the sound of that. "Oh?"

He fixed on a smile that didn't quite reach his eyes. "Just because I know all about your adventures in love doesn't mean you know of mine."

Her heart sank. "It is going well, then?"

"I'm feeling hopeful." His smile shifted into one more real, making his blue eyes dance while Emma's heart sank.

"Are you?" She tried to sound happy for him, but she didn't manage it very well. She tried again. "You think you have finally found someone worthy of the great Nicholas Forester?"

He chuckled. "I have found someone who makes me want to be the man she thinks I am. She pushes me to be better."

"Oh."

He must have seen her disappointment because he softened and crouched by her side, taking her hand. "If anyone can understand, dear Emma, you can. I could never forgive myself if I didn't fight for the life I want with the woman I love. I am a man of conviction. I don't know what will happen or if she will accept me, but you must know that I cannot in good conscience give up, just as you cannot surrender. We both deserve love, don't we?"

They did, and she couldn't help but smile despite the ache in her chest as she thought about someone else enjoying those smiles of his. "I suppose you are right. I would lose all respect for you if you allowed me to win. Even if I *am* going to win, I expect you to fight your hardest."

"And I will. I know what I want." He hadn't moved, and he watched her with an intensity that had her questioning things again. A man wouldn't look at her like that in the same breath as professing love for someone else, would he? She was hardly an expert in love, but she couldn't stomach the idea of falling for someone else when her heart beat so strongly for him.

Please be the man behind the letter, she silently begged him. If he wasn't, she didn't know what she was going to do.

Chapter Thirty-Three

THE DAY SEEMED BRIGHTER THAN normal as Nick walked along Park Lane, whistling a cheery tune to keep himself from running the whole way back to Calloway's. He had forced himself to remain at Harstone House for at least two hours, during which he'd pretended to listen to Miss Barton explain how she and Mr. Drake had formed a secret attachment in Tutbury. Really, he had been lost in a fantasy, dreaming of telling all his friends about how he and Emma had been so against each other when they were clearly meant to be a match.

He imagined telling their children the story and hearing them laugh every time Nick described the abysmal options he had thrown at their mother in his attempt to get her married off and out of his way, all the while not knowing that that would have earned her the inheritance and left him sunk. Thank goodness she hadn't been inclined to marry for anything less than the deepest love, just like him.

While he'd been at Harstone House, Emma's letter had been burning a hole in his pocket and driving him mad with temptation. She had written far more than he'd expected, which had him desperate to know what was inside. Had she decided it was a terrible idea and told her mystery suitor that they would never work? Nick would gladly argue the point. Had she come up with a secret plan to run away to Scotland and marry the moment they met? That wasn't such a terrible idea. Did she secretly know it was Nick, rather than some stranger, and she had written a whole lecture about deceiving her?

He swallowed as he neared Calloway's Mayfair house. Some of her questions in the breakfast room had made him wonder, and Harstone had been right when he'd said Emma was clever.

What if this ruse would only turn her against him? Nick's cowardice could easily be his downfall.

He wouldn't know until he read the letter, and he picked up his pace, eager to get inside and find some privacy.

"Nicholas?"

Nick didn't have to look behind him to recognize Lavinia's timid voice, and he was tempted to pretend he hadn't heard her. But his feet seemed to have a mind of their own, pulling him to a stop. He was one house away. If he had gone a little faster, he could have avoided her entirely.

Taking a deep breath, he steeled his nerves, then turned. "Lady Hayworth. What a surprise to see you on your own."

She turned pink, still as beautiful as ever. The last three years had been kind to her. "I saw you through the window." She gestured to a house across the street. "Hayworth wouldn't want me talking to you, but . . ."

Nick did his best to keep the growl out of his voice. "Perhaps you should do as your husband says. If you'll excuse me, I have—"

"That woman you were with the other day . . ."

Nick tensed. "What of her?"

"You are aware of what everyone is saying about her, are you not?"

Blast it all, what were they saying now? Nick should have hied himself to White's or ventured out to any soiree he could get into just to see what gossip may have been surfacing after his walk in the park with Emma. A single romp in public shouldn't have been anything worth noting, but Nick had been under so much scrutiny lately that he should have known there was nothing innocent when it came to an association with him.

"Tell me," he commanded, not caring when Lavinia startled at the gruffness in his voice.

She frowned. "I have heard she has been nothing but trouble since the moment she came to London. The hypocrite censures others for listening to gossip, all the while spreading her own lies. Did you know she convinced an entire roomful of ladies to disregard you? Clearly it was so she could try to take your fortune for herself by pretending to be all things good and virtuous."

Nick was clenching his jaw so hard that he wasn't certain it would open again, but he couldn't just stand there and let Lavinia speak of what she didn't know. "Miss Mackenzie's lies have been few and inconsequential, and her measure of me has always been accurate. She would happily live out her life in peace away from all of this nonsense, and I deserve anything she may or may not have said about me." He narrowed his eyes, studying Lavinia. "Why should you care what happens to me, anyway?"

That question seemed to catch her off guard. Or perhaps it was the first part of his response that had her staring at him open-mouthed and pink-cheeked. "I only thought to spare you from the—"

"*Spare me?*" Nick laughed, feeling no humor. "Spare me from what? The rumors? The lies? This *disease* upon Society that has everyone thinking they have the right to be a part of someone else's business simply because they think they know something? You know very well you are the reason I became a puppet of the *ton* when it should have been *you* tied to their strings. Good day, Lady Hayworth."

He took a step to move past her but stopped at the sound of her voice, small and full of shame.

"I'm sorry for what I did to you." She clasped her hands to her chest, her eyes on her shoes. "I never said. And I owe you my thanks for not exposing me when you should have. You took all the blame and made a mockery of your life when it was I who betrayed your trust."

"I wouldn't go so far as to call it a mockery." Nick really didn't want to have this conversation, but the pain in her eyes held him in place. How long had she been holding on to this guilt? Three years? Or had she come to her senses the other day when she'd seen him with another woman? It didn't matter why she had decided to apologize; he was desperate to get away from her and his own pain that was dredged up by the sight of her.

It seemed his broken heart was still damaged, perhaps beyond repair.

"Go back to your husband, Lavinia."

"I don't want to see you get hurt, Nicholas."

"How thoughtful of you, but you're about three years too late." And if she thought he would allow Emma to be ridiculed, she was sorely mistaken. He leaned in close to Lavinia, fixing his gaze on her even if she didn't offer the same courtesy. "If ever you held any affection for me—even if you didn't—please stop talking about Miss Mackenzie. I pulled her into this game when she had no need to play, and I fear I may have ruined everything for her. She doesn't deserve to be whispered about. Not like this." He put his hand over his heart. "I beg of you to help me fix this."

Lavinia peeked up at him. "What do you expect me to do?"

Shaking his head, he wished he had some grand plan to protect Emma from the harsh words she would undoubtedly hear about herself the moment she left the house. If he had still been held in high regard, he could have said anything he wanted about her and be believed. Men far better than him would have seen the incredible woman she was and fallen at her feet. If he tried hard enough, he could have convinced every man in London to give her the money she would need to live out her independent life exactly as she wished, with or without her grandfather's will.

"Lord Hayworth is well-respected and influential," he said, hating the taste of every word. "You are so often at the center of Society, so far above where I ever was. One word from you and Emma would be spared the misery of the life I have lived for the last three years."

Though she seemed to understand what he was saying, she still frowned at him, like his plan would never work. "Her connection to you," she said, cutting herself off and shaking her head. "I am not sure I could save her without ruining you."

For some reason, Nick almost smiled when that thought should have left him dizzy with nerves. "I don't care what happens to me. All of London can despise me for the rest of my life, as long as she never has to bear their scorn." True, he would be a terrible match for her if he sank lower than he already was, but Nick had to hope he was right in thinking Emma wouldn't care where he stood. If she loved him even half as much as he loved her, they could still make a match and get her the life she deserved. He wouldn't even have to stay with her if she didn't want him. He could become her gardener. Her butler. Anything she required, even if she asked him to live out his days on his own pathetic lands. A husband in name only—he would do it.

Shaking his head, he bowed slightly to Lavinia. "Do what you will with my name, Lavinia. I thank you for your apology, but the only thing I care about is Emma's happiness. Good day."

"That Miss Mackenzie seems to understand you in a way I never did. I am glad you found someone who makes you happy. Is she . . . that is to say, are the two of you . . . ?"

"I hope so." That all depended on what was in her letter. "Though, I have no idea why anyone—"

She put her hand on his arm, making him tense and pull away. "You are a good man, Nicholas. And I am certain she knows it. I may have been too much of a coward to marry for love, but Miss Mackenzie seems stronger than I ever was. I hope you have a happy life together. You deserve it, after everything."

Before he could reply, she scurried back across the street and disappeared into her town house, leaving him unsure how to feel. He had always wanted her to admit her fault in their failed engagement, but he felt no satisfaction from her apology.

Perhaps he hadn't needed it in the first place.

Feeling out of sorts, Nick wandered the corridors of Calloway's house with new eyes, like a man who had been so focused on the distant horizon that he hadn't realized just how far he had gone. Less than a month ago he would have given anything for a house like this. For a library stocked with more books than a man could read in his lifetime and servants aplenty and a title and prestige and everything else that came with being a wealthy aristocrat.

He'd wanted the Mackenzie fortune so he could tell the world he meant something and had value.

All this time he had claimed a profound desire to find love, and yet his focus had always been on the fortune.

As he settled in a chair in Calloway's study, Nick considered Harstone's question once more. *"What are you looking for?"* He had told his friend the truth when he'd said he wanted to find love, but he already had it. It coursed through him with every beating of his heart. But he still felt lost and unsure, so there was something still missing from his life. Money—he could earn it. Calloway would happily give him one of his many businesses and teach him how to make it thrive. Family—Harstone and Calloway were as much his brothers as if they had been born of the same mother.

The only thing he truly lacked was Emma's love in return.

Pulling out her letter and breaking the seal, he traced her elegant handwriting as if the lines might guide him in the direction he needed to go. Within these words that he was almost too frightened to read were his hopes and dreams. His future. And there was nothing for him to do but read and hope she was not about to break his heart.

> *To my last hope,*
>
> *I will be direct. I am not accustomed to asking for help, and I dearly wish I didn't have to now, but I must find myself a husband within the week, or I am lost. You are my only chance.*

"Well done, Emma," he breathed, grinning at her tenacity. She was bold for a lady of Society, but he had always liked that about her.

She wrote next about her requirements in a partner—most of them things he already knew—warning him that she would not be one to sit idly by while there was work to be done. Should she inherit the Mackenzie lands as she hoped, she intended to be an integral part of running the estate.

"I would expect nothing less," Nick said, as if she were there to hear him. "I know next to nothing about running an estate, so that will benefit us both."

He had said as much in his letter to her, and he loved that she still set her own expectations. This was the longest part of the letter, as she had a good deal to say about how involved she already was in her grandfather's estate, and Nick had never been more attracted to the woman as she essentially put him in his place for knowing nothing about running an estate. Her strength and confidence were quickly becoming his favorite part of her in a way he never could have expected.

The next part of the letter was softer in tone and included a list of some of her likes and dislikes, just as he had done for her. She seemed more timid about these details, but he drank them in, each one a window into her soul.

> *I suppose you would want to know more details about me before becoming trapped by my awful circumstances, though I don't know what you would most like to know.*
>
> *I enjoy reading novels almost as much as I enjoy telling stories. I hope to build my library over time until my home can no longer contain all the books. Some people may consider that frivolous, particularly when my estate is not especially large, but I like to think a good book is worth every penny. It sounds as if you may feel the same way.*
>
> *I actually like gloomy weather, though a sunny day has its value as well. It depends on the season and my mood.*
>
> *I have three adorable nieces, whom I love dearly, and I desire my own children with my whole soul. Before this necessity, I wasn't certain whether I would have that opportunity, and I pray you hope for children as well. I didn't have a loving father, and perhaps that is common. But could you find it in your heart to love your children, should we have them?*
>
> *Look at me, just as presumptuous as you! I too like roasted goose, though I enjoy turnips as well. I also delight in cats, music, roses, and beautiful bonnets.*

Nick felt like his cheeks might crack from smiling, particularly from her question about children. Could he love them? If only she knew how desperately he wanted a family and always had. Should all of this work out as he hoped, and should they be blessed with children, Nick would be the most loving father in the world. Those children would come second only to Emma.

He treasured every word of the letter, his only regret being the knowledge that he could learn these things face-to-face if he were only brave enough to tell her how deeply he had fallen for her.

But he wasn't brave. His heart was too fragile for him to throw caution to the wind, no matter how much he wished otherwise.

The last bit of the letter caught him by surprise when his name was mentioned.

> *I do not know if you and Mr. Forester are close, but I trust*
> *him wholeheartedly. If he thinks you and I would make a good*
> *match, I am inclined to believe him. I hope you feel the same.*

"You have no idea," he muttered, rubbing his jaw. But then his eyes fell upon the last line of the letter, just before she signed it with her name—simply *Emma*—and his heart constricted.

> *I am running out of time, sir, so if we are to make a match,*
> *we must meet in person before the week's end.*

He blew out his breath in a steady stream, unsure how to react to that. "Wasting no time, I see." He had known a meeting would need to happen, but a part of him had still been hoping for more time. If he wasn't worried that Mr. Mackenzie had less time than he hoped, he would refuse to play the old man's game, but . . . he had seen the look in the man's eyes. Mackenzie was holding on for as long as he could, and Emma needed more than her sister, who had her hands full with her daughters.

Emma needed someone who could hold her steady while she mourned the only father figure she had.

"Well, Emma," he said as he crossed to the writing desk and pulled out a sheet of foolscap, "I hope you will not be disappointed when you learn your mystery suitor is nothing but a liar."

No matter how much it frightened him, it seemed it was time for him to offer his heart and hope he didn't get hurt again.

Chapter Thirty-Four

For perhaps the first time in his life, Nick didn't care one whit what this roomful of people thought of him. He could feel their stares as he paced the length of Lord Norwich's drawing room, and he was certain most of the whispers were regarding him. He didn't care. The only reason he had come to this dinner party was to see Emma and give her his next letter in response to the one he'd received from her at breakfast this morning.

The problem was Emma wasn't here, and he was only able to pace for the span of three minutes before Lady Georgina approached him.

"I haven't seen you out much lately, Mr. Forester," she said after greeting him.

Nick reluctantly kept his feet in one place, forcing a smile. "I've been rather busy of late."

"Yes, so I've heard."

His stomach did a flip. He had quickly grown used to everyone disregarding the rumors about him that he had quite forgotten how it felt to have someone believe something. "And what is it you've heard?" he asked, too curious to make his question more subtle.

Lady Georgina smiled, and there was nothing flirtatious in the gesture. Simply friendliness, something he had experienced little of in the last few years. That made his stomach flip again. What was happening? "I know I shouldn't pay attention to all the gossip, but Lady Hayworth was quite convincing."

Lavinia had actually said something? But what had she said? How brutally had she cut him down to save Emma? Perhaps she hadn't done so at all and had instead chosen to tear them both down.

Though Nick was too stunned to respond, Lady Georgina didn't seem to mind. In fact, her smile grew at his silence, as if he had unknowingly confirmed something. "To think I listened to all that nonsense about you when you were not the cause of any of it. What must you think of me?"

"I don't understand," he finally admitted.

"Lady Hayworth told me about your engagement and how *she* was the one to break it off. To think you took all the blame and suffered the scandal to protect her! I cannot imagine how much that must have pained you."

Nick's jaw dropped, and he suddenly became aware of more people listening to the conversation than he'd realized. Most of the room, in fact. But he couldn't focus on that because he was slowly comprehending what Lady Georgina had just said. Lavinia had told the *truth*? Or at least a version of the truth that painted him in a better light and left *her* looking the fool? Why would she do such a thing?

"I am sorry to have misjudged you," Lady Georgina said, bowing her head.

Nick couldn't find any words, so he simply gawked at her, still trying to understand. Her sentiments seemed to be reflected in everyone else in the room, which made sense. Lavinia had always had a good deal of social influence, even without her husband.

He had to hope Lord Hayworth did nothing to punish her for speaking out, but he wasn't a cruel man. Hayworth may have pursued an engaged woman because her father was an earl, but he had always seemed to carry some measure of affection for her. Otherwise, Nick wouldn't have let her go so easily.

He had loved Lavinia, but the way his heart beat for Emma was so much stronger. Maybe Lavinia had made a match between him and Emma not only possible but ideal. Did Emma feel the same? Nick still didn't know. He wouldn't until he revealed the truth to her.

"I was hoping to make your better acquaintance tonight, but . . ." Lady Georgina smirked at him when his attention snapped back to her, her eyes taking him in from head to toe. "It is clear your affections are already spoken for. I hope she makes you happy, Mr. Forester. I think you, more than anyone, deserve that much."

Nick spent the next twenty minutes surrounded by people wishing to express their apologies for letting gossip get the better of them, and he was almost grateful that when Emma finally arrived with her sister, he couldn't break away to greet her. He needed some time to process this turn of events and wonder what it might mean for his future. It shouldn't have mattered, but regaining his social standing would give him a better chance at giving Emma the life she deserved.

Or maybe she would take it as a sign that they wouldn't suit and he should pursue someone like Lady Georgina, who would enjoy being well-known.

He decidedly did *not* want the latter outcome.

By the time he finally convinced the gentlemen to finish their port after dinner and allow him to break away from the endless conversations they had pulled him into—many of which involved what a catch Emma was—he was more than glad to see Emma sitting on her own. He had half expected her to be surrounded like he had been, given how much everyone was talking about her pleasant personality and clever stories.

Lavinia likely hadn't known about Emma's storytelling, but perhaps she had squashed any negative rumors flying about, leaving room for the good notions to circulate more naturally.

He slid onto the window seat beside her with so much eagerness that he crashed into the glass behind him, but he hardly cared when he was rewarded with a bright smile.

"I was starting to think you had forgotten I existed," she said with a laugh.

"Forget you? Impossible." Oh, he had missed her. He hadn't seen her since this morning, and that was far too long to go without her dimpled smile.

"I see your admirers have returned."

Nick glanced around the room, unsurprised to see several pairs of eyes on the two of them. It felt so familiar, and yet he had realized during dinner that he didn't care whether the *ton* loved him or hated him. The only person whose opinion mattered was right beside him, where she should be. "It seems Lady Hayworth has been working hard to repair what you so happily broke."

Emma snickered. "I know. You think the ladies were talking about anything else? I only just managed to extricate myself before you came out."

"Ah, so I have interrupted your alone time. I should leave you to it." He stood, laughing when Emma grabbed his arm and tugged him back down. But then he turned more serious. If he was going to follow through with his plan, she would forever be tied to his fate. "Are you angry that you've been dragged back into the gossip mill? I can tell them to leave you out of it, though I can't guarantee they will listen to me. I'm rather out of practice when it comes to commanding the crowds."

Narrowing her eyes, Emma gave him a playful shove. "You forget, sir, that I managed to undo what you built in three years with a single conversation. I think if anyone can convince London to leave us alone, it will be me. Besides, I hardly care what they think of me. It won't change who I am."

Lud, he could no longer remember a time when he wasn't madly in love with this woman. Unless he wanted to truly shock Society by kissing her right here and now, he needed to distract himself.

"I have another letter for you," he said, patting his jacket. "Though, I have no idea how to give it to you without anyone seeing."

"I don't care what they see. Give it to me."

Nick raised his eyebrows. "Now? Are you sure? You've seen how quickly word can spread through London, and if anyone thinks you're writing to someone you shouldn't be, you'll be—"

"Forced to wed?" Raising an eyebrow, she held out her hand, palm up. "I don't think my circumstances could be any worse than they already are, do you?"

In all honesty, he would rather she wasn't forced into anything at all, but there was only so much he could control about this situation. He handed her the letter and held his breath as she read.

"Oh," she said when she'd finished.

Of all the times for her expression to be unreadable, it had to be now? "What did he say?"

"He wants to meet at the Bartletts' ball tomorrow." She frowned, making Nick's stomach clench.

"That's a good thing, is it not?" He could barely breathe, wondering why she looked so disappointed. Either she knew it was him and didn't know how to reject him, or she wished it was him and didn't know how to tell her mystery suitor that she was already in love with someone else. Or perhaps he had no idea how to read this woman and he was wrong about everything. That seemed far more likely.

Folding the letter and gripping it between her hands, Emma gazed at it for a long while with a furrowed brow. "What if I meet him and I cannot love him?" she asked quietly.

Then, he will live out his days poor and heartbroken. Nick swallowed. He most assuredly didn't want that outcome, but two letters to the woman hardly counted as building trust. If only he could have been writing to her from the moment he'd met her. "I think he will understand that your duty is to your happiness and nothing else."

Looking up at him, Emma searched his face for a long while before she whispered, "What if he finds he cannot love *me?*" Her voice broke, cracking Nick's heart in the process. It felt almost as if she was asking *him* if he loved her, and he didn't want to learn he was wrong about that assumption.

"My dear, darling Emma," he said as gently as he could, "any man would be a fool not to fall in love with you, and I guarantee this man is no fool. Not in this case, at least." In every other instance, perhaps.

Tears pooled in her eyes as she stared at him. "Are you certain?"

He tucked a stray curl behind her ear, wishing he could hold her and show her how deeply he cared for her. They had already spent too long on their own, and he could see her sister getting anxious as she watched them. "I have never been more certain of anything in my life," he said, and then he reluctantly got to his feet. "Would you like to go home?"

Emma nodded, still clutching the letter like her life depended on it.

With all eyes on him, Nick quietly explained to Lady Harstone that Emma was feeling unwell, and then he offered to escort them both home. Thankfully, Lady Harstone didn't ask any questions, and the three of them were silent until they reached Calloway's. Lady Harstone had pretended to fall asleep on the way—she sat too stiffly for it to be genuine—but Nick appreciated the small bit of privacy regardless.

"Emma," he said, keeping his voice low. "Everything will be all right."

Her eyes traced his face. "Do you promise?"

"Do you trust me?"

"Yes." There was no hesitation in the word this time, which gave him just enough hope to keep going.

Picking up her hand, he brought her fingers to his lips, holding them there, as if he could suspend time with his kiss. "I have some business to attend to tomorrow," he told her, "but I will be at the Bartletts', right by your side. Spend the day with your grandfather and take heart. You will have your happy ending."

As tempted as he was to lean forward and press his lips to hers, he forced himself to instead open the door and step out into the winter chill. He wouldn't be able to sleep a wink tonight, but he hoped he had laid the groundwork well enough. With Emma watching him out the window until the carriage had vanished into the darkness, he had just enough hope to last until tomorrow.

Chapter Thirty-Five

Emma was inordinately nervous, something Elias picked up on immediately upon entering the sitting room where she waited for the rest of the family to be ready for Lord and Lady Bartlett's ball. He had been spending all his time with Catherine, so he and Emma hadn't spoken much since his arrival in Town, but that didn't stop him from sitting beside her now and taking the book out of her hand.

She hadn't really been reading it anyway, so she didn't mind.

"You seem different," he said simply.

Emma laughed once, but she was grateful for an easy way to turn the subject away from herself. "*I'm* different? This morning I saw you laugh so hard that you cried. It's as if you're a different person entirely."

He smiled, the gesture subtler than on most people but far more pronounced than what he usually showed. "I know my affection for Catherine must have surprised you. It surprised me as well, but when Forester said—"

"What?" Emma's jaw dropped, and she grabbed Elias's arm. "What did he say?"

"I haven't decided whether he meant it for my benefit or his own, but back in Tutbury he mentioned how quiet I am and how Catherine needed someone like me, someone content to listen. It got me thinking, and the more I interacted with her, the more I liked her . . . vivacity. It wasn't long before my affections grew beyond curiosity."

"Why didn't you tell me?"

"Why didn't you ask?"

Emma couldn't help but smile. "True. I suppose I am always so focused on myself."

"That isn't what I meant."

"But it is true, nonetheless. Otherwise, I might have realized before I did that Catherine had already given her heart to someone new. I think I've been a terrible friend to her."

Elias took her hand, shaking his head. "You've been the *only* friend to her. She has a good deal of enthusiasm, I know, and most people dismiss her. But what she really needs is someone to listen, just as Forester suggested. To stay by her side. I wanted so badly to write to you and thank you for being that for her, but . . ."

Laughing, Emma squeezed his hand. "But you were too busy with your clandestine courtship through letters."

"How else was I supposed to continue when you stole her away from me?"

"You've surprised me, Elias, falling in love with someone in only a few weeks."

He scoffed. "Hypocrisy if ever I've heard it. You've known Forester for just as long as I've known Catherine."

Emma spluttered. "Mr. Forester? What does he have to do with anything?" She didn't need her cousin to respond, however, and she let out a deep sigh as she pulled the most recent letter from her reticule and handed it to him.

Though he scowled at the sight of it, Elias read quickly, his eyes going wide. "You've planned a secret meeting with Forester tonight?"

"Yes. No. I mean, I *think* it's him, but I'm not certain who I'll be meeting."

"Emma!"

She explained the situation as quickly and succinctly as she could, in case they were interrupted by one of the others. Elias listened in silence, back to being fully stoic, something she both appreciated and hated. It felt good to confide in someone, but she had no idea what he thought of the mess she'd gotten into.

"And the way he looked at me last night, I could have sworn he felt . . ." She was too afraid to put a word to it.

Finally Elias spoke, pulling his eyebrows low. "Of course he feels for you, Emma! Anyone can see the way he looks at you, and I have half a mind to call him out for playing this ridiculous game with your heart."

As much as she hoped he was right, Emma couldn't help but laugh as she imagined her quiet cousin challenging the likes of Nick Forester. "You do know they say he is the best shot in England, don't you? I think a duel between the two of you would result in a heartbroken Catherine."

Elias narrowed his eyes. "Then, I'll challenge him to the sword."

"I guarantee that is a bad idea."

Harrumphing, he pushed to his feet and paced a few times. "I still don't like the idea of you meeting a potential stranger in secret."

"It won't be entirely secret. He chose a spot within sight of the ballroom." Another reason to think it might be Nick behind the letter. They had spent enough time together in public that no one would question the two of them speaking. Meeting an actual stranger would require more discretion should things not go well.

Elias glanced at the letter again. "And how will you know it is him?" He must not have read the entirety of the letter.

"He will have a blue ribbon in his buttonhole."

"How quaint."

Emma scowled at him, not sure she liked this emotive version of her cousin. His disdain was clear in his voice, but if he had been here in London the whole time, he would understand why he didn't need to worry. This was Nick, the man who continually came to her rescue and put her before himself.

Standing, she met Elias toe-to-toe and leveled him with her best glare. "I hardly think you have any room to judge me when you secretly wrote love letters to an unmarried woman, Elias Drake."

He clenched his jaw. "I accept your censure, but it wasn't a month ago that you were disparaging the idea of marriage altogether, and you were determined to hate everything about Mr. Forester. Are you choosing him because you have no other options? I know you want your grandfather's estate, but at what cost?"

Emma narrowed her eyes. "My admirers have not been in short supply, and while I was fully determined to hate Mr. Forester, that was only until I came to know him. I love him, Elias."

Admitting those words out loud should have frightened her, but it didn't. She felt rather peaceful about the idea, which told her all she needed to know about the depth of her feelings. There was so much still to learn about Nick Forester, but she knew they could make a happy life together, assuming that was something he wanted as well. She wouldn't know until she asked, which she planned to do tonight regardless of who would be waiting for her on that balcony.

She needed to know whether Nick could ever be an option.

Taking a deep breath, Elias considered her words before offering his arm. There were voices out in the corridor, which meant most of the family had gathered. "And what if this mysterious suitor is not Nick Forester?" he asked. "You don't have time to gamble on this."

Emma didn't have an answer to that question. As much as she liked to believe she could come to love someone else, her heart beat so strongly for Nick that she genuinely feared that outcome. For everyone's sake, she had to hope her suspicions were correct.

Besides, she knew there was more to this than the inheritance. "He's dying, isn't he?"

Elias dropped his gaze. Though he said nothing, the sadness in his eyes was clear. He was almost as close to Grandfather as Emma was, and she suspected Elias knew far more about his health than he let on. If she could do this one thing for Grandfather—show him that she would be happy and no longer alone—perhaps his passing would be easier to bear.

Tabitha, Alvaro, and Catherine were all waiting in the entryway, and Emma fixed on a smile before anyone else picked up on her nerves and sadness. But that smile lasted only long enough for her to realize that Nick was not here.

"Is Mr. Forester not joining us?" she asked, though it was not as if Nick couldn't find his own way to the ball.

As Catherine latched on to Elias's arm, Tabitha and Alvaro shared a glance.

"I believe he will meet us at the Bartletts'," Tabitha said, brushing her skirts. "He just left an hour ago."

Emma's heart skipped a beat. "He was here?"

Though Alvaro chuckled, Emma hardly saw any humor in her realization. Why would Nick not at the very least say hello? She had thought he would be far from Harstone House today, or she would have sought him out herself.

"He and I were discussing business," Alvaro said brightly. "I am lending him money to rebuild his estate, and I fear I overwhelmed him with talk of everything he will need to do to bring it back to being profitable. The poor man was rather in a state of anxiety and needed a moment to refresh before he joins us."

Emma could hardly breathe as she processed this. Nick was going to rebuild his estate? But what did that mean for her letter writer? If Nick was the one writing to her and intending to marry her, he wouldn't need his lands. He would share the inheritance with her. Did this mean he had given up because she was soon to be engaged to someone else?

"Oh," she said weakly, wondering if she would have the strength to carry on tonight.

Did she have a choice?

"Come along, dear," Tabitha said, reaching out for Emma's hand. "We don't want you to be late."

Though she likely meant late for the ball, Emma half wondered if Tabitha knew about the clandestine meeting. How, Emma didn't know, but she prayed she was doing the right thing as she followed her family into the night.

Chapter Thirty-Six

Lord and Lady Bartlett were an exceptionally sweet couple who greeted Emma warmly despite them having never met. Lady Bartlett was full of life and energy, her smiles wide and her enthusiasm practically spilling out of her, while her husband seemed the opposite, more subdued and calm. But anyone who looked at them could see the love they felt toward each other, and Emma immediately liked them.

"Are you thinking of spending Christmas here in Town this year, Harstone?" Lord Bartlett asked.

Alvaro chuckled when Tabitha gave him a warning look. "Much as I would like to, we will be returning to Staffordshire until the Season begins." He squeezed Tabitha's hand when she gave him a grateful smile.

While the men began discussing some government policy of sorts, Lady Bartlett took Emma's hand, as if they were old friends. "Are you the Miss Mackenzie that Nicholas Forester is looking for? He arrived ten minutes ago and immediately asked if you were here yet."

Emma's cheeks warmed despite her overwhelm, and she couldn't hold back her smile. "Yes, I suppose that is me. He is here?" She rose up on her toes but couldn't see the ballroom from the entryway.

Lady Bartlett giggled. She was young, but even with her exuberance, she still held the title of viscountess well. "Ah, will there be an engagement in my ballroom tonight? You look as if the sun just came up."

Emma's eyes went wide; she had no idea what to say to that. She could hardly make any assumptions, but then again, the whole point of meeting tonight was to make arrangements so the banns could be read on Sunday. She didn't want Lady Bartlett to start telling everyone that Emma and Nick would be getting engaged tonight, in case another man entirely would be waiting for her on the terrace.

Thankfully, Lord Bartlett seemed to catch on to his wife's enthusiasm and pulled her against his side, giving her a loving look. "Beth, we talked about this."

"Yes, Graham, I know," she said with mock annoyance. "I shouldn't frighten our guests by pretending we are the best of friends." She gave Emma's hand a squeeze, as she hadn't yet released her. "Perhaps we shall become friends in time."

Emma laughed. "I fully plan to live out my days in the country, but you are always welcome to come visit."

"Oh, I do love the country."

Lord Bartlett chuckled. "You hate the country."

Her smile turned softer, all her attention now on her husband as she pressed her fingers to his cheek. "I met *you* in the country. How could I hate it?"

Laughing as the pair got lost in each other's eyes, Alvaro gestured toward the ballroom. "Shall we?" Once out of earshot, he explained. "They are not yet a year married, and I've been told their story is quite a humorous one."

"I heard they both pretended to be untitled and fell for each other anyway," Catherine added with a sigh. "It all sounds so romantic."

Based on the mild disgust on his face, Elias seemed to disagree. "I don't think anyone should pretend to be something he isn't."

Emma glared at him. It seemed he was still against Nick's potentially dubious methods, and hopefully he would keep his disdain to himself throughout the night.

"Oh look," Catherine said. "There is Mr. Forester!"

Emma's heartbeat doubled in speed when she caught sight of him.

Though he was on the other side of the ballroom talking to the Duke of Tipton, he glanced behind him as if he had heard his name and caught Emma's gaze. He grinned at her and then discreetly pointed to His Grace, widening his eyes in mock awe and mouthing, "It's a duke!"

Emma bit her lip to hold back her laughter, wishing she were at his side instead of all the way over here.

"Good evening, Lord Harstone." A man Emma had met once but couldn't remember pulled her attention away from Nick. "I was wondering if I might ask Miss Mackenzie to join me for the next set."

"Yes, of course, Mr. Lewis," Alvaro said.

Emma reluctantly agreed to the dance, taking Mr. Lewis's arm and reminding herself that she wouldn't be able to spend the whole evening with Nick anyway. She still had several hours before her appointed meeting time on the balcony, and dancing would be her best way to spend those hours before she went mad with anticipation.

But dancing was a mistake.

The moment the men of the *ton* realized they could dance with the famed Emma Mackenzie, she couldn't get a minute to herself. She danced the supper set with a kind but quiet man who was so nervous that he nearly tripped over her as he led her into the dining hall, and his lack of conversation made it too easy for her to watch Nick laugh with Lady Georgina. Emma didn't especially love that. When supper was over, she hardly had the chance to catch up with Catherine before she was whisked away again for another dance. Even Lord Bartlett stood up with her once, though he wasn't much of a dancer and they spent the set in silence, something Emma actually welcomed after a night filled with tedious small talk.

It wasn't until just before midnight when Emma finally heard the voice she most wanted to hear.

"I believe this next one is promised to me."

Emma could have cried, she was so relieved. Though her current partner seemed reluctant to let her go, he dutifully handed her over to Nick, who tucked her arm through his and held her far closer than he needed to.

"You have been quite the prize tonight, dear Emma. I thought I might never get you away." He gave her a soft smile—a favorite of hers—and led her to the edge of the ballroom. The terrace waited just beyond a set of doors, and Emma was suddenly overcome with nerves.

"What if he isn't here?" she asked, gripping his arm and staring at the empty terrace through the windows. "I haven't seen any ribbons all night, and I must have danced with every eligible bachelor in attendance."

"Yes, I noticed." There was an edge to Nick's voice, but he softened before he looked at her. Reaching up, he stroked her cheek with a tenderness that brought tears to her eyes. "Where has my brave Emma gone? You have nothing to fear."

He was wrong. She had everything to fear because Nick wasn't wearing a ribbon in his buttonhole, and he was making plans to revitalize his lands. What if she was mistaken, just as Elias had said? What would she do if she was asked to marry someone else when she felt such affection for Nick? She wasn't certain she could face that pressure.

When a tear escaped onto Emma's cheek, Nick frowned. "Emma," he whispered, leaning in close. He took up her hands, clasping them to his chest. "Do you trust me?"

"You know I do."

His eyebrows pulled low as he studied her face, like he was searching for the source of her fear. Little did he know that he was at the center of it all. What if she told him that she was in love with him? Would he still send her out onto the terrace? Maybe he would admit that he was behind the letters. Maybe he would ask her not to go out there and instead remain with him. Or maybe he would tell her that she was nothing but a friend to him and her only hope would be meeting her in two minutes.

"Nick," she whispered.

"Are you ready?" he whispered back.

"As I'll ever be." Reluctantly releasing his hands, she walked backward to the doors without taking her eyes off him. He gave her a reassuring smile, but there was worry beneath the optimism in his eyes. Not knowing what that might mean, Emma forced a deep breath and then stepped out onto the terrace.

Two minutes. Two minutes, and then she would have her answers.

But those two minutes came and went, and Emma wrapped her arms around herself to stave off the chill.

Five minutes, but she told herself not to worry. He was probably caught in a dance.

When nearly ten minutes had passed, Emma could no longer keep her chin up. What if he didn't come? What if Nick had left her out here so he could propose to Lady Georgina without interruption? What if—

The door opened, and Emma's breath caught in her throat. It was Nick who stepped through it, his eyes sad as he slowly approached her. Either he knew as well as she did that her mystery suitor had failed her, or . . . She was too cold and heartbroken to think about the alternatives.

"He didn't come." Emma didn't know how to feel right now, and she kept her eyes on Nick, willing him to explain.

He looked miserable. "He was frightened."

"By what?"

Reaching into his jacket pocket, he pulled out a length of ribbon and ran it between his thumb and forefinger. Emma's breath caught, but he didn't seem to notice. "He feared you wouldn't trust that his love is real. He feared he had done nothing to make him worthy of you. He feared—he *knows*—you deserve so much more than a liar and a coward who couldn't find the courage to tell you how much you mean to him except in a letter." He held the ribbon up, glancing between it and her face. It wasn't in his buttonhole, but it was most decidedly blue, a detail she hadn't told him. "I tried to match the color of your eyes," he said with clear disappointment, "but they change so often that I didn't quite manage it. Perhaps I should have chosen gre—"

Emma grabbed his lapels and pulled him forward until their lips collided. At first, he didn't move a muscle, standing completely still, as if a statue. But then his hands jumped up, cupping her jaw, and the kiss changed, igniting into a fire that burned so hot she thought she might melt. Nick's lips moved against hers with an intensity that Emma matched eagerly. She tugged on his jacket, taking a step back, and he followed until they were out of sight against the wall. And then he dove deeper, mapping out every inch of her lips with his own until she eventually pushed him back so she could breathe.

"I'm sorry," he said immediately, his lungs heaving.

Emma narrowed her eyes. "You had better not be apologizing for that kiss, Nicholas Forester."

Laughing, he brushed his thumbs across her cheeks. "Definitely not." To prove it, he kissed her again, this one achingly slow and tender. "I am sorry for lying to you. I should have told you it was me from the beginning, and I didn't intend for tonight to go in this direction, as much as I enjoyed your boldness." As if to prove himself, he took a step back, leaving Emma cold and wanting. "I will not speak for you, Emma, and I leave this choice to you. But you should know that Harstone will inherit the Mackenzie lands if you do not, and he has promised to allow you full use of the estate. You do not need me in order to live the life you wish." He swallowed. "You should also know that I love you with everything I am. I failed in finding you a husband who can be what you need, but I want nothing more than a happy life for you, Emma. Whether or not I am a part of it."

Her heart seemed ready to burst out of her chest. "What of your estate?" she asked. It was the one thing that didn't add up.

He cocked his head. "My estate?"

"Alvaro told me you are borrowing money to rebuild it."

Groaning, he ran his hands through his hair and glared into the ballroom. "I told him not to tell you," he grumbled. "I couldn't be sure you would accept me after this deception, and I have been sufficiently humbled to know I need to take control of my own life where I can. Regardless of what happens tonight, I want to do what I can with what is mine so you can be guaranteed what is yours."

Stepping forward, Emma reached up and ran her fingers through his hair just as he had done. For the last few days, he hadn't kept it nearly as neat as he used to, and she loved the way the blond waves seemed to have a mind of their own. He seemed so much more real now than he had when they first met, and he watched her with so much hope in his blue eyes.

"Oh, Nick, to think how I misjudged you." She pulled him down until their foreheads pressed together, and then she closed her eyes and focused on how right this felt. Like they were created to fit together.

The man could be infuriating at times, but he had a good heart, and he was likely the only person in existence who understood and embraced her oddities without ever once trying to change her.

Nick's arms snaked around her back and pulled her closer until she was flush against him, her head tucked under his chin. He spoke slowly, like he was having a hard time getting the words out. "I was so convinced you hated me for so long that I never thought you could . . ." She felt him swallow.

"I love you more than you could ever know, Nick Forester."

His breath hitched, and thick emotion choked his words when he spoke. "Everything I have, everything I *am*, is yours, dear Emma. I thought I might never be whole again, but you pieced me back together every time you forced me out of hiding and made me face the man I had become. Your spirit and bravery have given me the courage to think I might be happy again, and I will do anything to return that to you a thousand times over. There are no words to express how deeply I love you, and I never want to leave your side for as long as I live. If you'll have me."

Emma had never felt happier than she did now as she stood there in his arms. "Are you asking me to marry you, Mr. Forester?"

He chuckled, and the sound rumbled through her. "I am asking if you'll allow me to be your husband and follow you wherever life takes you."

"Even if I never want to set foot in London ever again?" She didn't mean that, mostly, but she was curious to see what he would say.

Instead of answering, Nick pulled back and whispered a kiss on her forehead. "Good riddance."

She grinned. "What if I want to run the estate and leave you to run the household?"

"We'd probably be better for it. I was raised by a housekeeper, after all." He kissed the tip of her nose.

"If I spend every other night with my nieces in the Harstone nursery?"

"I'll allow that only until we have our own nursery full of children." His next kiss found her mouth, and Emma got lost in it, imagining a future full of kisses and children and so much happiness that it couldn't possibly be real.

But if she knew anything, she knew a life with Nick Forester would be so much better than anything she could possibly imagine.

And she couldn't wait to see how their story played out.

Epilogue

Three weeks later

"I thought we'd find you hiding in here." Calloway's voice was full of amusement.

Nick didn't bother looking up from the floor as he paced. "I am not hiding." He was absolutely hiding, though he clearly hadn't done a good job of it if Calloway and Harstone had found him this easily. He supposed the library at Harstone Court wasn't exactly a secluded place. Sighing, he turned to find his friends standing in the doorway with grins on their faces. "Please tell me you were both this nervous."

Harstone shook his head at the same time Calloway said, "Not in the slightest."

Nick groaned. "I thought you found me so you could help me feel better."

Chuckling, Calloway came into the room and wrapped his arm around Nick's shoulders so he could force him onto the sofa. "What made you think that? We're only here to ensure you don't run away before the deed is done."

"I'm not going to run away," Nick snapped, clenching his hands into fists. "I'm more worried about Emma. She hasn't changed her mind, has she?"

His friends looked at each other, apparently having a silent conversation between them, their brows furrowed.

Nick gulped. "What? What's happened?"

Calloway and Harstone burst into laughter, which didn't exactly make Nick relax, but at least he could assume nothing was wrong.

"Whatever happened to the man who was afraid of nothing?" Harstone asked as he settled beside Nick on the sofa. "I think your age has softened you, no?"

Calloway took a seat in an armchair, his eyes dancing. He hadn't been happy like this in years, since before his father died, and Nick enjoyed the sight of his friend laughing. Even if it was at his expense. Marriage had been so good for the man, and Nick was eager to see Calloway's wife, Lucy, again. At least, he assumed Lucy was here, though he hadn't seen her yet. He hadn't seen anyone.

That was what happened when a man took to hiding in a library before the sun had even come up.

Nick forced in a deep breath, holding it in his lungs in the hopes that it would settle his nerves. But no, it only made him lightheaded. "You really weren't nervous on your wedding days?" he asked his friends.

Calloway's smile softened. "I was terrified. I kept wondering if Lucy would realize she could do a lot better than a boring old baron like me."

"Always selling yourself short," Nick muttered at the same time Harstone said, "Don't be ridiculous, Calloway."

Shrugging, Calloway seemed to be thinking back on how he and his wife met as his eyes grew distant. Their circumstances had been less than ideal—like Nick, Lucy had been pretending to be someone she wasn't—but somehow they had still managed to build a friendship of trust between them. Nick had liked Lucy immediately, partially because he had seen her lies (and the necessity behind them) and recognized a kindred spirit.

"I can't help wondering what would have happened if we hadn't met the way we did," Calloway said wistfully. "We may have both been in London, but I don't think we would have found each other."

"I know that feeling," Harstone agreed. "Meeting Tabitha on the road in Tutbury felt like fate; we wouldn't have met if I had remained in Town."

Nick grunted. London was overrated. "Perhaps I'll never set foot in London again. It has never done me any good."

Calloway frowned. "About that . . . Olivia is going to make her debut this Season, and I was hoping you could assist with her come-out. No one knows Society better than you do, Forester."

Cringing, Nick wished he could argue that fact. If it was anyone but Calloway's sister, he would absolutely refuse, but he had known the girl almost since the day she was born. He could hardly leave her to face the gossips on her own. "Are you sure that's a good idea?" he asked hesitantly. He hadn't told Calloway all the details of what had happened over the last couple of months, and he still wasn't exactly certain where he stood with the *ton*. There was a high chance he would do more damage than good by associating with her.

"Of course it is," Calloway said with a laugh. "You know how much Olivia looks up to you, and she would be a lot more confident going into her first Season if she knew you were there to walk her through. I'm likely to make a mess of it, and technically this will be Lucy's first Season as well. Besides . . ." He got a ridiculous grin on his face. "Lucy and I may be a bit distracted, considering she is with child."

Nick's jaw dropped as Harstone cheered. "So soon?" Nick said breathlessly.

"We've been married for five months now."

"I know, but . . ." Nick shook his head. It was strange enough that Harstone had three children, and Nick had almost lost hope that all of them would find their happy endings. He and Calloway were both thirty years old at this point, and for a time, it had seemed as if they would both be on their own for the rest of their lives.

Calloway narrowed his eyes. "Forester, are you crying?"

"No!" But he cringed. He had promised himself he would stop lying, but it was a deucedly difficult habit to break. "Yes. I am happy for you, Simon. Truly."

Grinning, Calloway stood and pulled Nick up with him so he could wrap him up in an embrace. "And I am happy for you, my friend. You deserve this. So do you think you could stand to spend a few months in London with me in the spring?"

Nick had rather hoped he could avoid the *ton* a bit longer, but how could he abandon Olivia? "I will have to talk to Emma first."

"Good answer," Harstone said with a grin. "Now, are you ready to speak your vows and give Mackenzie a reason to stop fretting?"

Thankfully, Emma's grandfather was still holding on, though he seemed to get more ill with each passing day. Nick and Emma had both spent a good deal of time with the old man, learning together about the estate and what had made it thrive over the years. Not only had Nick been grateful for the education, but it had also given him a chance to see how skilled Emma already was. He trusted her to keep him from doing anything that might damage their future, and that had made the last few weeks far less terrifying than they could have been.

"He and your housekeeper have both been complaining all morning that you are likely to run away," Calloway added with a smirk.

"I have not been complaining," a soft voice said in the doorway.

Nick brightened at the sight of Mrs. Murray, tears filling his eyes again when he saw her smile. It had been years since he had been able to visit her, and letters had most definitely not been enough. "You came," he breathed, hurrying forward to offer his arm to her.

She snickered and patted his cheek. "You think I would miss a joyous day such as this? Come, or you will be late to your own wedding."

Though he dearly wished his parents could have been here, having Mrs. Murray at his side as he made his way to the waiting carriage outside felt as close to family as he could get. He had half expected her to remain at home rather than make the journey. Choosing between Derbyshire and Tutbury to hold the wedding had been a nearly impossible task. Mr. Mackenzie may still be alive, but there was no plausible way he could have made the journey from Staffordshire, and Nick couldn't have deprived Emma of having her grandfather give her away.

"I will be honest with you," Mrs. Murray said as they walked. "I wasn't convinced this day would come while I was still alive."

Nick laughed. "Yes, we are all surprised someone settled for a lout like me."

She swatted his arm in the way she had when he was an unruly boy dragging mud into the house. "That is not what I meant, you silly boy. No, I feared you would be too afraid to open your heart again after what that wicked woman did to you."

"How do you know about that?" Nick had never confided in her everything that happened with Lavinia. Perhaps, if he had trusted Mrs. Murray with his heartache, she might have had some advice.

She clucked her tongue. "Your letters changed after you broke off your engagement, and I knew you couldn't have made that decision to part ways on your own. She hurt you, and I had half a mind to hie myself to London and give her a stern talking-to. She could have begged you to take her back."

"I'm glad you didn't," Nick said, though he wouldn't have thought so three years ago. "Otherwise, I wouldn't have met Emma."

As they reached the carriage waiting to take them to the church, Mrs. Murray hummed while Calloway and Harstone stopped a ways away to give them privacy. "You found a woman who is entirely suited to you, my dear Nicholas. And I can see she makes you happy. That is all I have ever wished for you."

Nick swallowed the emotion that threatened to choke him. "Have I ever told you how deeply grateful I am to you?" he asked, bending to place a kiss on the old woman's cheek. "I don't know where I would have been if you hadn't stepped in after my parents were taken from me."

After dabbing at her wrinkled cheeks shining with tears, Mrs. Murray swatted him with her handkerchief. "Now you've gone and made me cry," she snapped, though her smile spoke of her happiness. "You were the son I never had, Nicholas, and I thank God every day that I was given the chance to know you. Now, let's get you to your bride!"

When they arrived at the church, it seemed all of Tutbury had shown up to celebrate the union, though Nick knew they were there for Emma, not for him. He couldn't blame them. Emma Mackenzie possessed the most beautiful soul he had ever known, and he was lucky she had settled for a man like him.

When he caught sight of her walking toward him from the back of the church, smiling behind her veil and wearing the blue bonnet he had recommended when they first met, his breath caught. Suddenly he felt as if all of this was a dream. The words of the vicar sounded muddled and hazy, and Nick wasn't entirely certain he said the words he was supposed to when it was his turn. But the moment they were declared husband and wife and Emma leaned in to accept his kiss, everything fell into place, like all of the broken pieces of his life finally fit back together.

"Are you ready for this?" Emma asked as they stood hand in hand and gazed at each other, like they were the only two people there.

Nick grinned. "With you by my side? I am ready for anything. I love you, dear Emma, and I will love you always. My wife."

She brushed her thumb across his cheek with a giggle. Lud, he was crying again. "My husband," she replied, and she said the words as if they meant the world to her.

Nick had been chasing this moment his entire adult life, but no matter how wonderful he thought his wedding day would be, he never could have expected Emma. She was so much more than he could have dreamed, and as he led her out of the church and to the carriage waiting for them, he knew the future would be nothing but bright.

About the Author

Dana LeCheminant has been telling stories since she was old enough to know what stories were. After spending most of her childhood reading everything she could get her hands on, she eventually realized she could write her own books, and since then she has always had plots brewing and characters clamoring to be next to have their stories told. A lover of all things outdoors, she finds inspiration while hiking the remote Utah backcountry and cruising down rivers. Until her endless imagination runs dry, she will always have another story to tell.

Dana loves connecting with readers and talking books!
Website: lecheminantbooks.com
Facebook: @authordanalecheminant
Instagram: @authordanalecheminant